M000118104

WATERBORNE

A Novel by

J. Luke Bennecke

Black Rose Writing | Texas

©2021 by J. Luke Bennecke

All rights reserved. No part of this book may be reproduced, stored in a retrieval system or transmitted in any form or by any means without the prior written permission of the publishers, except by a reviewer who may quote brief passages in a review to be printed in a newspaper, magazine or journal.

The author grants the final approval for this literary material.

First printing/ First Hardcover printing

This is a work of fiction. Names, characters, businesses, places, events, and incidents are either the products of the author's imagination or used in a fictitious manner. Any resemblance to actual persons, living or dead, or actual events is purely coincidental.

ISBN: 978-1-68433-674-6 (Paperback); 978-1-944715-98-4 (Hardcover)
PUBLISHED BY BLACK ROSE WRITING
www.blackrosewriting.com

Printed in the United States of America
Suggested Retail Price (SRP) $20.95 (Paperback); 25.95 (Hardcover)

Waterborne is printed in Book Antiqua

*As a planet-friendly publisher, Black Rose Writing does its best to eliminate unnecessary waste to reduce paper usage and energy costs, while never compromising the reading experience. As a result, the final word count vs. page count may not meet common expectations.

For Jim Balcom, P.E.,
an inspirational civil engineer, mentor, and friend.

FACTS:

1. Light-water reactors, used at both the Chernobyl and Fukushima disasters, are the most common type of nuclear reactor in use today. The United States Department of Energy oversees the operation of 99 light-water nuclear reactors, providing 20% of U.S. electricity.

2. Molten Salt Reactor technology was developed in the 1950s, consumes existing spent nuclear fuel, and will not melt down.

3. California has a population of 40 million people, each of whom uses 109 gallons of fresh, pure drinking water every day during summer months.

4. In 2015 CRISPR gene editing technology matured to the point where biologists could accurately change the genome of living organisms, including viruses.

WATERBORNE

CHAPTER 1

August 1st – Stockton, California
11:15 p.m.

Mass murder can be complicated. But profitable.

From a vacant corner of the Chili's parking lot, behind a four-foot-high wall of cropped manzanita shrubs, Gunther Pertile scanned the area for civilians. Not a soul in sight. He whipped out his Glock 9mm — with suppressor — aimed at each of the two main overhead lights and squeezed off two muffled rounds. Glass shattered, falling to the ground as the entire scene went dark.

He dismounted his jet-black Harley, then slid off his helmet to reveal the short, curly hair he'd recently bleached to no longer be the dark-haired, dark-eyed killer on the FBI's most wanted list.

Running his fingertips along each of the four loaded mags inside the pocket of his leather jacket, he calculated the time to empty all sixty rounds. At three rounds per second and another three seconds to swap each mag, he could finish in just over half a minute.

One dead every half second.

Not bad.

But he tossed aside his mass shooting fantasy, forced himself back to reality, drew a deep breath and relished the security of his weapon. After two decades as a sniper, he knew tonight's assignment — his actual job — would succeed.

Piece of cake.

His weapon holstered, he glided through the front door of the restaurant and took a window seat.

A flash of blue pulled into the parking lot. The target — a civil engineer named Jake Bendel — wore a gray fedora hat, jeans, a light blue dress shirt and plaid charcoal sport coat as he exited a Tesla and strolled toward Chili's carrying a laptop, several rolls of paper, and a three-ring binder. Inside, the hostess escorted him to a booth on the room's opposite side. Physically, the target's height and weight matched the profile the boss had provided. At a height of just above six-one, maybe two hundred pounds, Gunther evaluated the level of effort to accomplish the abduction.

Within tolerance.

After Bendel sat, he ordered dinner and worked, checking his Apple Watch every few minutes.

Gunther took a slow sip of ice water, studying the mostly vacant dining room of the restaurant.

Eventually, the target's food came and he ate — still checking his watch. Gunther smiled.

The other members of the assault team had already taken care of Jake's friend, Dave, who most definitely would not be dining at Chili's tonight.

Or anywhere ever again, for that matter.

Gunther finished his water and set the glass on the table.

His Android read 11:55 p.m.

Perfect.

He dug a hand into his pants pocket and wrapped his fingers around a syringe filled with enough Trihypnol to subdue a professional wrestler. With the quarter-inch-long needle capped at the tip, he'd avoid accidentally injecting himself with the hypnotic drug.

Trihypnol was the perfect concoction for tonight's events. Once administered, the victim would remain fully awake, but in a highly suggestible and altered state of consciousness—alert and fully mobile for up to four hours. The famous Dr. Jake Bendel would later crash like a pelted pigeon and sleep for half a day, with zero memory of the evening's activities.

Bendel stuffed the last piece of halibut into his mouth, chewed, and washed it down with a final swig of beer.

Game time.

CHAPTER 2

August 1st
11:55 p.m.

Jake shifted in his seat, alone in an oversized padded booth, as he stabbed the last dry bite of cold halibut with his fork. From inside his leather folder, he slid out his favorite pen, the one personally awarded to him by the Governor for his previous efforts. Inscribed on the side, above a line with his initials "J.B." read: *Sûr System - Moving America Forward without Traffic Congestion.*

While scanning the construction plans sitting off to the side of the table, he wrote several notes for himself, focusing on the remaining year of scheduled tasks—hundreds—all accurately displayed in the form of bar charts, dates, and percentages of completion. After setting the pen onto the plans, he raked his fingers through his thinning hair, wishing he'd worn his comfy construction boots instead of the black leather dress shoes pinching his toes. He took a long swig of Budweiser, then rubbed his eyes, trying to relax.

One final survey of the inside of the restaurant for Dave Trainer, his longtime friend, yielded nothing. Still no sign. If Dave wasn't coming, Jake could get more work done at his home office than in this restaurant.

As he packed up the multi-paged schedule, Jake's mind churned through potential solutions to the project delays and he waved the waitress over.

Jake's waitress strolled up then slipped the check and its black plastic tray next to the napkin dispenser. He plucked his wallet from his jeans and tossed an American Express onto the tray.

After closing a manila folder stuffed full of the latest progress reports, he thought about the largest water treatment plant. Three months behind schedule—unacceptable on a five billion-dollar project. The construction delays needed serious reining in, for sure, to keep the governor off his ass.

A tall order.

Maybe with twelve-hour shifts per day, seven days a week. Jake blinked rapidly, running the numbers in his head. The shit ton of overtime would totally obliterate the already bulging budget.

But the governor demanded excellence, especially from her project director. She'd brought Jake on board to solve California's drought by finishing all five plants in record time. At her request, Jake had engineered the concept of pumping and treating seawater with energy created by a new form of cheap, safe nuclear power. The clean water would provide a basic human resource to most of California's booming population for decades.

Now, only three of the five plant combos were finished and ready to go online.

Jake piled up his used silverware on his plate, glad he hadn't ordered steak. He'd thought about it a few times the last couple of years, but ever since the infamous Los Angeles auto crashes and terrorist threats two years ago he hadn't been able to eat red meat. Partially because he'd seen too many of the victims. Partially because his wife was one of them. And partially because the press had initially blamed him for the carnage.

Too much death.

That's why he planned to meet Dave here tonight. As a master computer hacker, Dave had played a key role in stopping the terrorists responsible for the crashes. Coming head-to-head with evil like that had messed them both up pretty bad, so Jake had invited Dave to a seafood dinner as part of their ongoing healing process.

But now the guy had stood him up.

No text. No phone call. Nothing.

As he waited for the waitress to bring his card back, he noticed a muscular black man with short, bleached blond hair and a salt and pepper half-length ZZ-Top beard sitting alone across the room, nursing a clear drink. Vodka on the rocks, perhaps.

Jake checked his watch: two minutes after midnight. He needed to go home.

The waitress returned, he picked up his card, threw on his fedora hat and rose to leave.

As he walked toward the door, the bearded man also rose to leave. A credit card slipped from his hand and landed in front of Jake on the low-pile carpet.

Jake bent, scooped the card up off the ground, and jogged after the man.

Ꮽ

Gunther strode across the parking lot as Bendel raced after him.

So far so good.

"Excuse me, sir! I think you dropped this."

Gunther smiled and turned around. "Thanks, bro." Jake gave him the card and spun toward his Tesla.

As Jake extended his arm to open the driver's door, Gunther pulled out the syringe from his pocket and closed the distance between them while placing a thumb snugly on the plunger. Before Jake could open the car door, Gunther lunged forward, bumping the engineer forward while injecting the Trihypnol into the meat of his neck.

6

Jake stumbled but caught his balance. Gunther stabilized his target, saying in a drunken, slurred tone, "Sorry, dude, didn't mean to—"

Jake whirled around and stepped back, eyes blinking. He shook his head, brushing imaginary dust off his arms. "Watch where you're going, man, I—"

Gunther said nothing, instead turning his gaze to the corner of the parking lot and motioning toward the target.

Headlights popped on as the unmarked black van parked in an opposite corner of the lot sped forward and pulled up next to Jake.

The side door swooshed open and the rest of the abduction team, two men wearing dark green ski masks, black jackets, and leather gloves, leapt out and surrounded Jake, who stumbled sideways in a failed attempt to escape. The largest of the abductors jabbed a stun gun and ten thousand volts into Jake's rib cage, then heaved him into the van.

As Gunther hopped into the cargo space of their vehicle, another man jumped out and dashed toward the Harley. Gunther slid the door shut and nodded to the driver who hurled the van onto an empty street and accelerated west.

The abduction had taken less than ten seconds.

Another success.

Two of the masked men secured Jake's wrists behind his back with 3/8-inch yellow nylon rope. Same with his ankles. Jake's aggressive efforts to free himself eventually gave way to slow, clumsy movements as the Trihypnol coursed through his veins.

Gunther thought of his boss and the several dozen Jihadist souls sent to Allah two years ago because of Jake's actions. But now the Almighty had called on their sleeper cell as chosen ones, to send yet another message to the American infidels. One final, symbolic act of religious supremacy before the heroes would ascend to the Kingdom of God.

And those 99 virgins, or whatever.

What a bunch of extremist Allahu Akbar bullshit.

Gunther was in this for the money.

And the unbeatable rush.

The sense of control.

Power.

The assassin pulled up Jake's torso, sitting Jake's drugged body upright on the van floor as Jake's head flopped around like a fishing bobber. "He's all yours."

The woman in the passenger seat unbuckled her seatbelt, climbed to the rear of the van, leaned forward, and lifted Jake's chin as she stared into his half-open eyes.

She slapped his cheek, but he only smiled. "Whew. Just a nightmare." He chuckled, glancing around the van before taking a second look at Gunther.

"Glad you think this is funny," the woman said. "Good news is you won't remember a damned thing."

The van drove across a deep pothole, forcing everyone to bounce. Jake gave a weak shake of his head, likely trying to clear the fog and regain clear focus.

She continued. "You're going to do me a favor." She brought her face to within an inch of his. "Jakey boy."

Jake's face morphed into a distant, confused daze.

"I understand your daughter, Carlie, has a three-month-old son. Living in New York. Would be a shame if anything were to happen to them."

He furrowed his brow, tilting his head.

She finally had his attention.

The van turned a corner and sped up as streetlights streaked by in a blur before the team entered the I-5 north, ultimately headed toward the coast to put Jake to work.

"You tousha my family," Jake said, still slurred, to the woman, "and I'll hunt your seck ass down and bash in that pretty li'l face of yours."

"Sounds like we have an understanding then," she said, smiling, leaning back and crossing her arms. "Tonight, you'll live. But you're going to wish we'd killed you."

CHAPTER 3

August 2nd
10:55 a.m.

Jake was used to the nightmares every night for the last two years. Ever since Viktor Johnston murdered his wife, orchestrated the attack on the freeway, and threatened to come back for Jake. Today, however, instead of waking up from another nightmare about Viktor strangling him, Jake awoke to the sound of a cat purring in his ear, along with the chirps of multiple wrens outside the first floor office window. Unable to sleep in a bed since his wife's untimely death two years ago, Jake lay instead on the lush leather couch in the rear of his downstairs office.

Out of habit and with his eyes still closed, he stretched out his arm with full intentions of snatching the thin Ultrabook computer from atop the coffee table to create a new Google Doc and type details about last night's nightmares. His therapist had told him to document his daily feelings and impressions of his dreams as a coping mechanism to process the nightmares.

But for the first time in months, no memory of bad dreams.

No dreams at all.

Odd.

Good, but odd.

No laptop, either.

Crap, I slept in my clothes again?

Now, with his conscious mind fully awake, he felt the familiar surge of emptiness and anxiety as he remembered Cynthia was no longer in his life. *Guess it's time to get up.*

After feeling in his pocket for his good luck Sur System pen, he rolled off the couch, picked up his fedora hat from the floor and set it on the coffee table. Jake's black and white tuxedo kitty, Lazy Bones, enjoyed a good rub down and a scoop of kibble from a fresh bag.

After stumbling upstairs to brush his teeth, Jake threw on a pair of black exercise shorts, stuffed the pen into the pocket, and put on his favorite white tank top, the one with the green and gold Cal Poly Pomona Civil Engineering logo. With his Apple Watch secured firmly to his wrist, he wandered back downstairs to the kitchen for a hefty cup of caffeine. While filling a clean glass full of water, he focused on how the water had been purified at one of the combo treatment plants he'd helped design and construct. As he sipped the water he relished the fact that, just weeks ago, ocean fish were swimming in the liquid now in his stomach.

Technology is amazing.

After shoving aside a stack of mail on the counter, he slid open a lower drawer to grab a mocha coffee pod, tossed it into his Keurig brewer and hit the "on" button. His phone vibrated. Paige Terner.

"Good morning, sunshine," Jake said to his fellow engineer and longtime friend. The sounds of car horns mixed with a rustling wind noise.

"I'm like totally freaking out right now. On my way over to your pad. Be there in five," Paige said, ending the call.

He noticed a text message from Dave:

Sorry about last night, bro. Something came up . . . will make it up to you later

Jake replied and checked on his coffee brew, staring absentmindedly around his large kitchen. Nobody needed 6,000 square feet of house to live in alone, but Jake and Cynthia were only a week away from closing escrow when she passed. Plus, the extra room was perfect for when Carlie and her extended family visited.

But the man who had killed Jake's wife in the fire might still be alive, and no doubt, the guy would murder him in his sleep if he got the chance. With Jake's construction engineering business brimming with multi-million-dollar contracts, he had plenty of cash to buy every imaginable security measure.

The Bendel McMansion stood out among the other high-profile homes in the west Stockton neighborhood of Brookside, across the San Joaquin River from the country club, and on the tip of a man-made island. Flowing water surrounded the property, all from several water bodies feeding the Old River via the farming communities of Orwood and Discovery Bay, which then dumped into the Clifton Court Forebay, where the 700-mile long California Aqueduct started its journey south.

Even with a security system on steroids, Jake felt unsafe inside his own home. He'd been experiencing severe anxiety, panic attacks, and insomnia ever since the incident two years ago. When he did manage to sleep, vivid nightmares of Viktor chasing him and threatening his family prevented Jake from getting any meaningful rest.

He and Paige had grown close over the last two years since their near-death bonding experience sponsored by the now-famous international terrorist. Viktor had abducted the two of them on a private plane which he and Paige had to land after Viktor jumped.

As a civil-engineer-turned-comedienne, Paige struggled to put her life back together with her newfound career. But she'd hit a dead end. Last month, she had confided in Jake some people had a natural gift for making others laugh, but despite her dedication, thousands of hours of practice, dozens of classes, and beaucoup bucks, that natural ability eluded her. Wasn't in her genes. She now felt like a failure at not only one but two separate careers and suffered constantly from similar symptoms to Jake's: heavy anxiety and panic attacks.

Birds of a feather . . . brothers in arms . . .

The doorbell rang. Jake snatched his coffee mug from the machine and blew on the surface as he shuffled to his front door.

CHAPTER 4

August 2nd
11:30 a.m.

Paige had dyed her normally short, bleached blond hair a bright fire engine red.

Jake remarked about her hair color, but she ignored him, dashing to the kitchen table to sit on her favorite wooden chair.

"Smells good," she said, glancing around the kitchen. "You make a pot of coffee or —" She rolled her eyes. "Jake, you know those pods aren't recyclable, right? Those things are horrible for the environment. Have you seen the island of trash in the middle of the Pacific Ocean? I mean, it's like twice the size of Texas. Huge. Man, you need to get on board here and make coffee without those trashy pods." Her soft, blemish-free skin creased in concern.

He strolled over. "Easy, cowgirl. Sounds like someone's having a rough day, and it's only . . ." Jake looked at his watch. "Just before noon. Must be that red in your hair." He winked, then stepped toward the sink.

"Shut up." She slumped in her chair. Lazy Bones jumped onto her lap and she started petting him. "You're right. Sorry. I'll take one of whatever you're having. Screw it. I just broke up with my girlfriend."

"I saw that coming from a mile away. You two weren't a suitable match anyway," Jake said, popping another coffee pod into the machine and starting it brewing again. "Maybe for the best."

"Crap. You're right. But I can't seem to shake this anxiety. I thought maybe it was the relationship, you know, but now . . ."

Jake nodded and turned to the pile of mail. "Maybe what?" he asked, leafing through the letters. The third one caught his attention. IRS. *Great.*

"I know you don't like to talk about it, but . . ."

Jake opened the envelope and scanned the letter.

"Wonderful. Just what I need. Not only are my power plant and desalination projects behind schedule, but look," he said, handing the letter to Paige as Lazy Bones jumped off her lap and strolled out to the living room.

As a defense mechanism, instead of thinking about the contents of the letter, or what Paige was suggesting, he focused instead on the new form of nuclear tech used in the plant combos. How scientists at MIT had perfected a form of clean, safe nuclear technology a few years earlier. How they had finally cracked the code to generate cheap nuclear power effectively with zero chance of a meltdown.

She glanced over the document, already over her breakup, handed it back to him, then put her elbows on the table, dropped her head into her hands and raked her fingers through her short hair. "Bummer. Is this your first time dealing with that shit?"

The coffee stream dribbled to a stop. With his back to Paige, he grabbed the hot mug of mocha, turned and set the steaming beverage on the table in front of her. "I've had credit card numbers stolen before. That was a pain. But a letter from the IRS threatening to freeze all my bank accounts because I owe over a million dollars in back taxes? Jail time for tax evasion?" He slid another chair next to Paige for himself. "Obviously a clerical error or something. No way in hell my CPA screwed up that bad."

Paige sipped from her mug. "You got something on your neck." She reached over and rubbed just below his hairline, then hopped up to get a better look.

Jake ran his fingertips along the nape of his neck. Sure enough, a welt. And a powerful urge to scratch the raised area. "Must be a mosquito bite."

"Maybe it's Viktor. Not the bump, the tax problems," she said.

He laughed. "We've talked about your paranoia."

"We both know he's still out there." She set her cup onto the table next to the letter and stared dead into his eyes. "You refuse to think about this, but why hasn't the FBI, with all their resources, found the body of that ISIS son-of-a-bitch? You said yourself you weren't sure if there were three parachutes or four. If there were four when they dragged us on board the plane, and we know there were only three when we landed . . . deductive logic, man."

Jake looked at the ceiling, pondering her comment. "Fine. But I know, or knew, him. He'd want revenge. It's been two frickin' years already. Nothing. He'd have blown us up by now. Or at least tried."

"He's a planner, Jake. A schemer. You know this. He strategizes, he thinks, and when every detail has been thoroughly vetted and he has backup plans for every move, considering every scenario, then he attacks. Then he . . . like . . . comes after us." She tapped her fingers on the side of her mug. "No. It's not paranoia, dude. He's out there, biding his time."

"Wow, I'm so glad you came over, Paige. You and that dark cloud hovering above you." Hunger struck Jake's belly. From the fridge he pulled out a half-empty container of almond milk, and from the upper cupboards he grabbed a box of Wheaties and a bowl, but a sharp pain in his lower back forced him to pause. He touched his back, feeling a stiffness in the lower side, a soreness even, like he'd been in a boxing match last night. He tried to ignore it.

"Old age sucks," he said, retrieving a spoon from the drawer next to the fridge and limping back to the table to dive into the cereal.

"Tell me how dinner with Dave went last night," she said. "Haven't seen that dude in, like, months."

Jake finished chewing, lifted another scoop to his mouth, thinking, then stopped. He set the spoonful of cereal back into the bowl, waiting for a memory of the previous night to enter his mind. "He didn't show. I have a vague recollection of waiting for him at Chili's. I ordered food. One beer. But then . . . oh, I got a text from him. Something came up." He trailed off the last word.

Paige rubbed her chin. "Hope you're not turning into an alcoholic. One drink, ten drinks. Same difference."

Jake bit his lower lip. "I never drink more than one beer at a time. Never." He tried to remember something, anything, from last night. "Good news is, I must have slept pretty well. No nightmares. But my arms are so . . ." He rubbed his biceps and forearms, repeatedly stretching his fingers out and closing them into a fist. "They're killing me. And my lower back feels like a bull stomped on me."

Paige took an extra-long swig of her mocha, then set the cup on the table. "Okay. You have a lump on your neck. Sure, it could be a bug bite. But you also have sore muscles and you have no frickin' clue what happened to you last night after Chili's. Do you even remember driving home?"

Jake looked up again, searching for his last memory of the night. He remembered leaving his house, driving to Chili's. He tried to remember parking. "Nope. Nothing. Now you're scaring me."

Paige stared into her coffee, quiet.

Jake sighed. "I need a change. Time to retire from engineering. Play golf every day. I'm done with the old life. Too many memories of Cynthia. Painful." He looked around, up to the kitchen ceiling and waved an arm. "This enormous house I don't need anymore. I was hoping my legacy would be strong, positive, lasting. And maybe it will be if I leave the game now. I'm fifty-one. I want my life to mean something to Carlie and little Andrew. Was hoping the world would be a better place after I lived my life than if I'd never been born, but so far, not happening."

She frowned, squishing her thick black eyeliner into tiny bunches. "Some deep shit there, man. Like twenty thousand leagues deep. But I feel you, dude. I just can't think about moving on until I know he's gone."

"I'm serious. I thought I'd avenged Cynthia's death when we got Viktor, but if that sick monster might still be out there, I can't deal with this constant possibility of him—."

Out of the corner of his eye, he noticed movement, slight, a shadow behind the opaque cream-colored curtain covering the French door to the backyard. He jerked his head toward the door and sure enough, a fuzzy silhouette of a bearded man moved across, behind the curtain, with a slight hunch in his back. A second later, the shadow slid out of view.

Jake's eyes widened. He slid his chair back from the table, grabbing Paige's hand while pointing toward the door. "Tell me you saw that," he said, voice shaking.

Paige turned to the door. She blinked several times. "I see a curtain covering the window door." She looked to Jake, then back to the door. "And I'm paranoid?"

Jake rose, staggered toward the back door, one step at a time and said, "Not paranoia. Viktor. I can feel him. I'd know that shadow anywhere." He reached his trembling hand to the brass doorknob, twisted, and threw open the door. A blast of warm, humid air entered. Down on the concrete porch slab covered with vines and daylilies stood an orange and white cat. Jake scanned the entirety of his vast, grassy backyard all the way out to the water flowing in the river and beyond. No humans. Only the sounds of a gentle breeze rustling through the oak and palm trees scattered willy-nilly, mixed with bird chirps. And a cat's meow.

But then a motorboat engine fired up. Jake darted his gaze to the dock as a covered Bayliner sped away, out into the river. Jake sprinted from his home, across a hundred yards of grass, then skidded to a stop at his wood-planked dock, but the boat was too far away to identify the driver.

Footsteps came running up behind Jake. Paige slowed to a stop next to him.

"That boat just launched off my dock," he said, panting. "It was Viktor. I know it."

Out of breath and with her hands on her knees, Paige craned her neck up to Jake. "Whoever it was, he's long gone."

Back at the porch, Jake squatted to pet the cat who purred at the attention.

Paige entered the kitchen, saying, "I think it's time to bring in Cavanaugh."

"No way." He stormed after her, slamming the door closed. "Not unless we have something concrete. He'll laugh if we tell him I saw a shadow and a boat."

Even after transferring up to the San Francisco FBI office six months ago, Special Agent Jose Cavanaugh had stayed in touch with Jake over the last two years. Every month or so, Cavanaugh would give Jake an update on the search for Viktor's body.

"You have CCTC cameras?" Paige asked.

Jake hustled into his office, loaded the security website and checked the video feeds over the last few minutes.

"Are you kidding me?" he asked, Paige hovering behind.

"Why's everything blacked out?"

"Says the system went offline nine minutes ago." Jake pushed away from his desk, stood, and walked back into the kitchen.

Paige sat and downed several gulps of mocha. "No way that's a coincidence, man."

A shiny, white cardboard box sat on top of the mail pile on the counter. About seven inches long, a half-inch tall, thin, with a blue bow affixed to the top.

Jake stepped toward the counter. "Did you put this here?" he asked. "While I was outside?"

Her eyes went wide, lips and chin trembling with fear as she stood and took a slow step backward. "Are you listening to yourself?"

Jake studied the box. "You put this here."

"No. I have no clue what the hell that is or where it came from." She continued backing away from the package as he flipped the enclosure over, then pried open the lid.

In the center of the box lay a blue ball-point pen with gold writing engraved on its side. He took the familiar-looking pen into his palm, brought it close and read the words aloud: "Sûr System - Moving America Forward without Traffic Congestion."

But the second line read: "V.J."

Jake's body tensed.

"Maybe you're not paranoid after all," he said, stepping toward Paige and showing her the pen. "Each team member who worked on the Sûr System had his or her own set of customized pens." He dug out his version of the SS pen from his pocket. "Mine looks just like this but has my initials, J.B., inscribed." He bobbed the pen up and down in the palm of his hand. "Feels heavier than mine." He handed the V.J. pen to Paige.

She rubbed her fingers along the wording and swallowed hard. "But these initials are—" The blood drained from her already pale face.

ಶ

August 9th
12:30 p.m.

"Are you sure?" Jake asked the security technician from down on the ground.

Up on the roof of the Bendel home, with the bright sun beaming from directly behind the guy, he nodded. "Taking pics now. Hold on, I'll be right down."

Two minutes later, Jake slid on his reading glasses, accepted the guy's iPad, and zoomed in on the bundle of gray CAT-5 cables.

"The cut looks clean, no frayed wires," Jake said, studying the pic and trying to figure out how someone could've cut the cables without Jake hearing a single suspicious sound. The saboteur would've needed a ladder and tools and time to climb up, step quietly across the shingles, open the roof-mounted security panel, snip the video cables, climb down, then carry the ladder off the property and escape with no detection whatsoever.

"Sorry it took us a week to get out here, man," the technician said. "Been swamped with recent work. Rash of break-ins 'round here. Pros and cons of the biz. Get it?" He chuckled.

Jake handed the iPad back, not in the mood for any humor. "Email that pic to me. Cops said they won't file a report without proof of wrongdoing. Said my system was probably malfunctioning and I was just seeing things."

The tech pointed to the pic of the cut cables and shook his head. "Whoever did this was a pro. They knew precisely which wires to neutralize. You said you were inside when the video feed went offline?"

Jake nodded. "Even with this pic, though, I feel like the cops don't believe me anymore."

"Why's that?"

"Weird things have been happening over the last few weeks. Water main shut off. Power surges that tripped all my breakers. Three times now, actually. Weird banging noises on my second story window in the middle of the night. Nothing ever caught on the CCTV's, but I've filed several reports and without any evidence, they probably think I'm nuts. But now I have this."

The technician bent over and picked up a cardboard box with a dozen new wi-fi cameras. "You got another problem."

"Hacker?"

"Yep. Even after we upgrade you to these wireless babies here, someone's been deleting encrypted video files from your secure server." He shook his head. "Not cool, man. But that's above my pay grade."

Jake's thoughts turned to Viktor, how the psychopath enjoyed toying with people.

The tech continued. "I can tell you one thing, sir: you ain't safe until you upgrade your system and I get you back online."

CHAPTER 5

August 16th
10:25 a.m.

FBI Special Agent Jose Cavanaugh kicked his feet onto the mahogany desk, leaned back and sank into the sleek leather chair in his newly renovated office on the twelfth floor of the eighteen-story Federal Building in downtown San Francisco. The expansive windows offered an impressive view of the surrounding buildings and famous bay below.

Man, I'm one lucky S.O.B.

He opened a news app on his iPad Pro to a live press conference of the ribbon-cutting ceremony at Point Pinole Regional Shoreline in Richmond, California. Politicians from all around had gathered to celebrate the opening of the newest Molten Salt Reactor and Desalination Plant—dubbed the "MSR/DP" by the press. This system promised to provide cheap, fresh drinking water to millions of Californians.

Cavanaugh popped a handful of trail mix into his mouth and chewed while watching reporter Terri Lopez, from the ABC-10 news San Francisco, standing in a field of tall brown grass overlooking San Pablo Bay as she started her coverage of the event.

Terri gave her report, taking several steps to her left while putting an arm out to guide her viewers' attention from the rolling beige hills and scattered clouds behind her to the massive brown and green concrete structures nestled in a clearing of overgrown eucalyptus trees. A series of monumental, fifty-foot tall cylindrical storage tanks, hundreds of towers, tubes, and countless electro-mechanical objects that made up the desalination plant dominated the backdrop.

Through the tiny speaker on Cavanaugh's iPad, Terri described the plant as a last resort in California's battle against a brutal, decades-long drought caused by global climate change. She explained how environmentalists had initially protested the construction of this plant, but when oceanic biologists partnered with Dr. Jake Bendel and his team of civil engineers, they'd crafted a strategy to minimize impacts to the local ecosystems for fish and other wildlife. In certtain cases, they'd even enhanced the systems.

The camera panned right, bringing Jake into frame next to Terri. He wore his trademark gray fedora hat, a dark gray sport coat over a blue-and-white-striped dress shirt, and black slacks. The matching thin tie and worn leather construction boots completed his unique style of professional engineering manager.

Lookin' good as usual.

Cavanaugh tossed another handful of nuts into his mouth.

"Before we get started," Terri said through a mouthful of gleaming white teeth, "I want to congratulate you on the success of the Sûr System, or SS, as everyone is calling it. How does it feel to have single-handedly solved the problem of traffic congestion nationwide and have saved the lives of 40,000 people a year?"

She aimed the mic at Jake, who clasped his hands below his waist. "Thanks, but the credit goes to the entire team. It's remarkable what we can do with great ideas, goals, and strong leadership. The Sûr System was designed and implemented by thousands of professionals who worked tirelessly for many years. The cost was borne by the taxpayers of our great nation, so we're all in this together. It was an enormous effort and everyone on the team deserves a pat on the back."

A stiff breeze blew through, threatening to knock off Jake's fedora, but he grabbed it with his right hand and re-centered it atop his head.

"Now let's talk about these MSR/DP's you're involved with," Terri said. "Tell me more about how this desalination plant is different from others that have already been constructed in California."

"Close to ninety-eight percent of the water on earth is saltwater. Of the small portion of fresh water available to us humans, about eighty percent is frozen. So we really don't have a lot of fresh water to begin with and, of course, the drought in California has been going on for the better part of two decades now. Global climate change is a genuine threat to humanity, and the leadership here in California decided it was time to take advantage of our 800 plus miles of coastline to solve the water needs of our citizens. We tapped into the Pacific Ocean not only for us to drink, but for us to irrigate twenty-seven percent of California's land, all used to grow crops." He swallowed, shifted his stance and adjusted his hat.

Cavanaugh recalled the first time he'd met Jake, how much the man had matured on camera over the last two years.

"Yes, but specifically, what makes this and the other plants you've designed different and better?" Terri asked again, prompting Jake to clear his throat.

"Phase one of the overall plan will build five desalination plants. Each facility is paired with a safe, high-tech, relatively new nuclear engine based on a design we call a Molten Salt Reactor, or MSR. Typical desalination plants are notorious energy hoarders that use millions of kilowatt-hours every year. The primary reason more haven't been built is because of the high cost of electric energy needed to pump the saltwater in from the ocean, through the reverse-osmosis filters, then uphill through pipes and into the existing aqueducts and other water infrastructure. Fortunately, scientists at MIT resurrected technology from the 1950s and perfected it. They've come up with one of the safest, cheapest, most efficient methods of making electricity ever."

"Sounds like this isn't a typical nuclear reactor," Terri said.

"Not even close. I'll get to the reasons why in a second, but for now I'll just say the MSR you see behind us," he said, gesturing toward the plant, "generates up to 500 megawatts of power for about a million dollars per megawatt, or about five hundred million bucks. The ninety-nine nuclear power plants operating throughout the U.S., constructed in the seventies and eighties, all use a completely different technology called 'light-water reactors,' that cost roughly thirty times as much —" he counted the issues on his fingers — "create a ridiculous amount of nuclear waste, and are inherently unsafe because of the potential for meltdowns, like at Chernobyl and Fukushima."

Terri blinked, moving the mic closer to her mouth. "Wow. I had no idea."

"Here's an analogy: think of a light-water reactor as an old, 1950s Edsel, spewing exhaust, always breaking down, costing a ton of money to maintain. By contrast, an MSR plant is like a brand new all-electric Tesla. Fast, efficient, safe, and with zero carbon footprint."

"Amazing," Terri said, swiping her hair across her forehead and around her ear. "Initially, your project faced opposition from environmentalists, fighting the governor for creating new nuclear reactors, but apparently, you were instrumental in sitting down with them and having rational discussions. Can you tell us more about that?"

Jake scratched the back of his head. "Happy to. We discussed the environmental benefits of these new plants. Let me give you an example. Those old nuclear reactors from the seventies I mentioned earlier, many of which are still in use and I'm personally not a fan of, only use about three percent of each of their uranium-enriched rods — the number one reason we have so much nuclear waste in our country. Tons of it. But with these new reactors, we can use the spent rods from the old power plants as a source of power. Think about that. Every day we use these new plants, we're reducing the stockpile of nuclear waste to generate cheap power. That's part of why these are good for the environment. With this cheaper cost to generate electricity combined with a high-tech desalination plant, we can recapture the initial capital investment in less than ten years. The ongoing operations and maintenance costs are a fraction of what they would have been with the old tech, too."

Terri raked her fingers through her bleached blond hair. "And the bottom line?"

"We're making fresh water for less than it costs to pump it out of the ground, which until now has been the cheapest way for civil engineers to provide water to everyone. The fifty billion dollars in public-private partnership revenue bonds will add fifty percent more water supply than we currently generate from snow runoff and rain. More than enough to handle the drought and the next fifty years of population growth in California. And all the extra salt is dried, packaged and sold to help pay off the bond. Healthy stuff, tastes great."

Cavanaugh slid the last few bites of trail mix from the plastic baggy into his mouth, tossed the wrapper into a trash bin, and slapped his hands together to dust off the salt. *Okay, Jake, time to bring it home.*

His cell phone vibrated.

CHAPTER 6

August 16
10:35 a.m.

In a quiet town north of Modesto, near Naraghi Lake, parked along a quaint, tree-lined street lined with World War II era cookie-cutter houses, the boss had watched most of the interview with Jake, but couldn't take anymore. He slammed the cover shut on the tablet. Gunther sat next to him in the passenger seat of his gunmetal gray 7-series BMW. They scanned the neighborhood for threats.

He shifted in his seat, turned to Gunther and said, "Now they have four plants online. Everything's going according to plan, and the arrogant jerk still has no idea what happened two weeks ago." His voice sounded deep and gravelly, a sign his age was catching up to him.

Gunther retrieved a shiny black box the size of a deck of cards from inside his leather jacket and caressed the red button on top. The remote detonator fit snugly in his hand, ready to arm the trigger. He squinted, biting the tip of his tongue. "It's all gonna be worth it boss. We be gettin' paid soon and got bigger things to worry about, like not fucking up this demo job. We piss off Linda, we screwed."

"Or Tracy," the boss said, studying the small bungalow a hundred yards away in the middle of the block, his voice still dry and deep.

Gunther wiped his face up and down several times. "At least we had fun fuckin' with him. I liked how you used them rubber bullets on his window. I'll bet that freaked his ass out."

"Nothing about this is fun, you moron."

"Listen to me, boss. We got that dyke's house right there, filling up with natural gas." He pointed toward Paige's house. "Selim's tracking her and she ain't got no idea." Gunther looked at his phone, checking several WhatsApp messages. "She gonna be home in a little over two hours, dependin' on traffic. Bitch drivin' down from Sacramento, about—"

"Yeah, yeah, I know. Seventy-five miles north of here," the boss said, gritting his smoke-stained teeth while stroking his chin covered with white stubble. "You just make sure you press that button when she goes inside. We'll see how much of an expert assassin you are if the arson investigator rules this an accident. So far, I'm not impressed." Linda had told the boss the dolt sitting next to him was one of the best assassins she'd ever worked with, but now he questioned her recommendation, wondering if she'd even worked with any assassins. This mouth-breather was probably her first. He had a strong tendency to gloss over details, important stuff that could make the difference between a successful job and going to federal prison. Or getting killed. "I'll be blunt. To hell with Linda or Tracy, you muck this up, I put a bullet in your skull."

"Chill out, boss. The Bendel job went totally sweet. You tellin' me I fucked that up somehow?"

He ignored Gunther's pathetic attempt to start another argument, then leaned over into the back-seat area, grabbed his backpack from the rear floor, unzipped the main compartment and grabbed a burner phone. "Gonna call the pen and see where it's at."

"For the record, boss, I know you think it's cool you built that wireless voice transmitter into one of your old SS pens so we can listen in, but you should have added a better GPS." He tilted his head back, yawning. "Then we'd be able to listen to Jake and Paige's conversations *and* know where the hell the pen is."

"Goddamnit, boy, we already went over this. The pen's fine without GPS. It's no big deal to call the thing and get a ping to triangulate the location. Besides, adding the cell tech to the pen made the little suckers too heavy and adding a GPS transmitter would have made them feel like they had lead inside."

The boss dialed the number assigned to the pen they'd left at Jake's house two weeks ago, the one Paige had taken and lost—at least Gunther did something right—underneath her seat. Jake's pen, the one he thought of as a good luck charm, had been secretly swapped with a modified version, too, and listening in on all his conversations was almost like cheating.

Almost.

Damn, I'm good.

After a silent ring, the pen "answered." At first all he heard were rustling noises and wind, then he heard Paige calling someone on her phone. He ran a tracking app on his tablet, which showed Paige on a digital map sixty miles north of their current location, driving south at exactly sixty-five miles an hour, probably in Jake's Sûr System, so he continued listening to their conversation—sounded like with Agent Cavanaugh.

Poor stupid bitch.

But her troubles would be over soon.

CHAPTER 7

August 16
10:37 a.m.

"Paige Terner. To what do I owe the pleasure?" Cavanaugh asked, muting the iPad.

"It's Jake. I mean, it's Viktor," she blurted out. "I think we saw him a couple weeks ago and I wanted to tell you then, but Jake said it's a local PD issue and he's been trying to file a report and getting nothing but bullshit from them because his security cameras caught nothing which means someone screwed with them and I haven't heard anything from Jake and this has been chewing me up and I took the pen with Viktor's initials on it as proof, but then I lost it, and I can't take all this anymore and needed to call and tell you. Or maybe I'm just feeling anxious because I feel like shit and am probably coming down with a cold."

Cavanaugh heaved his legs off the table, hitting the floor with a thud. He stood, responding, "Where the hell are you right now?"

"Jake's at some ribbon-cutting ceremony north of San Francisco and I got one more set to do at a gig here in Sacramento, then I'm gonna drive to my house in Modesto, the one where we had the Halloween party last year. You remember."

"I don't understand," he said. "Tell me what you mean by 'you think you saw Viktor.'"

She explained the shadow, the boat, the pen, how she took the pen to take it to the police, but somehow lost it. And how Jake still believed Viktor was dead, or at least that's what he wanted to believe.

"I'm sure someone's messing with you guys. Jake's right. There's no way Viktor's still alive. But the fact Jake's CCTV's didn't capture anything worries me." He took a step toward his office door and turned, knowing Jake was, in fact, *not* correct, that Viktor could very well be alive. "There were hundreds of those pens made. Somebody just got one and is playing a joke on Jake. He's got a lot of friends. Some are downright sinister. I wouldn't put a stunt like that past them."

Cavanaugh did his best to sound confident with Paige, but chills found their way up his spine. Could have been a boater needing directions, but with the pen showing up? At the same time? No way that was a coincidence.

He didn't believe a word he was telling her.

A long pause before Paige spoke again. "You could be right. But what if you're wrong and Viktor *is* alive?"

She didn't believe him either. He told her he'd look into it, asked her to call him again if anything changed, everything would be fine, and they ended the call.

Cavanaugh sat back in the chair and un-muted the iPad to continue the end of the interview.

Terri gleamed her bright smile at the camera, then back to Jake. "You mentioned safety. Like you said, when people think of nuclear power, they usually think of meltdowns, like the ones at Three-Mile Island, Chernobyl, or Fukushima. How were you able to deal with safety? Aren't all nuclear power plants basically the same?"

Jake adjusted his hat and looked directly into the camera lens. Cavanaugh remembered how upset Jake got when he'd asked him the same question last year. Cavanaugh leaned forward to get a better view of his iPad, curious how Jake would handle it.

"MSR's have an inherent safety mechanism built into the design. They use what we call a 'passive safety system.' With the old tech, if the plant lost power, the cooling pumps stopped working and, if the backup generators failed, the nuclear reaction would spin out of control and explode and you'd get a dangerous, radiation-laced meltdown. But the MSR's need electricity to operate, so if the power is cut, they automatically shut down. It's virtually disaster-proof."

Cavanaugh shifted his crossed legs, turning his attention to several new emails in his inbox. One from the governor.

A small crowd of people gathered behind Jake and the reporter. "You told me earlier that other plant combos are coming online soon."

Cavanaugh turned up the volume on his iPad, scanned the first sentence of the email from the governor without really reading it, and continued listening, impressed by Jake's performance.

"The governor has a total of five plant combos planned, up and down the coast of California. Three've already been constructed, all like this one. And the first one was more of a pilot or proof-of-concept that, honestly, exceeded our expectations. This one here behind us is the fourth and the largest by far. The fifth one, even bigger than this one here, is under construction near San Luis Obispo and was scheduled to go online the same time as this one, but we're about six months behind schedule. I'm headed down there tomorrow to meet our guys and try to get things on a fast track for delivery. By the way, since we're selling half the power back to the grid and we have an eco-friendly bottling plant a half-mile away from the site to sell bottled water, we're already generating a positive cash flow for the State of California. And no, the water doesn't have any radiation." He chuckled. "In fact, there's more radiation in a typical bottled water you buy in a store, one made from water pulled from the ground. The whole thing's a win-win-win for everyone."

Terri leaned toward Jake. "Any final comments?"

Jake stared at Terri for a beat before responding. "As a civil engineer, heck, as a human being, I believe clean water is a basic right we need to give to all Americans. It's great to watch these plants come alive like this."

Cavanaugh continued reading the email from the governor.

His stomach dropped.

CHAPTER 8

August 16th
10:40 a.m.

Terri thanked Jake for his time, then ended the interview. A faint scent of saline water and beach algae filled Jake's nostrils as he shook Terri's hand. A group of people had assembled for the ceremony, and she trudged off through the thick, tall grass to the next victim as a flock of seagulls flew overhead, their squawks echoing throughout the area. Jake's phone rang. Glare from the high sun reflected off the iPhone screen.

"Hey, hey! How's my favorite daughter doing?" Jake asked Carlie, now twenty-six years old and a recent graduate with a master's degree in communications theory from NYU. She'd been married now to Daniel Cavanaugh, the younger brother of FBI agent Jose Cavanaugh, for the better part of a year.

"I just saw you on the news from here in New York. Wow! National celebrity! Pretty fancy, Dad," she said, her voice pitched high and excited.

Jake rubbed his fingers along the blue good luck charm in his pocket and felt his mood improve. He always enjoyed talking with Carlie, especially after he'd lost her mother in the fire two years ago. As he turned to face the bay, Governor Fairchild blocked his view.

An inch shorter than Jake and thin as a plastic straw, the governor's bright politician smile gleamed in the midday sun. A woman in her mid-fifties stood next to her, with drawn-in eyebrows and graying brown hair, possibly a wig. Probably an attorney. Or businesswoman.

"Thanks, Sweetie, but I gotta run. Can I call you later? Give my best to Daniel and baby Andrew," he said to Carlie, putting up his index finger to the governor.

"Wait, Dad. Are you still coming out to New York next week to visit us?"

"We'll have to talk about that later. The governor of California is waiting patiently to talk with me. I love you. Bye."

The governor put out her hand for Jake to shake. She wore a ruby-red sleeveless dress that ended below her knees, and a "California First" button on her lapel. "Dr. Bendel, it is truly a pleasure to see you here. What a marvelous job you've done bringing this whole idea together."

"Thanks, thrilled to be here. Finally," Jake said.

"I'm so glad you could clean up the mess caused by the labor union and get this project to the finish line, albeit five months late. And the San Luis Obispo plant. I believe that's even further behind schedule, so I hope you're not losing your magic touch. We can't afford any more delays." She looked into Jake's eyes with a harsh squint, still shaking Jake's hand. "The funding from our partners relies on us delivering a high-quality product on time."

She turned toward the woman at her side and ended the handshake. "Nevertheless," she said, crinkling her eyes and revealing that bright smile once more, as if her dig at Jake had been erased, "I'd like to introduce you to Linda Bennett, CEO of BioStall. They're based in Cupertino, near Apple headquarters."

Jake shook off the criticism from the governor by telling himself he'd process her comments later, although deep inside he knew he could have kept these projects on schedule if he hadn't been so fixated on Viktor. Not sleeping well hadn't helped, either. He blinked to ground his focus on the current conversation before rapidly scanning the face of his new acquaintance. A sense of familiarity about her hit him in his gut. She wore a traditional business suit, navy blue, with a collared white silk shirt and matching pumps.

"Pleasure to finally meet the Superman of Engineering," Linda said, shaking his hand with a firm, confident grip. "I've had my eye on you for quite a while. It's amazing what you've been able to accomplish in such a short amount of time."

Jake wet his lips and pressed them together. "Thank you. Just been lucky, I guess. Right place at the right time."

Linda waved a hand. "Oh, come now, Dr. Bendel. No need to be so mod—"

Governor Fairchild answered her phone, covering the receiver with one hand. "Gotta take this. You two keep talking. Back in a jiffy," she whispered as she wandered away.

Linda crossed her arms, then said with a wink, "I'll bet you have a few other ideas hidden up your sleeve."

Jake stole a glance over her shoulder at the governor, who continued talking. "Of course," he said. "We have some serious issues with our national power grid. Room for improvement."

She squinted. "You know Tracy Ciacchella?"

Jake thought for a moment. "Nope. Friend of yours?"

"Sort of. Tracy's a Silicon billionaire venture capitalist who's invested in dozens of biotech companies over the last couple of decades, including BioStall, my company. We're going to help a lot of people fight cancer. Like what you've done here by pairing new desalination tech with new nuclear power tech, we're combining the power of supercomputers and quantum processors with usable artificial intelligence, then linking it all with human genetics engineering. If all goes well, we'll have cures for Parkinson's, Alzheimer's, and many forms of cancer within two years. Then we can write our own ticket and finally gut out all the corruption and collusion in big pharma."

Jake raised his eyebrows. "Impressive."

"We're taking giant risks, but the ends are gonna justify the means. I'm sure you'd agree," she said, leaning toward Jake, touching his shoulder.

He nibbled his lower lip, contemplating her assertion. "Perhaps. Totally depends on the situation, though. Need to get down into the weeds. Into the details. That's where you find all the answers." He hoped his generic response didn't offend her.

A hefty man with close-set, narrow eyes and weighing north of 300 pounds waddled his way to Jake and Linda. Wearing a beige cowboy hat, brown suit with a pressed white shirt and a turquoise bolo tie, he introduced himself as Tex Murphy.

Linda asked Tex what he did for a living.

"I'm in the oil business," he responded with a deep-toned, gravelly voice laced with a heavy Texan accent. "Sorry, the 'energy' business." He chuckled, handing Jake his business card. Jake gave him a card, too. "A lobbyist for Exxon Mobile. Wanted to introduce myself and ask you a question, Dr. Bendel, if you don't mind, sir."

"Shoot." Jake enjoyed the popularity his micro-celebrity status had brought him. For a few minutes, his anxiety had abated.

"You realize with your Sûr System, people are carpooling more and driving less, buying more electric vehicles, and demand for gas and oil has plummeted about forty percent, which has a lotta folks in my industry running for the hills." Tex adjusted his hat. "Profits are hard to come by. If things don't change, and soon, this might be the end of Big Oil as we know it."

Inside, Jake felt a twinge of delight. He'd been aching to take down the oil giants for decades. The sooner they stopped pulling oil from the earth, the sooner the planet could nurse itself back to health. The Sûr System was a timesaver too—Jake estimated all the productive time he'd had over the last two years driving all across California using the SS. Whenever he entered the dedicated freeway lanes, the SS took over, driving the car itself, leaving extra time to work on his laptop. Those extra hours had accelerated the design and construction of these plants and reactors.

"I'm sorry, is there a question in there?" Jake asked, trying to hide his weakness with politics.

Tex gave a bellowed laugh and patted Jake on his back like they were old high school buddies. Linda frowned at Jake, confused.

"Son, are you a civil engineer or one of these hippie-dippy environmentalists?" Tex asked, still chuckling.

Before Jake's plan, nuclear energy in the U.S. had all but failed. The environmentalists — and the general public — hated any tech with the word "nuclear".

A stocky woman about Jake's age with salt and pepper hair in a tight bun, wearing a necklace with a large, gold cross lying in her cleavage, stared at him from ten yards away, standing in the shade of a large tree. She gripped a bottled water in her hand. Jake rubbed his fingers along the shaft of his Sûr System pen, ignored the woman and responded to Tex.

"Sir, healthy civilizations rely on civil engineers. This means that for mankind to survive, we have to work environmental factors into our plans. It's a balancing act. We can't have business running amok with no regard for the environment. At the same time, we can't ignore the capitalist nature of man and focus solely on protecting the environment. There needs to be give and take. That's how we could bring these new power plants and MSR's into existence without harming the sensitive underwater ecosystems."

"Well, not to dilly-dally around, son, but I believe you've pretty much put me out of a job. With gas demand down so much, our dependence on foreign oil has been cut by half, but our American oil refineries are also drying up. Now with these here nuclear plants all safe and efficient, heck, we might not even have a business model in five years, so I wanted to come by and thank you for putting a lot of folks out of work." Tex took hold of Jake's hand and embraced it between his own two.

Jake stood still for a moment, stunned, before turning to Linda.

"You could always shift industries and work in bottled water," Linda said.

Oil man grinned. "You've got my card, Dr. Bendel. Hope ya have a nice day." He put his hands into his pockets and shuffled off toward the ocean.

The governor ended her call and returned to Jake and Linda.

"Jake, I need to ask a favor," the governor said, pulling him away from Linda. "Excuse us a moment, Linda." After a few paces the governor said, "I've got the CDC crawling up my ass on an urgent issue. I just emailed your FBI buddy, Cavanaugh, but you and I need to talk in private, away from these reporters, so you're going to come to my office tomorrow morning for a brief chat. Eight-thirty a.m. Sharp."

Jake noticed the gold-cross-wearing woman still staring at him in the distance and thought about how he'd need to reschedule his meeting tomorrow at the San Luis Obispo plant. She crushed her empty water bottle and tossed the crumpled plastic into a recyclables basket, never taking her eyes off him.

CHAPTER 9

August 16th
12:30 p.m.

As the self-driving network—the Sûr System—whisked Jake along the median lanes of State Route 99 toward Southern California at 65 miles an hour, he worked on his laptop to tweak and crash, or speed up, the project schedule to prepare for tomorrow's meeting with Governor Fairchild. He needed to get to Paige's house and since the car drove itself, he could focus his attention on various construction task durations of the San Luis Obispo project instead of driving. While passing through endless acres of farmland and thousands of dairy cows roaming free atop dark brown dirt, the stench of cow manure and urine filled his nostrils.

After finishing, confident of the scheduling adjustments he'd made, he folded his laptop and called Paige, asking if she'd watched the interview. She told him she'd been too busy to watch and had a stuffy nose, headache, and her throat felt like an inferno whenever she swallowed. Also, she got stuck in Sacramento traffic, but was now twenty minutes from home. She wanted to lie down and sleep.

"Well crud, that's not cool," Jake said before curling his lips, pausing, and calculating how to say his next sentence. "But, I need your help."

She let out an audible sigh. "Okay but only if you bring me a cure." Good ol' Paige, even when she's down, still cracking jokes. "Several of my friends up north are sick and so is my old man. I'm hearing rumors the government's trying to cover up something, but everyone's saying it's fine, just another flu bug going around."

Jake remembered the governor's request for a meeting. "I'll tell you what I know, but not over the phone."

"So this isn't the flu, dude? Crap, I don't want to deal with this right now. I need sleep."

Jake exited the self-driving lanes and entered the old-school, human-controlled lanes of the freeway. With all the commercial vehicles traveling inside the Sûr System lanes of the median, the outer two mixed-flow lanes were uncongested. He floored his Tesla and zoomed through eighty miles an hour up to ninety-five in less than two seconds, taking the increased risk of a speeding ticket—or jail—as the rush of acceleration flooded his gut.

"Perfect. Ten minutes to take a cat nap. I'll be at your house around one."

CHAPTER 10

August 16
12:35 p.m.

Gunther bared his teeth. "We get to take out two engineers with one stone. I like it." He continued fiddling with the detonator trigger.

Gripping the steering wheel, the boss shifted in his seat again to ease pressure on his left butt cheek, which had become numb sitting for so damned long. "Patience. I've waited six years now to get this prick. In a half-hour, it'll all be over. But only if you screwed nothing up."

The various tasks the boss had assigned to Gunther scrolled through his head and a sense of dread punched his gut.

At 12:45, the boss said, "I'm going back inside the bitch's house to make sure you put all those vent covers on right." With his gas mask and backpack dangling from his hand, the boss pushed open the door.

Gunther leaned over the driver side seat. "Ain't no time, boss, they both almost here. Trust me. Everything's gonna work."

The boss gave Gunther an intense stare, letting the moment sink in, knowing seconds counted. "You think I got this far by trusting insect-brained idiots like you?"

Gunther's dark face melted.

After slamming his door shut, the boss flipped the black hoodie over his bald head and trotted with a slight hobble across the hot pavement, past several large trees toward the back door of Paige's house. His knee and hip joints, ancient and damaged from a lifetime of military-level abuse, panged from severe arthritis; but he powered through, not wanting to show weakness to the assassin.

The gas mask slid smoothly over his head and face. The in and out of his breathing became the only sound as his hand turned the doorknob and he snuck inside her back door. Sweat sprang from his forehead and armpits. Not only was the temperature over a hundred degrees outside, but they'd turned off Paige's air conditioner so Gunther could cover all the vents in the house to prevent the natural gas from leaking outside.

Wearing my stupid sweatshirt doesn't help.

The boss estimated the inside temp at ninety-five degrees.

Allah only knows how many lesbo orgies have happened here.

For a split second, he rotated the mask away from his face, inhaling the proprietary masking agent Gunther designed and had sprayed throughout the house to cover the scent of the mercaptan. The boss wanted Paige to smell roses, not gas, when her body exploded into a million pieces of charred meat.

With Paige only minutes away and the mask secured, he zig-zagged from the kitchen to the bathroom to the living room to each of the two bedrooms, checking each vent cover for proper placement. Sure enough, all the vents were covered.

Except for the kitchen.

By far the single largest and most important vent because Gunther had placed his detonation here. Without enough gas in the kitchen, the spark wouldn't ignite the explosion, and nothing would happen.

I swear I'm gonna strangle that Gunther asshole myself!

Fortunately, the boss had two backup vent covers in his backpack. After pulling one out, he climbed atop the yellow and blue-tiled countertop and started attaching the cover with a screwdriver. They might have wasted too much time allowing gas from the stove line to escape into this vent.

Another Gunther error.

Now, with the vent covered and the kitchen filling with gas, the blast would easily take out half the house. If there was enough time for enough gas to fill the kitchen, and the ignition device would still work, the gas from the kitchen stove should combine with the open gas line piped into the bathroom from the garage. With all the other vent covers preventing any gas from escaping to the outside, nothing but rubble should remain when they blew the unholy wooden sin shack back to Allah.

Gunther had hidden the self-incinerating detonator inside her ceramic, lime-green, cactus-shaped cookie jar, where — according to Gunther — the device would create enough of a spark to cause the explosion, evaporating all potential evidence for the arson investigators to find.

Next, the boss checked to make sure the detonator was online with the transmitter Gunther held in his calloused hand. But the jackass had also forgotten to activate the damned thing. The boss flipped the switch to the "on" position, but nothing happened.

No red light.

Defective.

Reaching into the front pocket of his backpack to grab the backup detonator — one with a timer — the boss heard the automatic garage door opener jolt the house.

Paige.

His pulse quickened and he scrambled to remove the busted detonator, replacing the tiny device with the new one after setting the timer for one o'clock — eight minutes from now — but he dropped the old one on the hardwood floor and froze, hoping the noise hadn't tipped off Paige to his intrusion.

"Dammit," he mumbled before pausing, listening as he synchronized his watch with the timer.

Paige would walk through the interior garage door any second now.

The boss finished connecting the new detonator and flipped it to the "on" position.

A red, blinking light. *Praise Allah.*

Toe-to-heel, with long silent steps, he flew through the living room, but the moment he slid through the back doorway, Paige opened the door. As quiet as a snake, he slithered outside, gently closed the back door, trotted across the backyard grass and into the bushes and trees behind her house, only turning back for the briefest of moments to see if she'd seen him. After jogging back to the BMW, he sat safely next to Gunther.

Finally, after years of planning, the chance had arrived to wipe two know-it-all asshole engineers from the face of this godforsaken planet.

Praise Allah.

CHAPTER 11

August 16
12:58 p.m.

Jake had stopped by a Safeway on the outskirts of Modesto to pick up a quart of orange juice, zinc pills, and aloe juice for Paige. He needed to talk with her about Cavanaugh, but could at least bring over a few key homeopathic items to ease her symptoms.

He pulled alongside the curb across the street from Paige's house on Lakeview Court. Several other cars were parked in the street, including a black BMW too far away to see anyone inside. As he reached across the passenger seat to pick up the Safeway bag, a thought hit him to call Paige first, so he grabbed his cell phone and called, but she didn't pick up.

Puzzled, Jake hung up, waited a few seconds and tried again. No answer. He assumed she must be sleeping and knew from experience that she never awoke well from a deep sleep. Professor Everton, Paige's dad and Jake's mentor from his Cal Poly days, had described her as an "angry tiger" whenever anyone woke her up.

No sooner had Jake decided to wait a few minutes, the shock wave blasted out both driver's side car windows.

CHAPTER 12

August 15
12:58 p.m.

The boss had arrived back at his parked BMW just before Jake pulled up in his blue Tesla. Gunther and the boss sat two hundred feet away from Jake's car, keeping a careful watch on the engineer through the glaring reflection of the sun off his windshield, but all they could see was a partial silhouette of Jake's head and upper torso.

"This is ridiculous," Gunther said. "We know the dyke's inside. What the hell is that stupid piece of shit waiting for?"

The boss rubbed his chin and checked the timer on his watch, calculating risks and options. "One minute until the house blows, there's less than a twenty percent chance we get him if he stays there. A piece of shrapnel or the blast wave could take him out. Assuming the level of gas inside is sufficient now."

"We fuck this up and our heads are gonna roll down Tracy's bowling alley." Gunther tossed the detonator trigger onto the floor. "I been doing this shit for two fucking decades. Never been caught. Not once. You gotta always make this shit look like an accident. I've used this natural gas gig on at least a dozen people. Works like a goddamned charm." He gave a toothy grin.

The boss tweaked his jaw left and right, thinking about Gunther's incompetence, and how he'd failed to properly activate the kitchen detonator. Now he wished he'd set the timer for a few minutes longer, maybe for 1:04. But the dumbass had a point. He wanted to call Linda and explain the situation, options, and probabilities.

Before he could call, Paige's entire house exploded into a massive orange and yellow fireball. Shards of wood scattered across the front yard as the house turned into a raging inferno with thick black smoke billowing out from all directions. The blast wave hit their BMW and gave them a solid rattle. Out of instinct the boss ducked, assuming hundreds of tiny pieces of windshield would splatter onto his face. Car alarms echoed off the surrounding houses.

Lifting his head a few seconds later, the boss peeked through the steering wheel and his now cracked windshield. Jake's windows were blown in. No silhouette.

We got lucky.

The boss fired up the engine, pulled away from the curb and bolted straight ahead toward Jake's car, passing through the dark clouds and falling ash between his parked car and Paige's house. While slowing to look inside Jake's car, he saw several police units headed their way, sirens blaring. Unable to determine whether Jake was still alive, the boss floored the V-8, the tires chirped, and they hauled ass south, away from his first genuine act of terror in two years.

Damn, that felt good!

"Boss, we gotta go back and make sure Bendel's dead," Gunther said, waving his arms around like a crazed monkey.

"Tell me how the hell these cops got here so fast," the boss said, zipping past them one at a time as they zoomed toward the destroyed home. Behind the string of squad cars came two red fire engines and a paramedic ambulance, all lit up like a Christmas parade.

A minute later, they merged onto the 99 freeway north, back toward their abandoned munitions bunker between Waterford and the Modesto Reservoir, twenty miles east of Modesto off Highway 132.

Finally, the boss's chest relaxed and he drew in a deep breath.

"If we didn't get that bastard engineer in the explosion," he said, "he'll die knowing his buddy Paige was blown apart into millions of tiny pieces of trash. He'll be on the defensive. He'll make a mistake. And we'll be there to get him."

CHAPTER 13

August 16
1:01 p.m.

The explosion created a shock wave that blew out the window just inches from the left side of Jake's face and pelted his cheek with hundreds of glass shards. The deafening boom forced him to throw himself across the passenger seat, out of pure instinct, away from the driver's side and away from Paige's house.

The muted distant sounds of car alarms pierced the neighborhood. Jake's ears rang with a high-pitched droning hum as he peeled his hands away from his face, then hesitantly opened his eyelids. He anchored himself to the steering wheel, pulled himself upright, and noted the smell of charred wood and melted plastic permeating the hazy, gray air.

Seconds later, five black and white police squad cars, with red and blue flashing lights and sirens blazing, all screeched to a halt in the street between Jake and the remains of Paige's house. Two massive fire engines and a paramedic followed, driving onto the front grass and parking as a dozen firemen hopped out, buzzing with energy, hooking up their fabric-covered flexible hoses to the engines.

Most of the roof was gone, scattered across a two-hundred-foot radius from the center of the foundation. Two exterior walls of the wood-framed structure remained vertical, orange and yellow flames licking their tops, spewing black and brown smoke skyward to the east, away from the parked vehicles. Heat from the fire pushed on his face. Loud crackling noises made their way through the twanging in his ears.

A two-man fire crew dragged multiple hoses across the front yards of two houses to the north, where a yellow fire hydrant sat perched near the back of the curb. The burly men hooked up the hose, along with a tee splitter, to the pumper nozzle and rotated the operating nut at the top, freeing up thousands of gallons of potable water at fifty pounds per square inch of pressure.

Absurdly, Jake wondered if any of the water used to douse the blaze had come from one of his desalination plants, perhaps the . . . *Oh no, I must be in shock . . why the hell am I thinking of the water?*

Paige.

No! No! No!

A paramedic approached Jake. She wore a navy blue short-sleeved shirt and matching pressed pants. "Sir, you're bleeding on your forehead and cheek. Is it okay to examine you?" the woman asked. Jake heard what she said—barely—and took several seconds to respond.

After blinking several times while darting his gaze between the house, the firemen working to put out the inferno, and the female paramedic, he jostled the door handle, but his fingers merely fumbled around.

She opened Jake's car door and offered to help him exit. He stood and stepped toward the house, but she grabbed his wrist. He said, "No. You don't understand. That's my friend's house that just blew up. Paige Terner. I need to help, I need to—"

"First things first," the EMT said, guiding Jake to the rear of a parked ambulance ten yards to their south and motioning for him to sit. She affixed an oxygen mask to Jake's face, over his mouth and nose, and advised him to breathe easy while she checked his pulse and blood pressure before cleaning up the cuts on his left cheek and above his eye with antiseptic bandages.

A little while later, an unmarked black 4x4 Ford Explorer with government plates and black tinted windows sped down the street, skidding to a stop next to Jake and the ambulance. The driver's side door opened. Agent Cavanaugh hopped out and stood in the middle of the street, scanning the scene with squinted eyes before locking in on Jake. Cavanaugh set his hands on his hips, pushing open his navy blue sport coat, then took several steps toward Jake and knelt at his side.

"Looks like you've gotten yourself into another mess, my friend," Cavanaugh said.

Jake slid the oxygen mask from his face. "I'm confused," Jake said. "I just talked with Paige an hour ago. I thought you were in San Francisco."

Cavanaugh slid aside an orange tackle-box full of medical supplies and sat next to Jake. He put his palms on his knees and leaned forward. "I was in the chopper on my way down to L.A. when she called me and said she thought she saw Viktor in her house."

"That was two weeks ago and at my house, not hers. I have proof my security system was sabotaged, but I've been getting the run around with the local PD and was gonna call you, but—"

Cavanaugh waved off his arm and shook his head. "No, my friend. Today. Her house. About thirty minutes ago. We rerouted and saw the smoke plume as we were landing at the local field office just now."

Jake stared off into the distance at nothing. Dozens of questions popped into his head, tangling with the others, adding to his confusion.

"She called me, said she felt sick, maybe the flu."

Cavanaugh raised his eyebrows and inhaled. "She claimed she saw our mystery terrorist running through her back yard, or what's left of it. And now this happens." Cavanaugh stood. "Let me check around. Need to tread lightly here, this is a local investigation for now, but I want to know if they've found any human remains — sorry — any evidence of murder."

Jake felt sick to his stomach. Not knowing the outcome of this attack on his friend added a whole new level of anxiety. Cavanaugh stood, patted Jake on the back, and jogged toward one of the cop cars.

The EMT finished one final butterfly bandage and determined no reason for him to be transported to a hospital. She said he should feel lucky.

A Stockton detective walked up to Jake, introduced himself, flashed his creds, and started lobbing questions. The guy said he recognized him from that morning's broadcast of the desalination/nuclear plant opening. Even so, after another half-hour of grilling questions, the detective shook Jake's hand and advised him not to stray too far in case they had more questions.

I feel like a suspect.

How quickly any of us can fall from grace.

The detective also said there's a possibility they might hand over the case to the feds, but that depended on whether the explosion was ruled an accident, arson or terrorist attack. The detective said that from his perspective it looked like an accident, but they needed more evidence. One of the two remaining walls rotated and collapsed inward, blowing more debris and smoke toward the street.

After what seemed like forever, the firemen put out the blaze, leaving the smoldering remains in various piles of charcoal rubble streaming with gray smoke. Only one wall now stood. Most of the firemen packed up and headed out. One fire engine remained. After working with fire investigators and walking through the site multiple times, Cavanaugh made his way over to Jake, who'd been sitting in his car for the past hour, struggling to find logical answers to the questions in his head.

"Got good news and bad news," Cavanaugh said. "Which do you want first?"

Jake rubbed the back of his neck, thinking. "Bad news."

"This wasn't an accident. Someone tried to murder our friend, Paige." He leaned onto the car door and peered inside, his face just inches from Jake.

"Tried?" Jake asked.

"No body. There's the charred remains of a cat, but nothing human. Looks like Paige is still out there. . ." He stood upright, scanning the neighborhood. "Somewhere."

"Holy crap," Jake said half to himself, staring blankly at the asphalt while letting out an overdue exhale. "What do we do now?"

"*We* do nothing. You're going to go about your life as you normally would. However, in light of the fact that I received the call from Paige about her sighting of a known terrorist—one who, as you know, we haven't been able to find after he jumped from your plane two years ago—and that this is now a missing persons case, I'm making the call to shift jurisdiction to the Bureau. I've already spoken with my Assistant Director in charge, and she's agreed to let me head the search. Personally. Not only for Paige, but for whoever the hell did this, whether or not it's Viktor."

An overwhelming sense of relief came over Jake. He wanted to help but failed to put the sentiment into words.

Cavanaugh crossed his arms and looked down at Jake. "There's something else, buddy."

Jake looked up at Cavanaugh, who gritted his teeth.

"Say it. Nothing could be worse than knowing Viktor might still be alive," Jake said.

"We have an issue at the state level, has Governor Fairchild mentioned anything?"

"No," Jake said, formulating several questions.

One of the policemen said from the front yard, "Agent Cavanaugh, come quick. You need to see this."

Cavanaugh looked at Jake and put his hand on his shoulder. "Forget it, I'm really not at liberty to say just yet. But I'd like your input as soon as I am, so I'll have to get back to you. Stay close."

Jake's mind rattled through a thousand ideas. "Crap. I'm scheduled to go to New York in two days to visit Carlie and your brother," Jake said.

"Not anymore. Stay close. I'm a phone call away." Cavanaugh met the cop, then they disappeared behind the last remaining wall of the house.

CHAPTER 14

August 17
7:25 a.m.

Jake wrapped his hands around the hot venti-sized Starbucks cup of café mocha while scanning the empty helipad at the Stockton Airport where he stood, waiting to take a ride to meet the governor. He took a sip, careful not to burn the roof of his mouth, then stuck his hand into the pocket of his black pinstriped suit pants, rubbed his fingers along the good luck charm pen, and retrieved his iPhone. No voicemails or text messages from Cavanaugh or Paige or Dave. The angry cut above his right eye, held together by a fresh bandage and caused by a hefty shard of window glass from the explosion, stabbed him with sharp pain. He stuffed his phone into his pocket, touched the gauze-laden bandage attached to his forehead, and winced.

Inevitably, his thoughts turned to Paige and all they'd been through with Viktor and his terrorist crap. The EMT from yesterday was right, Jake considered himself lucky to be alive. Had he decided to knock on Paige's door, rather than wait for her to pick up one of his calls, he'd be as dead as Paige's cat. Assuming Cavanaugh was correct, and Paige had made it out of her house alive before the explosion, Jake wondered where the heck she could be and why she hadn't tried to contact him yet.

Then his focus turned to the power plants, the scheduling problems, that lobbyist Tex at the ribbon-cutting ceremony the day before, the weird lady staring at him, all creating an overall heightened level of chaos muddled with confusion inside his tired brain.

After considering reaching out to Governor Fairchild and requesting a postponement of their meeting at her office this morning at the Capitol Building in downtown Sacramento, he decided against it. He'd learned over the years that keeping his mind occupied, and away from dark thoughts, helped keep him on the sane side of the sanity sandbox. Briefly — on an instinctive level — he felt the tug to mourn the loss of his dear friend Paige. But without a body or anything concrete from Cavanaugh, he leaned in, needing to find answers, struggling forward with his "normal" life as Cavanaugh had advised. . . *whatever the hell that meant.*

A stiff breeze blew across the tarmac as he called Carlie, telling her about what had happened to Paige's house and how he might have to postpone his visit to New York. She shared her concerns but understood and he promised her he'd check in again soon.

After hanging up with Carlie, he sent out a reschedule notice for the meeting at the San Luis Obispo plant, and changed the time to tomorrow morning at 10:30 a.m. He checked his email, six unread, all from creditors threatening in one form or another to "take appropriate legal action" if his debts were not satisfied in a timely fashion. He rolled his eyes in disbelief at how someone with his level of notoriety could become a victim of such a gross error by the IRS, knowing full well he owed no debt to any bank or lending institution. Using an app on his phone, he logged in to his Wells Fargo online savings account to check the balance, which included his 401(k) and cash savings.

Two weeks ago after receiving the letter from the IRS, he'd checked and had just north of five million dollars. But now, when the screen showed the balance, his stomach dropped: negative three hundred sixty-five dollars.

His pulse quickened; adrenaline surged through his veins. He looked to the sky. "How the hell can this be happening?" he asked nobody, fighting the urge to throw his phone onto the ground. His retirement nest egg, the money he'd worked so hard to accumulate over the last three decades of civil engineering service, the money he would live on the rest of his days and planned to give away to Carlie and various charities after he died, had evaporated into the abyss.

Pondering an eternity in IRS hell but before he could make a call to his CPA, the clapping sound of an approaching helicopter pumped through the air, faint at first, but growing stronger in volume with each passing second. A minute later, thunder and wind oscillated all around Jake as a dark turquoise and white CHP Airbus helicopter descended onto the tarmac. Jake tented his squinted eyes as the high-pitched scream of the jet engine wound down.

The pilot wore a khaki jumpsuit and helmet with black goggles. He gave Jake a hand signal to walk toward the craft.

Jake trotted to the passenger door, careful to steer clear of the tail rotor, and pulled on the handle. The downward thrust of air from the spinning rotor blades pushed Jake's thinning bangs into his eyes, but he climbed inside, slam the door closed, brush aside the hair from his face, and introduce himself to the pilot.

"Nice to meet you, Dr. Bendel," the man said. "Heard a lot about you, sir. Thank you for what you did a few years back. My family and I love the SS."

"You're very kind," Jake replied. The comment took him off guard, but he appreciated the compliment.

"I'm Sergeant Dubree. Heard you're a fellow pilot?"

Jake set his coffee into a cup holder and buckled his seatbelt, nodding. "Got a few hours in fixed wings, yeah."

"I'll be flying you to the governor's office this morning. Gonna be a little bumpy; hope you didn't eat a big breakfast." Dubree chuckled, then announced into his mic and to the flying community on 122.95 megahertz, his intention to depart runway 29R. He pulled up on the collective-pitch lever, the craft responded by lifting off the ground and as the earth dropped away from Jake, Dubree pushed forward on the "stick," and they floated forward down the runway at a heading of two-niner-zero, nearly a straight westerly direction. After a few seconds, they banked right on a northerly heading toward Sacramento.

They climbed to elevation 6,500 on the way to their destination fifty miles away. At a cruising speed of 130 knots, and after tolerating moderate turbulence over several water bodies and hills, Jake kept his breakfast down. Thirty minutes into the flight, they started their descent to the California Highway Patrol State headquarters heliport. When Jake exited the craft after landing, another CHP officer met him to provide escort into a full white CHP cruiser. After a five-minute, mile-long ride north to the Capitol building, Jake exited and found himself escorted further by two different CHP officers into the governor's office on 10th Street in downtown Sacramento.

CHAPTER 15

August 17th
8:30 a.m.

The sharp beige walls, plush cream carpet, oak chairs and mahogany desk inside the governor's office had always given Jake a sense of awe and respect for power. The flag of the California Republic, with its red, white and green colors and dark brown California grizzly bear, displayed prominently against the walls, draped in the corner from atop a golden rod.

Governor Fairchild stood from behind her office desk, then strolled toward Jake. "Please, Jake, come in. Make yourself comfortable," she said, motioning to a stout, padded chair with a rainbow floral pattern on the seat. "Would you like some water?"

Jake shook her hand, gave his usual pleasantries, and accepted the offer of a beverage.

She motioned to her assistant standing near the door, who disappeared to get the water. "That's quite the bandage you've got there," the governor said, leaning forward for a closer look at Jake's head. He'd never been this close to her before. The scent of her perfume was similar to Cynthia's.

"You should see the other guy," he joked, hoping it would make him feel better. *Nope.*

"I heard about your friend's house. Awful. Just awful," she said, shaking her head. "Tell me how you're feeling."

I feel like crawling into a hole.

"I'm alright," he lied. "It's been so long since I've seen you," he said, again trying with humor. Still, *nothing.*

She ignored his failed attempts at humor. The assistant arrived with two bottles of water, handing one to Jake and the other to her boss. "Please close the door on your way out," the governor said to the assistant.

The instant the door clicked closed, the governor sat in the chair directly opposite Jake, their knees merely inches apart. She leaned forward. "We have a major issue with the water supply, Jake. I need your help." Jake sensed urgency with a splash of panic in her voice.

He furrowed his brow while unscrewing the cap and noting the label on the bottle: Cal Pacific Agua – Ride the Wave to Hydration. Shaking his head a tad and remembering how much he'd fought to find a better slogan for their bottled water product, he took a sip of water, which tasted great and felt good sliding down his throat.

After replacing the cap, he said, "You told me yesterday, Governor. Funding is in jeopardy because of the delays. But don't worry, I'm going to—"

"No, Jake," she interrupted. "The schedule delays are the tip of the problem iceberg." She crossed her legs, then set her bottle of water on a short wooden table. "I'm talking about poison. A mysterious waterborne illness is poisoning people. And crops. The CDC is threatening to go public. They've given me seventy-two hours to find and contain the cause. Obviously, this information cannot be shared with anyone."

Jake looked at his bottle, then to the governor.

"Don't worry, our bottled waters are all fine. The poison's apparently in the stuff we're pumping."

Half-relieved the water he'd just ingested was fine, his mind flipped through thousands of pages of blueprints for the desalination plants, all detailing the engineering effort that went into designing the drinking water systems. The top priority was, and had always been, to provide safe water to citizens. He pictured the multiple-reverse osmosis filters, charcoal filters, pumping systems, and chlorine injection systems that went into the process of sucking the water out of the ocean and treating it for residential and commercial use.

"No way," Jake said. "Not from my plants. I've tested and drank the water myself. Each plant pumps out some of the cleanest, purest water mankind has ever seen. I'll bet my life on that."

The governor stood. "We've known each other a long time, yes? Since before my days as a politician? You've earned my trust and I know you mean what you say. But let me show you something." She walked over to her desk, rotated her laptop to face them, then pulled up a map of California. Jake leaned in for a better view. "The five MSR/DP's are here at these spots." She pointed to thick, red circles near San Francisco, San Luis Obispo, San Diego, Eureka, and Los Angeles. "These tiny red X's are instances of poisoning caused by an unknown pathogen. I've got the CDC looking into this mess now, but so far they haven't discovered the cause and their patience has evaporated." Jake noted the red X's were all concentrated around each of the four functional water treatment plants, but there were no X's around the San Luis Obispo plant, possibly because it was behind schedule and not ready to open for another five months.

"I don't understand. You're saying there's a correlation between the water we're pumping out from the new treatment facilities and these so-called poisonings?"

She leaned over, resting her hand near the keyboard. "Exactly. And only in less affluent areas." She clicked a few keys and moved the cursor with her mouse, which changed the view to a new map, like the other one, but with orange Xs. "Now these locations here—" she pointed to the clusters of orange icons " —are where farmers have reported wilting crops. Totally unexplained. Like the plants are dying from dehydration, even though they're getting plenty of water." The governor stood straight then crossed her arms.

More questions entered Jake's head, colliding with the existing ones. "Again, not possible. Water from the plants is good stuff. Civil engineers have been providing water to civilizations for almost two centuries now. Sure, we're not perfect, and we've made some mistakes, but the technology we're using now is solid. No way."

She motioned for Jake to sit and they took a seat. She curled her lips in a forced smile. "Let me explain it to you from a different angle, yes?"

Jake sat back, then crossed his legs. "Shoot."

"You were the major idea guy on this. You came to us with this crazy proposal about solving the drought in California. You and your team came up with the locations for the plant combos, yes? You coordinated and spearheaded efforts to improve the Molten Salt Reactor technology so it could be constructed relatively inexpensively and safe for our citizens and the environment. As far as I'm concerned, you're the man on this. And we're forever grateful. We truly are."

Jake felt a gigantic "but" coming.

"But if the public gets wind of this poisoning, even the perception of it, whether it ends up caused by the treatment plants or not, we're looking at political suicide. I backed you a hundred percent. You know this. I helped secure the fifty billion in revenue bonds. I put my name on the line with you. If this goes sideways after the taxpayers have invested this kind of money, both our legacies are shot. You, me, my entire administration. Totally screwed."

The governor saying her legacy was in jeopardy hit him square in the gut. And his, too. After all he'd done for civilization. All the lives and money he'd saved. All the ideas he'd come up with using his civil engineering background and connections to make the world a better, safer, more joyful place. He'd end up being remembered as a crazy psycho who poisoned and killed God-knows-how-many people while causing billions of dollars in crop damage.

He raked both hands through his hair, then re-crossed his legs.

The governor continued. "Obviously, this is stressing you out. Hell, when I found out I felt like jumping off the Golden Gate Bridge, but here's the thing, Jake." She leaned forward, staring directly into his eyes. "Sometimes we need to expand beyond our natural-born capabilities, push those comfort-zone boundaries, and leave the legacy we were destined to leave. If we don't, future generations will look back on us with shame. Now's the time for action, yes? We have to fix this. Now."

Jake furrowed and released his brow before blinking several times. "Let's play hypotheticals. Assume the hypothesis is correct and the water supply is, in fact, the cause of the mystery illness. Have you run any tests? What data do we have to support the theory?"

The governor snapped her fingers. "Now we're talking." She took a deep breath. "To answer your question: yes, we've done a ton of tests, not only internally at the State Department of Public Health, but also in conjunction with the feds at the CDC. According to the preliminary data, it's some new, hard-to-detect virus, maybe even a modified poliovirus, but one that takes about two weeks to fully infect its host. But we're nowhere near anything conclusive at this point."

"I know just enough about bacteria and viruses to hold a conversation," Jake said. "Enough to kill and prevent those little bastards from getting into our drinking water. But are you saying someone weaponized my water by injecting it with an engineered virus?"

The governor stood, then turned her back to Jake while crossing her arms. She took several steps toward her desk before turning back to Jake. "The first three plants were tiny compared to the one we opened yesterday, and even that one will be dwarfed compared to the plant we're constructing in San Luis Obispo, yes? We need answers, Jake, and we need them now.

The conspiracy theorists are gonna say it's Big Brother or the alt-right trying to get rid of us liberal Democrats in California. We need the truth."

"I'm no bioterrorism expert. You know that."

She nodded. "But you're one of the most well-read, knowledgeable scientists I know. You designed these damned things. We'll let the viral experts keep digging on this, but in the meantime, I need you to focus on figuring out how this crap is getting into the water supply. That's what you can do to help. Tell me you will."

"This is a lot to take in, governor. To be honest, I'm not sure my head is screwed on tight enough right now to tackle this."

"I really need your head to be fine right now, Jake. More than fine. I know this is outside your comfort zone. I know you're still mourning the loss of your wife. I know you're still stressed out about not finding that Viktor son-of-a-bitch and of course, yesterday's explosion. But I need your help. You've got two hours to make your decision."

CHAPTER 16

August 17th
9:30 a.m.

Jake traveled along a reverse travel itinerary from earlier, driven from the governor's office to the CHP helipad, where Sergeant Dubree flew him back to the Stockton airport in the same helicopter.

While descending, Jake whipped out his phone to check his email. Between multiple junk emails he found a message from Governor Fairchild, something about environmental activists using quadcopter drones to cause construction delays on major transportation and infrastructure projects. To stop the interference, the state had just purchased several dozen "Drone Killers," and the governor's office—knowing how much of a drone enthusiast he was—had sent one to Jake to run some tests.

No time for any of this.

He flagged the email to look at later. They had bigger problems right now.

Safely back on the ground in Stockton, Jake hopped into his Tesla, sped home without the benefit of air-conditioning because of the two blown-out windows, hurried into his office, flipped open his laptop and buried himself in water purification research for a couple of hours.

Confident in the knowledge his systems were not causing the illness, he texted the governor with his decision at 11:29 a.m., one minute before the deadline.

He agreed to help her determine the cause of the waterborne pathogen, poison, or whatever was causing so many people to get sick.

For the next ten hours, he lost himself deep in research before crashing at his desk around midnight.

His Apple Watch alarm jolted him awake at 6:30 a.m. on August 18th as sharp sunbeams penetrated through three large picture windows placed high on the dominant eastern wall. He jumped up from the living room couch, not remembering how he got there—again—startled and disoriented. After wiping a trail of saliva from his chin, he glanced around the living room, then came to, realizing his meeting in San Luis Obispo was in four hours. He needed to meet with the project development team and coordinate their efforts to rein in the project delays and get the plant finished as fast as humanly possible.

After a quick shower and shave, he threw on a clean pair of jeans, his comfy construction boots, a dress shirt, tie, and gray sport coat.

The 0.45 caliber pistol, stuck in its leather holster, sat innocently on the couch arm and stared back at him. He hated guns, but outside Paige's former home after the explosion, Cavanaugh had re-issued a loaner weapon to Jake, the same one he'd used during the CDM attack two years ago. "Remember your training. Two hands. Gentle squeeze on the trigger," Cavanaugh had told Jake. "But only if necessary. Insurance."

He tried to ignore the weapon and instead, pulled out two hard-boiled eggs from the fridge and chugged a bottle of raspberry smoothie with extra pea protein. Grabbing his favorite backpack from the floor next to the couch, he scooped up his fedora hat, the holster and pistol before jogging out the front door.

But a thought hit him, mid-swing of closing the door, forcing him to stop dead on the porch.

I need to call Dave and reconnect. It's been two weeks since "something" came up.

Plus, his hacking buddy might give him some insight into all this IRS nonsense.

Dave had given him a special chrome USB drive six months ago. Had an American flag imprinted on the side. As a paranoid hacker, Dave had customized the drive for Jake, telling him to use the tool "for emergencies only." The compact drive had the latest firewall and log-in-busting code available, hundreds of customized hacker programs that would allow the user to access any computer and sort through any data, even if encrypted. The ultimate spy USB drive. According to Dave, more powerful than any the FBI had by a factor of ten.

I wonder if I could use this to find out who hacked into my alarm system?

Since the front door was still half-open, Jake hustled back inside, went into his office, and slid open the upper right desk drawer. Making a mental note to call Dave today, he grabbed and pocketed the chrome drive with U.S. flag imprinted on the side, then headed back outside.

After locking the door, he turned to run toward his car but stumbled over a brown cardboard box that sent him crashing against one of the two white columns holding up his second-story porch. He stopped, knelt, and read the address label. Something from the governor's office. Probably the *Drone Killer*. After picking up the one-foot by two-foot nondescript, rectangular, box, he hustled toward his driveway, tossed the box onto the passenger seat, threw the gun and holster into the rear seat and hopped in.

Once he entered the southbound onramp of the I-5 freeway, he approached the smooth, asphalt-covered self-driving lanes on the left, in what used to be a dirt median before the Sûr System upgrade. With his Apple Watch connected via Bluetooth to the Tesla, Jake gave the verbal command, "Auto Engage". Two seconds later, a voice came through the speakers and said in a soft, sultry voice, "Sûr System engaged. Have a pleasant drive, Dr. Bendel."

He released his grip on the steering wheel. It retracted and buried itself deep inside the dashboard, where two panels folded outward before closing to form a firm leather wall where the steering wheel used to be. The brake and accelerator pedals locked in place as his drive became hands-free. A fifteen-inch diagonal touch screen in the center console displayed a map. Jake gave verbal instructions to his San Luis Obispo destination and the system calculated a three-hour and twelve-minute drive.

Just barely gonna make it.

Jake and millions of other commuters were still getting used to the Sûr System. People needed time to get accustomed to allowing a computer to control their vehicles. He himself still found the process unnerving because he had been driving under human control since he was sixteen, almost four decades ago. Having a computer in control still felt both odd and yet simultaneously refreshing.

He slid back his seat, cracked open both eggs, peeled off the shells and started eating his breakfast. Zipping along the center of the freeway at seventy miles an hour, while chewing and swallowing, he flipped open his laptop to continue where he'd left off last night with his water purification research. His notes helped him formulate the beginning of a plan for flushing out how the mystery virus had wiggled its way into the water supply.

Most likely culprit: the chlorination system. Not enough chlorine getting into the water to kill the virus.

After an hour on the road passing through mostly agricultural areas in the San Joaquin Valley, he mentally switched gears and plowed into the Gantt chart critical path schedule for the San Luis Obispo power plant/desalination plant combo project.

The chart showed hundreds of individual tasks as line items on the left, with start and end dates for each task shown as a green or red horizontal bar, and relevant costs. He updated the schedule dates based on what he knew about the project, then determined the critical path for the construction project to be several sub-tasks of the water purification system of the desalination plant. The structural components, including the concrete footings, steel framing, foundations, and electrical had all been completed, as had ninety-seven percent of the work for the Molten Salt Reactor. Only testing remained for the reactor which would still take at least three more months. He calculated the best-case scenario for getting the entire plant combo package online.

The end of November. Right before the holiday season.

Another hour and a half whooshed by before his car approached the exit onto State Highway 41, which did not have the Sûr System. His dashboard flashed multiple lights accompanied by internal sirens and vibrations on his Apple Watch, all warning Jake to take back control of the vehicle. The dashboard panels in front of his seat rotated open, the steering wheel slid forward to its original position, and Jake was ready to resume control as the Tesla coasted down the southbound exit ramp to Highway 41. He gave the verbal command to the onboard computer. "My controls," he instructed the machine.

"Your controls, Doctor Bendel," came the sexy digital voice.

Jake grabbed the wheel, switched his turn signal on and, with a green light at the intersection, rolled right onto the state highway and drove another seventy miles toward San Luis Obispo. Low on electric fuel, and with a few minutes to spare, he stopped at a local gas station to rapid charge the car batteries.

But the system denied his credit card.

After trying his other two cards—both denied—he opened his wallet. Two twenty-dollar bills. He calculated forty bucks would be enough, barely, to pay for the electrical charge needed to get to the meeting on time. Jake hurried inside the mini-mart and paid the cashier. The charging process took ten minutes.

Cashless, Jake continued driving west to Baywood and Los Osos, then onto the dedicated paved road leading to the decommissioned Diablo Canyon Power plant, where an ancient light-water nuclear reactor had been partially demolished to make way for the new plant combo.

From a cliff overlooking the deep blue Pacific Ocean, the facility was perched safely a hundred yards above the crashing waves below. The spot had been designed geographically as the perfect location to construct the largest of the five plant combos. When fully online, this new facility would generate 5000 megawatts of power and enough safe, clean drinking water for a third of California's thirty-five million residents.

His phone rang: Carlie – Mobile.

"You want the good news or the bad news," he said as his front tire slammed into a pot hole.

"Bad news," she said.

"I'm running late for a meeting and only have a minute. Also, something's happened to my bank account and credit cards, I'm suddenly destitute."

"Maybe identity theft. My friend had that happened, she–"

"And Aunt Paige's house was blown up."

"Is she alright?"

"No idea." A flock of seagulls flew past, on their way out to the ocean ahead. "But your favorite brother-in-law is working on it."

"Good."

"Sorry, Sweetie, I have to run," Jake said. "It's great to hear your voice, though."

"Hold on, Dad. What's the good news."

Jake took a beat. "I guess I don't have any."

She chuckled. As he pulled off the paved road onto the gravel-strewn construction parking lot, his phone vibrated with another incoming call.

Carlie replied, "Just wanted to check in and see how you're doing. Call me back when you get a chance?"

"Absolutely."

After coming to a stop, he glanced at his iPhone.

The five-and-a-half-inch screen read: Paige Terner – Mobile.

CHAPTER 17

August 18th
10:23 a.m.

He pressed the "answer call" button on his Apple watch.

"Jake? You there?"

Recognizing the familiar voice coming through his car speakers, Jake said, "Oh my God, Paige." A tear broke free, dripping down his right cheek while another tear threatened to do the same from his left eye. "I can't believe you made it out alive." He raked his fingers through his hair. "You okay? Where are you? I want to—"

"Jake listen to me. I can't talk long. Someone's been following me and this phone isn't secure," she said.

"But I think—"

"Jake!" she cut him off. "Viktor's alive. I saw him."

Jake rubbed his left temple, not wanting to argue, but knowing Paige had made this claim many times over the last two years. "Cavanaugh told me you called and told him the same thing, but there's no way. Must be a mistake."

She shot back, "No. Trust me, dude. It was him. After what we went through, I'd know that evil shit anywhere. When I got home yesterday, after talking with you and telling you I felt sick, I saw his face through my window." She let out several rough hacking coughs. "I walked through my house and the place smelled like some crazy-ass, super intense rose garden. I thought maybe a can of air freshener had exploded. My eyes were watering and I had a coughing attack, but when I tried to open my backyard window to let in some fresh air, I saw a man jogging into the backyard trees. I put my face against the glass to get a better look. Dude was the same height as Viktor, same walk, same pot belly, same vibe. Same crazy gray Einstein side hair and bald head. He stopped to turn back and look at me and Jake, I swear—" she paused, taking several breaths. "I recognized those eyes."

Jake shuddered.

Those soulless, empty, psychopathic eyes.

"Viktor. Is. Alive. You gotta believe me."

Jake scanned the construction parking lot now full of construction trucks and SUVs. Backup beeps from a loader echoed around the surroundings. His watch read: 10:26 am.

"I sat out front, calling you several times, but you never picked up."

"I couldn't get the damned window open. It was stuck or locked or something. I coughed my way out the back door, the same one Viktor must have used, and I ran into the bushes. I saw him get into a black Beemer with some weird-looking black guy who had short, blond, curly hair, and a beard. I waited in the bushes to see what they'd do next. I watched you, too, and I called Cavanaugh and told him what I smelled. He told me to get away from the house. He must have called the local cops and fire department. Anyway, just as I got a hold of my breathing, a blast of hot wind hit me from the side, along with the loudest clap of thunder I'd ever heard. Shit knocked me on my ass. Scared the hell out of me, dude. Lying on the ground, I propped myself up onto one knee just long enough to watch Viktor pull away from where he was parked. He drove right by your car, slowed, and took off heading north."

She was sure she saw Viktor and sounded quite convincing. But how did he survive the seven-thousand-foot fall from that airplane two years ago? People's memories were not foolproof, scientific fact and Jake knew this. Brains were malleable. She *wanted* to see Viktor. But the last thing Jake needed was a fight with his friend. Plus, he really had to get into his meeting.

Now.

"Sorry about your house and your sweet little kitty. If that son-of-a-bitch is alive, where've you been since yesterday? Why haven't you called? I've been worried like a cashless crack addict."

She laughed but ignored his questions. "Not on this line, but maybe you're the one who should go into the comedy business. We can swap places."

He moved on, trusting her. "No thanks. I'm perfectly happy as a civil engineer. But as happy as I am to hear your voice and know you're alive, I have to go, Paige."

"10-4," she said.

Jake glanced toward the construction trailer to the north of the parking lot and switched the call to his watch while exiting the Tesla. "I'm gonna be late for this meeting here in San Luis Obispo, but then I'm going to head right up to—um—I have no idea where you're staying. Your home was incinerated."

Two white seagulls flew over Jake's car on their way out to sea. A FedEx truck arrived at the trailer and parked. Several vehicles pulled into parking slots near Jake, where a bunch of his construction engineers, managers, and inspectors left their trucks and walked toward the construction trailer.

"I'm staying with your mentor at his vacation place. You know the one," she said. Her father had a tri-level in north San Francisco.

As he shut his door and headed across the parking lot with his wrist near his mouth, Jake considered the long drive up to San Francisco without the two driver's side windows, voided credit cards, and no cash in his wallet. Against his instincts, he buried the worry deep in his belly, knowing he'd need to address the seriousness of that fiasco later. "Okay, I'll get up there as soon as this meeting's done, and we'll figure something out. And I have something engineering-related I need your help with."

CHAPTER 18

August 18th
10:29 a.m.

Jake jogged toward the double-wide construction trailer on the edge of the project site. Normally, he enjoyed getting to these monthly meetings a half-hour early, giving him a chance to discuss important topics with key players prior to the actual meeting.

But not today.

As Jake approached the trailer, a slender delivery man in his early twenties hopped out of the FedEx truck, holding a cardboard package half as big as a shoebox. He handed it to Jake, who signed mindlessly on the wireless pad. The box weighed more than Jake expected and had Jake's name and the address of the trailer on the label, with a return address in Modesto, California. With the box in his right hand, he jumped up the triple-step metal-framed staircase, threw open the door to the room. Every single one of the thirty or so engineers, managers, inspectors, electricians, mechanics, and administrators was staring at him.

Out of instinct, he flashed his winning smile to hide his embarrassment for being tardy. It was unacceptable — hypocritical even — for the guy responsible for bringing the construction of a four billion-dollar project in on schedule to be late to such a critical meeting. Set the wrong tone.

A long, rectangular wood-laminated table sat in the center, with attendees scattered around the perimeter of the room. Jake spied his empty seat at the head of the table, then took several steps toward his chair. The room smelled of sweat, dirt, and old seawater. Four people stood in two of the far corners. Not enough chairs, he thought, before coming up with a quip he hoped would help distract everyone from his tardiness.

"Whoever designed that damned Sûr System ought to be shot," he said. The room erupted in chuckles and laughter. "Would have been on time if I could've driven a hundred miles an hour, but no . . ." he trailed off as he sat.

He grabbed an agenda from a pile of papers in front of him before handing the package to the office engineer on his right, who gave him the latest Gantt chart and three-week look-ahead schedule.

"Thank you all for coming," Jake started as the room settled. With all eyes on him, he continued. "I had a rather upsetting discussion with Governor Fairchild yesterday and, to put it mildly, she's not really impressed with our performance. I take full responsibility but I need your help getting this project finished ASAP. We were originally supposed to be finished two months from now, but—" he looked down at the Gantt chart schedule "—if I understand this, we're looking at finishing in about eight months. That's six months late."

The project superintendent's face turned red and he started defending himself. In his usual rough baritone voice, he said, "But you gotta understand, we—"

Jake put his hand in the air to stop the man from speaking. "Hold on, let me finish." Jake maintained eye contact with the guy for a couple of extra seconds before continuing. "At this point, it's impossible to get this plant combo open in two months. I've studied the schedule, have a few ideas, and I'm going to set a new goal for us. Let's talk about getting to the finish line in five months. Shave three months off the current schedule. I think I can sell that to the governor. For the next ten minutes, all of us are going to brainstorm on ways to crash this schedule. I want to hear input from everyone."

For the next hour, after the initial brainstorming session, the rest of the meeting went well. Some people in the group who normally didn't speak much, if at all, had excellent suggestions about doing multiple tasks simultaneously. The team ended up surprising Jake with its creativity. Commitments were revised and the new schedule had a high probability of getting the project done in five months.

After dismissing everyone, Jake pulled the project superintendent aside and requested a tour of the project site. The two men left the trailer, then wandered through the various components of the construction site, including the nearly completed Molten Salt Reactor, the desalination plant, and the demolition of the once mighty Diablo Canyon light-water nuclear reactor.

As they strolled across the final filtration area of the desalination plant, a black man with short, curly, bleached blond hair and a short ZZ Top-looking salt and pepper beard crouched over one of the chlorine tanks, fiddling with the injector system. The man wore a leather jacket and black motorcycle boots, the ones with the large chrome ring mounted on the ankle side.

The guy struck Jake with a sense of familiarity, but distant, faint, reminding him of someone from a dream, perhaps.

Jake stopped to ponder, racking his brain for an answer, but the superintendent yelled, "Hey you. Get the hell away from those chlorine tanks!"

The man pulled a hood up onto his head and bolted away. The superintendent, with his bulging belly bobbing around, ran after the potential saboteur, disappearing out one of the rear exit doors into the parking lot.

For a second, Jake considered running after the guy, but at this point he'd be too far behind. The chlorine tanks needed an inspection. With the construction details etched in his mind, Jake crept up to the set of tanks, retrieved the designs, then compared the dimensions, spacing, and components to what lay in front of him.

Motorcycle thunder roared outside from the parking lot, along with skidding rubber. Jake squinted, cocking his head the instant he noticed a discrepancy between the layout of the chlorine tanks and the design plans. An extra cylinder, a foot tall and several inches in diameter, with a chrome finish, was strapped to the main chlorine tank, which had a thin, two-foot-long black tube bored into the output valve.

A tiny red light blinked from atop the cylinder.

The superintendent jogged back to Jake. "Little shit got away. The office engineer's on the phone right now with 9-1-1, but that fucker's long gone."

Jake stared at the cylinders, his focus razor sharp, so the words barely registered.

"Hey Kevin, come over here and check this out. I don't think this is supposed to be here," Jake said, motioning to the cylinder.

The superintendent leaned in close. "Huh." He blinked several times, rubbing his chin. "We just signed off the final inspection on these tanks yesterday. I guarantee you that fucking thing wasn't there, whatever the hell that is."

Jake's heart jumped into his throat. This could the source of the virus contamination, but what if this was a bomb? Placed here by one of those extremist eco-terrorists the governor had mentioned?

The plant combo projects had initially been opposed by multiple environmental groups, out of habit, because of the decades-long abuse instituted by both the state and federal governments that allowed big corporations to rape the environment shared with all other life on the planet. But once Jake opened communications and explained the positive benefits of eliminating tons of existing stockpiles of nuclear waste, most of the groups came around and turned their efforts to supporting the projects. But not all groups were on board, and some liked to fight just because the plants represented the progress of man.

Jake remembered the words of his mentor, Dr. Everton, who told him during grad school at Cal Poly Pomona, "You can make some of the people happy some of the time, but you can't make all of the people happy all of the time." This rang true to Jake and he knew some people were out there who would never be satisfied, no matter how beneficial a project was to people and the environment.

Jake grabbed Kevin's upper arm, yanking, as they ran toward the back door. "This whole place could go up any time. We gotta get out of here. Now," Jake said.

A hundred yards away, Jake skidded to a stop in the gravel then turned around, half waiting for an explosion.

Nothing.

He and the superintendent hustled back to Kevin's office in the construction trailer. They made a second call to 9-1-1 and told the operator about the potential bomb. Over the next hour, dozens of police vehicles arrived, including members of ATF, who used a fancy x-ray machine to determine the device contained no explosives.

The lead ATF agent held the cylinder in front of Jake. "I have no idea what in God's green earth this thing is, but I can tell you with 100% certainty, it's not a bomb. We're gonna take it back to our lab and analyze the contents." Jake thanked the officer who lifted his arm and made a circling motion to his team to move out.

"Need the results ASAP, especially if there's anything biological in there." Jake called the superintendents of the four operational plants and asked them to search their facilities for similar canisters. Then he sent a text to the governor with an update, that they'd found something suspicious.

As the various police units left the project site, Jake focused his attention on the mystery box from FedEx.

With his curiosity piqued yet again, Jake walked into Kevin's office, picked up the box. The delivery date was today.

Odd, especially because the meeting was originally scheduled for yesterday.

He turned to Kevin. "Tell me I'm not losing my mind. You guys got my invitation to reschedule the meeting yesterday? Or the day before?"

Kevin's eyes looked to the ceiling, then to Jake. "Yesterday."

"Who else knew about the meeting reschedule other than the guys here today?"

Kevin took a beat then shook his head, which included a rather large, flappy bulge in the front of his neck. "Nobody."

Jake remembered the other package in his car, the one from Sacramento, but ignored it for now.

The two sat, Kevin handed Jake a pair of scissors, Jake sliced open the white box, stabbed his hands into the pool of white and pink Styrofoam pellets and retrieved a glass jar filled with liquid. The metal lid had the word VLASIC printed on top, but brown paper was wrapped around the entire circumference of the glass portion of the jar which prevented Jake from viewing the contents.

"How thoughtful of someone to help you feed your pickle addiction," Kevin said with a brief laugh.

The smell of formaldehyde immediately transported Jake back to tenth-grade biology class, where they had to dissect fetal pigs.

Although Jake enjoyed pickles, he wondered why someone would go to the trouble of hiding the contents with the brown paper. He moved the jar closer to his nose to confirm the source of the stench. Yes. The jar reeked of formaldehyde. Definitely not pickles. Jake's heartbeat fluttered into overdrive.

While looking down at the jar held in his left hand, he placed his right hand on top and with his thumb and index finger, pinched a piece of the brown paper and tore downward, slowly. About halfway through ripping the paper, he stopped.

His entire body went numb.

A detached eyeball was staring back at Jake, suspended inside the murky brown-gray fluid. Jake nearly dropped the jar. Kevin stepped back from behind his desk, kicking his chair onto its side. Jake tore off the rest of the paper and found, on the bottom of the jar, a three-inch strip of cream-colored masking tape pressed onto the glass. There, in thick black marker, someone had drawn a simple smiling face.

And two upside down words.

Jake righted the jar and read the name.

Dave Trainer.

CHAPTER 19

August 18th
2:03 p.m.

Cavanaugh had spent the better part of the previous day overseeing the arson investigation at Paige's house. With twenty-two years working for the bureau and dozens of criminal investigations, he'd learned to trust his instincts. Last week, he'd read an article in Popular Science about how all humans have a cluster of neuron cells attached to their intestines, which he found odd. But it gave a whole new meaning to the phrase, "Trust your gut."

Twelve hours ago, in the dead of night, he'd driven from the remains of Paige's house in Modesto back to the San Francisco Federal Building, grabbed a few hours of shut-eye in the designated sleep room, then injected a major dose of caffeine into his system via three cups of rich coffee — brewed with beans grown in Venezuela, his native country — before staggering to his office on the twelfth floor.

He pried opened his laptop, set it on his desk, and searched for information about newly discovered strains of viruses, ways the little buggers spread, and contamination rates among humans.

His mind wandered back to Viktor Johnston. Over the last two years, Cavanaugh had used all available FBI resources —

unsuccessfully — to recover the damned body, but logic dictated one of two scenarios had unfolded. Either Viktor's body did, in fact, land in a lake, unpopulated hot spring, backyard of a vacant house, et cetera, in which case they'd never find it; or the son-of-a-bitch genius was still alive.

The neurons in Cavanaugh's gut told him the pieces to this Viktor Johnston puzzle — whether the psychopath had cooked up this entire plan before he faked his death two years ago or was now pulling the strings from a secured location — added up to more than what the neurons in his prefrontal cortex were telling him. A red flag warning.

Proceed with caution.

At Cavanaugh's request, Jake had consulted with the FBI part-time over the last two years. Ad nauseam, the two had spoken about the nitty-gritty details of every tiny event leading up to Viktor's death. Jake was under severe duress during the plane flight when he and Viktor fought over the pistol. Jake had been drugged and was conscious for maybe ten or fifteen minutes when Viktor ultimately leapt from the plane, so the likelihood of Jake mistakenly accounting for three parachutes on board before and after Viktor jumped was high. Given that fact, the probability of Viktor jumping to his death without a parachute and landing in a location where no one found his body was low. Over a hundred federal, state, and local police had searched unsuccessfully for three months.

No parachute, no body.

Sipping on a fresh cup of coffee, Cavanaugh thought back to one of his earlier training classes at Quantico. The instructor had discussed the problem-solving philosophical principle of Occam's razor, a concept that stated if there are several possible ways that something could have happened, the simplest one is probably correct. Here, the simplest outcome of Viktor's jump from the plane was that he was alive.

Cavanaugh stood, arms folded across his chest, and paced in a circle in front of his desk, staring at the faint ghost of a coffee stain in the carpet. If Viktor was alive, why hadn't he been picked up on the proverbial radar? They'd cast a wide digital net that would ping any use of Viktor's credit cards, phone numbers, and possible aliases. All state, local, and county law enforcement agencies had been issued a BOLO and APB, and Cavanaugh had updated them every single month to keep the information request fresh in the minds of the hunters.

Nothing.

And if Viktor was alive, why hadn't he shown himself yet? Done something grand and awesome? All they had right now were maybes — maybe he was at Jake's house; maybe he was at Paige's; maybe he was part of this water virus thing. What the hell was he waiting for?

So many unanswered questions, with no logical strategy to flesh them out.

His cell phone rang.

Jake.

Before Cavanaugh could greet the engineer, Jake blurted, "Dave Trainer's eye. Pickle jar. San Luis Obispo—"

Cavanaugh sat in his office chair. "Slow down, amigo. You're not making any sense. Take a deep breath and tell me what's happening."

Jake exhaled, but as the details poured through the phone, Cavanaugh rolled his shoulders, stood, and worst-case scenarios ran through his mind like a slide show.

"Stay where you are," Cavanaugh said. "I'm gonna make some calls, but I promise an agent will be at your site in the next hour and take the jar to a local forensics lab and get the DNA analyzed. Trainer's already in the system because of the work he'd done for us as a hip pocket-informant, so we'll know later today if this is some kind of sick joke or aggravated kidnapping."

Jake informed Cavanaugh of the call with Paige.

Cavanaugh replied, "Thank god. I'll call her ASAP and bring her in."

"Any updates on her house?"

"These fire and explosion investigations take time, but I assure you we've got everyone working hard and fast on this. Answers will show up soon. Trust me. Either way, I've decided we need to move forward under the assumption that Victor *is* alive, so that bastard's gonna be the lead suspect for the explosion. I've been briefed on the poisoning of the water supply and we got the CDC working behind the scenes. And now this potential Dave kidnapping. I'll discuss everything with my ADIC and get her on board with combining these three federal crimes into one investigation. I'm going to personally oversee every aspect. Speaking of which, I need get ready for a meeting with the CDC in a half hour."

The two ended their call and Cavanaugh shifted gears to refocus his efforts on viruses. Governor Fairchild had asked him to keep the outbreak and all information related to it out of the media for as long as possible, to give the CDC and Jake a chance to fix the situation before the whole thing blew up from a relatively localized disease outbreak into a full-blown, uncontrollable epidemic. Or worse, a pandemic. He understood Fairchild's need to keep a low profile for political reasons but his responsibility to the public conflicted with her request. He hoped the meeting with the CDC would provide answers to give him what he needed to move forward with a reasonable strategy.

After logging in to the FBI server that ran the mapping software tracking the progress of the virus, he memorized the latest data sets showing the locations of the infected people and the affected crops. Satisfied with the update, he snapped his laptop shut, then hustled down to the seventh-floor conference room. Eight representatives from the CDC sat in chairs along the perimeter of a black oblong table. Brief introductions were made before Cavanaugh seated himself at the end of the table, facing the door.

The power seat.

Dr. James Rosen, a tall, cinnamon-colored man with large, squinty eyes, and a pudgy belly, jumped right in, holding nothing back. The Deputy Director for the Office of Public Health Preparedness and Response, he wore a somewhat wrinkled suit and said, "Agent Cavanaugh, I can appreciate the reasons for the governor's request for preventing this outbreak from going public, but we have a responsibility to let the public know what's going on. Immediately." The man's mahogany eyes blazed. "From our initial analysis, the virus appears to be spreading at an accelerating rate. If we don't stay ahead of it, lives may be lost unnecessarily."

With a furrowed brow, Cavanaugh leaned forward onto his forearms and said, "Dr. Rosen, it's not just a matter of what the governor wants. We need to be aware of the potential for panic. Social ramifications. No pun intended, but if something this big leaks out about the water being contaminated, we're looking at the potential for protests and a major uprising. Billions of dollars in negative economic impact. Thousands of violent deaths, all in addition to the casualties caused by the virus. Neighbors will be shooting one another. Fighting over bottles of water." He leaned back in his chair and crossed his arms. "No. We need more time. I assure you of every effort of cooperation on our side, but you're going to give us forty-eight hours."

Another tall man, with broad shoulders, thinning blond hair, and pale complexion with fading freckles, sat to the left of Rosen. Rosen had introduced him as Dr. Willis. Cavanaugh tried to get a read on Willis, but the guy averted his gaze whenever Cavanaugh looked his way. Perhaps a shy medical doctor.

Or perhaps he was hiding something.

Dr. Rosen squinted his eyes, wheels apparently turning inside his head. He scanned the faces of his seven medical colleagues, leaned in, and discussed in whispers about the ramifications of waiting another two days. They seemed to come to an agreement among themselves.

"I understand and appreciate your position, Agent Cavanaugh," Dr. Rosen said. "We'll give you 'til August 20th at 8:30pm, but not one second more. There's a reasonable possibility this could spread faster than we expect and if it does, we'll all be in hot water. Like you said, no pun intended. I expect you to keep my staff apprised of every single detail as your investigation unfolds. We'll continue to monitor and sample and study throughout the state. We expect you to stay in constant communication with us, Agent."

CHAPTER 20

August 18th
6:45 p.m.

On the third floor living room of Professor Everton's tri-level home on Twenty-First Street, north of Golden Gate Park in San Francisco, Paige gave her dad a warm embrace, squeezing him tight as she looked north out the large bay window to the Golden Gate Bridge. Beloved by the engineering community—and the thousands of Cal Poly Pomona students he'd taught over the last three and a half decades—his retirement from the university as a structural and transportation engineering guru a month after Viktor disappeared had been a healthy choice.

"I feel awful," her dad said. "This is all my fault. I'm the one who convinced Jake to go after Viktor in the first place."

She ended the hug, then gripped his upper arms. "No, Dad. Your relationship with Jake had nothing to do with my house exploding. Viktor's at fault here. Pure and simple."

He let out an audible sigh before taking a seat on his long, taupe-colored sixties-era couch. Then he coughed several times and sneezed.

From the glass coffee table, Paige scooped up her ceramic mug, full to the brim with hot black tea and a dash of honey. A tall storage cabinet stood against the west wall. She glanced around the room, inhaling the comfortable, harmonious mixture of old and new furnishings, along with the scented hints of charred marijuana, fresh jasmine, and that smell all old people seem to adopt after they turn seventy.

"I know," he said in a strained, raspy voice, grabbing a tissue from the box on the coffee table, then blowing his nose. "But I'm also the one who gave Jake the advice about working with the FBI. He initially wanted to bolt. Run for the hills. But I thought he'd be missing an opportunity to mature professionally if he, well, never mind. That's all in the past now, I guess." He tossed the snotty tissue into a small wastebasket before peering down at his clasped hands. "I don't know what I'd do if I lost you, Paigey." He hadn't called her by her childhood nickname in decades. A wave of gratitude washed over her as she pressed her palm to her smiling lips.

She took a sip of tea, relishing the familiar taste as it slid back along her tongue, down her throat. "The point is I'm alive," she said, also grabbing a tissue and wiping her nose. "My poor kitty didn't make it, but I did. I'm here with you right now. We're safe."

Everton wrinkled his forehead, squinting, looking inward. "Not so sure about that," he said.

She set her mug back onto a *Molten Salt Reactors / Desalination Plants - Clean Water for Californians* coaster resting on the coffee table. "Jake's driving up here now. Should arrive in the next couple of hours. We can figure out what to do next. Come up with a strategy."

He grimaced with a slight shake to his head. "I'm afraid you don't understand."

She furrowed her brow.

He continued. "I'm hesitant to tell you . . ."

"Dad, you can tell me anything. You know that."

"Honey, I can't express how happy I am you're alive. I only want you to feel joy in your life."

"I know, Dad. But I'm a big girl now. Have been for two decades. Tell me what's bugging you."

A warm, humid breeze blew through the open windows, fluttering and billowing the gossamer curtains.

"Some weird stuff's been going on, but I purposely kept it from you because I thought maybe I was finally going senile in my old age. Or maybe all that pot has finally kicked in and I'm going paranoid. Or maybe it's this damned cold I picked up a few days ago and I'm not thinking straight."

She leaned toward him, putting her hand on his shoulder. "You're gonna get better. We both will. You've had colds before, Dad. Paranoia and pot-head-itis aside, talk to me."

He repeatedly rubbed his hands along the top of the beige corduroy pants on his thighs, then stood. After raking his hand through the few strands of white hair on his head, he walked in a slow circle while looking at the lime green shag carpet beneath his shoeless feet.

"Okay, fine," he said.

She sat upright on the couch, tucked her left foot underneath her rear, tugged on her earlobe, then whirled her hand in the air for him to continue.

He swallowed. "A month ago, I was doing some research online for a structural engineering book I'm co-authoring with another former professor from Cal Poly Pomona. When I went to the Google page and entered 'structural engineering erosion,' I'd expected to see results for some of the latest work being done in the field of erosion control. Even some slope stability techniques and other new stuff coming out from the various schools across the country and —"

"Dad," she interrupted, knowing he tended to ramble, a personality trait many professors had. "Get to the point."

"Sorry. Yes, well, when I pressed the Enter key, instead of getting the usual results, the feed of topics had things like 'FBI fails to catch Viktor Johnston – Case remains open,' and 'Viktor Johnston's body still not found,' and several other articles and blog posts by people following the Jake Bendel saga."

Paige wondered how the hell something like that could happen. Someone would have to hack into Google, which was impossible. Or maybe the hacker had made malware that mimicked a Google search, which would give customized results that had nothing to do with the search criteria.

But why screw with an old man like that?

"Totally bizarre," she said, rubbing her chin.

"It gets worse," he said, taking several steps to the opposite side of the living room. He crossed his arms on his chest. "I refreshed the screen, cleared my cache, then reentered the same exact search parameters. The next set of results all related to deadly virus outbreaks. Ebola. The 1918 Spanish Flu. Cholera. HIV. COVID-19. There were also links to blogs that talked about how incompetent the CDC has become since its founding in 1946, how big government is our enemy and all that alt-right conservative paranoia crap those types of people talk about all the time."

Paige massaged the nape of her neck, thinking. "Sounds like your computer caught a virus of its own, maybe some weird version of malware. I can run some tests and—"

"Someone's been following me," he said.

Paige looked sharply up, eyes wide.

He continued. "Two guys, actually. Every time I walk to the market or Starbucks a couple blocks away, there are always these same two guys tailing me. They try to hide and fit in with the other folks walking around, like they're trained, but this old coot hasn't forgotten some of the tricks I learned while working for the CIA back in the sixties."

"You never worked for the CIA, Dad," she said. "Maybe you are going senile."

He chuckled. "Hell, I wasn't supposed to ever tell anyone. They promised they'd take me out if I did. Had to sign all this non-disclosure paperwork saying I'd keep their dirty secrets, et cetera, but screw it. I'm an old man now. Damn their secrets."

Paige tilted her head and paused, studying her dad, then coughing. "Okay, for the moment, let's assume you did actually work for the CIA during what—the Vietnam War? I don't understand what that has to do with these two pricks following you."

He shook a pointed finger at the ceiling. "Right. So I'm checking mirrors and reflections in glass windows, pretending to look inside at clothing and food or whatever, and I see these two guys following me. I'd say this happened maybe a dozen times recently. They never got too close, but they were always there."

"White guys?"

He shook his head. "Middle-Eastern. One had a full black beard, the other had a mustache. Their clothes fit in nicely for this city and they did a good job of blending in, but they just didn't account for my photographic memory and assumed I had no military training." He coughed twice and grabbed another tissue from the box. "You remember my old buddy, Alex?"

"Of course."

"He's from Egypt and one of the nicest men I know. I've found, as you probably have, devout Muslims are some of the most humble, friendly, caring, and peaceful people I've ever known. It bothers me how a small percentage of Muslims get radicalized and ruin the reputation of the rest. Sad, really."

Paige crossed her arms and bit her lower lip. "Political commentaries aside, this changes things. If you're under surveillance, we need to figure out by whom."

"Anyway, Alex is good with computers and data, so I called him up. This is gonna sound totally out of the galaxy, but going back to my cold, I'd say at least a dozen of my friends have the same damned thing. Very contagious."

"It happens."

"Yes, but here's the thing: only my male friends are sick. None of my female friends. None. Zero. Nada. In fact, we were joking about this when we were at the theater two nights ago. We all seem to know a ton of people who are sick, but none of us know any women with the cold. Maybe me being paranoid again, I don't know."

"Okay, now you're freaking me out, but I'm sick, feeling better today, but I'm a female, obviously."

"Interesting you mention that, sweetie. We've never talked about this, but now's as good a time as any. When you were born, you had both sets of genitals, male and female. A condition you may have heard of; it's called hermaphroditism. But your male parts were, for lack of a better term, non-functional, so your mother and I decided when you were a baby to have them surgically removed. That's why you have a scar down there."

Paige took this revelation in stride, somehow unsurprised, but giving herself the chance to process it later. She nodded.

"Anyway, two of my friends have been sick longer than me and we're thinking this ain't no cold. It's a full-blown flu. One of them vomits every hour, is coughing up blood, and has a crazy high fever. Guy's been bed-ridden for a solid week. He went to the emergency room two days ago and they turned him away, saying they were already full up and couldn't help him. But the point is, I've been doing my own research and I'm close to finding some answers about this bug I have. Might be related to the water and I have a theory of who might be behind it. Crazy?"

"No, but thanks for dropping these bombs on me. I wish you'd told me all this earlier, Dad. I'm calling Jake right now. Something's wrong. Something's very wrong."

CHAPTER 21

August 18th
7:00 p.m.

Jake's trembling legs took him down the three steps outside the construction trailer as he received a call from Paige, but let it go to voicemail. He could call her on the way up to Frisco, but right now he needed to fix this. Exactly what "this" was, though, eluded him.

Dave Trainer had stood him up for dinner two weeks ago because "something came up." Until that day two weeks ago, they were on excellent speaking terms and Dave still hadn't returned the two voicemails. And now some sick bastard had sent a pickle jar with Dave's eyeball. Allegedly. As much as Jake wanted to avoid flaring his anxiety, he had to split his focus on two tasks: helping Governor Fairchild and finding Dave.

Paige and Everton would provide a good sounding board for figuring out what to do next.

During the drive up to San Francisco, Jake took a half-hour detour east to stop at his house in Stockton for a quick shot of home-brewed coffee and to give love and food to Lazy Bones.

After walking toward his home office, coffee cup in hand, Jake checked his jeans pocket and made sure he still had his blue Sûr System pen both his good luck charm and symbol of his grit to fight Viktor. On his iPhone, a new email had arrived from

Wells Fargo showing the wire transfer from Carlie had been deposited into his business bank account, which used a different tax identification number. Not much cash, but enough to keep paying for minor expenses over the next few days until his CPA could untangle the IRS mess.

He had higher priorities to deal with and Carlie's money would help.

Once inside his office, he closed the door to keep Lazy Bones out, then called Governor Fairchild's office.

"I just got off the phone with Agent Cavanaugh about what happened at Diablo. The eyeball in the jar," the governor said, her normal confident tone tainted with audible signs of strain.

"I have a bad feeling about everything that's happening," Jake said.

"We need to stay strong, yes? Tell me you're still on board with us on this, Jake."

Jake leaned his butt against the edge of the desktop. Heart rate skyrocketing, he said, "I talked to Cavanaugh too. He's telling me Viktor's alive, which logically means the guy's somehow involved in Dave's kidnapping, Paige's house explosion, and this viral attack here in California."

"You knew Viktor pretty well," the governor said.

Jake's legs surged with restlessness. He needed to move, opened the office door and stretched his way toward the kitchen. "He's a plotter, a schemer. He's setting me up for failure. Or death. I'm in his cross-hairs, but not knowing what to expect or when he's going to attack, isn't helping. But to answer your question, yes."

The governor sighed relief. "Good, glad to hear you've decided to help us, Jake, and I'm sorry you're going through such anxiety right now." She paused. "So, I need you to dig deep with what I'm about to tell you."

On entering the kitchen, Jake grabbed a towel hanging from the side of the cabinet under the sink, and, out of habit, began scrubbing a small blot of coffee on his caramel-and-black-marbled granite countertop. His chest thumped hard and fast.

The first stage of perspiration drizzled down his forehead, but he wiped his brow with his hand, smearing the sweat onto the towel.

"Might as well give it to me," Jake said.

"The virus is spreading faster than we'd initially assumed, but only men are getting sick, and exponentially. Also, vast fields of crops are dying. Not sure how much longer I can keep the attack a secret."

"I had a feeling you'd say that," Jake said, thinking of Cynthia, drawing strength from her memory. "I get it. I'll meet up with Cavanaugh ASAP to strategize and implement a plan."

The governor paused again, this time for several seconds before continuing. "He's going to be at your house any minute."

"Who? Cavanaugh?"

"Jake, as bad as that news is, there's more."

Jake dropped the towel on the floor, then kicked the rag against the cupboard. As he walked back toward his office, he couldn't imagine how the situation could get much worse. He expected Viktor to come up with a brilliant plan, but he braced himself for the curveball from the governor.

"Go ahead," he said.

"An hour ago, my office received a threat and accompanying video on a thumb drive," the governor said. "The package is allegedly from one of our political foes, an advocacy group that call themselves Californians for Honest Engineering. This is a legit group, Jake, I've dealt with them before, they mean business."

Jake had flashbacks to the framing job Viktor did two years ago by plastering trumped-up charges in the media and blaming him for Viktor's terrorist attacks. Jake felt a fresh wave of dread rise from deep inside his belly.

"Wonderful. Let me guess. I've done something awful and there's some doctored video that proves it," he said.

"The video shows, without a doubt, the two people who've been poisoning our water supply. To reiterate: it's clear who the perpetrators are. We've had our IT guys analyze the details of the file and we have a legit video, not that computer-generated Hollywood stuff."

"So the footage is real." *Can't be me.*

"Yes, and it shows you and your buddy, Dave Trainer, poisoning the water supply. Both your faces are caught, clear as day, multiple times from several camera angles. You guys look tired, your eyes are half-open. But it's definitely you."

"Me? And Dave?"

"Yes."

"Terrific."

"The threat from the advocacy group is that if we don't charge you with multiple crimes in the next two days, by 8:30 p.m. on August 20th, including a slurry of federal-level shit, the video will go public."

Advocacy group, my foot. Viktor's name is all over this.

Jake worried about where Dave had disappeared but found hope in the possibility he might still be alive. Jake also realized his entire career was now on the line. Again. But the fact that someone had painted Dave and him as terrorists, as two guys who legitimately intended to cause harm, to instill hatred and fear in the hearts of innocent people, made Jake reconsider all he held sacred. He pictured himself in jail for the rest of his days. He needed to defend himself, his family. He needed to find his friend. He needed to speak, but nothing worthwhile came out, only an excuse.

"Not possible. The footage is faked somehow," Jake said, the urge to argue mushrooming inside, along with a primitive instinct to run somewhere and hide. "Can we get a second opinion on the validity of the video?"

His phone pinged with a text, a link to a video.

An audible sigh came through Jake's speaker, like a whine. "Already did. I wouldn't be having this conversation with you unless I was absolutely one hundred percent sure this is you. I just sent you a link to the video, the same link the FBI has. Watch it."

Jake watched the fifty-second video and sure enough, it showed Dave and him clear as day. He scanned his office, thinking of a response.

Nothing.

The governor continued. "We've enjoyed a long and mutually beneficial relationship, Jake, but I'm in a pickle here, yes? I'd like to think I know you, that you'd never do anything sinister. But this goddamned evidence is strong and if you did do this, I can't for the life of me figure out why. So many innocent people. So much economic damage to the farmers. Billions of dollars."

"But Dave's eyeball is in a jar. Clearly, he's being framed, too."

"Or it's a double-cross, either way, I don't care. This is politics and it looks bad for both of us."

Jake swallowed hard. "Governor Fairchild, I swear to you on my wife's grave I have no conscious awareness of any sort of sabotage. My goal in life is to help people, not poison—"

"Spare me the holier than thou crap, Jake." She sounded irritated now but tried to rein herself in. "I must be losing my mind." She paused, mild static on the line. "Or it's the fact Cavanaugh reminded me how Viktor did this same thing to you before, so against my better judgment I've decided to give you a mulligan on this, but that's just between you and me, and taking Cavanaugh at his word he's going to be on you like glue. I have to report this to the state police and they're gonna want to bring you guys in for questioning but because of our long-standing relationship, my gut tells me you didn't do this, so I'm going to take a tremendous risk. My political career's at stake here. I'm screwed if you're innocent and I don't figure out a solution to the poisoning. And I'm screwed if you're guilty. We still have two days before the CDC deadline to go public, so you have two days before I call this in and throw the book at you and we haul you off to jail. I want you to make every attempt to figure out where the hell this tape came from and clear your name—for both our sakes. Figure out why and what in God's name you—

or someone—put in the water supply. I'm going to text you the phone number of my contact at the CDC office here in Sacramento. You're going to call him the instant we end this discussion, which, by the way, never happened."

Jake sat in his office chair, gritting his teeth. "Yes, ma'am. Thank you. I'll do everything possible to help us get out of this mess."

CHAPTER 22

August 18th
7:20 p.m.

The phone vibrated with a text message from the governor. The phone number and the name "James Rosen" appeared. He tapped the number and the phone dialed the CDC doctor.

After a few seconds of brief introductions, Rosen requested a video Zoom call. Jake ended the cell call, propped open the laptop on his clutterless desk, the usual ring tone played, and Rosen answered.

The man's thick black eyebrows pinched together below his shiny, bronze, bald head while his eyes, likely tired from extended working hours, bored into Jake's.

With a hint of a Middle-Eastern accent, he said, "Dr. Bendel, you need to get up to speed on what we know about the spreading disease. We've obtained quite a bit of data in the last couple of days as far as our understanding of how this virus is spreading, the type, and likely origin. I hope you have a few moments to wander down this scientific journey with me."

Jake agreed. The medical doctor explained that, to their knowledge, none of the women who drank the water from the new desalination plants had been affected. But men who it presented symptoms similar to something called polio, which was caused by a poliovirus. He continued to inform Jake that viruses were particles of either RNA or DNA, were neither living nor dead, and unable to do anything until they found an appropriate cell with internal mechanisms to commandeer and reproduce themselves.

"If the ability to replicate is one of life's attributes, then polio is a chemical with a life cycle," Rosen said.

"You're saying viruses are like 'living' chemicals," Jake said.

"Exactly. They have structural uniformity, like crystals, but can only self-replicate inside living cells." The doctor reported all sorts of additional technical data.

Jake struggled to remember the basic chemistry he'd learned ages ago at Cal Poly Pomona. He sat in his chair, slumped over, trying to keep up with the doctor.

"Sorry to dump so much technical info on you, Dr. Bendel, but suffice to say, from these elements, the virus forms its ribonucleic acid, genes, and—"

"Laymen's terms, please, sir," Jake said.

"Fair enough," Rosen said. "Testing has been a challenge because the process requires a specialized concentration step prior to isolation and detection. We've tried adsorption-elution techniques, both of which failed. What did work, however, was precipitation."

"Tell me what that means."

"Bottom line, Dr. Bendel, this virus is man-made."

Jake bolted upright in his chair.

Rosen continued. "Someone modified a poliovirus-- chemically--so it's like poliovirus, but immune to detrimental effects of chlorine, the typical agent, as you know, used by water treatment facilities to strip viruses from water. This is an enterovirus, with a delayed toxicity, which means it sits dormant in the human body for up to fourteen days before replicating. Once enough replication has occurred, the symptoms of poisoning present, which include vomiting, headaches, high fever, and potential damage to the central nervous system, including paralysis and death, if not treated in time. We still don't understand how the virus is targeting only men, but we're working on that."

"Holy God." Jake wiped his sweat-filled eyebrows. Lazy Bones rubbed his back along Jake's legs.

"As part of our contact tracing efforts, we've interviewed a sample of the affected male population. They all drank the water straight from their faucets and did not use a filter — well, some of them did. The charcoal filters found in some systems like Brita don't remove viruses from the drinking water. Some neighbors of the affected, some of whom have reverse-osmosis filters installed in their homes, are asymptomatic."

"We use reverse osmosis filters in our desalination plants. Are you saying those will filter the virus?"

"Yes, but my guess is someone is adding the virus after your filtration process."

Made sense.

Jake considered the possible political fallout from this nightmare. Most people in lower socioeconomic areas of the state drank their water straight from the tap because they assumed the government — civil engineers and water districts — had made their water safe to drink. Californians in more well-to-do areas typically had higher-end water filters installed in their homes.

That must be why the virus seemed to be affecting people in the less wealthy geographic areas of the state.

Jake raked his fingers through his hair. "Tell me you have a timeline for the virus and a way to treat the damned thing."

"Unfortunately, Dr. Bendel, these things take time. Vaccinations can take years to develop and I'm sorry to say, these viruses are unlike anything we've ever seen, particularly regarding how they're affecting plant life, too."

"I don't follow," Jake said, leaning the side of his head onto his palm, with his elbow resting on the desktop.

"This is just my personal theory because we have no evidence to support it but I believe there are two different viruses in the water. Normally, the poliovirus only affects humans, which is what's happening with the first virus, but there could be a second version that's also affecting crops across California." Jake pictured a map in his mind, but he needed to create a much more detailed, real-time one that plotted the affected areas with their relative locations to the MSR plant-combos. "Oddly enough, neither version seems to affect any other forms of animals other than humans. No livestock have been affected, which is something else we can't explain."

Jake let the latest tidbit of information soak in for a few seconds.

"You're saying that since the virus—or viruses—are man-made, whoever designed them purposely wanted to only affect human males and plants," Jake said.

"Precisely. And there's something else."

Jake stood from his chair, took a few steps out onto the thick rug in front of his desk, and said, "I'm all ears."

"We modeled the spread of the virus, making several assumptions. Even though the initial data showed the virus was spreading at an exponential rate, we now believe the virus does not spread from human to human, like a flu or cold virus."

Jake shifted the weight in his stance. "I'm sorry. I still don't follow."

"Our models show that if this virus was spreading from human to human, the entire planet would have been infected by now. We're talking a major pandemic of historic proportions. Ten times worse than COVID-19. We broke down the chemical composition of the virus and—you're not going to believe this—but if the virus had been created with one extra sulfur atom, it would have, in fact, been spreadable by human contact and we'd all be sick right now."

Jake's mind scrambled to comprehend the massive potential consequences. "One single sulfur atom. I don't get it. If the geneticist who created this virus wanted to cause all this damage and terror, did he forget to include the extra sulfur atom?"

"No, Dr. Bendel. I believe we're looking at a terrorist with a heart, if such a thing exists. Bottom line: if you find the source of the infection and remove it, the outbreak will cease, the virus will stop causing damage. Period. We still must deal with what's already been done, which right now looks like upwards of maybe several hundred thousand infected men, along with several millions of acres of crops."

Jake's mind formulated a strategy. "Step one will be to find the source of water contamination and curb the spread, which I may have already done, waiting for results now from the FBI lab. Step two will be to treat the infected humans and crops. Somehow. Can we use existing polio vaccines for this?"

"We're looking at all options."

They ended their video call and Jake immediately dialed Cavanaugh.

"You spoke with the governor?"

"Yes, you're supposed to be here by now. Something about glue."

"I was planning on it, and I watched the video, but honestly, I got bigger fish to fry right now. If anyone asks, I'm there with you, but we need to connect soon."

"And the lab results on the eyeball?"

"Nothing yet," Cavanaugh said.

Jake updated Cavanaugh about what he'd learned from Rosen, and Cavanaugh took the news in stride.

Jake continued. "Earlier today when I called you about the eyeball, in my panic I forgot to tell you what we found at the Diablo Canyon plant." Jake described the hooded man and how he got away.

"Jesus, Jake, these are key details."

"You're right, I'm sorry, but anyway, without going into too many technical details, we're using what's called *dry calcium hypochlorite* to treat the water exiting the desalination plants. It's a powder. When it contacts water, it forms free chlorine and does an amazing job of killing all sorts of bacteria and most viruses."

"I thought you said you weren't going to get into too much detail," Cavanaugh said.

"We found a cylinder, about the size of your thigh, attached to one of the chlorine tanks. We thought the thing might be a bomb, but ATF said there were no explosives inside. They have the canister now and are analyzing it. We should bring the CDC in."

"Not yet." Cavanaugh shared info about the deadline from the CDC — they still had 47 hours — and agreed with Jake that the suspected chrome cylinder at Diablo Canyon could be the smoking gun for how the terrorists were infecting the water supply, but they had no proof.

Yet.

"I'm going to send agents to each of the other three desalination plants and have them search for the same type of cylinder."

"I already talked with my guys at the other plants and they have found nothing."

"10-4. If there were canisters, they're gone now. Just a theory, but either way, I'll coordinate with the local PD and get that cylinder transported up here to my office ASAP. I'll have several agents on my team mobilize to the three operational water plants and shut them all down. We need full investigations at each of the contamination sites."

Jake rubbed his temples. He'd never thought the brand new MSR/DP's would have to be shut down so soon.

Cavanaugh continued. "We need to figure out what's inside and then I'll loop in my new contacts at the CDC. If that thing is chockful of killer viruses, we need to proceed with extreme caution."

Jake ended the call. Sitting at his office desk, he propped open his laptop. He needed to get up to San Francisco to see Paige, but needed to spend more time researching how a virus could differentiate between a male and female body.

But then he remembered he had a self-driving car. Duh.

After gathering what he needed, Jake ran upstairs, stuffed a backpack full of clothes and toiletries, fed and said goodbye to

Lazy Bones, then zoomed northwest in his Tesla toward San Francisco.

Once plugged into the SS on Interstate 205, he continued his research. He'd assumed, like most people his age, that men, and women were essentially the same biologically, with obvious differences in anatomy and various hormone levels. After fifteen minutes online, while his car drove him north, he discovered there had been several monumental studies done in the last decade that proved significant differences in human males and females, including the physical brain. Every cell in a female body differs from a male's at the chromosome level. He realized he needed to let the doctors at the CDC do their research and his time would be better spent searching for Viktor, getting a handle on the extent of the viral spread, and working with Cavanaugh to help answer questions about the water treatment process.

He took a call from Paige.

"I've been trying to get ahold of you. Something's not right," she said. "Two guys have been following my dad."

Jake digested her information and, after swearing her to secrecy, got her up to speed with the spread of the virus, his financial troubles with the IRS, and the eyeball.

"I knew it. Goddamnit, I told you. Viktor's done something to Dave," she said, panic in her voice.

"You were right all along. I'm sorry, but I need your help. We both need to get up to San Francisco and coordinate with Cavanaugh. I'm headed west on the 205 right now."

"I'm already here. I'm like five minutes from the Federal Building, dude. Hurry."

Jake peered out his left window to the south. Beige rolling hills, with spots of green oak trees, blurred past in the distance. "Get with Cavanaugh. I'll be there in another hour. There's one more thing I haven't told you yet, but I need to tell you in person."

CHAPTER 23

August 18th
7:45 p.m.

As Cavanaugh slurped the last drip of cold black coffee from his *I Heart Venezuela* mug, Paige appeared at the doorway to his office. She'd already called ahead, and he'd cleared her through security on the ground floor. With an FBI Visitor badge clipped to her black *I See Dumb People* t-shirt, she walked into the room and sat in one of two chairs opposite Cavanaugh.

"Jake's driving here now, should get here in another hour," she said.

"We don't have time to wait," he said, standing from his chair, walking to his office entrance, and closing the etched glass door. "I have bad news."

Paige's eyes, bloodshot from the dry weather and likely caused by her suffering from seasonal allergies or a cold, were pegged wide open. She reminded him of the clichéd deer in the headlights image.

Cavanaugh took a few steps toward Paige, hovering over her while she sat. He crossed his arms and explained about the eyeball in the jar.

"Jake already told me." She pulled out a fresh tissue from her pocket and blew her nose.

"Just received word from our forensics lab. I haven't told Jake yet and I'm sorry to be the one to tell you this, Paige, but the DNA on the eyeball is a perfect match for Dave Trainer."

She grabbed onto Cavanaugh's forearm through his suit coat sleeve. In a halting voice, she said, "There must be a mistake. Can't be Dave."

"Our guys don't screw up." She looked up at the tiled ceiling, pools of unspent tears forming in both eyes as she blinked. "The good news, if you could call it that, is that just because Dave lost an eyeball, doesn't mean he's dead. I realize that must sound cold, but—"

"He's not dead. You're right. We need to find him, instead of sitting here talking."

Cavanaugh agreed. He reached for his cell and dialed the lead doctor at the CDC.

"I was just going to call you, Agent Cavanaugh. We've discovered something, well, rather odd," Dr. Rosen said. Cavanaugh walked to the corner so Paige couldn't hear the details.

"Go ahead," Cavanaugh said.

"The discovery is preliminary, but from what we can tell, there appears to be a possibility of some rather rare, genetic side effect to the virus," Dr. Rosen said.

Images of Nazi Germany and the horrors from World War II flooded Cavanaugh's mind.

"Not sure I follow, doctor," Cavanaugh said, placing his phone to his other ear.

"If our lab results are correct, the men affected by this virus may end up with modified DNA. We're not a hundred percent sure, but that's what it looks like at the moment. We're still gathering data."

"Jesus. If what you're saying is true, this is an entirely new level of criminal behavior," Cavanaugh said in a hushed tone, so Paige wouldn't hear much. "Not sure we even have laws against that."

"We're going to keep running tests, but it's not looking good. Agent Cavanaugh, according to my timeline, you have less than forty-eight hours left to sort this out before we go public. We're already doing the preliminary set up for quarantined isolation of approximately 200,000 infected males, but that's going to be hard to keep quiet. Plus, if we're wrong in our analysis that the spread of the disease is limited, we might even need to set up quarantine areas within a ten-mile radius of each of those water treatment plants."

"Yeah, yeah. I gotta run. You find anything else out—" Cavanaugh said, noticing his phone flashing an incoming call from one of the field agents, "—let me know ASAP." He ended the call with Dr. Rosen and answered the new call, which he put on speaker.

"Sir, we tracked the FedEx package back to an abandoned munitions bunker just outside of Modesto. We're headed there now."

Cavanaugh calculated the distance to Modesto at about a hundred miles. "Get there. Send me the address via text and I'll meet you there in an hour."

He ended the call and stood, grabbing Paige's upper arm. "You're coming with me," he said, racing with Paige out of his office and heading up to the roof.

They jogged toward the elevator and, noticing the confused look on Paige's face as they entered the elevator, Cavanaugh said, "Call Jake and tell him to reroute. I want him there with us in Modesto. We're taking the chopper."

CHAPTER 24

August 18th
8:15 p.m.

Linda Bennett forced a half smile as the Morton's Steakhouse waiter finished the pour of a 2011 special selection Pinot Grigio. He twisted the bottle, arched his back and watched as she maneuvered the crystal glass to her nose and inhaled the rich, musty scent before taking a sip. As the liquid flowed over her palette, the words "complete" and "elegant" came to mind. She nodded at the waiter who added another six ounces before jamming the bottle into an icy cold wine bucket.

She took another taste, relishing the memories of enjoyable outings she and her husband of nearly a quarter century had experienced in various countries across the globe. Her MBA from Stanford, a year after they married, virtually ensured her of substantial business success, although at the time she had no idea of the specific field she would pursue. A deep, instinctive desire drove her to make money and change the world, to make it a better place than when she arrived those many decades ago. Her passions for biology and computer technology had merged in the nineties, contributing to her immense financial success.

While waiting for her dinner guest to arrive, the scent of marinated beef and freshly baked rolls wafting in the air. The mini-chandeliers strained to illuminate the dim atmosphere. A dozen round dining tables were scattered throughout the interior, draped with bleached white linen cloths and immaculately set with silver utensils nestled against fine china plates. In the distance to her left, the deep oak bar cabinetry sat prominently against a wall cluttered with a plethora of colored hard liquor bottles. To her right sat a cherry wood wine barrel, wrapped with four chocolate brown steel straps, surrounded by the sounds of clanking forks on plates that blended with the light background mix of human conversations and the occasional outburst of laughter.

Her brown wig, with streaks of gray speckled throughout, felt off kilter, likely because of the spiked level of stress caused by her intense OCD. To restore balance, she raised her hand to her ear, then gave a subtle tug on the false hairpiece to make the necessary adjustments. Her mind wandered to her eyebrows, ensuring she'd remembered to pencil them in as part of her pre-dining bathroom ritual.

Ten years ago, while defending herself through a horrific business-related lawsuit, the stress of the legal trauma had triggered an autoimmune response that caused every strand of body hair to fall out. Her doctor called the syndrome *alopecia areata*. Although she hoped the hair loss would be temporary, her body never renewed its ability to grow hair. One benefit from the disease was not having to shave her legs. But wearing a wig in public always felt awkward, like everyone was staring at her head, poised to laugh at any moment.

She took another sip of wine, drew back inside her powerful mind, and considered her recent actions.

And the virus.

Nobody on the entire planet could have created that virus the way she and Gunther did.

A work of art.

She knew many people would suffer from her creation, but she kept a firm grip on sanity by selling herself on the ultimate benefits for the greater good. The hefty high-eight-figure donation from Tracy in exchange for her viral expertise would help keep Linda's company, BioStall Industries, flush with cash to find a cure for Irritable Bowel Syndrome, a condition that Linda and about thirty million other Americans suffered from. Her goal was to find a cure not only for IBS but also all forms of cancer.

She reached into her leather purse to retrieve her good luck charm: the gold Cross pen her Aunt Diana had given her as a gift when she graduated from Stanford. Linda recalled the many contracts she'd signed with it. She set the pen on the table, then took a healthy gulp of wine, which had now started to provide those epic, stress-alleviating benefits.

"Linda, my dear friend, so good to see you," Tracy said from behind, surprising Linda into spilling several drops of wine onto her suit. Tracy strolled up to Linda, hand out to shake, trying to hide the slight limp caused by a one-inch difference in leg length.

Linda forced a smile and shook Tracy's hand, which felt cold, before offering her dinner guest a seat opposite her at the square table.

"Will your husband be joining us?" Tracy asked.

"You think he'd understand what we're doing, or why?"

"I hear your work is a splendid hit with several thousand Californians," Tracy said, eyes fixated, drilling into Linda's prefrontal cortex.

"I guess we're skipping the pleasantries this evening."

"Indeed. Time is of the essence."

"We've talked about this," Linda replied. "Not entirely my work. I coordinated with Gunther. You know—"

"These trivial details are of no concern," Tracy said. "You are pulling the strings. I don't know how or where you found Gunther, and I honestly don't care. But the brains of a henchman and a biological weapons engineer merged into one man is quite astonishing, to say the least. It's as if God himself is watching us, providing the right tools to do this job to save humankind from itself."

"So you keep saying. But there's nothing in the news about the infections yet," Linda said, leaning back in her chair.

"It is of critical importance for you to stay focused on the big picture," Tracy said. "I go to sleep every night knowing we are doing the right thing, something the U.S. Government and its gaggle of worthless politicians have all failed to do. We are the ones taking action. We are the warriors. We are taking the risks and will be judged by history as the genuine heroes of the modern world."

Linda took three large gulps of wine, emptying her glass with an exhale, arm stiff as she set the crystal piece back onto the tablecloth. "Don't worry, I'm still on board a hundred percent and Gunther is still on target to take out the engineer per your instructions. Our mole at the CDC will use the modified drones tonight. But I would've felt more comfortable if we could've tested our product more thoroughly before the release two weeks ago."

Tracy scooped up a menu and glanced across the inside. "I am absolutely famished. Let's have a nice dinner, shall we? I can fill you in on all the details."

Before the blackmailing, Tracy's confidence used to give Linda a jolt of energy. But not anymore. Linda hid her second thoughts, misgivings, and remaining seeds of regret. She thought about her husband and the sacrifices she'd made to get to this point and felt like a deflating balloon.

"You go ahead. I've lost my appetite."

CHAPTER 25

August 18th
8:00 p.m.

Thirty minutes into his westerly drive from his Stockton home to San Francisco to meet with Agent Cavanaugh, Jake received an urgent call from Paige. She told him she was getting into an FBI helicopter with Cavanaugh to fly to an abandoned munitions bunker near Modesto, based on new intel about Viktor.

Jake exited the SS as the sun dipped below the coastal horizon, the entire scene lit up with bright shades of orange and pink. After crossing underneath the I-205 at the nearest interchange, he hung an illegal U-turn, peeled out and before long was driving south on the I-5 toward Modesto to meet Cavanaugh and Paige.

Jake's mind turned to getting the San Luis Obispo project back on schedule. He mulled over the ideas the group had come up with earlier that day to accelerate the schedule but had questions, so he called the construction manager, Omar Abu Ali, to get them both on the same page.

"Didn't have time to talk with you much yesterday afternoon, with the eyeball in the jar and everything," Jake said, yelling over the sound of wind coming in through the two window openings on his left, while a wave of nausea hit him after thinking what might have happened to Dave.

"We've beefed up security around the entire construction site," Omar said through the phone, with the slightest of Egyptian accents. "I brought in a whole new crew of armed guards and we're giving everyone ID badges. No badge, no work. Period. We can't afford to have any more problems."

Through the left side of his cracked Tesla windshield, a low, full moon peeked through patches of thick, haloed clouds surrounded by a pastel-colored eastern sky. Jake purposely stayed out of the SS lanes to get to Modesto as fast as possible, risking the old school human-controlled lanes. And a speeding ticket from the CHP. Zooming past a triple trailer truck safely inside the SS going seventy miles an hour, Jake easily broke the speed limit as power lines supported by ancient, massive truss towers flew past. He recalled a shortcut he'd taken once before and exited the freeway to local streets.

"Still got the governor breathing down my neck on the schedule, so I need your A-game, Omar," Jake said.

The two talked for the next fifteen minutes about the risks associated with paralleling sequential tasks. Omar told Jake he was at his desk at the San Luis Obispo construction trailer, reworking the Gantt chart critical path schedule.

But Jake soon realized his idea to shave time off his drive to Modesto had failed. He found himself in the middle of a two-lane road lined with thousands of almond trees illuminated by a dim, setting sun. He needed to check his navigation app on the dashboard screen, but wanted Omar to finish crunching the numbers on the schedule.

"Okay, boss. Those changes will help us reduce the delay quite a bit more," Omar said. Clicking noises came through the phone's receiver, then after several seconds Omar returned. "Wow. We're looking at chopping that goddamned delay down from six months to three," he said with a chuckle. "I might need your help negotiating with the contractor on these changes, but if they buy in, we're looking at having this bad boy fully operational in three months, the day after we complete testing the MSR."

A warm, much-need injection of confidence flowed through Jake's veins. As he wrapped up the call, a swarm of blinking red and green lights appeared a few hundred yards in front of him, floating mid-air. He first thought they might be a miniature cloud of tiny airplanes, imagining a terrorist scenario where two-pound blocks of Semtex explosive were affixed to the bottom of each drone, and the aerial vehicles were programmed to hit certain infrastructure targets. He tucked the idea way back into his head, reminding himself to talk with Cavanaugh about what the FBI was doing to prevent that type of potential attack in the future.

Before he finished his thought, the lights stopped moving relative to his car. Both he and the lights were moving south at the same speed of thirty-five miles an hour, as though they were tethered, leading his Tesla down the potholed road. He realized he'd been distracted and hadn't pulled up the map app. Not wanting to pull over, he instead turned right onto a dusty road heading west, hoping the floating objects would go on a different vector, or maybe that the lights were just an illusion.

But the flying objects changed course with him, continuing to float fifty yards in front, maybe thirty feet off the ground. Jake slammed on his brakes. The lights stopped, too. He leaned forward over his steering wheel, eyes squinted. There, hovering in the air with the specs of moonlight reflecting off their shiny rotating propellers, were four octocopters arranged in a left-to-right line, each four feet in diameter, with something black dangling beneath.

Jake had flown quadcopter drones over the years and, as a private pilot, found them fun to fly. And without the risk of air sickness. He knew the technology existed to stream live HD-quality video to any nearby source, but as these drones stared down at him, unmoving, lights blinking, he put the Tesla in reverse and backed up nice and slow. The drones kept their same relative distance to his car, locked on.

"Shit," Jake said. He assumed those flying creatures had a maximum speed of maybe fifty miles an hour, unlike the newer tiny drones that held Guinness Book of World Record speeds just under two hundred miles per hour.

He floored the gas pedal, surging thousands of volts to the massive motor to outrun the drones. Spinning the steering wheel hard left, he spun his tires while making a half-doughnut, then sped east back toward the paved road.

But the drones hovered in his rearview mirror.

Within seconds, he raced up to over a hundred miles an hour. The drones faded backward into the distance.

With a loud, clapping boom, his rear window shattered. He whipped his head around to get a better look. Bursts of yellow and white flashes appeared below all four drones.

Gunfire from drones?

Multiple pings and pangs pelted the exterior of the Tesla. He swerved side to side, speeding east along the local road, heading toward the interstate freeway a mile in front of him. He floored the gas pedal again. The car leapt forward, speeding up to a hundred and thirty miles an hour.

The video display system in the center console of the dashboard exploded. Sparks flew onto his lap. He swerved onto the shoulder, scraping a low-set guard rail affixed to the top of a box culvert. Once across the culvert, his front right tire bogged down in the loose sand, sending his Tesla into a flat spin before skidding to a stop near the almond groves.

Nauseous and dizzy, he rotated his head to regain his bearings, but more rounds hammered his car. The I-5 freeway taunted him from a quarter mile away, with the bridge over the local street and streaming lights from dozens of cars and trucks crossing back and forth.

The term sitting duck came to mind. He'd thought he could outrun these things. Mistake. Any second now one of the rounds would sail through his body and he'd bleed out in the middle of nowhere. His life to that point, with the death of his wife, his new grandson, his daughter's marriage to Daniel, all he'd accomplished for the world using his civil engineering genius—would be for nothing.

He thought back to how the FBI had failed to find Viktor's body. Deep inside his belly, he knew the bastard was alive. Now someone was controlling four gun-enabled drones, peppering his Tesla with God-knows-what-sized rounds of ammo. The drones probably . . .

Drones!

The box!

He craned his head toward the brown cardboard object sitting on the passenger seat. Several thoughts collided inside his head.

An opportunity to survive.

He ripped open the top flaps, then retrieved the camouflage green Hulk-looking bulky rifle with *DroneKiller* printed on the side in black. Another round flew past him. He floored the Tesla, peeling out again, east toward the freeway, steering the car with his knees while trying to figure out how to operate the device. He remembered reading about how these anti-drone devices used radio-frequency jamming to kill the control signals the drones used to operate.

Many of Jake's recent tech purchases were powered by lithium-ion batteries, which held an initial charge from the factory for months, if not years, unlike the old nickel-cadmium rechargeable units from the nineties. He hoped the DroneKiller already had a charge. His life depended on whether the stupid little piece of electronic energy storage had juice or not. Another round tore through the roof. His chest heaved in and out, his pulse pumped in his neck.

With the army of four drones following him a hundred yards to his west, approaching fast and firing dozens of rounds per second, he flipped the dark green power switch on the side of the green machine to the "on" position. A tiny green light appeared. A whining, high-pitched noise emanated from the device.

This might work.

He crossed the southbound ramp intersection. No traffic other than up on the elevated freeway above. With the bridge to his east, he slammed on his brakes, skidded to stop, shifted the transmission into park, and pushed open his door. After crawling out of the Tesla, he hustled behind two large guardrail barriers. The ten-gauge steel beams were an eighth of an inch thick, enough to provide decent cover from the rounds coming at him at an angle.

Crouched low, Jake slid to a stop while several dozen pangs popped off from the guardrail. He closed his eyes tight until the firing stopped, then bent at the waist, aimed the anti-drone beast backward to his mechanical assailants, and pulled the trigger. The green gun made a pulsating, faintly audible squeal. Jake stared at the drones and in less than a second, instead of alternating green and red, the lights on all four drones changed to solid red.

No green.

More importantly, the gunfire stopped.

With his finger still holding the trigger locked, he stood, facing west, toward the drones, which hovered in the air, motionless.

Now who's the sitting duck?

Without taking his eyes off the drones, he continued aiming the green rifle at the computerized mini-army as he walked back to his Tesla and opened the rear door. He retrieved the holster with the 0.45 pistol Cavanaugh had given him. Holding the drone killer in his left hand, he jiggled the pistol loose with his right and the holster fell to the ground. His thumb flipped the tiny nickel safety lever to the red dot.

Armed.

With the pistol aimed at the drones, the scientist in him needed to know how this all worked, so he released the trigger on the green DroneKiller rifle to see what would happen. Within seconds, the drones came back to life, the green lights flashed, and all four drones went back into attack mode, coming at his car and firing their weapons again. He flinched, pulled the trigger again on the DroneKiller, then crouched over as the pulsating noise returned and the drones froze.

Before the drones could have another chance to come alive, he walked toward them from fifty yards away. The volume of the buzzing noise, which sounded like a swarm of bees, increased. The drones hovered twenty feet above the street as he approached, low and alert, like a cat stalking a wounded mouse.

Now five yards away, he cocked the hammer of his pistol, aimed at the left-most drone, and fired off a round. The deafening blast jolted his eardrums. Instant ringing. Sparks exploded from the guts of the drone, forcing the thing to crash to the ground. He repeated his assault in rapid succession on the remaining three unmanned aerial vehicles, grateful the governor had sent him the DroneKiller, as he shot the helpless bastards from the sky. The drone on the far right side took several bullets to disable, but ultimately swirled onto the ground with its three brothers.

With two rounds remaining in his magazine, Jake released the trigger of the green machine and scanned the area, wondering if the drone operator was close by or at some remote location. Satisfied of his safety, he picked up the remains of one of the assassin drones, hauled it back to his Tesla, and threw the damned thing into the trunk for Cavanaugh's team to examine later. Then he got in his car, prayed that it would move, and shifted to drive.

Miraculously, the Tesla still worked.

CHAPTER 26

August 18th
8:25 p.m.

Under a darkening sky, first twinkling stars becoming visible, Viktor Johnston shuffled along five feet behind Gunther as they meandered through the empty field toward the door of their operations center outside Modesto, California. The tall dry grass collapsed beneath each step of his ten-inch black army boots, while a mild breeze rattled through the dehydrated flora. From a hundred feet away, they approached the facility they'd been using for the last year as an operations base to coordinate their ultimate attack against the California liberal infidels.

A gopher scurried away, disappearing into the misty darkness hovering over a vast field to their right. Viktor continued plowing through the scattered, low-lying scrub brush before Gunther turned his head and fell back by his side.

"Well, boss, word is our little plan's startin' to come together," Gunther said. "Our inside man at the CDC is telling me they've unofficially tallied over a hundred thousand sick guys. All with my virus running through their veins. And money coming to my bank account."

"I'm elated to hear you're so enamored with your work," Viktor said, taking several more steps toward the bunker, a football field-length earthen hump piled high during World War

II, with two large, rusted blue steel doors at the entrance surrounded by one-foot-thick retaining walls holding back the soil. The midsection of Viktor's back throbbed, burning. "We were lucky the Trihypnol worked so well on Bendel, but boy, you really fucked up at that dyke's house."

They approached the gateway doors, half above grade and half below, then stepped down four concrete steps to the entryway. Gunther punched in his six-digit PIN, the box beeped, and the door lock clanked. With a hefty pull, he swung the door open. "I figured someone with your genius-level IQ could've figured out a better plan when Jake showed up," he said.

"How about you shut that hick mouth of yours," Viktor said, popping two Vicodin and swallowing with saliva. They glared at each other. "I'm a plotter, a strategist, need time to think. But either way, don't blame me. We hired you, as a simple man, to handle two simple tasks and so far, I'm not impressed."

After they entered the massive, camouflaged earthen hump, hidden from any passing aircraft or the nearest street a hundred yards to the north, Gunther flipped on the light switch set into the reinforced concrete wall and Viktor slammed the heavy door shut.

"You'll see," Gunther said. "Bendel might not be dead yet, but he's served his purpose. No way he's gonna escape the fact he's involved. And what he did to the water! Gotta give you mad props for coming up with that idea, man. The dude put my virus into the water of one of the treatment systems he designed. Genius."

"Linda's virus."

Inside the bunker, the musty air filled Viktor's lungs and he hacked. The arched ceiling of the enclosed area hung above them like a protective dome, with cream-colored paint flaking away and incandescent bulbs strung along the center at ten-foot spacing for the entire length.

Graffiti art dotted the face of the arching walls. One image displaying a gigantic, engorged penis and oversized testicles, colored with rainbow pastels. On the opposite wall, a ghost white reproduction of a skull with Darth Vader-looking teeth was painted between two human-sized representations of a machete and an automatic weapon. In red, someone had painted a biological hazard symbol at the rear of the bunker.

"Low risk operation," Viktor said. "We threatened to kill his daughter if he didn't do as we asked. We had him at gunpoint, but the arteries in his brain fed him the most potent psychological compliance drug known to mankind. Couple all that with the drug-induced amnesia and the operation could hardly go wrong. Either way, flattery won't help you score points with me. You need to step up your little game. Period."

The concrete floor, covered with a layer of clay dust and various shoe prints, supported five gray steel desks, a server rack, desktop computers, and the twelve-by-twelve-foot biological weapons lab next to a large crate, both stuffed in the corner of the opposite end of the subterranean hideout. A smooth, thin layer of water puddled in the opposite corner. The server rack stood several feet away from the water and mixed dozens of blue and yellow CAT-5 wires that ran along the base of the wall to the other computers and desks. At the rear of the interior, a closed steel door guarded the rear connector tunnel to adjacent bunkers hundreds of yards away.

They walked toward their desks, echoes of footsteps breaking the silence.

Viktor longed to sit in the padded chair to rest his throbbing back, knowing his old body was falling apart. He felt unsure how much longer he could take the pain. Or life in general.

His still-healing right femur fired off a fresh shot of pain and he winced, burying the muscle burn, trying to hide any sign of weakness from Gunther.

Two years back in Glendale, California, that hard landing on top of a brick wall in the middle of an abandoned park had split Viktor's thigh bone clean in two. Every time he felt that pain, he kicked himself for not making his brother upgrade the parachutes in the airplane. Instead of choosing thirty-five-foot military surplus canopies, he should have paid the extra few grand for parafoils, the ones with the ram air design. The landing could have been nice and soft, but no, his lazy brother went cheap. Busted leg. But he was dead now, so screw him. Viktor was lucky to float down without a soul in sight. After stuffing the chute into a trash can near the base of a mulberry tree at a park, Viktor had hopped on his good leg and dragged himself to a nearby homeless encampment, paid five bucks to borrow a burner phone, and called his personal pilot, who'd driven four hours in the crashing rain to pick him up.

That same night, they flew to Bogota, Colombia, which allowed him to escape the manhunt involving, he was told later, over a hundred federal agents. There, totally off the FBI radar, he received much-needed medical attention. Even wore a cast on his leg for two months, which preceded a half a year of physical therapy to strengthen his leg muscles. A Colombian doctor gave him special doses of human growth hormone to speed the healing process, along with dozens of testosterone shots and micro-current treatments to improve overall recovery.

While recovering in Colombia, Allah had gifted him with a plan for revenge against the men who had prevented a well-deserved martyrdom. Viktor reached out to several underground colleagues, including the primary funding source for their failed attack on the national freeways. Eventually, Viktor met up in Mexico City with Linda Bennett, CEO of BioStall industries. She told him about her need for someone with his skill set to coordinate a large-scale viral attack on California. But she didn't have all the details, just knew the end game.

She told him the mastermind, someone named Tracy Ciacchella, would support the effort.

Linda ponied up the cash and hired this Gunther dickhead to work for him. According to her, Gunther was supposed to be a highly trained henchman, hitman, and chemical and biological weapons expert. Her plan synced with Allah's gift. While the enemy worked to design and construct desalination plants in California, the details for the attack solidified in Viktor's head, and he implemented a full-fledged revenge strategy. He'd make a shit ton of money from Linda and continue the Jihad by killing a few thousand useless liberal infidel Californians, all in one shot.

Brilliant.

But now Gunther's incompetence put the entire plan at risk—and his sky-high level of arrogance.

Viktor shook his head to bring himself back to the latest argument about how Gunther had screwed up. "Right now, you're batting five hundred."

While sitting across the bunker at an identical desk, Gunther unfolded his laptop. "I don't give a shit about your fucked-up baseball stats, but don't you worry none, old man, I'm all over this shit," he said. "Sure, I messed up on the detonator, but I enjoyed myself when we grabbed Bendel a couple weeks back. Brought back wonderful memories . . . something about grabbing someone, forcing them to do something against their will and knowing they'd have absolutely no recollection of it later is . . . what's the word? Invigorating?"

One of the overhead lightbulbs flickered and went dead.

"Just check your goddamned email and be sure to connect us to the secured server. I'm gonna give Linda an update. She needs to know about your screw-ups." The servers used a satellite internet connection, bounced and routed via multiple IP's in Europe and the Middle East.

Inside the biological containment unit, a blue-green glow pulsed in the corner of the main bunker room, behind clear plastic vertical sheets.

Gunther typed away on his keyboard. "You know I got all my training from Uncle Sam," Gunther said.

"I don't care."

"Yeah, boy." He stopped typing long enough to rub the palm of his hand back and forth across the top of his hair. "Reagan administration. During all that Iran-Contra shit back in the 80s. They was worried about the Central American drug war, hand-picked a few of us snipers to learn all there was to know about chemical and biological weapons. Showed us how to change the DNA of the little bastard viruses, too, in case we needed to make a vaccine, but we knew what was what." He continued typing, staring at his laptop screen. "A personal army of biological terrorists."

This guy's crazier than I am.

Gunther continued. "Simple, really. We just took the vaccinia virus for the polio strain. Immunotherapy. Fortunately for my bank account, I'm pretty good at instructing viruses to transmit shit."

"You've bragged about this before." Viktor stretched out his back, a small portion of the pain easing a bit. "I didn't care then, and I don't care now."

Using a satellite phone wired to an external dish mounted on the surface above the bunker, Viktor connected the call to Linda. "We're at the Modesto hideout working on phase two," Viktor said. "Tell me you have word on the rate of spread."

Through a bit of static on the line, she responded with a crackling voice. "Not yet. You got Gunther under control? What's the status of Dr. Bendel?"

"Last I checked, he's headed north up to San Francisco, but we heard all his phone calls because of the pen. He got Trainer's eyeball. That's the good news." He looked at the computer screen, to the map showing the precise location of Jake, but it showed him only a few miles away from their operations base. "This can't be right," he muttered mostly to himself, his heart pounding deep inside his chest like a double bass drum.

More static. "And the bad?"

He looked away from the screen, trying to focus on the conversation. "Paige is still alive."

"How?"

"Also, someone spotted Gunther at the Diablo Canyon plant when he was hooking up the last of the viral load canisters. Bendel, apparently. If Gunther had taken care of that son-of-a-bitch yesterday as planned, we'd be a hundred percent ready." Gunther looked at him, glaring. "He says nobody saw his face at the plant and he thinks he got away with no one following him, but he's here with me at the bunker."

"Fuck," Linda said, speaker distorting. "We needed Bendel and Paige gone and that canister in place. If I tell this to Tracy, we're all dead." An impatient snort funneled through the receiver.

"If you want a scapegoat, I'm looking at one right now," Viktor said, blowing an air kiss to Gunther, who stopped typing.

"The full implementation of your plan won't work unless all five canisters are planted, so the infection spreads at maximum rate," she said. "Especially the San Luis Obispo plant, that's the biggest one. You know that."

Viktor ruffled his fingers across his gray stubble, half-expecting to find his old beard, but he'd jettisoned the Grizzly Adams look while hiding in Colombia, opting for a radical change to help hide his identity.

It felt invigorating to throw Gunther, a trained assassin, under the bus while he was sitting ten feet away. Viktor's hand wandered to the rear of his waist, rubbing his fingertips across the smooth, cold nickel of his Ruger 9mm.

"We're working on a plan to get us back in the game. Gunther's putting together the details now."

More static. "Tell me again how long it takes the virus to change the male sperm cells," she said.

Several overhead lights flickered for a few seconds. "Incubation period is one month. No symptoms for about two weeks from the time the guys drink the contaminated water. The virus works its way into the testicles and alters the fundamental properties of the single piece of DNA code you asked us to modify. Half the males will die. The survivors will eventually mate, and their children will never know fear or anger, so they're easier to control."

"Those two emotions will be as foreign as English to a twelfth-century Chinaman."

"You and your boss are getting what you want."

"Despite Gunther," she said.

Viktor smiled.

She continued. "Over generations, and once we implement the virus worldwide, without the feelings of fear or anger, all wars will end and humans can finally live in harmony. And you didn't answer my question. How long does the DNA modification take?"

"Since you made us spend so much time creating the stockpile of vaccine," his eyes scanned the bunker and settled on the large crate in the corner, "we didn't have enough time to do proper scientific testing so we don't know for sure, but according to Gunther's calcs, he's estimating the change should already be present once the symptoms show. He said there's a slight chance it will happen one to two months after the symptoms present. But only time will tell."

"Goddamnit," Linda said. "This whole thing better not fall apart. I knew I should have pushed back for more time."

Without looking away from his screen, Gunther chimed in. "Less than three percent chance. We're good, tell her not to worry about that shit, man. And she owes me some money."

The muffled chopping of helicopter blades pierced the calm air inside the bunker, echoing off the rounded ceiling. Viktor ended the call with Linda and stood stiff as a lamppost, tilting his head to help calculate the source of the noise. "Stop typing," he said to Gunther, as the sound grew louder each second.

Instinct took over. "Go," he yelled to Gunther, running toward the back end of the bunker, near the biological containment unit. Grabbing the handle of the horizontal steel trap door flush with the ground, he heaved up. After hobbling down the ladder to the darkness below, he pulled the tiny chain to illuminate the walk-in-closet-sized space.

They didn't call this a munitions bunker for nothing.

On the dirt floor near his feet sat two rows of AK-47's, four RPG's, and five metal boxes of ammo. He grabbed three of the machine guns and handed them up to Gunther, who pulled them up out of the hole, then Viktor hauled himself up the ladder and made his way to the rusted, rear metal door as

Gunther hustled toward the front of the bunker, flipped two desks onto their sides, and dug in, ready to fight.

Viktor yanked the door handle, flakes of rust clinging to his palm, and rotated open the hefty mass with an ear-piercing, high-pitched scraping sound, then pulled it shut and turned on his phone flashlight to illuminate the pitch-black void. The smell of rotting fish floated by as he jogged through the cobweb-infested rectangular concrete tunnel.

In his rush, he realized he'd forgotten to recheck Jake's location on the laptop. While running with a substantial limp down the tunnel, before he had a chance to rethink his escape, a deafening blast shook every cell in his aging body and his ears rang. Rapid gunfire erupted behind him from the other side of the metal door.

Probably the feds.

He hoped Gunther would get taken out after they breached their Modesto safe house.

Still trotting along through the hallway, he veered right twice and after several dozen yards further, made a left, then went a good quarter mile while passing several side doors that led to other bunkers. The underground journey ended with a rebar ladder embedded into the concrete wall in front of him, leading up to an iron manhole. He climbed the ladder.

His spine screamed in pain, even with the numbing effect of the Vicodin, but against his instincts, he leaned the top of his back into the underside of the cover, thrust hard, and a moment before his legs gave out, the lid popped off.

The sweet smell of grass erased the stench from below.

CHAPTER 27

August 18th
8:40 p.m.

Cavanaugh yanked off the lime green David-Clark aviation headset the instant their black Bell 205 FBI helicopter touched down in a field on the outskirts of Modesto. Now thirty yards from Viktor's supposed hideout, Cavanaugh extracted his service weapon from its holster as two other choppers settled in and twelve agents, armed with MP5/10 submachine guns and SIG Sauer 9mm pistols, filed out and took positions around the front perimeter of the bunker.

Cavanaugh took a knee, wrapped his other hand around the pistol grip, looked at his demolition lead and gave a sharp nod. The demolitions guy hustled to the entrance, pasted the C-4 charge, armed the wireless detonator to the metal door, and jogged back to the small herd of crouched FBI agents.

"Go," Cavanaugh said into his throat mic before turning on his body cam, which gave a live feed via satellite link to Washington. He glanced at Paige, partially hidden behind a boulder.

A brief second later, orange and yellow flames shot out in the dark, illuminating white and gray booms of smoke. The blast wave hit the front of Cavanaugh's body and pushed him off balance.

With the smoke thinning out, five agents climbed through the remains of the doorway and jumped down the steps. Various orders were barked, followed by the pecking sounds of automatic fire.

A bullet-ridden blue Tesla with a missing rear window scraped to a halt behind Cavanaugh and Jake hopped out, crouched low. He ran to Cavanaugh with his head down.

"Dammit, Jake, get behind that boulder next to Paige," Cavanaugh said. "You guys get shot it's my ass." Before Jake could comply, the gunfire stopped.

"Cavanaugh," Jake said. "I need to talk to you about—"

"All clear," one of the agents said into Cavanaugh's earpiece.

"Not now, Jake. Stay here. Do not move. We might've finally caught your buddy, Viktor."

Cavanaugh aimed his weapon to the ground at his side and trotted to the entrance. Once inside the bunker, through the opacity of smoke and dust, he noted the computers, desks, server stack, and an odd-looking cleanroom in the rear corner. Two of his agents were finishing the arrest procedure on a tall, muscular, black bearded man wearing a dark gray Metallica shirt. The man had an arrogant smile pasted across his face and an odd tick in his right cheek that twitched every few seconds as the agents marched him to Cavanaugh.

"I'm FBI Special Agent Cavanaugh, and you are?" Cavanaugh asked.

"Katie Perry," the man responded with a chuckle.

"Right. Where's Viktor?"

"Name sounds familiar," the man said, looking at the ground. "Viktor Newman? From *The Young and The Restless*?"

Cavanaugh waved his gun at the three agents to his left and motioned toward the rear of the bunker. "I want this place torn apart. Now. Every square inch. Find Viktor."

Jake and Paige appeared, standing at Cavanaugh's side. Jesus, this guy couldn't follow an order to save his life.

∞

The cuffed man apparently recognized Jake.

"Ah-ha! Dr. Bendel, in the flesh," the guy said, smiling, wrists cuffed behind his waist. "What a pleasure it is to finally meet the big man himself, the engineer responsible for poisoning the California water supply. How d'you do it? I want to hear all the juicy details." The man laughed and pounded his right foot several times on the dusty concrete floor.

Jake squinted his eyes, glancing at Cavanaugh, then back to the black man, and recognized his face.

The saboteur from the San Luis Obispo plant.

"You seem to know who I am, but I don't recall your name, sir." Jake leaned forward and raised his eyebrows.

In an instant, the black man's cuffs were off. He swiped something from a hidden pocket in his jeans and lunged at Jake. Paige screamed.

He stabbed Jake in the side of his thigh with a syringe.

"Jesus!" Jake said, recoiling and extracting the needle from his leg, then rubbing.

&

Cavanaugh punched the assailant in the ribs, hard, then grabbed his wrist and twisted while the arresting agents helped regain control. The trio drove him into the floor.

"Gunther Pertile," Gunther said with an even bigger toothy grin, face plastered into the concrete floor, wiggling underneath all three agents, puffs of dust billowing out at every breath. "So nice to formally make your acquaintance. Consider that a combination welcome and parting gift."

Gunther's right thumb was tweaked backward unnaturally. Shithead must have broken it without wincing and slid his hand through the cuffs.

Cavanaugh grabbed the empty syringe from Jake and held it in front of Gunther's face as the two agents lifted Gunther to his knees. "Tell me what the hell this was."

"I'm sorry, suh, I'm just a poor ignorant house slave. I dunno what you'z talkin' about."

Paige stepped forward, leaned down, and slapped Gunther's face. Cavanaugh wrapped his arms around her and pulled her back.

"You lying son-of-a-bitch," Paige yelled. "I saw you outside my house before you blew it up. With Viktor. You killed my cat." Tears formed in her eyes, but she wouldn't allow them to break free, and Cavanaugh's respect for her grew.

Gunther gave a silent smirk.

An agent named Shaun Smithouser, whom Cavanaugh had tasked with searching through the various electronic components strewn across the floor in the middle of the bunker, yelled, "Got something here, sir. Hard drive. He tried to wipe it clean, but I caught it. Not sure what's left."

Cavanaugh acknowledged the find but turned to Jake and ordered him to sit, to slow his heart rate and the absorption of whatever was in the syringe. "Excellent work, Smithouser." He turned back to Gunther. "You two, get this piece of crap out of my sight."

Jake ignored the order.

The two agents recuffed Gunther with plastic tie-straps but underestimated the criminal a second time. As they pulled Gunther up to stand, he jumped two feet in the air, swung around a hundred and eighty degrees, kicked both agents in their balls, came down and landed with his elbows on top of their hunched backs. He ran toward the rear of the bunker and as he passed Smithouser, tried to swipe the hard drive.

Cavanaugh aimed the sights of his Glock directly at the midsection of Gunther's back and double-tapped the trigger. The blasts echoed off the interior walls as two copper slugs seared into the man's back. Gunther slammed his cheek on the corner of an overturned desk and crashed to the ground.

Jake dashed toward Gunther, who was lying on his back.

"Get the hell back here, Jake," Cavanaugh said.

Jake skidded beside Gunther and knelt, Paige following. Blood soaked through the Metallica shirt and out from beneath his back. Gunther coughed blood, and streams of crimson ran down both sides of the bastard's face as he looked up at Jake, still smiling, somehow still amused. Jake slid his hand behind Gunther's head to help him breathe.

"Bio . . . Stall," Gunther managed to say between coughs filled with blood spray.

"Is that what you injected me with?"

"Bitch . . . owes me a lotta . . . money."

"Those attack drones. Was that you? Was that Viktor?" Jake asked.

Gunther laughed and inhaled deeply before exhaling his last breath.

"Goddamnit," Jake said, dropping Gunther's head on the floor. Paige bent over, spit on the man's chest, then broke down crying. Jake stood and embraced her.

"Call the local coroner and get this piece of trash outta here," Cavanaugh said. He turned to Jake. "You gotta start listening to me, man."

"BioStall," Jake said, ending the hug, a distant look on his face. He snapped his fingers. "Linda Bennett. I met her two days ago. CEO. What the heck did he mean this is a welcome and parting gift?"

"No idea. But we can sure find out," Cavanaugh said. He touched his earpiece mic and barked orders to the agents outside to get him answers. He handed the empty syringe to an agent standing at his side and told the guy to get the contents analyzed ASAP. The agent ran back through the bunker entrance and disappeared.

"Jake, we have no idea what you've been injected with," Cavanaugh said. "Need to get you to quarantine, or a hospital."

"No," Jake said. "There's too much at stake." He retrieved the blue Sûr System pen from his pocket and rubbed his fingers along the shaft. "If I show symptoms of something, I promise I'll go."

Cavanaugh felt a twinge of curiosity about the pen.

"Now's not the time to be a hero. I'm going to have you airlifted to Modesto General."

"I said no. I'm not going anywhere. I need to stay here."

"I'm going back out to the chopper," Paige said.

Cavanaugh clenched his jaw and pinched his lips together.

To Paige, he said, "No. Stay here." To Jake, "You could be affected with a contagion. I'll put you under arrest if I have to. You're getting a cursory examination to get you checked over briefly. Period. End of discussion."

"Fine."

"I'll get a team out here." He called and requested a medical team to come to the site. They said they'd be there within the hour and he informed Jake.

"Now, you asked Gunther about attack drones. I'm confused."

"Four drones tried to kill me, all armed with automatic weapons. I brought one for you. It's outside in the trunk of what's left of my Tesla."

"We'll take a look in a bit. Paige, see if you can help Smithouser with that hard drive."

Over the next ten minutes, the agents tore apart the entire bunker and found the door at its rear. Two agents walked into the dark tunnel to see where it led.

With Jake sitting in the corner trying to slow his pulse, Smithouser continued working with Paige on Gunther's nearly fried hard drive. They had propped up one of the desks, got their portable printer online, and plugged in the drive to his laptop to analyze the contents. Smithouser explained to Jake how they were now using the latest in sophisticated decrypting tech, including a third party software "tool" similar — but vastly superior — to the one the FBI used to decrypt the contents of the iPhone owned by the shooter responsible for the San Bernardino terrorist attack back in 2015.

"Got something, sir," Smithouser said, motioning to Cavanaugh, who stood next to Paige in the rear corner of the bunker, near where several agents were processing the makeshift bio lab.

Cavanaugh jogged to Smithouser, who had already printed multiple sheets packed full of chemical calculations, viral statistics, and biological data.

"From what I can tell, and we'll need to confirm with the bioweapons guys," Smithouser continued, "this evidence points to the possibility these guys manufactured two unique versions of the same virus."

Cavanaugh leaned in. "Anything solid?"

"Something about the poliovirus and human sperm cells, not sure exactly, though," Smithouser said.

"Transmit everything you got to our team working with Rosen's team at the CDC," Cavanaugh said. "We need answers and we're running out of time."

Jake grabbed Cavanaugh's upper arm and pulled him to the side, away from the various agents buzzing around inside the bunker.

"You said Viktor would be here and from what I can tell, there's zero trace of the guy," Jake said. "We're chasing a ghost. I'll bet he is dead and someone wants us to think he's still alive. Some kind of sick, real world, terrorist prank."

Clanking tools echoed off the interior walls and Cavanaugh inhaled a deep breath of the stagnant air.

"Viktor's alive," Cavanaugh said. "I can feel it. Paige saw him. This work, everything you see around you, this is all one hundred percent consistent with his criminal psych profile. To a frickin' tee. Gunther knew who you were. He had a special syringe filled with God-knows-what, made just for you. Everything points to Viktor being alive. You're supposed to be a genius, I'm surprised you don't see it. Or you don't want to."

Jake blinked several times, wheels apparently spinning, then looked at the ground. "I need to think. I'll be in my car waiting for the medical team."

CHAPTER 28

August 18th
9:30 p.m.

Jake and Paige wandered past several agents processing the crime scene, taking photos of Gunther's blood puddle on the dust-laden concrete floor, marking each significant piece of evidence with a short numbered yellow plastic tent, and taking notes about the details of the events since they all arrived not less than an hour ago. They shuffled up the steps out into the crisp night air. A glimmer of the moon's efforts broke through to the east, sparkling and reflecting off the atmosphere, outlining several long, thin clouds floating in the sky.

So many variables.

Deep in thought about everything that had happened to him since Cynthia died in the fire at the Long Beach gala two years and two months ago, Jake's mind bounced from the chases, to the explosions, to the near-death experiences of the past several days. The obliteration of Paige's home. Multiple Viktor sightings by several people. Inconclusive evidence. The virus. The video of Jake and Dave. The IRS financial trauma. The unknown substance he'd been injected with. The mysterious pen left at his house.

Jake's pulse pounded hard inside his head.

Paige sat in the front passenger seat of the Tesla while Jake extracted the remains of the warrior drone from his trunk, tossed the thing on the ground, opened the door and sat.

He turned to Paige. "Sorry you had to see that Gunther guy die like that."

For the next several minutes, she remained in a hunched-over position, tears streaming steadily down her cheeks and plopping onto her jeans.

"The weird thing is I really don't care about my house. I don't, but I do miss my fluffy kitty. That bastard killed my cat without a second thought. And I know he's behind Dave's disappearance. And all the people they're planning to kill." She raised her head and wiped the tears from her eyes, trying to regain her strength. "But I disagree with Cavanaugh on bringing out a medical team. We need to get you to a hospital. It's like a ten-minute drive from here."

No way.

Jake drove them fifty yards to the north, away from the scene crammed full of helicopters, a half-dozen black SUVs, crime-tech vans, and over fifty federal personnel buzzing around, searching for answers. He parked under a large oak tree as the coroner's van passed by.

"Not just yet. I need to think. Gimme some time," he said, adjusting his seat. He leaned the backrest to a forty-five-degree angle and closed his eyes. He started a simple meditation exercise to clear his mind of Gunther's shooting, Paige's reaction to seeing Gunther, the bunker . . . all the messy details cluttering his mind and lost track of time for a bit.

His thoughts drifted to the Santa Barbara pier, where he and Cynthia had spent countless hours walking, eating, kissing, and loving each other on dozens of romantic excursions over the years. So many amazing memories there at his happy place, where he could travel in his mind to relax and stave off impending panic attacks.

Now in a deep state of concentration, during inhalation of a slow, calming breath, the rear driver's side door flung open and someone jumped in, rocking the car. Before Jake could turn around, a forearm wrapped around his neck, pressing against his windpipe. He felt a sharp, metal object dig into the base of his skull.

Paige turned and let out an audible gasp.

A deep, gravelly voice pierced the otherwise quiet environment inside the car.

The man sounded relaxed. His breath smelled of old cigarette tobacco mixed with the putridity of stale coffee.

"Jakey boy. It's been too long."

CHAPTER 29

August 18th
10:08 p.m.

Paige pushed her body against the interior of the passenger door of the Tesla, screaming while covering her mouth with both hands.

Jake faced forward, struggling to breathe. Someone had him in a headlock, with a clump of his hair in a firm grasp and the tip of a sharp object jabbed into the back of his neck.

He darted his eyes right, toward Paige, who trembled uncontrollably, then snuck a peek in the rearview mirror to confirm his gut instinct was correct.

Nothing but shadowed darkness.

No face. Only the echo of a voice from his nightmares. The gravelly, base tone of the man responsible for starting the fire that killed his wife, the psychopathic genius who had jumped from the plane on that fateful evening two years ago. In Jake's fantasy replay of events from back then, he'd pointed the gun at Viktor and, instead of taking the higher moral ground and allowing Viktor to escape by jumping from the plane, Jake pulled the trigger, shooting the techno-genius-engineer-turned-terrorist dead center between two wrinkled, beady eyes. Jake had yearned for a do-over, a chance to take down Viktor and blow chunks of his diseased brain out the back of his ugly head, splattering them like cat vomit across the inside fuselage.

But now, Jake could barely steal another glance toward Paige. Or breathe. His eyes widened, heart pounding like a jackhammer inside his heaving chest, mouth dry as a distant desert.

She nodded, non-verbally acknowledging Jake's worst fear.

Jake pictured the man in the back seat. For the second time in one night, his life's work, all he'd accomplished—Cynthia, Carlie, his grandson, his civil engineering feats—flashed in his head.

He knew his luck had finally run out.

CHAPTER 30

August 18th
10:08 p.m.

After Jake and Paige had left the bunker, Cavanaugh's team continued to comb through the terrorist assets inside. Additional lights had been set up in the corners. Agents continued buzzing around, collecting samples, taking photos, and searching for clues. One of Rosen's team, a CDC scientist, Dinesh Mehta, finally arrived and Cavanaugh escorted him to the rear of the bunker where the makeshift lab had been erected by Gunther and whom ever else he'd been working with.

Viktor?

Viktor.

But as far as hard evidence — proof — Gunther seemed to have been the sole inhabitant of this bunker-turned-terrorist-camp. The dead terrorist, and whom ever the scum had possibly been working with, had constructed a twelve-foot by twelve-foot bio lab, surrounded by sheets of thick, clear plastic hanging in the left rear corner of the bunker, against the two reinforced concrete walls. The plastic sheets extended up to the arched, corrugated metal ceiling above, connected with screws and Velcro.

The lab had a tall zippered door and two gray metallic desks inside. Several beakers and test tubes were visible through the windowed door of a biosafety cabinet placed next to one desk, while a white confocal microscope sat atop the other, attached to a laptop. Two bright yellow, curly breathing hoses hung from the ceiling next to a ventilation fan and a mini-fridge was tucked underneath the left desk on the concrete slab.

Looked harmless enough.

Cavanaugh reached to pull the plastic zipper and open the door to the bio lab, but Dinesh grabbed his forearm.

"Agent, sir, we are unsure if any airborne pathogens are contained inside this barrier sheath," the scientist warned, with a thick, pitchy accent. "We need hazmat suits."

Cavanaugh blamed himself for not remembering to follow protocol and thought about his two grown sons going through the rest of their lives without their old man. The CDC guy might have saved his life.

His phone rang: Dr. Rosen from the CDC. Dinesh and Cavanaugh stepped back from the lab as he took the call.

"Talk to me, Rosen," Cavanaugh said.

"Sir, we are diligently working around the clock to unlock the unique DNA sequence of this virus, but it appears we are getting mixed results."

"I can help. My guys and I are here outside Modesto with Dinesh in an abandoned army munitions bunker and we found and killed at least one terrorist before we interrogated him. But we secured a hard drive that has enough recovered data and notes to show the potential of two separate viral strains."

Dinesh walked along the perimeter of the lab, arms folded across his chest, glancing up and down at the various components contained inside.

"It would be of great appreciation, sir," Rosen said, "if you could kindly provide us with this newly discovered data set as quickly as possible."

Cavanaugh pulled a toothpick from the stash inside his jeans pocket and stuffed it into his mouth.

"My guy's cleaning it now. There's another computer, a laptop, inside what looks like a portable bio lab. Once we secure that hard drive, I'll upload all the data to you via the secure shared server. I need to know the latest infection numbers."

Cavanaugh worked the toothpick in between his teeth and squinted.

Dinesh whispered, "I'm going to get my hazmat suit on. You should do the same." He took several steps toward the front entrance of the bunker.

"Well, sir," Rosen said, "all of our information is preliminary. It is a target moving, so we cannot give firm numbers, but it unfortunately appears the rates are continuing through acceleration. And sir, we continue to confirm that no female humans are contaminated. Only men."

Cavanaugh slid the toothpick out between his lips and threw it to the ground. "Call me back when you have more info." He ended the call and followed Dinesh outside to put on his hazmat suit, wondering where Jake went.

CHAPTER 31

August 18th
10:12 p.m.

Jake debated whether to respond to the man's veiled greeting or remain silent. He chose the latter.

"Oh, Jakey Boy," the man said from the back seat. "I've waited an eternity for this critical moment in your quantum existence." The man's voice sounded calm, familiar, confident. "Hope you've enjoyed our little game of hide-and-go-seek."

Jake scanned the area in front of his car, trying to see if any of the agents had made their way over.

Not a soul.

"That was you at my house two weeks ago. The pen. The dock."

"It's amazing how much can be accomplished under the blind eye of a disabled CCTV system." Viktor pushed the pointed tip further into Jake's skin. "And of course, the little magic trick of utilizing the IRS to help make your nest egg disappear. Poor, desolate Jakey Boy, a pauper. Oh, and my favorite touch is the video of you and your buddy, Dave, both caught on camera for the world to see. But you have no memory of it! Ha!" Viktor said through a smile. "Beautiful irony. Now, give me one good reason not to jam this four-inch blade deep into that arrogant skull of yours and screwdriver your brain."

His tone changed, becoming deeper, angrier. "Shut down the Superman of engineering once and for all."

The man's voice, combined with the scent of his putrid breath and the fact that Jake could not see his assailant, reminded him of the night Dave Trainer had stood Jake up at the Chili's restaurant in Stockton. A brief flashback of bumping into a man . . . then waking up the next morning with a swollen, red welt on the side of his neck and thinking the bump was a weird bug bite. Unable to remember how he drove himself home that night. A van. A black van.

Wait a second. Gunther.

Jake's mind moved the pieces of this puzzle into position. Made more sense now. Trainer missed their dinner because Viktor had kidnapped him, cut out his eyeball, held it in formaldehyde and later Fed-Exed it to Jake at the construction site.

Why? Just to paint me as a scapegoat?

He needed more time. But only if he faced his fears. Rolled the dice of his life.

Again.

"So there *was* a fourth parachute," Jake said, trying to stall.

The man behind him grunted in agreement.

"Funny thing," Jake said. "And speaking of irony . . ."

Jake glanced again at Paige, who had a stare of incredulity pasted on her face.

"Tell me," the man said.

"My wife died in the fire you started. When you and I struggled on the plane, I got the upper hand and as much as I wanted to shoot you dead, get my revenge, Cynthia's spirit appeared and talked me out of wasting your ass. You're alive today because of my dead wife. A woman you killed. Irony."

The man paused, apparently taking in the information.

"Bullshit. I jumped before you had a chance to take me out," the man said.

"Agree to disagree." Jake strained to keep his voice box working but knew he sounded weak. "Either way, I chose not to kill you because that's not the type of person I am. But you are. You're going to do whatever you're going to do, but my conscience is clear."

Jake fully expected Viktor to drive the knife or spike or whatever he had into his brain any second and then check out of his life.

The humid air seemed void of oxygen. And hot. Dozens of sweat beads streamed their way down Jake's forehead to his eyebrows, which acted as a dam, ready to burst. Jake attempted to breathe slowly. Calmly. If Viktor wanted Jake dead, he would have already murdered him. No, he must want something. Jake willed himself to relax, play things cool. Keep the psychopath at bay.

Likely out of understandable frustration and pain, Paige blurted out a last-ditch effort to save her friend. "Let him go, you sick fuck."

The man chuckled.

Jake closed his eyes. *Not helping, Paige.*

Paige's good intentions had probably just pushed the man over the edge. Toward murder. The tip of the knife drilled into Jake's skin, but likely not enough to cause any permanent damage. Jake winced at the stabbing pain. The blade retreated from Jake's neck, but Viktor kept his grip. The cocking sound of a gun filled the interior of the car. Paige gasped and put her hands up, palms facing outward. Stinging sweat poured into Jake's eyes.

"I still need something from you, Jakey Boy, but not this mouthy bitch who's should've been in a million pieces of charred meat right now." Jake assumed the man had pointed a gun at Paige and was ready to pull the trigger.

"Tell me what you want," Jake said, interrupting whatever Viktor had planned. "I'll do it. Anything."

Several thick seconds passed.

Jake heard the gun's hammer uncock. Viktor shook Jake's head and released the death grip on his neck. Jake turned toward Paige. Black eyeliner tears streamed down her cheeks.

Jake turned around and finally set his eyes on the man in the back seat.

There, leaning back, as relaxed as a bartender on vacation, sat the man who had caused the terrorist attack in Los Angeles, the death of Jake's wife, and immeasurable terror to the American public two years ago.

Viktor Johnston.

Back from the grave.

In the flesh.

Seeing Viktor sent chills through Jake's spine.

His once-gray beard with black streaks running throughout had disappeared. And his head was fully shaved. A tiny moon and star earring was pinned to his earlobe. His red, crooked nose crinkled as he smiled, baring mangled yellow teeth. He held a revolver above his thighs, pointed at Jake and chuckled again.

"I can tell by the way you're sweating that Gunther was successful."

Nothing came to mind. Jake only blinked.

Viktor continued. "You get the honor of being our first test subject. We made a special virus just for you. I can see our product working. In your eyes."

Jake furrowed his brow and cocked his head but didn't speak.

"Gunther had terminal cancer. In a couple more weeks he would have been called up to sit at the right hand of Allah. His last task on this earth was to ensure our special virus made its way into your bloodstream. I'm sure that rings a bell for you."

Jake touched his hand to his thigh where Gunther had injected him with something. The efforts to relax waned and he wiped the sweat from his eyes with his fingertips.

"Yes, Jakey Boy. You're now going down an irreversible path. As you lie in your bed, with a hundred and six fever, sweating your little panties off, writhing in pain, you're gonna think of me. You're gonna think of how I warned you not to interfere, and how you continued fighting me. Fighting my master plan."

Still pointing the gun at Jake, Viktor opened his door. He exited the Tesla and yanked open Jake's door.

Viktor motioned with the pistol. "You two morons, outta the damned car."

Jake and Paige complied. Viktor sat in the driver's seat. "Gimme the key-fob," Viktor said. Jake dug into his pants pocket and handed it to Viktor. "Stay here for ten minutes. If you say anything about this to that Cavanaugh asshole, someone you love will die. I hope by now you know I never bluff."

Jake struggled to control his trembling body.

Viktor zoomed north, away from the tree, the bunker, and the two engineers.

CHAPTER 32

August 18th
10:15 p.m.

Cavanaugh and Dinesh retrieved their gear from the cargo hold of the helicopter and helped each other put on the neon yellow suits.

The night air had only brought the ambient temperature down to eighty degrees. Inside the suit, it was easily twenty degrees hotter. Beads of sweat appeared on Cavanaugh's face. Moisture prickled under his armpits.

Before he latched on the headpiece to seal the infernal sauna, he called Governor Fairchild's office. The secretary immediately patched Cavanaugh through.

"Agent Cavanaugh. I could use some good news," she said.

"Other than the fact that we found one of the terrorists, there's not much news I'd put into the 'good' category," Cavanaugh said.

"Tell me you at least killed the bastard."

Cavanaugh kicked a softball-sized rock. Dinesh grabbed a black nylon side pack, put the strap over the top of his shoulder, and leaned the object against his waist. He walked back down the steps into the bunker and disappeared.

"Affirmative. But it would have been better if we could've gotten him to talk."

"Understood," the governor said. "I'm hearing from our people at the CDC they're making progress on the DNA sequencing."

"Yes, ma'am. I was just on the line with our guy at the CDC and his team is trying to decode the DNA strands and create a faster way to track the infections, but that's all gonna take time."

A warm, stiff breeze blew through the area and for a brief second, the air cooled Cavanaugh's sweat-covered face. He closed his eyes and inhaled.

"We're up to around 400,000 infected," the governor said. "Eighty-five percent chance that twelve deaths are directly attributable to the viral outbreak. Still running tests, but we're running out of time before we need to go public."

Cavanaugh scratched his head. Another agent walked by and Cavanaugh motioned to his wrist. "Quarter past ten, sir," the agent said.

"The CDC gave us forty-eight hours and we're burning through it fast, but so far we're just scratching the surface on how deep this terrorist infection goes. We need another lead. I'm going to send the data we recovered on a bunker hard drive to the CDC and hope they can come up with something useful."

The governor thanked Cavanaugh, they agreed to regroup later tomorrow, and ended their call.

Cavanaugh stuffed his phone into his pocket and slid on the headset of the hazmat suit and air filter. No more breeze. Nothing but hot, stale, humid air inside. *Wonderful.* Fortunately, the clear front goggles he peered through had a special coating of anti-fog chemical to prevent his breath from obstructing the view as he walked back down into the bunker.

Next to the bio lab, Dinesh poked a hand-held viral and bacterial agent scanner through a tiny opening in the plastic zipper door, pressed a couple of buttons, and several seconds later, a green light blinked on the scanner top. The scientist looked at Cavanaugh.

"No need to vacate the premises," Dinesh said with a thumbs up. "Your agents can continue working while we investigate the interior of this lab." He zipped open the makeshift laboratory and walked inside. Cavanaugh followed.

Dinesh retrieved several test tubes from his side pack. He carefully extracted samples from Gunther's beakers and Petri dishes using different eye droppers. After picking up two microscope slides, he set them into a secure socket inside his pack, then gave the inside of the lab a final look around and nodded.

"Okay, we're all set. Need to get these specimens back to our lab for analysis," Dinesh said.

"I'll get some guys in here to pack the rest of this up," Cavanaugh said.

Cavanaugh exited the bio lab, yanked off the headpiece of the hazmat suit and shook his head before inhaling the relatively cool bunker air. He raked his fingers through his hair, which felt like he'd just had a shower, then approached Smithouser, who was continuing his attempts to hack the contents of the drive. "Tell me you got something," Cavanaugh said, still wearing the body portion of his suit.

"Almost. Give me five minutes," Smithouser said.

Cavanaugh exited the bunker. The hazmat fabric made a squealing, hissing sound when he walked. He asked two agents to help him out of the sauna suit. Once back in his street clothes, he scanned the entire crime scene for Jake. Nothing. Cavanaugh hustled back inside the bunker and jogged to Smithouser. Before he got an update, Dinesh called him over.

Peering in from outside the bio lab, Cavanaugh found Dinesh crouched near the mini-fridge. "There's something back here," he said to Cavanaugh, reaching around beneath a desk.

"I need to check in with my technician," Cavanaugh said, taking a step toward the opening of the bio chamber. "I'll be right—"

"Wait. What's this?" When the scientist stretched his arm behind the mini-fridge and retrieved a three-ring binder, Cavanaugh took a step back inside the chamber to get a better look.

CHAPTER 33

August 18th
10:24 p.m.

At the rear of the bunker, inside the bio chamber, Dinesh flipped through the pages covered with hand-written notes, chemical formula diagrams, purple, and blue virus structure diagrams with labels like animal virus, envelope proteins, DNA, nucleocapsid, and retrovirus.

Cavanaugh had no clue what the labels meant.

"Genius," the scientist said, pointing his finger at several journal entries, sliding left to right, and tapping his fingertip on one particular note.

"Talk to me, doc," Cavanaugh said.

"Looks like our friends very busy, they were."

"Does this explain why only men are getting flu-like symptoms?"

The scientist ignored Cavanaugh's question, flipped a page, then another, then another, scanning the information through his thick, coke-bottle glasses.

"Here. Right here," the scientist said.

Cavanaugh whirled his hand. "Tell me what you think they were working on. Short on time. Best guess."

The scientist slapped the binder closed, staring with wide eyes at Cavanaugh before backing away.

"You don't understand," the scientist said, plowing through the bio lab opening and scurrying back to the entrance of the bunker.

Cavanaugh raced after Dinesh, following closely behind. Outside the bunker, Cavanaugh said, "Tell me what I don't understand. Doc?"

The scientist yanked off the headpiece to his hazmat suit, lungs pumping hard. "Get me out of this suit. Now." Cavanaugh waved two agents over, who helped the man start to remove the suit.

"I'm waiting," Cavanaugh said.

The scientist scratched his head compulsively. His breathing was rapid and shallow. In a panic, his eyes darted from left to right as he scanned the entire area outside the bunker.

"You gotta get me back to the CDC," the scientist said. "Now."

"Not until you tell me what the hell's going on!"

Rapidly, almost incoherently the scientist muttered a rapid response. "There are two versions of the virus. One is targeted to human sperm cells. To us, it will present symptoms like a regular flu virus. To the victims, it will feel like the flu, which is bad enough and will likely kill, I don't know, hundreds, maybe thousands of people. But that's not the real problem."

"I don't follow," Cavanaugh said.

Dinesh slowed, more confident, loud. He looked deep into Cavanaugh's eyes. "When a virus attacks human sperm cells, we are talking about modifications to the DNA of human offspring. Someone's trying to alter our *genome*. But what I don't understand is in the other virus, there appear to be components that affect plant genomes, too. Never seen anything like it. We are needing some serious help to be analyzing this."

Cavanaugh paused, contemplating the additional information.

The scientist stepped out of the legs of the hazmat suit and continued. "If the data in this notebook is accurate, they've created a virus that basically, for all of the intent and purpose, will look and feel like an ordinary flu. But what will happen, is that the male sperm cells will be modified in such a way that when that man's seed is used to fertilize a human egg, the offspring will have . . . genetically modified traits."

"By default, babies share genes with their parents but aren't identical. It's part of evolution. I thought—"

"No!" Dinesh said, cutting off Cavanaugh. "This modification is specific to the human brain, targeted to a portion of the brain stem. From what I can tell, they are trying to somehow reduce the size or impact of a part of the human brain that handles certain primitive emotions like fear and anger." Dinesh paused, rubbing his chin and blinking rapidly. He opened the binder and shoved it into Cavanaugh's belly. "They circled the word EGO here on page twelve and put a line through the center, like a no-smoking sign. I am guessing they think if they infect enough people, they can eliminate the human ego, or at least the portion of it that has to do with fear and anger."

Cavanaugh thought for a second and remembered a discussion in a philosophy class he'd taken decades ago. Would it be so bad if humans could evolve out of our animalistic instincts and eliminate certain types of fear and anger?

"But this will not work, sir, it is purely amateur effort," Dinesh argued, mostly with himself. "You cannot just make genetic modifications like this. The side effects could be—" He turned, jogging toward Cavanaugh's chopper, with Cavanaugh in tow. "Agent, you must fly me back to the CDC. Now. It is most imperative I show this to Dr. Rosen."

CHAPTER 34

August 18th
10:32 p.m.

Jake and Paige ran toward the bunker and found Cavanaugh slamming a helicopter door closed, then ducking, trotting away from the downward thrust of the chopping, rotating blades blowing heavy wind and debris everywhere. Cavanaugh spotted Jake and Paige and tented his eyes with a hand. The jet engine whirred strong, fast. The helicopter lifted off and flew in a northwest direction, ascending into the night sky.

Cavanaugh tilted his head to the side and pursed his lips. He looked over Jake's shoulder, off in the distance, to where Jake had parked his Tesla. "Looks like the earth swallowed your fancy electric car. I told you I—"

"Viktor," Jake said, out of breath, hunched over. He pointed to the minor puncture wound on his neck. "Bastard was here, had a knife at my neck and a gun aimed at Paige. Said that guy you shot, Gunther, infected me with a virus. I'm an experiment. A test subject."

"We need to get him to a hospital now!" Paige said.

"Shit." Cavanaugh yelled back to one of his men, "Get me some medical transport out of here ASAP! And get me that CDC guy on the line."

Jake felt a tinge of nausea. He touched his forehead with the back of his hand. Too hot.

Was this caused by all the excitement? Or from the damned heat? Or was it a fever, meaning he was on his way to certain death, like Viktor said, because of billions of tiny viral particles streaming through his blood, infecting God-knows-what inside his body? The world spun and he felt an overwhelming urge to close his eyes.

"No. Not yet," Jake said, waving off Cavanaugh. "Viktor also threatened to kill Carlie or my grandson."

"Goddamnit."

Still out of breath, Jake grabbed Cavanaugh's arm and said, "I gotta show you something." Leading the group around to the side of the bunker, Jake reached to the ground and picked up the assault drone.

Paige helped Jake hold the drone so Cavanaugh could get a good look.

"Shit. This is like a bad frickin' nightmare. I knew someone would figure this out eventually," Cavanaugh said. "I've been warning my FBI peers for the last several years about terrorists attaching weapons to drones." Cavanaugh squinted and moved in for a closer look. "M4 carbine. Automatic." He released the magazine, peered inside, and pushed in the top spring to remove the last remaining round. "Thirty-round mag. Military grade." He held up the round, pinched between his thumb and index finger. "Two-two-three Remington. Standard issue for U.S. Army and Marines." Robotic arms had been connected to the trigger, along with tiny shock absorbers. "Impressive in a sick sorta way. Laser sight." He pointed to a black tube affixed to the top of the gun. "Night vision camera."

"This thing and three others just like it attacked me about fifty miles north of here. My Tesla looks like a shiny blue sponge."

Cavanaugh scanned the area. "Speaking of which, where is—"

"Viktor stole my car."

"Jesus, Jake, use your head," Cavanaugh said, baring his teeth, and starting back toward the bunker. "You should have told me that first. Every second counts."

Two blurred versions of Cavanaugh floated in front of Jake as he and Paige followed Cavanaugh back toward the bunker. Cavanaugh barked echoing orders to several other agents to follow and apprehend the suspect fleeing north in a Swiss Cheese blue Tesla. Jake coughed and leaned over, hands on his knees. A slow, thick fog rolled into his mind.

Paige put her arm around Jake, leaned over and put her head next to Jake's. "You look awful."

CHAPTER 35

August 18th
10:37 p.m.

Cavanaugh watched from the ground as his good friend ascended in a second Bell helicopter with Paige and two of his best field agents.

"Godspeed, Dr. Bendel," Cavanaugh said to nobody in particular.

His phone rang.

The field agent leading the investigation into Dave's eyeball and the water poisoning provided an update. Cavanaugh had informed the agent a woman named Linda Bennett was now a suspect for providing the virus likely causing the infection spreading throughout California. The agent's team had since procured several pieces of circumstantial evidence, but nothing concrete linking her to the outbreak. Yet. The agent had two of her best cyber sleuths digging into Linda's finances and they had followed the money trail to what appeared to be the driving force behind the entire operation.

"Hold on a minute," Cavanaugh said. "Sounds like you're telling me Viktor's just a pawn in all this, that he's not the one calling the shots."

"Sir, that's exactly what I'm saying," she said, her voice strained, yet confident.

Cavanaugh put his palm to his forehead and turned around, looking up at the dark sky.

"This changes everything."

Smithouser appeared in front of Cavanaugh, rubbing the back of his neck, blinking rapidly.

"I gotta run," Cavanaugh said, ending the call and turning to Smithouser. "Talk to me."

"Sir, we've decrypted the hard drive and found something. You gotta look at this."

After the two men reentered the bunker, Smithouser sat in the chair at the old desk and zoomed in to a full-color, still image of a video on his screen. The date stamp showed August 2. He pointed to a man, crouched over.

"Right here is Bendel, and here's Dave. They're at the combo plant outside San Francisco, the one providing water to over two million residents." Next, he next pointed to a system of tanks and tubes, next to Bendel. "These here are the chlorine tanks. The ones that give injections to the treated water to help keep the water clean during its journey from the desalination plant to the end users."

"I've already seen this video," Cavanaugh said. "It showed up at the governor's office yesterday and she shared it with me. Some radical environmentalist fringe group claimed responsibility for taking the footage and threatened the governor to go public if Jake was not arrested within two days." Cavanaugh looked at his watch. "Anything on the news about this?"

The agent shook his head. "Negative. But that's not what I wanted to show you." He swirled his fingertip in various places on the touchpad, typing as needed. Various windows popped open and closed.

Agent Cavanaugh leaned in for a better look.

"Get to the point, son, I need to fly outta here and get down to Los Angeles to interview a suspect."

"Sorry, sir. Here it is," Smithouser said. He pointed to a list of files, with types and dates.

Cavanaugh focused his eyes on the screen. Several video files popped up.

"Sir, I pulled up the metadata for these MP4 video files. Each one has a date stamp and identification code for the device that did the recording."

"Again, I know all this. Please get to the point, dammit," Cavanaugh said.

Smithouser blinked several times, obviously thinking as he bounced his knee and rubbed his palms down his pant legs.

The junior agent slid on two light blue latex gloves, leaned over across the table and grabbed ahold of a Sony video camera.

"This camera right here has the same identification code as the video," Smithouser said. He popped open the slot and retrieved the memory card, which had fingerprint dust on the outside. He held the card by the edges between his thumb and index finger and lifted the card to Cavanaugh's face. "There's a partial fingerprint right there. I took a hi-res photo with my phone and uploaded it to our server in San Francisco and we got a hit."

Smithouser hit the "Enter" key on the keyboard and a new screen appeared with an image of a middle-aged woman with graying brown hair and a bunch of facts. The title of the window read "Linda Bennett – CEO, BioStall Industries."

CHAPTER 36

August 18th
10:43 p.m.

Tracy Ciacchella unlocked the door to the penthouse suite at the Four Seasons Los Angeles Wilshire Hotel, pushed through the hefty wood opening and set her black leather briefcase onto the tiled floor. The door lock clicked, and Tracy drew in a long breath while leaning against the wall, then looked up at the chandelier.

The decor of the room's interior would dazzle the starriest of the Hollywood elite. Presidents had stayed here. The richest of the rich. Yet, to Tracy nothing mattered except the plan. The master plan. The one that would fix society's ills and save planet Earth from its worst enemy: the infestation of mankind.

Tracy strolled to the minibar, downed two 50 ml bottles of Grey Goose Vodka and disrobed before taking a long, cold shower to clear her mind of negativity. Once dry, she wrapped a fluffy white robe around her pale body, grabbed her diary from atop the nightstand, and plopped onto a modern-day version of a wingback chair.

Pen in hand, she wrote:

Why in the world do I keep doing this to myself? One would think a sixty-two-year-old billionaire would have a tad more confidence when dealing with moronic dolts. I worked hard in my accomplishments. I have earned every penny. Am I happy? Is my brother happy? My goddamned brother. Good questions. The Super Six investment paid off most generously. Now some old oil-industry buddies are causing a ruckus because their profits are down. Not my problem, but I shall indeed fix it anyway. And make even more money.

Am I glad I met Viktor Johnston? Yes. And No. Well, maybe. Such an odd fellow, really. None of this would have been possible without his religious fanaticism. Islam is amazing. Extremists have bastardized a perfectly peaceful religion and Viktor is certainly no exception. I could not have planned the whole attack better myself. So intense. So motivated to please the Almighty Allah. What an absurdity. Just a pawn in the big game of chess. I guess I shall allow him live a wee bit longer before finishing the plan. He has always wanted to be a martyr.

Tracy stood and walked back to the minibar, grabbed another two bottles of vodka, downed both, returned to the chair, and continued. She pulled out a paper from deep within the diary, with a graph on it that showed various phases of her plan.

Now that the proverbial cavalry is distracted with Gunther and Viktor, I am free to start Phase 2. The CDC will soon find the cause, but they're headed in the wrong direction. Making a second virus that kills plants, after I shorted such an enormous amount of ag stock . . . billions more for me. And no more war, or angry mobs . . . people will be like putty to us, the way they ought to be. But I anticipate things shall get worse before they improve. And with the stockpile of vaccine already made, I can certainly count on making billions more. Delayed gratification. Pick a philosophical phrase.

I make money no matter what.

Who knows? A run for president might be in my future.

She paused. *Focus, Tracy.*

She remembered meeting Viktor for the first time. Outside that concert hall in Chicago. Cold. Freezing. Ice everywhere.

Breath pumping out of mouths in clouds of mist. Hundreds of people funneling out of the front doors. That old lady had tripped on a ruffle in the red velvet carpeting. Totally random. He helped her up. Tracy commended him and they started talking. He explained, very proudly, about his work with the Super Six, led by Jake, and she'd thought their meeting couldn't be a coincidence. He complained ad nauseam about Jake, nothing good to say, really. The guy was driven, but too arrogant for his tastes, according to Viktor. He told her how the feds were looking for private industry folks like her to partner with. Six months later she'd signed the contract with those highway administrators and plunked down a half a billion bones of her own cash. Best investment ever. Four years later, the debt had been repaid forty times over. Easy money. Amazing how one chance encounter leads to making bucks. Had she not taken the risk thirty years ago with her first firm, though, she wouldn't have had the resources to invest anyway. The more money she made, the more money she could make.

America is beautiful.

And she needed to save her once-great country from ruin. Her plan would do this. And more.

Tracy's mind turned to Tex, her principal contact at the Shell Oil Corporation, and made a mental note to set up another meeting with him to discuss their strategies for getting Big Oil back in alignment with the Military Industrial Complex. She turned back to the journal.

The viruses better work as Gunther and Linda promised. No women or children affected, only post-pubescent males. Certainly glad they inoculated me six months ago. The latest tally from the CDC seems to indicate over 400,000 infected and showing symptoms, so I must give the poor old bastard some credit. He will be well paid, though, so I can pay him no further attention.

Need to figure out what Viktor is up to at this instant. Will call him the moment the sun comes up and I have a chance to sleep. Need some sleep. So bloody tired all the time!

Tracy reached across the arm of the chair to the marbled wood drink stand and grabbed the pill bottle full of Vicodin. Two tablets slid out from inside the orange plastic bottle and made their way into her stomach within seconds. Her vision blurred, but not enough to stop writing:

Phase 2 will seal the deal, as they say. Leave a lasting legacy for me as mankind sings my praises. Eventually. Once the virus does gets to work and rids the masses of those bloody lizard brains, we can all live in harmony on planet Earth once again. If a few billion men are wiped from existence in the process, that is wonderfully acceptable as well. The survivors will undoubtedly thank me. Either we go down this path or choose Option B, which would be to wait for one of those childish psycho dictators with nuclear bombs to attack us.

Tracy felt the effects of the alcohol and downers kick in. With a spinning brain, she needed to wrap up it up.

If only I'd figured out all this earlier in life. Hell. Can't believe my brother's been such a success. Seems to have it all. Why can't I have what he has? Need to sleep. The plan will work. I know it. Is my jet fueled and ready to go? No matter. Must sleep. It is going to work. Has to. Must work.

CHAPTER 37

August 18th
10:52 p.m.

Jake found himself lying across the rear seat of a chopper, floating several thousand feet above the farmlands below. He tried to sit up, but Paige held him down, then wiped a handkerchief across his drenched forehead.

"Relax," she said in a soothing voice. "We're almost there."

Minutes later, the helicopter landed atop the helipad of San Joaquin General. Two agents hopped out with Paige and helped Jake out of the helicopter. He leaned on them as the foursome hobbled across the tarmac, into an elevator and down to the emergency room. One agent flashed his badge and instructed the nurse to admit Jake, something about national security.

"Get yourself checked out and let Cavanaugh know what's going on," the agent said. "We gotta fly back. Do not go anywhere without telling Cavanaugh first." The agents hustled from the waiting room and headed back up to the helipad.

Two nurses escorted Jake and Paige to a two-curtained room, where he disrobed and put on one of those wrinkly green and white floral-patterned hospital gowns. The cool air wafting through Jake's private parts felt good, but his head pounded and his heart bounced around inside his chest cavity like a racquetball in a clothes dryer.

After a series of blood tests, CAT scan, EKG, and various other medical procedures, the head emergency room doc walked in. He stood a couple of inches north of six feet tall, and sprinkles of white peppered his tightly trimmed jet-black hair.

"I'm Dr. Abuelhassan," the doc said with a warm smile. He folded an aluminum medical chart closed and crossed his arms. "I'm afraid I have some bad news for you, Dr. Bendel." He removed his reading glasses and stared directly into Jake's half-closed eyes. "I understand someone injected you with a syringe carrying an unknown liquid."

Jake nodded.

"We've been coordinating with your friends at the FBI lab. We've run a plethora tests and I apologize for having to be the one to inform you, but I can confirm you are a carrier of an altogether new type of virus. Good news is you're not contagious. Based on your vital signs, your temp at 103 degrees, swollen glands, etc. you are exhibiting all the classic signs of influenza."

"I've had the flu before, doc."

"The virus itself is most definitely not the flu."

"I'm pretty healthy, so I'll take some TheraFlu to fight the symptoms and I'll check myself out now." Jake slid his legs off the white sheets and tried to stand. "Thank you for—"

"Not so fast, Dr. Bendel," Abuelhassan said, placing an open palm onto Jake's chest and easing his head back onto the bed pillows. "I'm not finished."

Jake crossed his arms, struggling to focus. Every joint in his body ached.

"Paige, hand me my phone," Jake said, motioning to his crumpled pants in the corner. She complied.

"In addition," the doctor continued, "your liver numbers are very low, to where you are exhibiting liver failure. And the urine sample you provided had blood in it. I'm sure you feel your heart pounding erratically and we've confirmed with the EKG you're experiencing a significant heart arrhythmia."

"Jesus God, doc," Paige said. "What are you gonna do to get him patched up?"

Abuelhassan cocked his head and opened and closed his mouth several times. "That's the rub," he said. "Again, I'm sorry, Mr. Bendel, but this virus appears to be very fast-acting and your symptoms are already advanced. We'll do everything we can, but it's my professional opinion based on my three decades of experience working in the medical field, without immediate radical treatment, you have maybe a sixty percent chance of living another twenty-four hours."

Paige let out a gasp and squeezed Jake's hand.

Jake slammed his eyelids shut and tried to wake up from this nightmare.

"With a careful combination of some new experimental antivirals, pain killers, electrolytic fluids, liver cleansing meds, and beta blockers, your chances might increase to maybe eighty percent. With your permission, we'll get started immediately. But you need to stay here. In bed."

I have twenty-four hours to live, people are getting infected with water from my treatment plants, and this guy wants me to stay in some pseudo-sterile hospital bed? No way. Still, Jake gave the doc the okay. Abuelhassan rushed out of the room.

In a shaky, disbelieving voice, Paige said, "You're gonna get through this. Screw his odds. We've been through worse. Think about Cynthia. She'd want you to stay strong."

Jake's phone vibrated. Text message from Carlie. U NEED ANOTHER $800? WHAT'S HAPPENING?

A wave of chills flew threw his body. He replied to Carlie's text, saying he was fine, not wanting to worry her. Paige unfolded a warm blanket from the end of the bed and wrapped it around Jake.

"Your lips are the same color as that damned Sûr System pen you love," Paige said. Jake tried to swallow.

Nothing.

Dry as a Palm Springs pond in summer.

CHAPTER 38

August 19th
8:00 a.m.

Cavanaugh spent the early morning hours coordinating with field agents in Beverly Hills, where Linda Bennett was allegedly staying, to bring her in for questioning. He flew south at an average of 140 knots in the same black Bell 429 helicopter he'd flown in to get to Viktor's Modesto bunker. His pilot landed the chopper at the Beverly Center Heliport, southwest of Santa Monica Boulevard in West Hollywood, where a junior agent awaited their arrival in an unmarked black Dodge Charger. By the time the chopper landed, they still hadn't arrested her.

With the rotors still spinning, Cavanaugh exited and hopped into the black muscle car. The junior agent flipped on the reds and blues, then drove Cavanaugh two-and-a-half miles west to the Beverly Hills Hotel on Sunset Boulevard. Linda Bennett's office had indicated she was currently a guest at the hotel.

The bright desert sun blasted heat from its low point in the eastern sky onto the agents. After running through two red lights with sirens blaring, they parked in front of the famous hotel where more movie stars and prominent figureheads had stayed than there were ants on an anthill. The normally green grass showed signs of browning, likely because of the drought and mandatory water rationing in Los Angeles County. A large

American flag flew proudly atop the chartreuse and forest green-colored main building.

"The hotel register shows she's been staying up in the presidential suite for the last eight days, but we were unable to confirm occupancy," the agent said. "We waited so you could make the arrest."

"Goddamnit, son," Cavanaugh said. "I specifically told the other agent to move forward with the arrest. She better be there."

The other agent's eyes widened and blinked rapidly as he took the lead, hustling them through the front lobby before jumping into the elevator.

"Call hotel security and have them meet us at the room," Cavanaugh said.

As they arrived at the fourteenth floor of the Beverly Wing and the ancient elevator doors screeched open, the agents drew their weapons and approached the main door of the suite.

The junior agent performed the normal "FBI—Open Up" routine, then they waited thirty seconds.

"We could breach or wait for the security guard to swipe us in," the kid said.

"She's not gonna make a run for it up here. Give it a minute," Cavanaugh said.

A few seconds later, the security guard approached the two agents, Cavanaugh instructed the woman to unlock the door, and she complied.

The agents crept inside the suite, clearing the entire area before holstering their weapons. No one.

"I'm sorry, sir. I'll take the blame for this," the junior agent said, but Cavanaugh waved the kid off.

An empty fifth of Maker's Mark bourbon lay on its side, next to an ashtray containing the remaining few millimeters of two smoked marijuana joints, all of which sat atop a glass nightstand next to the California king bed. A black mid-sized suitcase sat opened on the foot of the bed, with half the clothes inside the case neatly tucked and the other half crumpled up and jammed in. On top of the clothes was a folded piece of paper the size of a 3x5 card, with cursive handwriting that read: I'M SORRY.

Cavanaugh snapped on blue latex gloves and picked up the paper.

"Whatcha got there, boss?" the junior agent said as Cavanaugh slowly unfolded the note.

"Someone tipped her off. She knew we were coming," Cavanaugh said, rotating the note to read the writing. "Not sure."

30272 Vanda Cupertino 90-93-96

Looking at the paper, the junior agent snapped on a pair of latex gloves. "The hell does it mean?"

"An address?"

"Yeah, but what about the numbers?"

"Shit. Get the forensics team up here ASAP, get our analytics team on this," he handed the paper to the agent, "and tell me what you guys find. I'm going back to San Francisco to talk to our friends at the CDC. Only thirty-nine hours left until our deadline. We need answers and we need them now."

As Cavanaugh stepped toward the room door, the junior agent received a text.

"Sir. You're gonna want to see this," said the agent, walking toward the flat-screen television mounted on the wall of the living room above an antique credenza. He tuned to KTLA-Channel 5, where a reporter offered breaking news.

The screen showed a wood-paneled podium in the center, with several microphones affixed to the top, bound with gray duct tape. The reporter spoke while the live video feed played, and text scrolled at the bottom of the screen: BIOSTALL CEO ADMITS GUILT.

What the hell?

Cavanaugh moved closer to the TV and squinted his eyes.

With the empty podium on the screen, the reporter discussed how this last-minute press conference was scheduled not more than thirty minutes ago, that they were waiting for the CEO of BioStall Industries to take the stage, and everyone continued to speculate what specifically she'd be guilty of.

Finally, Linda Bennett appeared in the frame, standing behind the podium.

Cameras flashed, sounding like mating locusts before reporters in the crowd settled down.

"I have a statement I would like to read." Linda held a three-by-five card in her trembling left hand. Cameras continued to flash at her and her brown-and-gray wig, which contrasted with her shocking pink power suit.

She pulled back a smidge, grimaced, and shook her head to swipe her bangs out of her eyes before looking out into the sea of reporters below.

"My name is Linda Bennett. I am the CEO of BioStall Industries, a leading pharmaceutical company that has enriched the lives of countless people worldwide. I want to set the record straight on a personal matter that has, unfortunately, influenced the reputation of our company. What I am about to tell you should have no bearing on the financial health of BioStall."

She cleared her throat and glanced up at the audience below.

Cavanaugh put his hands on his hips and took a wide stance in the living room of the presidential suite. "We got the location of the BioStall building in downtown L.A. Get the guys over there and arrest her."

"Four years ago, I had a six-month affair with a younger female employee who shall remain anonymous." The shocked reporters inhaled collectively, more cameras flashed and clicked.

"My behavior is unacceptable and reprehensible. I successfully hid my sins and kept them a secret for three years. Didn't tell a soul. My husband only found out earlier this morning. He was, of course, angry, which I understand. I hope he can one day forgive me." She paused, looking up at the ceiling, apparently holding back her emotions. "Then, a year ago, in September, I was approached by someone who'd discovered my secret and blackmailed me into doing something

I am ashamed of. The person offered me a lot of money to do something and to keep my mouth shut about it. I was threatened that if I did what I'm doing, if I went public with the threat, I would be killed. Murdered. But . . ." she wiped tears from her cheeks and focused her attention on the reporters. "This morning I visited a hospital in Santa Monica and saw all the sick men. One man in particular, only twenty-five years old, was so sick he couldn't even talk with his little girl who'd come in to visit. I realized at that moment I was on the wrong side of the fence and this needs to stop. Right now. So I come before you, all of you, hoping the authorities will do what they can to help. This has gone on long enough."

The junior agent ended his call to the other agents. "They're en route now. They say they'll be at the press conference in less than five minutes."

Cavanaugh smiled. "She better hurry and get out whatever the hell she's gonna say."

Linda took a deep breath and recomposed herself. "The blackmailer had found out about my affair and threatened to tell my husband, ruin my marriage of twenty-five years, unless I put my best biotech scientists to work to develop a new virus. One that would change the DNA of the affected hosts." Tears streamed down her cheeks, carrying small chunks of mascara. She wiped them away, sucked in a trickle of snot through her nose, and blinked rapidly.

"Shit. Now that cat's out of the bag," Cavanaugh said. "We really need to get our hands around this ASAP before that Bendel tape gets released. That will be one huge-ass fustercluck we can't afford to deal with right now."

CHAPTER 39

August 19th
8:15 a.m.

Viktor sat in the parking lot of a truck stop off State Route 99 in the south end of Fresno, California, pounding the meat of his fist against Jake's driver's side door. Tracy had sent him a text message fifteen minutes ago, wanting him to watch a live news story on the KTLA-5 website. He had whipped out his nine-inch iPad and watched, in disbelief, as Linda Bennett confessed to the media.

After he'd seen enough, he called his lieutenant, Selim, his second in command and one of the loyal members of the team who'd abducted Jake from the restaurant. A smart, committed nineteen-year-old Jihadist, ready to do the needful for the cause.

"Linda's at the BioStall building in downtown Los Angeles, off Wilshire Boulevard. I want you there in five minutes."

"Yes, Mr. Viktor," the young man replied in Syrian-tinged broken English.

"I want her taken care of. Make it look like her husband did it."

On the iPad, Linda continued her prepared speech.

"I believe in Karma and take full responsibility for my actions. I know I'll probably be responsible for the untimely death of thousands of innocent Californians, many of whom are sick with what will likely be diagnosed as a regular flu virus. To all of you watching this right now: I am truly sorry. Words cannot express the sorrow, the grief I feel for you and what I've put you and your families through. I am going to donate every penny of my twelve million dollars to a trust fund to help the people upon whom I've inflicted this horrible disease. This is not nearly enough to earn their forgiveness, but it's all I have."

She continued explaining details of what had happened. When she stopped reading, she looked up, adjusted her wig, and was inundated with questions from the reporters.

Over the next few minutes, although asked to reveal the name of the person who had allegedly hired her, she declined, only giving vague and elusive summary-level details about the virus.

Viktor couldn't help but grin.

There would be no security in the lobby of the BioStall building. Visitors needed to pass through security to get onto the upper floors of the building where all the juicy biotech research was locked away, but in the lobby, nothing.

On his iPad screen, Viktor spotted his young Jihadist at the corner of the stage. The man wore blue jeans with a gray t-shirt that had "Star Wars" emblazoned in gold across the chest.

CHAPTER 40

August 19th
8:30 a.m.

Jake had drifted in and out of sleep over the past few hours. He picked up the TV remote to turn off the CNN show about self-driving cars and how the economic benefits had been greater than expected, but a news flash interrupted the program.

Paige returned from the cafeteria, drained the last of a Diet Coke, crushed the aluminum can and tossed the crinkled mess into a recycle bin stashed in the corner.

"You look a thousand times better," she said.

Jake pointed to the TV. "Check it out. Something about that lady I met a few days ago at the ribbon-cutting ceremony."

The video showed a press conference, several FBI agents moving in to a podium and arresting Linda Bennett. A news announcer said via voice over, ". . . CEO of BioStall Industries. Minutes after she admitted guilt in participating in the unfolding story about a viral attack on Californians, as reporters were asking her questions, FBI agents have taken Mrs. Bennett into custody."

After watching the story for another few minutes, the announcer switched to a story about the Lakers—another injured player—so Jake turned off the TV, wanting to focus on his health. "That should be interesting. Cavanaugh's going to have a field day with her."

"She probably works for Viktor," Paige said. "But screw her. How the hell are you feeling?"

Jake rubbed his right shoulder, rotated it and winced. "They say my fever is down, but holy crap, do my joints ache."

Jake's phone vibrated on the bedside table, Paige picked it up. "Says Tex, no last name."

Tex ... Ah. Oil Man. From the Point Pinole Regional Shoreline ribbon-cutting ceremony, after the interview with Terri Lopez.

He motioned for her to hand over the phone. "I'm losing my mind in this place. Need to talk shop to help get my head straight."

She handed him the phone and he answered.

"I've been trying harder than a rattlesnake outside a gopher hole to get a hold of you at your Stockton office, Dr. Bendel, but they keep giving me the runaround," Tex Murphy said, his thick accent warping every word. "I apologize for givin' you a call on your cell. And I'd hoped to make my plea to you in person, but I guess if this is the best we can do, then so be it."

Jake put the call on speakerphone so Paige could hear. He thought she'd get a kick out of listening to the oil tycoon beg for whatever he was going to beg for.

"I'm listening," Jake said.

Paige leaned in over Jake's bed. Jake turned up the volume a couple of ticks.

"Dr. Bendel, I wanted to further explain to you man-to-man what's goin' on in my world. We're one of several key energy companies that provide power to billions of people all over the globe."

Jake had thought it sly when the oil conglomerates changed their business model to one that involved the creation of "energy." Sounded clean, but still involved extracting oil and coal from the earth and processing and burning the stuff, which released millions-year-old carbon into the sensitive atmosphere of Earth. A critical driver of climate change. But most people would never know it since the companies handling this were simply in the "energy" business.

"I thought we already had this discussion, Mr. Murphy."

Jake turned to Paige and shrugged his shoulders.

"Dr. Bendel, like you, I'm a father. Got four kids, eight grandkids. I'm a patriot. I want to offer my family and my country a world we can be proud of, and I know you think we're just a bunch of crooks, ruining the planet and all that fake news crud about climate change, but I believe we're all here to serve a purpose."

"I'm still listening."

Barely.

"Sir, if you keep headin' down this path, with all these so-called benefits and improvements for the environment, like reducing our dependency on oil to make cars more efficient and comin' out with these new-fangled nuclear power plants that are supposedly safe and clean, and all that other rigamarole you're doing with the power grid, you're hacking away at and killing thousands of American jobs, taking the food off the table of good, hard-working folks."

"Mr. Murphy, I don't have time to get into this with you," Jake said as Paige rolled her eyes. "I'm in the hospital right now and they're telling me I have less than twenty-four hours to live. I'd prefer to spend my last few hours on this earth doing something productive, not haggling over whether climate change is real. If I'm gone, you'll have one less person standing in your way to continue business as usual."

The man on the other end of the line paused. Click. The "call ended" text appeared on Jake's phone.

Jake performed an internal assessment of his body. He felt tired and weak, but the sense of death and the overwhelming urge to sleep had vanished.

The drugs Dr. Abuelhassan had given him were working, at least in the short term.

He looked to the ceiling and pictured what needed to be done. The SLO project was getting back on track. They now knew Gunther had coordinated planting the virus injection system to bypass the chlorination tanks at the San Francisco combo plant. The governor had already told him she thought he was innocent, but that extremist environmental group wanted Jake's head on a platter based on the damning video.

And now Linda Bennett's involvement added a new twist.

He hadn't heard from Cavanaugh in hours and wondered what the latest developments were. They had thirty-six hours remaining until the deadline imposed by Governor Fairchild.

His thoughts circled back to Dave Trainer's eyeball. Dave might still be alive, without an eye. But Cavanaugh's agent said something pertaining to plant-based DNA in the second virus, so why harm crops? And what the hell did that have to do with humans getting sick? And if Viktor or Linda had designed the viruses, why'd they choose to infect only men? How many were infected now? Was it possible to stop it before it spread further?

These questions only motivated Jake. More of his energy returned.

"Get me my pants. We're leaving," he said.

But before Paige could dig back into the bag to retrieve Jake's jeans, Dr. Abuelhassan entered the curtained room, studying the same aluminum chart.

Paige sat on a plastic visitor's chair, next to the bag with Jake's belongings.

"I'd like to continue to run some more tests. Your viral numbers are improving, seems like the experimental anti-viral meds are doing their job, but you're not out of the woods yet by any stretch of the imagination. I'll be back soon." The doc left the room.

Paige leapt up and handed Jake his pants. "For the record, I think you should stay here. You're in no condition to help anyone if you can't even help yourself."

He stood from the bed, extracted the IV from the top of his hand and removed the heart monitor pads.

A bout of dizziness hit and the room spun around.

"Don't listen to the doc, I'm fine."

As Paige helped him get dressed, he felt his Sûr System pen clanking against Dave's flash drive, the one with the flag, in his pocket—symbols of his renewed motivation—but a nurse ran into the room, panicked the heart monitor had gone flat.

"I can't let you leave," she said.

"There's a lot more on the line right now than my health and my life. If I'm gonna die tomorrow, I want to know I made a difference. Or at least tried to." He buttoned his dress shirt, slid on his socks and tied his shoes.

They stepped toward the doorway, but before they could exit, Abuelhassan blocked their path, shaking his head.

"I figured you'd be headed out soon. I've read about you. Nobody can keep you down. I've seen it before. Many times. Your instinct to control everything in your life is going to be the death of you."

Jake stepped around the doc. "I appreciate your psychiatric opinion, doc, but I gotta run." Jake turned to walk through the hallway toward the front entrance, but Abuelhassan grabbed his wrist and Jake jerked to a stop, off balance.

"Here." Abuelhassan handed Jake a packet of pills. "If you have any chance at all of making it out of your condition alive, take these every three hours. Tell me you understand."

Jake nodded.

"Good luck to you, sir," the doc said.

Jake and Paige hustled as best they could toward the elevator, down to the ground floor, and out the front door where he sent a text update to Cavanaugh. A wave of heat with a hint of freshly cut grass and jasmine flowers blasted Jake's face, and an image of Cynthia appeared in his head.

Jake texted Carlie an update, too, as he walked with Paige, who said, "I took a cab back to my dad's last night and grabbed my car. It's parked over there." She pointed toward a four-story parking structure.

After walking across the street, they found her orange 1965 Mustang convertible, hopped in, and Paige drove them out onto the local streets, heading north toward Stockton.

CHAPTER 41

August 19th
9:06am

Paige drove Jake fifteen minutes north to the offices of South Sun Global, Jake's company headquarters in the heart of Stockton, California.

South Sun had over a dozen powerful workstations that normally handled computer-aided drawings for massive civil engineering projects like freeway interchanges, bridges, water treatment plants, housing subdivisions, and power plants. The machines used the latest graphics cards, CPU's, software and the fastest memory available. Over the past six months Jake had been experimenting with a new form of artificial intelligence, or AI, for calculating environmental, social and biological trends.

Paige parked her Mustang convertible in the lot thirty yards from the entrance of the building, closed the top, and locked the doors. Half a football field of delicately manicured dark green fescue, bisected by an open winding concrete sidewalk, was between the lot and the building.

Jake struggled to stand, but Paige helped guide him along the walkway to the building entrance. His insides felt like a well-used rugby field and his joints screamed with pain, but he dug deep, finding shreds of inner strength to power himself to his office.

South Sun leased the first floor of a 10,000 square foot, two-story modern brick structure, along the Calaveras River near the center of Stockton. The grass surrounding the building gave off the scent of a recent mow, not affected by the drought. The deep bass of a ship horn blasted in the distance.

"Once we're inside, I'll set you up on one of the best machines we have," Jake said, stopping to catch his breath.

Paige studied her friend's face.

"You still look like shit, dude. I knew this was a bad idea, never should have listened to you. You should still be in the hospital," she said, helping Jake up the entrance steps.

Jake fumbled his keys to unlock the front entrance, but the door was already one inch ajar.

Paige looked at Jake, rocking in place. He expected an empty suite. None of his engineers should be working on Saturday. Red flag.

Jake felt a rapid pulse in his neck, all of his pain increased a notch, and he felt faint as his vision narrowed.

Paige whispered, "I didn't see your Tesla in the parking lot, but that doesn't mean Viktor didn't ditch your ride and find some other car."

"This is crazy. We need to call Cavanaugh," Jake said, hobbling back down the steps, where he dialed his FBI friend.

Cavanaugh spoke over the high-pitched hiss of static, yelling. "I'm back up in the helicopter now, heading to the San Francisco Federal Building. I hope you're calling from the hospital to tell me you're feeling better."

"I discharged myself and I'm with Paige here at my office in Stockton," Jake said.

"Jesus, I want you back in that hospital. Now."

"I have a fever and feel like crap, but we need to find out more about this virus." Jake arched his back and grimaced. "Paige is going to work on putting together an infographic map of the outbreaks to find some patterns."

"Fine. Linda Bennett left us a clue and I'm not sure if you watched the newscast she all but confessed to the attack. We had her under arrest and were gonna ask her about this note she left at her hotel room, but she lawyered up before we could interrogate her. Judge is a friend of hers and said since she had no priors and is such a prominent member of the community at large, wasn't a flight risk, blah, blah, blah, he allowed bail. Especially since she confessed. Her husband posted the money and she's free, but we put a tail on her for her own safety. As of two minutes ago, she's supposed to be headed back to her hotel suite in Beverly Hills, at least for now. They're gonna throw the book at her once we get to trial, but that's months, maybe years, away."

Jake closed his eyes. Bright, colorful stars flickered in the darkness. He struggled to breathe and coughed several times.

"Okay, but one other thing. Did you find Viktor? He only had maybe a five-minute lead on your guys, so—"

"Dude frickin' disappeared. Like he went down a rabbit hole. No trace of him or your car, unfortunately. We even tried pinging the GPS on your car. Nothing."

Jake rubbed his forehead and shot a glance at Paige.

"Great. We're here at the South Sun office and the door is unlocked and open. There's not supposed to be anyone working today."

Paige tapped Jake on his shoulder, he turned, and she pointed to a window with open mini blinds behind which two men were rummaging around inside Jake's office.

"Get the hell out of there, now."

"Hold on," Jake said, squinting to get a better look. His eyesight waned and the dizziness returned. Fevers could be a real bitch.

Jake recognized the two men. They both worked for Jake as design engineers, both Cal Poly graduates. Top-notch staff.

Viktor was not inside Jake's office.

"They're employees. I recognize them. If Viktor was in there, they'd know," Jake said. "Need your guy at the CDC to send me whatever data he can via email or Dropbox."

"Ten-four. I'll do that right when we end this call."

"We'll reach back out if we find something," Jake said, waving Paige to follow him back inside the office.

Jake ended the call with Cavanaugh, shuffled inside South Sun and greeted his two engineers.

"Dude! You look like hell!" one of the engineers, Gary, said to Jake. Gary was at most thirty years old, balding, with a thick goatee.

"So I've heard. Guys, this is Paige Terner," Jake said, motioning to his friend, who shook hands. "Whatever you're working on, stop. Got something infinitely more important. Today Paige is your boss. You three are going to put together a GIS map."

Gary looked at the other engineer, Shaun, who was the same height as Jake at six-foot-three, with a large forehead and thin blond eyebrows.

"Sweet," Shaun said. "Didn't feel like finishing those structural calcs today anyway. Sounds like we're gonna get deep into some heavy-duty data mining."

Paige took a step toward the two junior engineers. "Okay, dudes, we're in the middle of something and can't share all the details, but I need you to swear on your grandmother's grave you won't tell anyone about this."

Gary smiled.

"Anyone!" Paige said again, clenching her jaw, and staring up at both men. "Your boss has been injected with some virus and has a ton of drugs in his system right now and we're hoping he'll continue to recover, so he's not gonna be much help."

"I'm confused," Shaun said. He crossed his arms across his surfer build chest. His entire body was lean muscle, no fat, healthy as a young shark.

"You're familiar with the plant combos?" Paige asked.

"Of course. We both worked on the design and construction details of the hydraulic systems for the de-sal plants."

Paige brought her trembling hand to her forehead. "Good, because someone's infected the water supply coming from the new plant combos with a virus. We're expecting to get a bunch of data in a few minutes from the CDC. Thousands of people along the coast are sick, but only men. My dad is Professor Everton — you guys might have had him at Cal Poly. He's telling me a bunch of his friends are sick. Also, the FBI is saying that crops are dying, too. We need to put our heads together and, like, find answers the CDC and FBI haven't figured out. Make sense?"

The two engineers looked at each other. "Your dad's Professor Everton? That's so cool. I took his class my junior year, I — "

"That's not the point," Paige interrupted. "Sit down and fire up the GIS. We got a lot of work to do."

"I'll get you started," Jake said. "Then I need to go sit in my office and catch my breath. These three here are our best machines. Use them. This one here has the experimental AI software." He pointed to the computer to his right, sat, flipped the switch and the machine came to life. The AI beast welcomed Jake with a verbal greeting, which reminded him of the talking computer in the *Space Odyssey 2001* movie. Paige pulled up a chair and slid next to Jake, who entered his username and password.

Once logged in, Jake stood, turned and walked toward his executive office off to their left, where a large dark wood door and clear panes of glass separated his room from the main office work area.

He sank into his soft, brown leather chair and left the door open. He heard Paige barking orders to the engineers as he and focused his mind on Cynthia. Her loving memory had a way of dulling his pain.

CHAPTER 42

August 19th
2:00 p.m.

Paige stormed into Jake's office, bolting him awake from a deep sleep.

"Dude. You gotta see this," Paige said, grabbing hold of Jake's forearm and helping him stand. "Your CDC guy sent me the data and we've spent the last two hours compiling everything into the GIS. I used the AI software to figure out trends and projections. It's still running, but we have some cool stuff to show you."

Need to pop some of those Abuelhassan pills.

Jake downed the pills and then walked with Paige into the main office area. She pulled up another chair and Jake sat, amazed how several hours could fly by in a matter of seconds.

"Show him," Paige said to Gary.

Gary pointed to his screen, which had a colorful map of the middle third of California, from the whole Los Angeles area to north of San Francisco. Red, blue, green, and yellow circles of different sizes littered the coastline and had greater density near each of the plant combos.

"Each of these circles represents a cluster of infected men," Gary said. "The larger the circle, the more infected men. The red circles are the clusters that have been infected the longest, for two weeks or more. Green represents less than a week. Yellow, in between."

Jake's eyes darted across the map. "I don't understand what the blue circles are for."

"Damn, dude. Even though you're half dead, you don't miss a beat," Paige said. "Those are where farmers have reported mysterious crop deaths. Otherwise healthy crops of walnuts, tomatoes, grapes, strawberries, lettuce, almonds, and hay are shriveling up and dying, as though they're dehydrated, even though the farmers are giving the crops plenty of water."

Paige pointed to a photo on her iPhone, one sent by the CDC, and zoomed in. The image showed several rows of almond trees, discolored and wilted as he would expect them to look after a brutal California summer with no water.

"Hold on," Jake said. "These trees look like they've been poisoned, like someone gave them a massive dose of weed killer."

"That's just it, though, dude. They haven't been poisoned," Paige said. "The CDC did all their normal screening for poisonous chemicals, heavy metals, et cetera, and the water seems fine for plants. But we know there are two strains of the virus. We just don't know *how* the second one is killing these plants."

Jake crossed his arms and rubbed his chin. "Did you run the AI?"

A hint of a smile carved its way into the side of Paige's cheek. "This is where things get interesting."

She nodded to Gary, who jiggled the mouse and clicked several times, pulling up new windows on the thirty-two-inch widescreen, and then she pointed to a colorful graph with bars, dots, and curved lines.

"The AI ran, like, a bajillion analyses," Paige said. "More than you and I could do in several lifetimes, considering a host of factors like socioeconomic, population locations and trends, land use, terrain, roadway, and hydraulic infrastructure, and of course the data from the CDC with the infected human information." She tapped the tip of her finger on the screen at a large red rectangle. "Right here."

Jake scooted toward the screen and squinted. Below the rectangle read 98%.

"According to the AI, there's a ninety-eight percent chance the plants are being infected by a virus," she said. "Which tracks with what we found in that bunker and why the CDC's regular tests failed to identify the cause of the dying crops."

"But the CDC already suspected this. What's new about this information?" Jake asked.

Paige showed a new graph on the monitor, with various agriculture stocks, prices, trade info and more. She pointed to a large spike in the middle. "See this?"

Jake nodded, wheels turning in his head. "Someone's shorting stock?"

"Not just any stock. All the stock of all the agricultural corporations running the farms here in California. Billions of dollars' worth."

Jake continued to think. "You're saying someone, or a group of people, is betting on a downturn in California crops? And if they do, they make—"

"Hundreds of billions of dollars," Paige said, finishing his sentence. "According to the AI calcs."

Two images of the computer screen blurred together as Jake shook his head to maintain clarity. He put the back of his hand against his forehead. Still feverish.

"Excellent work, guys. Keep digging for more hidden nuggets of information like who, exactly, has been shorting those stocks, while I get Cavanaugh up to speed."

Jake shuffled back into his office, plopped onto the leather chair, but passed out before he could dial Cavanaugh.

CHAPTER 43

August 19th
2:30 p.m.

Viktor clicked the "Play" button on his laptop screen and smiled, relishing the impending victory.

He leaned back in the driver's seat of an ancient, rust-bucket brown Ford F-150 pickup truck, locked his fingers behind his head and watched as the video uploaded across its wireless journey from the laptop via satellite internet connection to twelve major television stations throughout Los Angeles, Sacramento, and San Francisco, after the feed had been routed through multiple IP's across Europe and the Middle East.

Millions of people are now watching Jake commit an act of terrorism.

Brilliant.

Before Gunther's death and in true terrorist form, he had set up an ingenious hack that gave them unimpeded access to the encrypted satellite feeds the television stations used to send and receive video signals. They had planned to commandeer the digital signals and replace the normal boring American bullshit shows with something to pique the attention of the media.

He'd eluded Cavanaugh's FBI goons after the threat to Jake and that dyke bitch friend of his earlier today by burying Jake's Tesla in a different bunker two miles north. The other bunker, used by Gunther and him as a backup location in case their primary bunker was raided, had been vandalized by local gangs over the years to the point where only a portion of the rounded corrugated roof remained.

The backup bunker had no front door and no front wall, only a large opening to drive Jake's Tesla through to the underground area. Viktor had parked the Tesla, crawled out, and placed twenty pounds of Semtex along the perimeter of the semi-circular corrugated metal roof. He then set twenty pounds of additional explosives next to the old brown pickup truck and directly underneath the Tesla. Then he'd leaned down to the detonator, pushed the red button to activate the sixty-second timer, and hopped into the truck before backing out of the bunker and speeding away.

Thirty seconds later, in his rearview mirror, the bunker imploded on itself, entombing the Tesla and any evidence leading back to Viktor.

Man, I'm good.

A two-hour drive west landed him in the middle of a 16,000-acre ranch farm owned by Tracy Ciacchella. During the drive, he'd planned and memorized a mental script of what he wanted to say to the masses once he commandeered the airwaves. The vegetation all around looked dry. Dead. The drought had been hard on the environment. Trees wilted. Wild grass showed no signs of green, only beige, and he imagined this would be how landscaping had looked when the Native Americans roamed free throughout the land, before the white man had invaded and stolen everything from the indigenous people. The tribes would be happy once his plan came to full fruition and the infidels dropped like flies. Their sinful casino revenues would plummet, but their lands would be saved.

Viktor shifted thoughts back to their benefactor. He'd dealt with Tracy during the CDM attack on the 405 two years ago and had no problem accepting the money to fund the effort. He relished the fact that the FBI had failed to follow the money trail back to Tracy. Boy, Tracy's team sure hid their tracks well.

Linda had been in contact with Tracy on multiple occasions during the planning of the current project, aimed at striking a historic blow to the heart of the liberal Californians.

Tracy was just someone with billions of dollars and power and similar plans to help tip their hand in favor of the Jihad, to eliminate greedy American infidels.

The 90-second video of Jake poisoning the water supply at the new San Francisco desalination plant—taken two weeks ago when they had abducted him—finished playing. A tiny blue light next to the pinhole camera on Viktor's laptop blinked on.

Showtime.

Viktor leaned forward in his seat to get a better view of the tiny window in the lower right corner of the screen which confirmed the camera gave a nice, full-size shot of his once-bearded face, deep wrinkles and all. His live video message would stream directly to media outlets across the state, overriding whatever moronic programming they had planned to air, forcing his message to be seen live by over five million Californians.

Sorry, All My Children. *I have something to say.*

After clearing his throat, he relished the energy of knowing his message would stream live to so many people. Next to piles of cash, mass media was a terrorist's best friend.

He recited his memorized statement he'd concocted during the drive out from Modesto to Tracy's ranch.

"To the decent, hard-working people of California: I am a concerned citizen. My name is of no importance, but like you, I am worried about what our government is doing to us. And you deserve to know the truth. Agencies of the federal government, the CDC, and the FBI are hiding vital information from you, my friends. Over the course of the past two weeks, over one million California men have been infected with a man-made virus. The video I just showed you is hard, irrefutable evidence that the so-called hero of the masses, civil engineer Jake Bendel, is nothing more than a conniving, greedy, mentally unstable man working against us. He is delusional after murdering his wife two years ago and now has intentions of bringing down our great nation. He is the bioterrorist solely responsible for injecting our treated water with a deadly virus, and many Californians will die because of his actions. You've seen the proof and now you know the truth. If you feel angry, if you feel betrayed, if you feel threatened—" he furrowed his brow and narrowed his eyes, staring into the tiny camera lens— "take to the streets and send a message to our leaders. Demand answers. Do what is needed."

He clicked the "terminate transmission" button on the screen and ended the video feed, knowing he'd planted a glorious seed of fear deep into the minds of the masses, one that would bear the fruit of infidel death.

Praise Allah.

CHAPTER 44

August 19th
2:35 p.m.

In the fourth-floor conference room of the San Francisco Federal Building, Cavanaugh, and several other agents stared at the seventy-two-inch TV screen and watched in horror as Viktor's video messages played in real-time. First the video of Jake poisoning the water, now full confirmation Viktor Johnston was alive.

Goddamnit.

Cavanaugh knew he'd been beaten. Two years ago, over a hundred agents had searched nonstop for three months looking for Viktor's body after he fell from the plane near Glendale. But Cavanaugh and his team had found no trace of Viktor. No parachute. Nothing. For the last twenty-four months, Viktor had haunted Cavanaugh. And the mighty FBI, with all its resources, formed no sort of tangible conclusion about Viktor's disappearance. Reminded Cavanaugh of the D.B. Cooper bank heist back in the seventies. The Johnston disappearance story had leaked out within a month of Viktor's so-called defeat. Conspiracy theories abounded like a plague, oozing from blog posts and podcasts. Several authors had even published entire books describing their theories of what happened on that fateful day in August. The world wondered, asking legitimate questions every day.

Until now, the FBI had no answers.

Viktor had pulled out all the stops. In the full spirit of his psychopathy, he'd revealed his presence to the world, distracted the public by pointing the finger at Jake, increased the likelihood of civil unrest and a delay in finding solutions, and skyrocketed the chances of Viktor's plan—whatever his end game was— coming to successful fruition.

"Son-of-a-bitch," Cavanaugh said under his breath, knowing full well that the video would condemn Jake and incite rioting across the state.

His phone vibrated: Governor Fairchild.

"Guess our little deadline came sooner than expected," she said.

"I'm worried how this looks for Jake," Cavanaugh said. "As far as I know, we're no closer to finding a cure or getting a handle on this than we were twenty-four hours ago, but we do have some evidence from the raid on the Modesto bunker that might pan out. We're working to find out—"

"I'm tired of hearing your excuses or anything about what might or might not pan out, Agent Cavanaugh. We need answers, like yesterday."

Cavanaugh agreed and assured the governor his team was doing everything humanly possible to stop the outbreak and catch Viktor and the group responsible.

"At least, thanks to Viktor, we've all but confirmed the new desalination plants are the source of contamination. No other evidence of any additional contamination, though."

"Your men didn't find any of those containers at the other four plants?" she asked.

"Negative. The working theory now is Gunther, and of course Jake and Dave at the San Francisco plant, temporarily installed the containers with the viruses, then removed them once the contents were dispersed."

"I have a meeting in five minutes with my senior advisors to determine whether we need to call in the National Guard to quell any likely riots."

Cavanaugh ended the call with the governor and dialed Jake, who muddled his way through a groggy explanation that he'd just woken up and that he and Paige were at South Sun working on sorting through the data from the CDC.

"I still can't believe you're not back in the hospital," Cavanaugh said. "Won't do any of us any good if you keel over there in your office."

In a voice that sounded weak, raspy, slow, he responded, "Greater good, Cavanaugh. This isn't about me, it's about finding out the extent of the damage so we can home in on solutions to stop the spread. We've discovered a link between the human viral spread and contamination for plants and crops. Here, I'll let Paige explain."

Shuffling noises came through the phone.

"Dude," Paige said, "if possible, I think it would be helpful if you could get some scientists out to some of the farms in the central and western parts of the state, within fifty miles of each of the three working treatment plants in San Francisco, Santa Barbara, and San Diego."

Cavanaugh looked at the television, where several agents stood watching the same reporter, Terri Lopez, and a scientist from UC Berkeley dissect Viktor's message. He stepped out of the room into the dim hallway.

"We already did that. They're out there right now," Cavanaugh said.

"Plants are susceptible to viruses," Paige said. "Just the way all living things are, including us. Research we found suggests it's very rare to have a virus that can infect both plants and animals, but from what I can tell on the GIS map we made, we've confirmed the CDC theory there are two different strains in the water, one attacking the men, and one the vegetation."

"Send me what you got and I'll get some additional technicians out to the local farms to do some crop testing,"

Cavanaugh said. "I take it you guys didn't watch Viktor's message on TV."

Paige gasped and told Jake in a muted tone. Odd shuffling noises came through before she asked Cavanaugh for the details and he explained.

"Okay," she said. "I'll send you some PDF maps of what we found so you can share with your buddies at the CDC and we'll watch the video. I'm sure someone has already posted it to YouTube."

They ended their call and Cavanaugh walked back into the room with the television.

"It's already starting," one of the agents said, pointing to the TV.

Cavanaugh stepped toward the TV and watched as the ABC affiliate broadcast a live feed from a chopper above the lower area of San Francisco. Down on the ground were several dozen people, a small mob, marching along a street, firing multiple gunshots into the air and throwing whatever loose debris they could find into the store windows near them.

Terri Lopez chimed in, with the high-pitched squeal of the helicopter engine humming in the background.

"From up here, we have an excellent view of what looks like the beginning of a riot. San Francisco PD is on site. Around the corner from where the mob is heading, several dozen officers are waiting for the rioters. It should be interesting to see what happens to those people when they round the corner."

Several seconds later, the screen showed the mob approaching the hidden cops decked out in full riot gear. Gas canisters shot from the police into the crowd and green smoke erupted all around the rioters, who dispersed like hornets from a busted nest. Except for two armed men, who emerged from the cloud and started firing at the police. Several cops returned fire and both men collapsed to the ground. The video signal stopped, sending the feed back to the two reporters in the studio.

"That may be our first casualty," Cavanaugh said. "Chaos and anarchy are what Viktor wants, but he's underestimated us again."

Cavanaugh rushed out of the office and headed toward the elevator with an alternative plan in his head.

One he'd need Jake's help with, assuming Jake didn't die.

CHAPTER 45

August 19th
3:00 p.m.

Inside the Los Angeles City Hall building on the southeast corner of Spring and West Temple, after hours of paperwork to get the bail bonds posted, Linda walked across the central rotunda of the police station. Sharp streams of sunlight beamed in high through tall windows above onto the Spanish tile floor.

She blasted through the doors to the furnace outside, her husband Frank following close behind. They dashed down the front concrete steps toward the bustling street below.

Car horns echoed off the tall buildings. Linda stopped on the sidewalk, rubbed the nape of her neck, turned around, and looked straight up at the classic L.A. City Hall tower constructed in the late twenties, with the twenty-eight-story skyscraper tower and the sloping walls.

Her wig nearly slid off her head.

She righted the hairpiece and noted a seething look from Frank, who had been silent since posting her $1.2 million bail. She'd expected a certain level of blowback from Frank. Any husband worth keeping would have been upset when a wife admitted an affair, especially of the lesbian variety.

They darted north along the gum-strewn sidewalk toward their new silver Audi seven-series parked two blocks up the street.

He broke his silence.

"I get it," he said. "You have needs and I haven't been meeting them. I get that."

She slowed her pace, allowed him to catch up, and wondered if the agents had found the note she left them in the hotel room.

The one describing the stockpile.

Frank walked at her side, careful to avoid dozens of multi-colored homeless tents.

"What I don't get is why you didn't come talk to me a long time ago," he said. "And why you thought it would be a good idea to air our personal laundry all across the goddamned country."

She looked up at the crystal blue sky. One cloud. One measly stupid cloud.

An elderly man approached the troubled couple, holding out his left hand, grasping a cardboard sign in his right that read, "The end is near. Your end is near."

Linda blew past him and continued a brisk pace heading north to their car, a hundred yards further.

"I cracked. I couldn't take the guilt anymore. The shame," she said without looking at Frank. "We haven't spoken in weeks. I want to be in control of my life. My conscience got the best of me. I wanted to come clean. I needed to come clean. Tracy and her hoard of criminals held the affair over my head like a guillotine. If I didn't meet their demands with the biotech work . . ." She slid her finger across her throat in a slicing motion. "But I realized I could either be dead with a secret or honest and alive. I chose honesty, especially after seeing those poor sick people this morning, knowing I was partially responsible. I'm ready to accept the consequences." She scanned the area for potential threats. Viktor and Tracy had likely seen the press conference and confession and with any luck, by purposely withholding the names of her criminal cohorts, she might be forgiven and salvage the rest of her life. She wanted a clean break. A fresh start with no more ties to anything related to the so-called Jihad.

"You mentioned a name: Tracy?"

"Never mind."

He paused. She hoped he'd forget she'd mentioned the name of someone with enough power to neutralize anyone on the planet without getting caught. Or the slightest twinge of remorse.

"But we're married," Frank said. "Twenty-five years. I'm supposed to have a say in what happens. You should've come talk to me. We could've figured this out together."

Her face felt red, flush with blood, pulsating between anger and shame.

They approached her car and hopped in.

"Try to keep it under the speed limit. They'll probably put a tail on us," Frank said, turning off the radio.

"Honestly, that would be for the best. You have no idea what these people could—"

With pursed lips, she fired up the V-8 and zoomed north, staying well under every speed limit. Instead of getting her things from the Beverly Hills Hotel, she made her way toward their second home in the Hollywood Hills. She'd been staying at the hotel to keep her distance from Frank, who'd taken up full occupancy at their home. He hated their primary residence up in San Jose, five miles from BioStall headquarters, because it reminded him of their teenage daughter, Kassidy, killed in an automobile accident five years ago. She'd been driving back to Stanford on a two-lane rural road when a worker, texting and speeding at seventy miles an hour, plowed into the rear of her KIA Sportage, stealing her young life on impact.

The tragedy had driven a spike through the once-strong marriage.

In silence, Linda and Frank wound their way up the spiral driveway to their three-story mansion, surrounded by house-sized privacy bushes, oodles of palm trees, and more gardenia, hibiscus, orchid, and hibiscus flowers than a Rose Parade. A wide swath of the Los Angeles basin loomed in the distance.

"I don't know what to tell you," she said. "I've already apologized. It's gonna take time."

"You're gonna need to keep apologizing. The more the better," he said.

"My therapist says I was just looking for attention, maybe a diversion from the pain of losing Kassidy. If that guy hadn't hit her, none of this would've happened." She jammed the gearshift into park. "By extension, he killed her, our marriage, and now God-knows-how-many innocent people. Shit. How could I be so stupid?" She touched her forehead to the steering wheel, eyes closed.

Frank touched his fingers on her shoulder. "C'mon inside, honey. Let me make you a nice stiff blood orange margarita." He rubbed her shoulder. "Or five."

She chuckled under her breath and they exited the car.

Once inside, the scent of the furniture and whatever their cleaning lady had used earlier to mop the floors reminded Linda of happier times. She dropped her purse next to the built-in bar, kicked off her scuffed black court shoes, wandered into the living room, and plopped onto her favorite cream leather chair.

Several minutes later, Frank handed her the icy, reddish-orange Tequila drink. She took a sip. It felt good sliding down her throat and, craving the numbness, she downed the entire glass in three gulps before handing the glass back to Frank.

After two more drinks, and plowing through a major episode of brain freeze, the alcohol finally kicked in. The room buzzed in a wonderfully dazzling blur. She smiled and sipped the fourth drink. The press conference, the threats, the affair—everything became muted, toned down while her heart raced and her mind finally went into chill mode.

"What else did you tell the police?" Frank asked.

She paused, taking a nice long draw on her drink.

"Just that I was in on a kidnapping a couple weeks ago, but other than that, not much."

"Jesus, Linda." Frank rubbed his palm across his forehead. "They already have your confession. If you're not careful, you'll end up in prison for the rest of your life. I'm surprised you didn't use your only true bargaining chip."

She squinted at him, raised her eyebrows, took another sip, and swallowed. "I have more than one bargaining chip. Two years ago I started repurposing one of my plants, one that manufactures polio vaccine. I have the power to stop all this. I can—"

"Damnit, you need to cut a deal. Tell them whatever they want to know about whom ever you were working for."

She stared at the carpet near her feet for several seconds "Why?"

"We could go with witness protection. Beats prison. Get some police protection and get our lives back together. I'm seriously worried about someone showing up and taking us out."

She finished a hefty swallow and bared her teeth. "That was my plan, but our stupid attorney advised against all that. He said we need to wait until later. After the hearing. Better leverage."

"You're lucky the judge considered all the charity work you've done over the last decade."

An idea hit her like a wrecking ball and she drained the rest of her drink.

"I don't know what the hell I was thinking," she said, looking at the ground. "I could've just disappeared. Then confessed. Shit."

"No idea what you're talking about," he said.

She slammed the glass onto the marble end table on her right. "In the corporate jet. Let's fly out of here. Tonight. You and me. Fresh start."

He stood.

"I'm going to bed." He kissed her forehead, wandered up the plush, carpeted stairs and disappeared.

She stood, walked to the bar, and whipped herself up a fifth margarita. With double Tequila.

Someone knocked on the front door.

Already here to kill us? No way. She pushed the idea from her mind.

Probably another jerk from the press.

She shuffled along the travertine tile floor and peered through the peephole. A brown, smiling man with his arms clasped behind him.

Instead of ignoring him—her first instinct—and with a hefty amount of alcohol coursing through her veins, against her better judgment, especially considering the press conference and potential threats, she unbolted the lock. The door swung open and she found, standing on her front porch, a short non-threatening man, likely of Middle-Eastern descent, grinning like a fool. He wore an unzipped black hoodie with a gray t-shirt underneath with a gold silkscreened "Star Wars" logo, blue jeans, and black boots. He sported a mid-length goatee.

Linda said nothing. Just stared at his face and tried not to fall over as she leaned against the satin white door. Her eyelids felt heavy. She had minutes before passing out.

"Greetings, madam. I am Sam," the man said, with a mild Arabic accent. Lines from Dr. Seuss entered her mind. "I am wondering if you might have a minute to discuss the Lord and Savior Jesus Christ. For it is foretold He shall be risen and as a witness of the Jehovah faith, all ye who stray not shall enter the kingdom of God forever and—"

She thought it odd for a missionary to come by in the evening, was usually Saturday mornings when they bothered her. She put up her hand and burped. "Not interested in your religious fables. Get the hell outta here. Trespassing." She started to close the door, but the man stepped inside over the threshold, his foot stopping the door cold.

Linda's body posture loosened, and she frowned. "The hell you think you're doing?"

"Trust me, Linda Bennett, you listen to what I have to say." He took another step toward her. She backed up. Her glass fell to the floor, shattering into a million crystal shards.

The instinct to scream hit her hard, but she squelched the urge. Didn't want to wake up Frank. Wait. *Not thinking straight.*

The man whipped out a black snub-nose pistol with a large cylinder attached to the muzzle. Silencer. He pointed the gun at Linda.

"You scream, you die, bitch. But I make this real easy for you."

She swallowed. No saliva. Desert. Her mind a complete fog.

With her hands raised, palms facing toward the man, he crept toward her. She continued to back up through the foyer, her pulse pounding inside her head and no ideas coming.

He motioned with his chin for her to continue into the living room. She sat in her favorite spot, the same leather chair.

Did Frank heard the glass break?

Black gloves covered both hands and he held a length of 3/8-inch yellow nylon rope in his left hand. She remembered that same rope used on Jake during the Chili's abduction.

"You don't have to die tonight, bitch. Do what you are told. You will live. Trust me." He smiled, revealing several yellow-stained teeth.

She didn't recognize him because he, and the other two abductors, already had their masks on when she'd arrived at the Chili's parking lot.

"Selim," she said, taking a gamble he was at Jake's abduction. He paused, pursing his lips, surprised she remembered his name. "Whatever Tracy is paying you, I'll double it."

"You will not use my name. You talk again, I pull this little trigger. You go bye-bye, bitch."

He leaned toward her, forced her arms behind her waist, tied her wrists tight with zip-ties, and wrapped the rope around her upper torso, binding her to the chair.

"Triple the amount."

He stopped wrapping and smiled.

"Last warning, bitch." He tap-tap-tapped the butt of his gun into her temple. "I got ten bullet in this mag." He cocked his head to the side. "It only take one and you go to Satan. Shut. The hell. Up."

She trembled, her bladder ready to explode, while trying to control her rapid breathing before swallowing again and thinking of a plan to escape.

The man jostled the rope tight and tied a knot.

He retrieved a red gag ball attached to a black leather head strap and fastened the device to her head. *Cliché.*

After releasing an extended exhale, he sat on the matching couch across from her, pistol aimed at her chest.

"Now we wait."

CHAPTER 46

August 19th
3:00 p.m.

Jake stood next to Paige and his two young engineers, all watching Viktor's announcement. Once Viktor's broadcast ended, Gary closed the YouTube window.

A wave of nausea hit Jake in the pit of his gut. Probably the deadly virus flowing through his veins. Or the anti-viral meds raging all-out war with his immune system. He needed to sit.

Normally when he felt this way, his energy evaporated like gasoline on a hot summer afternoon, accompanied by a powerful urge to sleep.

Not this time.

He felt wide awake. Manic. His hands jittered and his jaw trembled as colorful bright spots flickered across his vision. A long time ago, at a fraternity party back in college, a so-called friend had slipped him a tiny piece of paper. The guy had told him the paper would help attract more chicks by changing his pheromones, but that was a lie and the paper was laced with LSD. It was the only time Jake tripped. And, he thought at the time, the last.

"I got an email from my dad, but it's from, like, two hours ago," Paige said, tapping her phone. "Says he figured out who's behind all this and he faxed it to the cloud, and there's a link here." The three men stared at her. "Who uses a fax anymore?"

Jake pointed to the office copier, which had a built-in fax machine. "Over there," he said to Gary, as his phone vibrated: Cavanaugh. "Give the number to Paige and her dad." Gary took Paige's phone and started tapping.

Gary said, "It's a onetime fax service. I can type in a phone number and it'll send the fax through and delete it from the cloud."

Jake gave Gary a nod.

Now on Jake's phone, Cavanaugh said, "I got a plan but need to talk to Paige first," and Jake handed her the phone.

As she listened, she moved back a half a foot, increasing her personal space. A few seconds later her nostrils flared, tremors hit her hands and fingers, she squeezed her eyes shut, and covered her mouth. Tears formed and broke free.

"No," she yelled. "That's not possible. I just had dinner with him yesterday. And we just got a fax from him a few hours ago, well that's when he sent it." She shook her head and sobbed. Jake's phone slipped from her hand and bounced onto the floor. She squatted and covered her face.

The office copier started to warm up.

Jake blinked, trying to jerk himself back to reality, but he felt like he was slipping into a deep, dreamlike state even though he was still awake. Wide awake. Something was definitely wrong. He stepped to Paige and touched her shoulder.

She jerked her arm away and stood. "My dad's dead. Your friend. Your mentor. They killed him."

Jake massaged his throat, fighting the urge to pass out.

"They poisoned my dad," Paige said. "And all those people?" She stepped away from him. "Are you and Dave working with Viktor?"

Jake rubbed his eyebrows. "Jesus Christ, Paige, of course not. You know me better than that. Are you sure he's . . . what happened?"

She peeled her hand up across her forehead and raked her fingers through her short, red hair. "Yeah, but sorry. Stupid me. I just, um, like, that's you and Dave on the fucking video."

Memories of his mentor flooded his brain. The urge to deny the news of his death, to mourn, piled on top of the already heavy burden, but he had to shove this aside, ignore the facts for now, and keep moving forward. Time was running out.

Gary stood next to the copier, watching it warm up.

"It's us on the video, but someone did some fancy Hollywood magic. CGI. Something. I don't know. I have no memory whatsoever of doing that. I promise you. And don't forget we have Dave's eyeball in a jar. Think about what you're saying."

Jake looked at Shaun, his fresh-out-of-college engineer, who blew out his cheeks and released.

"We believe you, boss," Shaun said.

Jake took another step toward Paige but she put both hands up and took a deep breath. "I'm sorry I yelled at you, but gotta process this. I just lost my dad."

Jake gave her a one-armed hug. "Yeah. No. Of course. Take a couple minutes in my office. We'll keep working over here. But, Paige?"

She wiped multiple streaks of mascara from her cheeks. "Yeah?"

"We need you on this. To stop him. Especially if—if I don't make it."

She nodded.

Jake patted her on the back, then stepped toward Shaun. "I assume you sent everything up to Cavanaugh. All your data and maps and financial info from the AI program?"

"Absolutely. While you had your cat nap, but the system needs more time to figure out the name of the company that's been shorting all that stock. It's running right now. I'm expecting results in the next ten minutes," Shaun said, as Paige sucked snot back up into her nose, pretending to be all right, trying to focus.

She glanced up and down at Jake. "You don't look too good. I still say it was a mistake taking you out of the hospital. I think—"

A thundering voice boomed from all around. "Get rid of the others," the voice said.

Jake paused, confused.

"Tell me you guys heard that," he said.

They looked at each other, also confused. "Heard what?"

The voice repeated. "Get rid of the others." Jake looked around the office, searching for hidden speakers. The voice repeated the same sentence every few seconds.

Something deep inside Jake urged him to comply. Instinct combined with a lack of will power. Primitive. A sudden spark of rage filled his soul.

Gary was still standing next to the copier, waiting for it to warm up.

Jake said, "Leave," to Paige and Shaun, moving them along with his outstretched arm, toward Shaun, then to the front door. "Now."

Paige resisted and tried to argue. "But Jake, you—"

"Now, Paige," he said with a gruff voice, curling his lips and baring his teeth.

Shaun and Gary grabbed their black leather South Sun portfolios, said goodbye to Jake and Paige, and rushed out the front office door.

Paige squinted, taking a step toward him and peered deep into Jake's eyes, seemingly all the way to his spirit.

"I'm not going anywhere," she said.

"I'll be all right. I, uh, have to do something and don't need you here."

She raked her fingers again through her hair.

"Whatever it is, I—"

"No!" Jake said. "Go. Now. Before the other guys get to their cars. You need to ride with them. I need the Mustang."

"You sure you'll be—"

"Yes," he said. He continued to hear the booming voice. "Get rid of the others."

Either Paige was deaf or he was hallucinating, but he needed to get rid of Paige.

"Go take care of your daddy," Jake said.

She looked at him one last time, tears welling up in her eyes, lower lip trembling, breaths shallow and rapid.

"Fine," she said, reluctant, but turning and finally storming out the office door.

Jake got on one knee and stabilized himself with his fists on the floor. The voice changed messages.

"Turn South Sun into a bright, burning ball, shining for all to see. Burn South Sun to the ground. Burn it all." The message paused for the same three seconds and repeated over and over and over. No matter what Jake did, the voice continued on a loop.

He put his hands over his ears, drank two sips of ice-cold water, slapped his cheeks, and jumped up and down.

Nothing worked. The voice kept repeating.

Images and ideas popped into his head.

Five-gallon gas tanks.

Gas station three blocks away.

Matches.

"Send all your troubles up in flames. Your pain from Cynthia's death. Your professional failures. Your nightmares about Viktor. The virus killing millions. Everything. Clean slate. Do it. Do it now."

The voice boomed louder over and over.

The copy machine, the one that had an internal fax installed, rang and beeped with an incoming message, finally starting to print the fax.

So, this is what it's like to lose your mind. *Great.*

A single sheet of paper printed out. Jake snatched it from the tray, read it, absorbed the information from Professor Everton — noting the time stamp from eight hours earlier — before tossing it on the floor while staggering out the office door, to Paige's car.

After driving to the gas station, he filled up two red five-gallon buckets with eighty-seven octane gasoline, and paid for everything, including a box of matches he stuffed into his front jeans pocket. He drove back to the South Sun office and hauled the fuel inside.

"Good boy, Jake," the inner voice said. "Do the needful. Your pain will dissolve. I will disappear. You will be rewarded with heaven on earth. Cynthia will come."

He paused to catch his breath, leaning over onto a computer monitor as beads of sweat dripped down his forehead, stinging his eyes as he swiped his forearm across his brow.

After unscrewing the black plastic gas cap, he picked up the first container and poured gasoline onto the floor, skirting the perimeter of the office, splattering the flammable liquid everywhere. Onto the desks, computers, the AI machine crunching the data on who'd been shorting Ag stock in California, tables, filing cabinets, chairs, carpet, and the fax from Everton with information on who he thought was behind the attacks. When the first can dripped empty, he repeated the same procedure with the second container.

The voice continued.

"Do the needful." Three-second pause. "Do the needful."

With all ten gallons doused onto every bit of furniture and equipment in the office, he retrieved the box of matches from his pocket and hustled to the front door.

"Do the needful."

He slid open the tiny cardboard matchbox drawer, plucked out a wood match, and stared at the red tip. So much destructive potential, all inside this tiny dried chemical on the end of a sliver of dead tree.

"Do the needful."

Jake pushed the drawer back inside the case and slid the match across the lighting strip. A flame appeared out of thin air and he held the wood stick between his fingertips.

"Do the needful."

In the foyer, near the front door to the South Sun offices, Jake flicked the lit match away from his body, ten feet toward the center of the room, and immediately felt intense heat on his face as the room erupted in fire. Within seconds, the flame scurried along the floor, following the trail of gasoline fuel, up the sides of desks, and on to the computers and monitors.

The voice stopped.

Jake exited the front door. Outside, clean fresh air filled his lungs and beams of sunshine sparkled off the surface of the river. Dizziness filled his head, but he continued walking along the concrete sidewalk to the parking lot and the Mustang where someone sat in the driver's seat.

Jake tented his eyes for a better view. Paige.

She exited the car and walked to him, then slapped his cheek and stared into his eyes.

Two versions of Paige floated in Jake's field of vision, dancing like two opposing sides of a distant tug-of-war.

"The voices. I couldn't, um—" Jake tried to say.

He collapsed into Paige's arms. Dead to the world.

CHAPTER 47

August 19th
4:00 p.m.

As Jake fell, Paige caught his limp body as best she could and lowered him to the ground. She checked his pulse. Weak, rapid.

She called 9-1-1 from her cell, reported the fire, and requested a 'bus' for Jake, which a cop had told her was the insider term for an ambulance.

Sitting on the half-dead grass, she held Jake's lifeless form in her arms before bursting into tears, rubbing his arm, and hoping he'd come to.

How could he do this?

And now he loses his mind and sets his office on fire?

He's trying to hide evidence, but what?

She wanted to call her dad and see what he thought but remembered she'd no longer have that luxury, ever. The tears started anew. Part of her needed to go to San Francisco and say goodbye to him, but another part wanted to stay with her friend and wait for the firemen and ambulance.

And figure out what the hell was going on.

After fifteen minutes, faint sirens blared in the distance, approaching fast. Seconds later, two fire engines pulled up next to her in the parking lot, sirens winding down.

Firemen hopped out, unfolded and attached their hoses to a yellow fire hydrant twenty yards away. The fireman with the white hat barked orders to the others.

A paramedic hustled up to Paige and knelt, setting his black toolkit onto the sidewalk next to Jake.

Paige explained what happened, how Jake had been infected with a virus, the hospital, the fluids, and medicine they administered, including anti-viral drugs, how he discharged himself and drove here, their research, and then how Jake lost his mind.

Hallucinations, she assumed, hoped.

"Okay, ma'am, we'll get an IV into him right now and get some fluids going, then we need to transport him to San Joaquin General."

The paramedics worked on Jake for several minutes before a white gurney appeared, pushed by a third EMT. The three men hoisted Jake, still unresponsive, up onto the portable bed, strapped an oxygen mask around his head, and wheeled him toward their ambulance.

CHAPTER 48

August 19th
8:00 p.m.

Jake awoke, groggy with blurred vision, and found himself lying on a hard bed with white sheets. He moved his wrist up toward his face, reading the hospital admittance bracelet to the emergency room at San Joaquin General. He lifted the sheet and peered down the front of his body. Baby blue paisley gown. No underwear. His breathing felt shallow and labored and while a beeping noise emanated from his left, he touched the IV needle taped to the top of his right hand.

Not again.

Memories flooded his brain.

Paige entered the curtained room, holding a paper cup of coffee. She blew the surface and took a sip, but when her eyes met Jake's, she dropped the cup onto the wax tile floor.

"Crap!" she said, lifting her arms high, then kicking the cup to the corner and bolting toward her friend. "Jake, you're back in the hospital. They say you need to rest. You need—"

"You gotta get me out of here . . . no time," he said, pushing himself up into a seated position on the bed. "I feel fine, other than my joints. Holy God, do my joints ache. And my head . . ." He rotated his right shoulder and head, wincing.

Jake remembered the voice. The fire. Viktor's video.

The fax from Everton.

He laid his head back onto the bed and put his hands over his eyes.

"This is like a nightmare case of deja vu," he said.

"Wow, all that IQ and that's all you can come up with? They said you were hallucinating. Those antivirals must have had hallucinations as a side-effect."

"Viktor has zero creativity. He used the media last time to blame me for those CDM attacks. He's doing the same damned thing again and it's working. Unbelievable." Jake wiped his face up and down with the palms of his hands.

Before he had a chance to share information from the fax with Paige, a phone vibrated. Jake scanned the room. His pants were stuffed into a paper bag in the corner. Paige picked up the bag, reached inside, and handed the phone to Jake.

Carlie.

"Dad, you're not gonna believe what just happened," she said in a panicked voice.

Jake put the call on speakerphone.

Paige leaned in.

The thought of something happening to Carlie set Jake's pulse on fire. The frequency of the beeping machine increased. Only two years had passed since he'd almost lost her in the freak flood in Pasadena. Sure, a lot had happened since then, but still, he regretted not spending more time with her.

He'd fallen into the same trap as last time—too many people pulling him in every direction, picking his brain to find the best engineering solutions for the California drought, power system upgrades, and of course, the Sûr System self-driving vehicle network. Too much work. Not enough family time. Now Carlie was having another problem.

"Slow down, Sweetie," Jake said. "Tell me what you're talking about."

"Brook's dead. Murdered."

"I need context, Carlie. Who?"

He heard her take a long deep breath.

"Brook Pai, Andy's babysitter. We came home to our apartment after dinner. Andy's in his crib crying, the stereo's blasting some heavy metal crap, and Brook is lying on the floor without her dress. Half-naked. Strangulation marks on her neck."

"Tell me where you're at," Jake said.

"We're safe. We called the police and they're at our apartment doing their CSI stuff. But dad, that's not all."

Paige raised her eyebrows.

I don't know how much more I can take.

"Tell us," Paige said.

"The police found a text on her phone that hinted you did this."

"Me?" Jake said.

Jake heard shuffling noises on the line.

"Jake hi, it's me, Daniel. I've already let my brother in on this and we both know it's bullshit, but I wanted to tell you what the text message said:

JAKEY BOY.

DEAD BABYSITTER.

OH JOY.

KILLING CALIFORNIANS AND NOW A BABE IN NEW YORK.

FEED THE BEAST YOU MORONIC DORK.

Paige whispered. "Whoever wrote that's a horrible poet."

Jake handed the phone to Paige, pulled off the tape from the IV on his wrist, slid the needle out, and applied the tape with pressure to stop the bleeding.

"I'm chartering a jet and flying to New York. Need to be with my daughter. Fighting Viktor's terrorist crap isn't worth it."

"Jake," Daniel said. "We think we might be next. And Andrew."

Jake thought for a second. "Go somewhere safe. Now. Need to get you three off the grid. Go to Walgreens and buy a burner phone, then go to the place where we had dinner last time I visited, and text me."

Slight pause. "Got it," Daniel said.

More shuffling. Carlie, "Wait, dad, my boss said she'd take care of us."

"Who?"

"Well, my boss's, boss's—the lady in charge of the company I work for. Stacy or Tracy or something."

"I don't care if the pope offers you help. Don't. Trust. Anyone. Text me once you get the new phone and we'll go from there."

"But—"

"Nobody."

"Fine, but you might want to know your face is all over the news. It's crazy what they're accusing you of."

"Not again," Jake said, mostly to himself.

They ended the call. Jake hopped off the bed, fought a dizzy spell, and grabbed his jeans. Before he had a chance to slide his second leg inside, Cavanaugh strode in.

"You're not going anywhere this time. Bed rest means you need to rest. In bed," he said, guiding Jake back toward the centerpiece of the room.

Jake shrugged off Cavanaugh's hand and shook his head.

"How the heck did you get—"

"Don't ask. Bed. Now."

"My life. My choices. I'm getting the hell out of here. I'm done. No more Dr. Bendel. No more scapegoat. No more target. I'm going to get better and disappear with Carlie until this all blows over."

Jake slid on his black golf shirt and sat on an orange plastic visitor's chair to put on his socks.

"I'm afraid I can't let you do that," Cavanaugh said.

Jake stopped and craned his neck up. "I'm sorry if you don't agree with my decisions, but I—"

"You run now you might as well plaster a huge frickin' sign on your forehead that says 'guilty'."

"But I'm not. All I've done so far is try to help and look where it's gotten me."

Cavanaugh leaned over next to Jake.

"You're right. This ain't fair. It's pretty eff'd up, actually. I get it. But you gotta stay."

Jake continued putting on the other sock, then a beige hiking boot. He slid his hand in his jeans pocket, stroked his Sûr System pen, then gripped the flash drive, the one from Dave with the American flag on it.

"Give me one good reason to stick around this little funhouse of horrors."

Cavanaugh stood back up and crossed his arms. He took several steps around the room and put his hand beneath his chin.

"First of all, we still don't know the full effects of the virus in your system."

"I'm fine."

"Bullshit. And second, you just committed arson on your own office building."

Jake stopped tying his shoe and stared at the ground.

"And third, Dave Trainer. We found his body."

Remorse flew through Jake like a stiff wind. Paige let out an audible gasp.

"No!" Paige said. "First my dad. Now Dave? When the hell are you gonna do something, Cavanaugh?" she yelled, beating his upper arm and chest with her fists.

Cavanaugh embraced Paige, holding her tight as she wailed.

Jake felt a pain in the back of his throat and had difficulty swallowing. Watching his close friend erupt with emotion made him rethink his plan. He struggled to hold back tears.

Cavanaugh continued. "The workers at the San Luis Obispo plant were doing routine maintenance on the water storage tanks and found, well . . ."

"Tell me. I need to know," Jake said.

"Later—" Cavanaugh started to say.

"Tell us. Right now," Paige said.

Cavanaugh paused, calculating whether to share, then said, "It's gruesome."

Paige repeated herself, "Tell us."

"They found the body, face up. And his head floating next to it. Had a tattooed note on the chest."

The image caused another wave of nausea to flow through Jake, spinning the room. After a few seconds, he stood with only one shoe on, holding the other shoe, then shuffled to Cavanaugh.

"I can't take this anymore," Jake said. "I just want to leave. Please."

Cavanaugh continued, unfazed by Jake's pleas. "Tattoo read: 'the fate of every man in California' and when they scooped his body out, they confirmed the missing eyeball. Just an empty socket. Horrible way to go. I'm so sorry, guys."

Paige stopped crying, eyes puffy, pushing Cavanaugh away. Then she wiped her cheeks and said, "I don't know about you two, but this guy has got to be stopped. We can't keep, like, running. We need to fight. Here. Now. This is our chance."

"You're a lot stronger than I've given you credit for, Paige," Cavanaugh said. "Kidnapping is a federal crime, plus the way Dave . . . well, we have a plan to flush out this son-of-a-bitch and we need your help. No way you're going to New York."

Jake felt a breeze of cold air flow over him as he thought about Carlie and Andrew. "You want to use me as bait again?"

"Nope. We need your mind to help fill in the missing pieces to the puzzle. Don't worry about Carlie, I have a team handling her and my brother."

Jake felt a smidgen of relief.

Cavanaugh continued. "I thought you'd be on your death bed by now, so I figured you'd need to stay here, but you seem to be doing alright. Let me talk to the doc and see what he says. I got the chopper up on the roof, ready to take us to the Federal Building in San Francisco. That's our headquarters for this thing and you and the guy from the CDC need to put your heads together on this. Guy says it's a matter of life and death."

CHAPTER 49

August 19th
8:33 p.m.

Viktor pulled the rust bucket truck alongside the curb at the base of Linda's driveway. In the dark neighborhood of Hollywood Hills, he gazed up the vine-covered hill toward the Bennett chateau perched at the top. Stars twinkled in the distance behind the tree-shrouded home. His phone rang.

"Sir, the tune-up on your Piper is almost ready. Did you know your airspeed intake is clogged?" his mechanic at the Burbank airport asked.

"No."

Viktor instructed the guy to fix it, ended the call, tucked his .357 revolver into the rear of his pants and stepped out of the truck.

Selim had told Viktor someone tailed Linda to her home. Tracy's people confirmed the tail belonged to the FBI and sure enough, the only car parked on the deserted street looked like a federal vehicle. Shiny. Black. Chevy Tahoe.

Careful not to tip off the feds, Viktor reached underneath the seat and slid out a second weapon, a 9mm Glock, and rotated the silencer into place before creeping up to the passenger side of the FBI car. While the two men in the front seats ate In-And-Out,

Viktor aimed and put two bullets into each of their chests through the passenger window. Surprise!

Damnit, that felt good.

But what a waste of two perfectly good burgers.

He reached in, snatched a half-eaten burger, and ate the rest before wiping the Glock clean of fingerprints. After hobbling across the street, he walked up the driveway to the entrance and opened the front door to Linda's home like he owned the place. No stirring noises inside. Good. Total silence, except for Linda's sniveling in the living room.

He shuffled along the entryway tile, rounded the corner to the living room, and found Selim sitting on the edge of a couch, pointing a chrome and wood snub-nose .38 revolver at Linda. Viktor walked closer to the slumped-over captive and knelt on one knee. Black eyeliner dribbled from her swollen eyes down both cheeks. Wig off-kilter, she stared at the ground. Ashamed.

"Sorry I'm so late to the party," Viktor said. "Had a little car trouble in the High Desert. But not to worry. The fun's just beginning."

"Hubby is upstairs, Viktor," Selim said. "I used the inhalant like you said. Drugged him."

Viktor nodded to Selim's revolver. "Unregistered?"

"Of course, sir."

"Go finish Frank, but use only one shot. One. Make it look like a suicide, just like we showed you." Viktor held out the gun he'd used to murder the two agents. "Here. Wipe it clean, then put Frank's fingerprints on it."

Selim stood, bounced on his toes, and hustled up the stairs.

Linda tried to scream, but the red foam ball muffled her noises. Snot streamed from her nose while she struggled to free herself from the yellow rope. No use. She continued sobbing.

"We had a good thing going," he said, arms clasped behind his waist, circling around Linda like a patient predator. "You were part of our team. Tracy hired us to do a job. A simple task. Two virus strains, mass-produced by BioStall, infused into the water supply by Bendel. Voila, Tracy's vision for helping the world, with thousands of California men dying and several million permanently infected. Genetically modified. They'll be less angry, less likely to spit on the one true religion, Islam. The balance of the Jihad is tipped in the favor of Allah, praise His name. And massive crop damage to help fund future endeavors. All in one nice, tight, neat little package."

Linda struggled more, then her shoulders drooped. He yanked off her wig, exposing a pale bald head, then retrieved the revolver from his front waist and slid the tip of the barrel along the bridge of Linda's nose.

He chuckled. "You'd already done your job. The five-hundred-million dollars Tracy promised you was ready to be wired. So stupid."

A single gunshot blast permeated throughout the home, echoing off the interior walls.

Linda wiggled and squirmed and tried screaming once more, knowing she'd never again see her husband Frank. Her chin trembled.

"But no. You had to grow a conscience," Viktor whispered into her ear. "You could have just walked away. Taken the money and run. Started a new life." With his lips pressed tight, he let out a heavy sigh. "Now your dear Frank is dead. The world is the same as it was before you had your little press conference. It's as though you never even lived. A sad existence, really. Pathetic."

While squatting in front of Linda, he gave her a nice, strong view of the disappointment in his eyes. Images flashed in his mind: the online floorplans of her home he'd pulled from the County Records office. "It's a shame how angry your Frank got when he found out about your affair. Such a hostile man. Quick to lose his temper. He took out the two FBI agents, then drowned you in your own bathtub." Standing, he continued moving at a slow pace. "But the guilt was more than poor Frank could bear, so he went upstairs and took his own life. Classic murder-suicide. Open and shut case for L.A.'s finest."

Linda's shoulders quaked and her eyes opened wide before squeezing them shut and letting out a high-pitched, guttural scream into the foam ball.

Selim hopped down the stairs and walked toward them.

"All set," Selim said. "Stupid man shot himself through roof of his mouth. I did not expect brains to be so many splattered about. Very fascinating, this American suicide. Police will have quick judgment. Very simple."

"You made sure Frank's fingerprints were on both—"

"Yes, yes, of course, sir. Everything like you and Mr. Gunther showed," Selim said.

"Help me carry her to the bathroom over there," Viktor said, sliding on a pair of leather gloves before moving behind Linda and hoisting her chair up off the ground. Selim grabbed her ankles and she tried to kick, but no use. They carried her, still strapped in the chair, to the full downstairs bathroom near the rear of the mansion. A lone pedestal sink sat inside the blue-tiled, shiny white room, with a porcelain toilet tucked in the corner, and a combination shower-bathtub along the base of the tall wall.

They set Linda onto the bamboo flooring, then grabbed three tissues from a box sitting on the toilet tank and turned on the bathtub water full blast, careful not to get their fingerprints on any surface. Viktor pulled the drain plug stopper to engage the block and watched the water level rise the side of the sparkling white tub.

"Tonight, you will die," he said, smooth and calm. "I'm not entirely heartless, though. I'll give you a sedative to help make this easier. You're less likely to vomit when your lungs struggle for air. Will make you die faster, too, so there's less trauma."

Linda shook her head and continued to struggle.

Viktor looked at Selim. "Give it to her."

Selim retrieved a three-milliliter syringe from his pocket, popped off the cap, knelt at Linda's bare feet and ripped open her pantyhose. She tried to kick him.

"I'm doing you a favor," Viktor said, grabbing her from behind in a choke-hold. "Keep your foot still or I'll snap your pretty little neck."

She complied. *They always did.*

With her foot in his hand, Selim inserted the half-inch needle into the web between her first two toes and pushed the plunger all the way. He pulled out, covered the needle and stuffed the syringe back into his pocket.

Moments later, Linda's body went limp. Viktor removed his forearm from the front of her neck, stepped around to her side and peered into her eyes. Dilated pupils. Perfect.

"Untie her," Viktor said, and they went to work on removing the restraints as the bathtub was seventy-five percent full of water. Bendel's water. Full of viruses invented by Gunther. Mass-produced by Linda.

Ah, the sweet irony of this moment. Praise Allah!

Viktor leaned over the tub and turned off the faucet.

Without uttering a word, they hoisted Linda's sagging body into the bathtub and submerged everything except her face. She mumbled a few incoherent words.

"I would like to give you the honor of sending this infidel to Satan," he said to Selim. "Two in one night would be a momentous occasion for you, my young brother."

Selim smiled, baring a full set of crooked, coffee-stained teeth. "Thank you, great sir," he said, repositioning himself toward the front of the tub to get better leverage above Linda's neck. Selim set his left palm on Linda's chest. His right hand smothered her face. Viktor held down Linda's waist. Together, they pushed.

Linda's nostrils flared. A last breath erupted from her mouth, spewing droplets of water across Selim's arms. Muffled noises emanated from the water. Her arms and legs and torso spasmed for several seconds before succumbing to the violence. A distant, blank stare came over her face and several tiny bubbles clung to her cheeks and forehead.

Silence.

CHAPTER 50

August 19th
8:53 p.m.

As Cavanaugh returned to the hospital room, Jake sat up on the bed, wearing his street clothes, and asked, "Well?"

Cavanaugh stepped toward Jake and put a hand on his shoulder. "Doc's coming. Take a deep breath, we're going to—"

Jake slapped Cavanaugh's arm away. "I don't want to take a deep breath. I want to get out of here. The governor's gonna want to use me as a scapegoat. Dave had his goddamned eye yanked out before they decapitated him and left his body in one of my water tanks." He clenched his jaw, curling his shoulders over his chest and rubbing his legs.

Jake felt his body trembling and swung his legs off the bed, but before he could stand, Cavanaugh grabbed his shoulders. Firm and steady.

"Not so fast, cowboy." He stared deep into Jake's eyes. "I know how you feel. We're working everything from all angles and the world is crashing down on you and your instinct is to save Carlie and your grandson and run as fast as you can away from these threats. And Viktor and all his bullshit. I get it. But listen to me, you've been through this before. The Jake Bendel I know is stronger than this. You have reserves. Endurance. Now's not the time to give in to panic. We need you here, with your expertise, to finish this once and for all. Now's the time we take a stand and fight."

Paige sat in the corner, head in her hands. He glanced around the room at the television set, the floral watercolor painting, the plastic visitor chairs, the wax tile floor with gray speckles and scuff marks.

After inhaling a deep breath, he closed his eyes, then exhaled for ten seconds. Cavanaugh let go of Jake's shoulders.

"That's it, buddy," Cavanaugh said. "Let all that crap go. Carlie's a big girl, she'll be fine. Don't worry about her and Andrew. Stay focused on helping us fix this. We're close to finding answers."

There was a tap on the door and the emergency room doc shuffled in.

"I'm fine," Jake said to the doc, a short, portly man with a trimmed white beard and sunken eyes. "You've been running tests for hours now. I'm telling you."

The doctor glanced at his iPad, then removed his reading glasses, crossed his arms, and stared at Jake. Cavanaugh and Paige stood on either side of Jake's bed.

The doc shuffled to a stop at the side of Jake's bed. "Dr. Bendel, have you ever tried any experimental drugs? I'm not talking about weed or anything. Actual drugs."

Jake looked into Paige's eyes and thought about sharing his acid trip experience thirty years ago. "No. Haven't even smoked weed. That crap slows down your thinking and since I make my living with my brain, it would ruin my career."

The doc tossed the iPad near Jake's feet, unfolded his arms and rested his left forearm on the bed near Jake's waist. "Help me out. We found trace amounts of a relatively new drug marketed as Trihypnol. Based on the decay rate, you took some, either orally or by injection, about two weeks ago."

Paige asked, "How can you detect traces after that long?"

"That would be a long answer, miss, but suffice to say the technology now exists." The doc cleared his throat. "Did anything happen to you around that time? When you have a lost memory? Like a missing day or an evening where you don't remember what happened?"

Bingo.

"As a matter of fact, yes. I was supposed to meet someone at Chili's—Dave, actually—but he never showed up. And all I really remember is waking up on my couch with a bug bite on my neck the next morning. You remember, Paige." She nodded. "And a few days ago, I started having flashes of a black van in a parking lot, clearer than a dream but foggier than a memory." Something clicked in his mind. "And the video . . . the water . . . Oh no."

Cavanaugh leaned in, head tilted, mentally weighing this fresh evidence.

The doctor felt Jake's forehead. "Your accounting is consistent with the effects of the drug. You'd have been fully awake, entirely aware of your surroundings, but in an extremely suggestible state. The memory loss is a side effect. I've heard nightmare stories of men raping random women, murders, et cetera, all because the guys took the drug and someone suggested something."

"So it *was* me. That's how they got me to poison the water," Jake said, looking at Cavanaugh, who nodded.

The doc paused again. Jake evaluated all the crap Cavanaugh wanted him to set aside. The fight-or-flight mechanism throbbing inside his brain leaned heavily toward flying away. Never looking back. Just twenty-four hours ago he thought he'd be dead by now, killed by whatever virus Gunther had injected into his bloodstream. Memories flashed of the recent hallucinations back at South Sun. And the ramifications he'd face of eventually having to look his engineering partners in the eyes and admit he'd intentionally—well, while hallucinating—burned down the office building of their thriving business. And the fax! Did Everton feel threatened? Why didn't he scan it and send as an email attachment?

Jake turned to Paige. "It burned in the fire, but I got the fax from your dad and read it."

Cavanaugh looked puzzled. "Who uses faxes anymore?"

They explained to details from Everton's email and the time delay.

"It's fuzzy, but I remember Everton's fax saying he had proof a woman named Tracy Ciacchella is behind this entire plan. And Linda Bennett had mentioned Tracy's name at the ribbon-cutting ceremony. Tracy's the one at the top. The one pulling the strings for Linda Bennett, Viktor Johnston, everyone."

"If the fax burned in the fire, maybe Everton has a copy at his apartment," Cavanaugh said. Paige nodded in agreement. "I'll make a call and get some agents over there and start digging into who this Tracy person is."

Jake realized now would be a terrible time to die. No legacy. No way to protect his daughter and grandson. No way to continue to help however many people had already been infected. No way to get revenge for the death of his mentor, Everton. No way to see all five of his plant combos become fully operational and work to benefit the citizens of California.

No. Today would be a terrible day to die.

Or run.

The doc aimed a laser thermometer at Jake's forehead. "Fever's gone." A nurse rushed in and slid to a stop. She handed a small pile of papers to the doc who put on his reading glasses and glanced at the report.

"I have some good news, Dr. Bendel," the doc said. "Looks like you're out of the woods on the virus. Your white blood cell count is back to normal. The antivirals did the trick and you will not die today or anytime soon. Not from the virus, at least."

Paige jumped up and clapped her hands.

Jake failed to share her enthusiasm, reserving judgment.

"You sure?"

The doc looked back at the report, scanning the text. "Yep. You're good to go. Just try to take it slow the next few days and drink plenty of fluids."

Jake inhaled another huge breath and let out a hefty sigh. "Jesus doc. Almost gave me a frickin' heart attack."

Several thoughts hit Jake like wrecking balls. *I'm not going to die from this virus. I wasn't supposed to die. Not my time. Time. I still have time. I can make a difference.*

Jake's anxiety began withering away. He must be destined for something greater than he'd originally thought.

The pieces fit like the last ones to a gigantic jigsaw puzzle, but Jake struggled with exactly what to do first. He could figure out a way to protect Carlie. To clear his name. Restore his legacy. Talk to the governor and right his wrongs. Save millions of lives. Capture Viktor once and for all. This was no longer about getting revenge for his wife. This was about self-defense. Protecting his family. Protecting California.

Cavanaugh took a step toward the doc, probably sensing the renewed purpose exploding inside Jake. "We're leaving. Now. You're going to sign the release."

The doc paused, studying Cavanaugh. "Fine. I'll have you out of here in five minutes. Hold on." He disappeared behind the curtain.

Cavanaugh turned to Paige. "We'll take care of everything for your dad's funeral once this is all over, I promise. But for now, we need you with us." Paige nodded.

Ten minutes later, as they walked out onto the roof, Cavanaugh shared his plan with them. Paige and Cavanaugh climbed into an awaiting black Bell helicopter atop the roof of the hospital, but Jake stopped short of getting in, gathering his thoughts.

Yes. This is happening. Viktor is going down. I'm no longer going to live my life in fear. I choose to fight. I choose to live.

Jake climbed into the helicopter, homing in on what he needed to do to stop Viktor. He and Paige sat in the rear and Jake buckled his seatbelt. He slid the lime green headset onto his head, covering his ears, then adjusted the mic near his lips.

Cavanaugh took a seat in the front left seat and gave a whirling motion with his hand to the pilot. The whining pitch of the rotating blades and jet engine increased. The craft lifted off the tarmac and climbed high into the night sky, headed west toward San Francisco.

CHAPTER 51

August 19th
10:00 p.m.

During the half-hour helicopter flight, Cavanaugh provided an update on the deadly octocopter portion of the investigation — they'd figured out how to track the drone operator, but more work was needed to pinpoint the location — and shared additional details of his plan with Jake and Paige how to capture Viktor. They listened, asked questions and discussed the details. The trip was relatively smooth — until they crossed over the San Francisco Bay.

Jake looked at the San Francisco airport below, hidden in the blackness among amber safety lights and patchy fog. He estimated another ten miles to the Federal Building downtown.

Rough, gusting winds pummeled the side of the craft from the west, jolting the four passengers back and forth. Jake slapped his hands against the copter wall and ceiling to stabilize himself, but his long-dead motion sickness awoke with a vengeance, and his palms turned sweaty and tingly, while his face flushed with fresh, oxygenated blood. He fought the urge to panic by focusing his mind on Viktor and turning the fear into fuel to fight the man who'd made his life a living hell. Almost there.

Ten minutes later the copter descended, approaching the tarmac atop the Federal Building at the corner of Turk and Polk streets.

Jake peered out the side window at the glass pane walls of the eighteen-story gray rectangular structure below. He breathed through his nose and narrowed his eyes, keeping the nausea at bay, but not for much longer.

"Hold your breakfast," the pilot said, jerking the yoke around like a damned joystick on an eighties video game. "Gonna have to abort and land back at the airport. Not safe. Too much wind up here."

"No time," Cavanaugh said, pointing down at the round red circle fifty feet below them. "Land this thing. Right there. Now."

Paige grabbed Jake's hand and squeezed.

"I'm sorry, sir," the pilot said. "I can't—"

"Land now or you'll be flying test runs inside Kansas tornadoes the rest of your goddamned career."

The pilot paused, put his hand up, bit his lip and complied.

After a rough minute that seemed to last hours, the beast finally settled in and landed. Hard. Three agents appeared from nowhere to tie the craft to the helipad.

The pilot wound down the jets and everyone unbuckled their seatbelts and exited into the gusting wind. They jogged across the rooftop, walked through a thick metal doorway, and hustled down two flights of stairs to a carpeted hallway on the sixteenth floor, which led to a glass-enclosed conference room. Ten navy-blue cloth chairs skirted the perimeter of an elongated black matte table.

Cavanaugh motioned for Jake and Paige to sit. No sooner had they plopped down than several agents walked in with three laptops, an external monitor, and a webcam. Within minutes the agents had connected the equipment and left the room.

A baby blue window filled the external monitor.

"This'll be the war room for the rest of the investigation," Cavanaugh said, sitting and wiggling the mouse to the laptop.

"Dr. Rosen at the CDC couldn't make it here in person, so we're gonna have a quick Zoom call with him."

Before long, Dr. Rosen's tired face appeared in the chat window, introductions were made, and the formal portion of the call began.

"Dr. Bendel, it's good to see you up and about," Dr. Rosen said, though his face showed only anxious weariness. "I need to ask you some questions about your plant combos, if you're up to it."

"Shoot," Jake said, jockeying for a better position in front of the monitor and camera. Paige and Cavanaugh sat on either side of Jake.

"I've seen this video of you and another man supposedly injecting concentrated virus serum into the water supply at desalination plant number three, just north of here in San Francisco. Help me understand how the water made its way to so many other cities and towns along the coast. I need to understand the infrastructure a bit."

Jake launched into his explanation. "In a nutshell, we suck the ocean water in from the San Francisco Bay, extract the salt through various filters, give it a shot of chlorine to kill any remaining pathogens, then pump the water via submerged pipeline about forty miles to the east. There, it's dumped into a freshwater river that flows south about fifteen miles and feeds into the northern inlet of the California Aqueduct. As the water flows south, it branches off and feeds counties like San Luis Obispo, Santa Barbara, Los Angeles, Riverside—"

"Okay, we get the idea," Cavanaugh said, putting a hand in front of Jake. "Let's try to keep it brief. We don't have much time."

"As far as you know," Doctor Rosen continued, "the water from Plant Number Three ends up consumed by people, animals, and farms for a good four hundred mile stretch between San Francisco to the north, and maybe Riverside or San Bernardino to the south, correct?"

Jake nodded. "Correct."

Rosen continued. "Without a vaccine, the best chance we have to prevent further infection is to prevent consumption of the contaminated water while we flush the infected water from the system. Any idea how long that might take?"

Jake took a moment to think. "I'm afraid I couldn't say, not without a better idea of how concentrated the contaminants are and how long it's been since they were injected into each system. Plus the time to get teams deployed to flush all areas of the system. Suffice to say it'll be a good while. Perhaps—"

Cavanaugh checked his phone and cut Jake off again. He spoke urgently to Rosen. "Looks like we may have a break in the case. Can we wrap this up?"

Jake felt his heart jump into his throat. He looked at Paige.

"One more important note, agent," Rosen said. Cavanaugh paused and motioned with his hand to hurry. "We're nearly finished with a simple treatment. I'll have more information for you in the next few hours."

Cavanaugh thanked Rosen for his time, ended the call, and stood, checking a text message.

"Sorry we had to rush that, but c'mon. I think you'll want to see this," Cavanaugh said. He led the two engineers through another hallway to an elevator where they went to the third floor. The doors split open and they followed Cavanaugh through a maze of cubicles until finding a small man holding what looked like the various pieces of the octocopter attack drone Jake had given to Cavanaugh the day before.

The bald-headed man wore black, thick-rimmed glasses and his lower lip fell to one side. Brief introductions were made, and Cavanaugh asked the man to explain his findings.

"I've dissected this bad boy and found some interesting tidbits," the man said, eyes wide. "For example, this tiny chip here—" he pointed to a one-quarter inch circuit board jammed into a side slot of the drone— "acts as a backup homing device operating on an acute frequency in the five gigahertz range."

"English, please," Cavanaugh said.

"Digital radio waves are sent from the chip," Jake said, sliding the tiny electronic board out. He held the device between his thumb and forefinger and moved it toward his own eye for a better look. "One-way signal. Transmit only. No receiving signal capability, which means it can't be hacked while in flight and we—theoretically—wouldn't be able to track the drone to its owner."

The little man nodded. "I'm impressed." He retrieved the chip from Jake, set the tiny square onto his gray, laminated cubicle desk, and pointed to a thin object on the outside of the drone body. "But guess what? This little sucker right here is a flash drive with all sorts of fun, useful information." He unplugged a one-inch rectangle that reminded Jake of a Wheat Thin cracker.

"Tell me you hacked the data," Cavanaugh said.

"I wouldn't have texted you to come down here if all I had was a bunch of boring bologna," the man said with a wink. "I spent the last several hours attacking the encrypted drive with an all-out assault of the best decryption software in the FBI arsenal."

"I'm waiting," Cavanaugh said, crossing his arms over his chest.

The man gripped the side of a twenty-four-inch HD monitor on his desk and rotated it toward his trio of visitors.

"Not only have I cracked their encryption algorithm, but I've sorted the data," the man said. "There are GPS coordinates of not only the drone itself, but of whoever was operating the drone remotely. It looks like it was operated from here in San Francisco."

Wheels spun in Jake's head. During the drone attack, he'd failed to find anyone nearby who might have been piloting the drones, and assumed the person was off-site somewhere but had no proof. Drones like these had maybe a thirty- or forty-minute flight time, so whoever was in charge must have been within ten miles of Jake's position at that time to start the attack sequence. At least, that's what he thought. He'd assumed Gunther or Viktor was controlling the drones from their Modesto bunker hideout.

Logical.

"I would've bet the GPS coordinates of the pilot were within ten or fifteen miles, maybe in Modesto. But apparently not?" Jake said.

"A very reasonable assumption, my good man," said the little man, puffing out his chest. "But if you look here—" he pointed to the coordinates displayed on the screen "—and map out the lats and longs, the pilot was here in downtown San Francisco at the time you were attacked."

"We need more than that," Cavanaugh said.

"Ahh, but check this out." The technician opened another window on his screen and pointed to an aerial map of the San Francisco area. "The piloting signal came more precisely from . . . here."

Cavanaugh leaned forward toward the screen, squinting and furrowing his brow. "That can't be right."

Jake set his palms on the desktop and leaned in next to Cavanaugh for a better look at the map.

Next to the satellite map view of the building on the screen, in a rectangular text box, read a familiar description.

The San Francisco Department of Health.

Jake pushed off the desktop and stood straight. He rubbed his eyes, then looked dead at Cavanaugh, who had his lips pressed together in a slight grimace.

Cavanaugh grabbed the shoulders of the little man. "You're telling me the person who controlled those drones, the ones that attacked Jake, was not only in downtown San Francisco, but you're sure this building right here—" Cavanaugh pointed to the screen "—is the exact building the signal came from? The same building where the CDC is operating?"

"Correct on both counts, agent," the man responded, breath bursting in and out. "I can even tell you the floor."

Cavanaugh sat the man onto his chair.

"How sure are you?" Cavanaugh asked.

"110%."

CHAPTER 52

August 20th
5:01 a.m.

After confirming the location with the drone technician and letting everyone get a couple hours of sleep, Cavanaugh asked Paige to work with the technician and find out more about the drone data. Jake had been upstairs for the last few hours, drowning himself in coffee while reviewing CDC employee records with two other agents to uncover the identity of the person likely responsible for the drone attack. They'd finally narrowed it down to two possibilities.

Rosen definitely has a mole working at the CDC.

Cavanaugh received back-to-back texts. He read the first from Rosen. A request for another Zoom call. He read the second text. Governor Fairchild said she was headed to his office within the hour for a situation report.

"Great," he mumbled to himself. "Another local politician impeding a federal investigation." Cavanaugh's tolerance for politics had ended over a decade ago when a political firestorm erupted over an investigation he had nothing to do with, but for which he ended up taking the blame anyway because his assistant director in charge ordered him to. Cavanaugh hated the role of scapegoat. And what little remaining respect for politicians evaporated after the CDM attack two years ago, when his ADIC at the Los Angeles Federal Building was convicted of multiple felonies and sent to prison. The big boss had offered the ADIC position to Cavanaugh, but he declined, knowing he belonged in the field, not in cubicle hell. In fact, since the current ADIC in San Francisco used to work for him, they had an amazing relationship and the guy gave Cavanaugh tons of leeway with calling the shots.

Cavanaugh gathered Jake and Paige from their assignments and the three met back in the same conference room on the sixteenth floor. The conference-calling equipment sat in the same place as before and Jake heard the Zoom call ring, then Cavanaugh clicked the "connect" button on the screen.

"Talk to me," Cavanaugh said to Rosen.

"Sir, we have concluded our preliminary analysis of the human virus strain," Rosen said. "We are going to recommend a two-day treatment for the immediate symptoms of all infected hosts. Yes, it's homeopathic and sad this is all we could come up with, so believe it or not, the best course of action is to have every infected male drink a regiment of bentonite clay."

"You're shittin' me," Cavanaugh said. "This whole time we could have cured everyone with some frickin' dirt milkshake?"

Jake chuckled.

"Not exactly," Rosen said. "The bentonite is for the *symptoms* only. It does not *cure* the host."

"Goddamnit, Rosen, get to the point," Cavanaugh said, leaning closer to the camera.

"But this is only a band-aid. As you know, most viruses are very difficult or impossible to cure, since they don't respond to antibiotics, so the best way to deal with viruses is prevention through vaccination."

"Tell me what we're looking at as far as getting our hands around this," Cavanaugh said. "Is a vaccine even in the picture?"

"Unfortunately, no. The only way a vaccine would be possible is it had already been manufactured. At this point the best course of action is still to prevent consumption of the water, especially over the next forty-eight to seventy-two hours."

Paige let out a slow breath.

"Okay," Cavanaugh said. "What about the virus killing crops?"

"Still working on that, sir."

"Okay, but I still see a problem."

Rosen's thick bushy eyebrows squished together. "Which is?"

Cavanaugh looked at Jake, Paige, then up toward the camera. "We need to talk face-to-face. Meet me here at my office in one hour."

"But I don't think—"

"One hour," Cavanaugh said, ending the video call. "C'mon," he said, hustling toward the conference room door. "Need to get you up to speed on a plan I have to flush out Rosen's mole. We have some work to do before he and Governor Fairchild arrive."

CHAPTER 53

August 20th
6:01 a.m.

After a detailed brainstorming discussion with Paige and Cavanaugh on a plan to catch Rosen's mole, Jake entered their seventh-floor conference room, which looked exactly like the war room on the sixteenth floor, but twenty percent smaller, and without all the equipment.

Paige and Cavanaugh followed.

A large man wearing a dark gray suit with a bright blue tie pushed open the door for Governor Fairchild. "We'll be right here outside," the bodyguard said to Fairchild.

Jake introduced Paige to the governor and as they shook hands, Jake noticed the governor's face had turned several shades more grave than when they'd met at her office two days ago. She brought a trembling hand to her forehead and pushed her bangs to the side.

Cavanaugh cleared his throat. "Governor, before Dr. Rosen joins us, there's something you need to be aware of. We have evidence that someone inside the Department of Health has been working with the terrorists."

She sat. "Those are serious accusations. Have you informed Dr. Rosen of this?"

"Negative. I believe that would be unwise."

"You think he's been compromised."

Cavanaugh nodded, then looked to Jake.

"Do you have enough to confront him?"

"Not yet."

"So this meeting is a test."

Cavanaugh nodded again. They were silent for a few minutes, then began reviewing the points of the meeting while they waited for Rosen.

The conference room door flew open. "Sorry I'm late," Rosen said, bumping into the doorway and stumbling for several steps. He continued to apologize to Cavanaugh and Fairchild as he sat at the head of the table and placed two manila folders in front of him.

The governor requested an update. Specifically, she wanted to know how many people had been infected, how many were dead, where the CDC was with containing the situation, including the crop killer virus, and where the FBI was with catching the bastards who'd started this mess.

"I need to get back to the lab," Rosen said. "So if you will kindly allow me to jump in first." Cavanaugh motioned with his hand for him to proceed.

Rosen continued. "We are still waiting on the FBI to decrypt the data found on the hard drives recovered at the Modesto bunker, but at this point the data will likely be more of a formality. The icing on the proverbial cake, so to speak."

"Doctor Rosen, please. If you could stay on track here," the governor said.

Rosen apologized. "As you know, our analysis has discovered that the virus is, in fact, a modified poliovirus, designed—among other things—to target males. Non-fatal, we believe, for the most part. Deaths will likely be limited to humans with already compromised immune systems, but I must stress this is very preliminary at this point. We estimate this will be less than five percent of the infected males."

"That's good news," Jake said.

"Not exactly," Rosen said. "The virus still infects all hosts and causes permanent genetic damage."

Jake cursed under his breath.

"The specifics of the damage are unknown," Rosen said. "But we're continuing to run tests. The data from the hard drives we are hoping might shed some light."

Cavanaugh broke in. "What about the information Dr. Mehta found at the Modesto bunker?"

Dr. Rosen paused. "I'm sorry." Rubbing his fingers together, he darted glances to the governor, Jake, then back to Cavanaugh. "I'm afraid I don't know what you're talking about."

"The notebook. Dinesh found a notebook with, apparently, a ton of detailed information about genetic modifications that scared the crap out of him. Said he needed to get it to you ASAP, so he left immediately. That was," he glanced up at the clock on the wall, "thirty-two hours ago. Are you telling me he never brought it?"

"I haven't seen Dr. Mehta since I sent him to help you at the bunker."

Cavanaugh ground his teeth, furious. "And you didn't find that suspicious?"

Rosen looked defensive. "I received a brief update from him via email. He mentioned the makeshift lab, the encrypted hard drives, and something about a large crate full of vials, but since he said he found nothing significant, I didn't see a need to meet in person."

"Unbelievable. Have you tried to contact him?"

"Not since receiving his email." A note of impatience. "I've been rather busy."

Cavanaugh looked like he was about to respond, but Jake cut in. "Hang on. I don't see how a virus can cause genetic changes to the host," Jake said. "I thought that wasn't possible."

Rosen leaned back in his chair. "Quite. Statistically, we all have between five and ten potentially deadly mutations of our genes, but they are all recessive, so we'd need to have two copies of the gene to inherit any given disorder. One reason close relatives should avoid having children."

"Goddamnit, Rosen. What are you saying?" Cavanaugh asked.

Rosen took a breath. "Our DNA is constantly subjected to mutations. Every time a cell divides, there's a potential for accidental changes to be made. This virus appears to do that in a targeted, non-accidental way."

Cavanaugh stood, put his palm on his forehead, and turned. "This is a whole new level of bioterrorism. Even if we get the virus dealt in the next few days, you're saying there's a chance of these lingering effects?"

Rosen nodded.

"But we don't know what they are."

"No." Rosen continued. "We also discovered the virus has a two-week incubation period, which means once a host is infected, he'll feel fine for a couple weeks before symptoms present. You and I might already be infected and not even know."

"Jesus God," Fairchild said, burying her face in her hands.

"Well, how the heck did I get so sick so fast?" Jake asked.

"We studied your blood samples and the syringe Gunther used to inject you with," Rosen said. "You were injected with a modified influenza virus, still manmade. A third virus, if you will, but nobody else has been infected with it. Just you."

If that was supposed to make Jake feel any better, it didn't.

"And the other virus?" Governor Fairchild asked. "The one affecting plants?"

"Nothing yet," Rosen said. The governor looked up, wet her lips, closed her eyes and sighed.

Jake felt a renewed weight on his chest and struggled for breath.

Cavanaugh turned away from the desk and kicked the wall.

Rosen continued to inform the governor details of the bentonite clay and updated the team on the status of a vaccine. Or rather, the lack thereof. "As I said before, the only way we could have a vaccine at this point would be if we'd spent the last six months manufacturing it. Now, it's probable the terrorists created a vaccine for themselves, but even if we could find it or learn how to make it we'd never be able to manufacture enough in time."

"I see. Thank you," the governor said as she typed an email on her phone to her staff with an update.

"That's all I have," Rosen said. "If you don't mind, I'd like to get back to the lab."

CHAPTER 54

August 20th
6:25 a.m.

Viktor and Selim put the finishing touches on the crime scene at Linda Bennett's mansion by positioning the gun with the suppressor — the one used to murder the two FBI agents posted outside — in Frank's hand, fired one round out the window to ensure gunshot residue covered his hand and fingerprints on the gun, then set it on the floor next to Frank's body. They placed the pistol used to murder Frank in his hand. All had to look natural. Poor bastard shot himself after taking out two feds then drowning his cheating bitch of a wife in the downstairs bathroom.

After walking to the front door, Viktor fastened the deadbolt, shuffled back across the first floor of the estate to the rear sliding door, then double-checked the rear door lock while Selim opened and pushed out the bottom half of an adjacent, single-hung window to exit. The little man popped out the screen and set the aluminum frame onto the dewed grass below, then climbed out the window. Viktor followed him through the opening, then Selim pushed the window closed and replaced the screen.

Viktor slid off his gloves and stuffed them into his jeans pocket. They walked around the house to the front, down the driveway, and across the street to his truck. After a quick inspection of the Chevy with the two dead FBI guys, Viktor looked up to the mansion. Satisfied with his work, he jammed the column shifter of his truck into drive and pulled away from the curb. Nice and quiet. Clean. Fucking cops wouldn't have a goddamned clue.

Two miles down the hill, at the outer edge of a Walmart parking lot, Viktor dropped off Selim.

"Lay low for a few months," he told the young Jihadist. "I'll be in contact." After he said goodbye and slammed the door closed, he flipped a U-turn.

Viktor drove along a dark local street toward the 210 freeway. Now, with all the loose ends tied up, his simple plan involved driving back to the Burbank airport, where he'd parked his twin-engine Piper Seneca V. He looked forward to hearing Jake was finally dead, then plotting a nice, leisurely course south to Colombia, to recuperate from his latest attack and watch from a safe distance as the California economy plunged into the abyss. With any luck, the almighty U.S. of A. would follow suit.

His burner phone vibrated.

UNKNOWN CALLER.

Out of pure curiosity, he clicked the green answer button, put the call on speaker, and said nothing, only listened.

"Viktor. I know you're there," said the caller slowly, in a low-pitched tone. He recognized the voice he'd heard only once for a brief few seconds. Four years ago. But unmistakable.

Tracy Ciacchella.

"It's done," he said.

"Everything?"

"Yes."

"Excellent. Now, my good man, I need you to finish one more task before you fly back down to that hell-hole you crawled out from," Tracy said.

He knew of no other person on earth with the power to rival Tracy's. If she asked him to do something, anything, he'd consider the request an honor.

"Tell me."

"Gunther's virus failed," Tracy said. "My people discovered Linda had paid Gunther two million to disable any contagious traits."

Back when they started, Viktor had argued with Gunther about whether to make the waterborne virus contagious. From the beginning, Tracy had wanted to make it airborne, spreadable by coughing and sneezing. But Gunther only had experience with waterborne viruses. Tracy threatened to withhold payment if the virus was not contagious, which now meant Linda would not have been paid a single cent. Same thing with Gunther.

Backstabbing assholes. Dead, but still, backstabbers.

This meant Gunther had made under-the-table money twice because Viktor had also paid Gunther to design a *third* virus, one based on an influenza strain. This was the virus Gunther injected into Jake.

"And my guy at the CDC just confirmed something about your little friend, Jake."

This was it. For the last twenty-four hours, he had relished the assumption that Jake was dead already or would die soon. A journey he'd started years ago, a goal he'd set for himself to wipe the engineer from the face of the planet. Finally, confirmation of Jakey's death.

At least, it should have been.

"Don't tell me Jake's still alive."

"Indeed he is. And getting stronger by the minute," Tracy said.

Viktor hammered the steering wheel with the base of his fist and clenched his jaw.

That son-of-a-bitch. To add salt to this fresh wound, had he known about an inside man at the CDC, he could have done additional testing on the virus strains to make sure everything worked according to all three of Gunther's designs. Reduced their risks and increased the chances for success on this latest attack.

Goddamnit. Why hadn't they been told?

"Mr. Johnston, as you well know, I do not tolerate failure. You will take care of this matter at once," Tracy said, slow and confident. "Along with that Agent Cavanaugh. I'm sure that genius mind of yours will come up with a two-birds, one-stone scenario, yes?"

He took a beat. Amber streetlights passed by and multiple red neon signs that read "CLOSED."

"Already have several ideas."

"I need wrap it all up by the end of today, nice and tidy," Tracy said and hung up.

Viktor made two calls. The first was to give instructions for a hit to his associate in Sacramento. "I don't care. Stripper. Hooker. But it has be the same height, weight, build and must be delivered by 1 p.m."

The second was to Selim to request his services a final time. One more favor. For Allah.

Selim agreed.

That should be just enough time.

CHAPTER 55

August 20th
7:25 a.m.

Jake stepped out from the ground floor elevator of the San Francisco Federal Building, walking alongside Cavanaugh and Paige as they headed toward one of the classic, crazy steep streets to Starbucks for a much-needed infusion of caffeine.

Paige seemed distracted, but who could blame her? All she probably wanted to do was work out the funeral details for her dad. Heck, Jake wanted to help.

But the trio needed to clear their heads and regroup. They'd spent the hour after the meeting pouring over the data on Paige's maps and charts, finding correlations between hot spots of infected men and the water system infrastructure throughout the western half of the state. They needed a fresh perspective. New ideas.

They also needed privacy. Cavanaugh wanted to share the details of his unconventional plan with no one looking over his shoulder.

Jake's head pounded. The effect of caffeine withdrawal, grief over the deaths of Dave and Professor Everton, lack of sleep, a call from the Stockton fire department arson investigator a half hour ago, and the fact that he'd nearly died the day before from Gunther's viral injection all combined into one massive migraine. He hoped a Venti-sized wonder drink would help take the edge off.

After Rosen left, Cavanaugh had tried unsuccessfully to contact Dr. Dinesh Mehta of the CDC. He'd assigned two agents to track down the doctor and to let him know as soon as they had any leads. Jake could tell Cavanaugh wasn't too optimistic about what they'd find.

The latest data from the FBI and CDC field personnel showed that the human outbreak had finally been contained, but the effects on the crops were devastating. Symptoms had lessened in ninety-eight percent of infected victims of the bioterrorist attack, providing a thin ray of sunshine in an otherwise cloud-filled day.

Earlier that morning, during his meeting with Cavanaugh, Paige, and Jake, Dr. Rosen had indicated that the CDC had determined there was a genetic modification component to the virus, but until the technicians at the FBI finished decrypting the hard drive seized from Viktor's Modesto bunker, nobody knew for sure what permanent damage had been done to over a million men.

Except Dr. Mehta.

"We need to find a fresh lead on Viktor," Jake said, stepping over a pile of vomit on the sidewalk next to a blue homeless tent.

"You know this guy," Cavanaugh said. "Slippery. No phone to track. No digital footprint to decode. No citizen sightings. Nothing. It's like the guy's a frickin' ghost. Again. Pisses me off my team at the FBI is having such a challenge with this little prick."

"He's gonna screw up soon," Paige said, looking up at Cavanaugh from his side. "Seems like your plan's a hail-Mary pass, but if it works, it'll flush out the mole and then, hopefully, Viktor."

"Hope isn't a strategy," Jake said.

They arrived at Starbucks, ordered three massive drinks with triple shots of espresso, and sat in a quiet corner.

Jake took a sip and the fiery liquid soothed his raw throat, reducing the pressure of the pulse in his head.

They spent the next twenty minutes strategizing further details of Cavanaugh's plan.

Cavanaugh's cell rang. He answered..

"Great," Cavanaugh said as he stood and motioned for his two cohorts to follow him out. Jake pushed open the glass entrance door and they started their two-block trek back to the Federal Building.

"Excellent. We'll be right up." Cavanaugh ended the call as his walk turned into a slow jog. "The techs finally decrypted Viktor's hard drive they found at the Modesto bunker raid. Got some data for us."

They hurried back into the lobby, up the elevator to the twelfth floor, and made their way to the technician's lab. Two server racks sat in the corner, illuminated by cool, fluorescent ceiling lights. White ceramic tile covered the entire floor and the hum of whirling fans mixed with the pecking sounds of three technicians tapping their computer keyboards.

"What have you got?" Cavanaugh asked a tiny man sitting in front of a laptop and two external monitors, all of which displayed various forms of raw Python code, biological data, statistics, graphs, and more.

"Looks like you hit the jackpot," Jake said.

"Yes and no," the tech said. "Everything's here." He pointed to three windows on the monitors. "All nice and neat and ordered. But I got no clue what it all means."

Cavanaugh patted the tech on his upper back and instructed him to upload the files to the FBI shared server. Then he walked away with Jake and Paige following.

With his back toward the elevators, Cavanaugh made a call to another agent and asked him for a favor. Something about scientists and further analysis of data. Jake wanted to ask but knew better. Instead, he looked at Paige and raised his eyebrows.

As they waited for the elevator, Cavanaugh called Rosen and told him he had the data the CDC needed, and he'd send over a link in a few. Then Cavanaugh got a call from another agent, listened for several seconds and then smiled.

"Ten-four," Cavanaugh said and hung up. He turned to Jake and pointed his index finger at him. "We got what we need. You ready?"

"Yep."

The trio made their way up to their war room on the sixteenth floor, Cavanaugh logged in to the laptop set near the edge of the massive black table, found the data on the server and forwarded the link to Rosen, with a request for an immediate Zoom call. He nodded to Jake.

"Like we discussed. Call Rosen."

Jake fired up his laptop and they called Rosen via Zoom. The familiar ring tone played while they waited for Rosen to answer. Paige looked at Jake and gave a downward nod.

Jake slid his hand inside his jeans pocket, stroked the Sûr System pen for good luck, then felt the special USB drive, the one with the American flag, the one Dave had given him. A second good luck charm.

After several seconds Rosen's tan face appeared on the screen, scanning the now unencrypted data files while they made their video call.

"Got something," Rosen said. He adjusted his glasses, continuing to read and study the additional information. "This isn't good." He pulled his brows inward.

"Not again," Cavanaugh said with his hands on his hips, standing behind Jake.

A few moments later Rosen continued. "Looks like, at least according to the terrorists' notes and some of their test data, their virus was, in fact, designed to do genetic modifications."

"You already told us this," Cavanaugh said. "I need to know the specifics. Do we know what cells the virus will target?"

Jake looked up at Cavanaugh, then back at the screen.

Rosen's eyes darted back and forth between the camera and the data on his screen. He scratched his cheeks and blinked rapidly several times before answering.

"No."

"So we still have no concept of what we're dealing with," Cavanaugh said. "The genetic modifications could be anything."

Rosen wiped his forehead. "Correct." He adjusted his collar and tie. "I'm truly sorry. I wish I could be of more assistance to you."

"There's one more thing I'd like to discuss with you," Cavanaugh said, moving his face closer to the camera. He squeezed Jake's shoulder.

Rosen narrowed his eyes.

"Our investigation of a recent drone attack has led us to someone at the CDC. Someone in your office. Dr. Willis. One of the scientists you brought here two days ago for the meeting. The tall, blond guy. We believe he might be a mole working for Viktor Johnston, the mastermind behind these attacks."

Jake raised his voice. "This is bullshit." He pushed the chair away from the desk and stood. "You need to go over there right now and arrest the bastard."

Cavanaugh jerked his head toward Jake. "Settle down, Dr. Bendel. Let me do my job."

"I don't understand," Rosen said. "How do you know this?"

Jake stepped back and spun around.

"Two days ago," Cavanaugh said, "there was a drone attack near Modesto. Four drones followed Dr. Bendel and fired, from what we can tell, over 200 rounds at his car. Damned thing looked like a sponge."

"And you think Willis is responsible?" Rosen asked.

Jake turned back around and faced the camera. "We don't think it's him. We know it is."

Cavanaugh shoved Jake away from the camera.

"I'm sorry, you must have the wrong man. I know Dr. Willis. He'd never do such a thing."

"Could be," Cavanaugh said.

"Plus, I'm sure he knows nothing about any drones," Rosen said. "He wouldn't know the first thing about how to remote pilot a UAV."

"Again, no problem. Mostly a hunch," Cavanaugh said. "Circumstantial evidence. You understand, but we do have to follow up on the lead."

Jake pounded his fist on the table.

"This. Is. Total. Bureaucratic. Crap," Jake said. "We know it's Willis. You need to get over there and stop him before he does anything else. Or tries to escape."

Cavanaugh stood upright and faced Jake, pinching the bridge of his nose while closing his eyes. "I'm the law here, Dr. Bendel. Up to this point, you've been an invited guest at the FBI. We have to follow certain protocols here and I'm responsible for enforcing them."

"I don't give a damn about your FBI protocols. What if Willis gets away? What if—"

"Careful. You're on thin ice, Dr. Bendel. I need you to calm down, otherwise I'm going to have to—"

"No. I will not calm down. After all we've been through? Are you serious? Willis tried to kill me yesterday. I thought we were friends?"

"Yes, we are friends, but this is business. This is the law. An FBI matter. I'm the FBI agent here. You're going to do what you're told. You're going to follow—"

"No. I demand you get over there right now and arrest this guy. We can't afford to waste another second. I can't believe you're being so pigheaded on this. It's black and white. The man is guilty. You need to go arrest him."

Cavanaugh took a deep, calming breath to make sure the next words out of his mouth came through as clearly as possible.

"Dr. Bendel, as much as it pains me and I'm sorry to have to do this in front of Dr. Rosen and your friend, I'm afraid you've left me no choice." He blinked several times, calculating the proper tone for effect. "Your participation in this investigation is hereby terminated."

Rosen wiped his palm across his forehead, staring incredulously.

Jake glared at Cavanaugh, shook his head repeatedly and waved his two friends away. Paige sat motionless.

"I'm not going anywhere. You need me. You have to—"

"Do I need to have security remove you from the building?"

Jake threw up his arms. "Fine," he said, slapping the table. "I'm leaving. I don't need the goddamned FBI to figure this out anyway. I'll do this myself if I have to."

Several awkward seconds passed as Jake stormed from the room and slammed the door closed.

"My apologies, Dr. Rosen," Cavanaugh said. "Please keep working. We'll be in touch."

CHAPTER 56

August 20th
8:05 a.m.

Jake fled the FBI building and stopped dead on the sidewalk outside to collect his thoughts and focus on the task at hand.

He looked up at the gray overcast clouds, relishing the cool air on his flushed face. They hadn't yelled that hard at each other since the CDM attack two years ago—only that time it had been for real. His heart raced deep inside his chest from the adrenaline, but he knew what had to be done.

Jake walked southwest on Market Street and with a left turn on Polk and a right on Grove, managed the half-mile trek, even in his weakened state, to the CDC building. He texted Paige an update of his location.

She acknowledged.

Inside the CDC building, lobby security called Rosen, who authorized Jake's entry to the premises, gave him a temporary security badge, and escorted him to the third-floor office where Rosen worked.

The elevator doors opened, revealing Dr. Rosen waiting for Jake with an unreadable expression on his face.

"We need to talk," Jake said.

Rosen agreed, led Jake down the long, bright corridor, and opened an oak door with a brass Dr. James Rosen, MD, PhD nameplate glued on the front. Rosen motioned for Jake to sit in one of the two blue fabric chairs in front of his desk. A half-dozen degrees and certificates hung on the beige, orange-peel-textured wall behind the workspace.

Jake sat.

"Need to ask a favor," Jake said.

Rosen steepled his fingers and leaned back in his black leather chair. "Not sure you're in a position to ask for favors. Or if I should even be talking with you, Dr. Bendel. You're no longer part of the investigation. Last thing I need is to get on the wrong side of the FBI."

Rosen pressed his lips together in a slight grimace.

Jake took a deep breath. "Cavanaugh and I are obviously not on the same page regarding the possibility of Willis being a mole."

"As I said, he's not a mole," Rosen said. "No way this can be. I hope you did not come here to ask me to spy on my colleague."

"No. I want you to take Willis to brunch."

Rosen opened and closed his mouth. "Why?"

"So I can spy on him."

Rosen shifted in his seat, gave a heavy sigh and stayed quiet.

"I'm sure the guy is hungry. Don't ask me how I know this, but his badge data indicates he's been here since 3 a.m. without clocking out and it's—" Jake looked at his phone "—already almost 8:35."

Rosen frowned.

"I don't feel comfortable doing this. I'm a scientist, not a spy," Rosen said, crossing his arms on his chest. He arched his back and jutted his chin out. "And besides, Cavanaugh said it's just a hunch. I'm sure he's innocent."

"Great. Then help me prove he's innocent so I can move on to the next suspect."

Rosen remained stoic.

Jake continued. "Someone attacked me. I need answers whether or not Cavanaugh helps. I just need twenty minutes. I'll even spring for brunch. My treat." Jake pulled out his wallet and set five hundred-dollar bills onto Rosen's desk.

Rosen scratched his cheek, leaned forward and set his elbows on the front edge of his desk. His eyes narrowed. "You get caught, you take the heat. Non-negotiable."

Jake placed three more C-notes, the last of his cash from Carlie, onto the desk, stood and shook Rosen's hand. "Done."

CHAPTER 57

August 20th
9:21 a.m.

Viktor gazed out the window of his parked truck, watching the planes taking off and landing at the Burbank airport. He still had the better part of three hours before he needed to take off to Sacramento, enough time for his mechanic to finish replacing the clogged airspeed pitot tube.

Enough time to have a little fun.

To put the first piece of his strategy into place, he grabbed the burner phone—the same cell Tracy had called him on four hours earlier—from the passenger seat, plugged in the headphone adaptor cord, and turned on the GPS tracking feature.

With all the pieces set, he called Jakey Boy.

Five rings. No answer. Went to voicemail.

Crap. Click.

Three minutes later Viktor called again. This time, he answered.

"Carlie?" Jake asked.

"Not even close," Viktor said.

Pause.

"Game's over, Viktor," Jake said. "You killed Dave. Why, I have no idea, but your little stunt went nowhere. You tried to be some bad-ass bioterrorist, but all you did was get a bunch of innocent people sick with the flu. Big deal. Happens every year. Paige is alive and so am I. Never felt better, in fact. You couldn't even get your buddy Gunther to get me sick. He died laughing at you. Pathetic."

But Viktor couldn't help himself, chuckling and clearing his throat.

"Oh, Jakey Boy. You have so much to learn." A jet airplane taxied in front of Viktor's truck, heading toward the hanger where Viktor's mechanic continued working on the Piper Seneca. "I didn't kill Dave. In fact, I had a lot of respect for the guy. Was a genius at coding. A worthy adversary. A dead one, but worthy nonetheless."

"You lie so much you don't even know you're lying. Pathological."

"I'm a lot of things, Jakey Boy, but I've never lied to you. Your old pal Viktor's just a pawn in a big game filled with power brokers, criminals, and governments all across the globe. If you think I'm the top dog, you're not as smart as I thought."

"Bullshit," Jake said. "I know you. Your crazy mind thinks you're one of Allah's generals in some pseudo-holy war."

He rubbed the nape of his neck with one hand while stroking the steering wheel with the other.

"How quaint. This whole time you thought I was the puppet master. FBI has been little help, looks like. I'm not talking about Allah, praise be his name, I'm talking about this puppet show we're all in. You. Me. Just puppets. Someone else killed your friend."

"You're so crazy you can't even hear how nuts you sound," Jake said.

"I have barbs dug deep into my soul, and they go way up the power chain. Higher than me. People I answer to, you stupid moron." He ground his teeth, rethinking his strategy. "Fine. Come get me. Kill me. Lock me up. The Jihad will continue. More like me will follow. I'm fucking done with this hell anyway."

Pause.

"That night at Chili's," Jake said. "Two weeks ago. That was you."

Viktor felt a tiny grin eke out toward his cheek.

"No, but I was there in spirit," he said. "And in the eyes of the public, the only true court that matters, you poisoned all those innocent men. Of course, the Trihypnol worked like a charm. Another one of my brilliant ideas. All you needed was a splash of coercion and—you don't remember—but we didn't even have to hold you at gunpoint." Viktor chuckled. "We focused your mind on that sweet daughter of yours. A simple threat to her and boom, you did the deed for us. You even smiled when you injected the virus gel into the chlorine system."

He paused for effect. No response from Jake.

"Brilliant," he said, cocking his head to the side while scanning the blue cloudless sky above. "The world-famous engineer designs an amazing desalination system, something to provide fresh drinking water to millions, and turns right around and converts the damned thing into a bioterrorist weapon. Beautiful irony, you gotta admit."

Jake hung up.

Viktor smiled.

CHAPTER 58

August 20th
9:32 a.m.

From an empty meeting room in the CDC building where he'd been waiting for Rosen and Willis to leave, Jake ended the call with Viktor. He could only take so much gloating.

He tried to wrap his head around the possibility of someone else pulling the strings. This whole time, Jake had thought of Viktor as the mastermind. Could this be possible? Or was Viktor just messing with him?

After sending a text to Cavanaugh with a request to trace the call, Jake put his hand in his pocket and clenched the special USB drive Dave Trainer had given him. His thoughts turned to his buddy's tragic death. The pain the guy must have gone through. The floating eyeball in the jar.

But he shoved the thoughts and doubts aside. Focus. Make Dave's death mean something.

Jake emerged from the empty meeting room on the fourth floor of the CDC building and recalled Rosen's directions on how to navigate to Willis's office through the sea of offices, cubicles, and mini-labs. Time to find evidence against the son-of-a-bitch who'd shot at him with the attack drones. He took the staircase to get to the proper floor.

Paige confirmed via text she was tailing Rosen and Willis as the two scientists were walking two blocks away from the CDC, toward a local cafe. A five-minute walk each way, plus at least fifteen minutes for brunch should give Jake enough time to hack into the CDC computer and find answers.

Jake made his way to the scientist's office, opened the door, snuck in, and closed the door behind him. He rotated the thin, vertical crystal bar, closing the blinds hanging in front of the single pane window on the front office wall. He needed as much privacy as possible.

Jake felt Dave's presence as he sat at the desk and inserted the special drive into the USB port of the mid-sized tower computer.

Within seconds, the Windows PC opened up like a spring flower and the screen showed a desktop crammed with icons. Jake rummaged through several folders, rifling through files related to viruses and this latest attack on Californians.

Text from Paige: THEY GOT THEIR FOOD TO GO! THEY'RE ALMOST DONE . . . HURRY!

Shit.

Jake ran a customized software program on the special Dave thumb-drive to speed up his search, typing in keywords relating to drones, UAV's, and genetic modifications. Twelve hits.

Another text from Paige: THEY'RE ONE BLOCK AWAY.

Jake scrolled through more files, clicking on each hit from the hacking program.

Bingo.

He found an EXE file to run a remote UAV control system and double-clicked the file and a program called "Remote UAV" opened. He clicked the "File" dropdown, revealing a list of recent files, then opened one with the date of two days ago, the same day as the drone attack.

When the file opened, the screen showed a satellite map of the area outside Modesto, where the attack occurred. A preprogrammed pattern of colored red lines showed four drones. He found a record of the exact date and time the drones attacked, then took a picture of the screen with his phone.

Text from Paige: THEY'RE ENTERING THE CDC! RU DONE??

This evidence proved the CDC had a mole, one who had tried to kill Jake, but Jake wanted to know more details on the specific genetic modifications caused by Viktor's virus.

Searching through several more files, homing in on plausible assumptions, notes, formulas, anything, he speed-read thousands of lines in a matter of minutes.

With seconds before Rosen and Willis would come up the elevator, a snippet of text grabbed his eye: "Human gamete cells." He downloaded the file to the thumb drive and planned to review it in full once he left the CDC building.

Close enough.

After putting the computer back into sleep mode, he popped out his magic USB drive, stuffed it back into his front jeans pocket, jogged to the door, rolled the mini-blinds horizontal and peered out. Rosen and Willis were walking side by side across the sea of cubicles, headed his way.

An instant before they rounded the corner, Jake slid out and ducked into an empty cubicle across the hallway from the office. Rosen and Willis walked by with several bags of food and entered the office. They closed the door behind them. Jake darted out into the hallway, made his way down the stairwell, and slipped out the front of the building with, hopefully, the evidence he needed.

CHAPTER 59

August 20th
10:12 a.m.

Back at the FBI, Jake entered the sixteenth-floor conference room. Paige and Cavanaugh stared at him, waiting.

"I got it." He set the USB drive on the table.

"Alright, let's see what we have." Cavanaugh inserted the drive and Jake clicked open the file he'd found on human gamete cells. They all scanned the file.

"This confirms what we got from the decrypted hard drives—but this isn't from the drives," Cavanaugh said. "Does the document seem odd to either of you?"

They looked again. "It's been scanned in," Paige said.

"Right," Cavanaugh said. "But we didn't scan any hard copies for the CDC. The only hard copy I saw in that bunker—"

"—Was the notebook you said Dinesh found." Jake finished.

Cavanaugh nodded. "Looks like he made it back to the CDC."

"So where does that leave us?" Paige asked.

Cavanaugh started to answer but his phone rang. He held up a finger and answered. "Cavanaugh." He listened for a moment and his face became grim. "I see. Thank you. Keep me apprised." He ended the call and turned to Jake and Paige.

"They found Dinesh Mehta."

Cavanaugh called Rosen and informed him that the FBI had discovered something extremely important and that there had been a significant development in the investigation. He told Rosen to drop whatever he was working on and get over to the FBI building.

Immediately.

Fifteen minutes later the FBI security desk called and requested permission from Cavanaugh for Dr. Rosen to enter the building. Cavanaugh confirmed and sat at the end of the long black table in the war room to gather his thoughts. They had no further leads on Viktor and no answers to the true cause or extent of the virus attack. A dead end.

Game time. Everything hinged on the outcome of this meeting.

He shuffled through several reports and papers as he waited.

The sound of muffled footsteps came from outside the room. The guard opened the door to the sixteenth-floor conference room, escorted Rosen inside, and closed the door behind him.

Cavanaugh gave a warm smile to help lower any of Rosen's defenses.

Rosen walked to Cavanaugh and they shook hands.

"Thank you for coming. I know you're very busy at the CDC."

Rosen sat and placed his hands in his lap.

"I need to get back but I'm eager to hear about the breakthrough with your investigation."

Cavanaugh stood, pacing. He crossed his arms, rubbed the tip of his chin, and stared at Rosen.

"Something's been bugging me since the first time you and I met."

Rosen tugged at his ear. "Oh?"

Cavanaugh nodded. "I couldn't quite put my finger on it, but fortunately, they train us here to notice when someone's hiding something."

Rosen adjusted his clothes as if they chafed, uncomfortable.

Good.

Cavanaugh continued staring down at him. "I think you've been lying to me from the beginning."

"This assertion is most preposterous," Rosen said, eyes fixed straight ahead at the grey fabric on the wall opposite his chair. He rubbed his nose.

"I pulled a favor with one of my longtime agent buddies," Cavanaugh said. "We had our own FBI scientists analyze the unencrypted data from Viktor's hard drive from the Modesto bunker. In a matter of minutes, they determined, as I'm sure you did, that the virus does, in fact, modify the DNA of the host."

"We know this. I told you before."

Cavanaugh continued. "You lied when you told us the specific genetic modifications were unknown. In fact, according to our guys, there is ample evidence to the contrary. We know the specifics. That was lie number one."

Rosen rubbed his arms, scanning the empty room.

"Fine," Rosen said. "I withheld the specifics from you about the virus affecting human gamete cells. I thought you might use the information to take the credit for the find and—"

"Nice try. We're way beyond you weaseling out of this, Dr. Rosen." Cavanaugh grabbed a single piece of letter-sized paper from the table and slapped the document against Rosen's chest. Rosen jumped, pulled the paper away from his body and read the text.

Cavanaugh continued. "You and I both know the terrorists wanted to use viruses to modify human sperm cells. They're changing the DNA code in the portion that generates cells in the brain area. They intend to reduce the size of the amygdala and hippocampus, which, as you know, make up the limbic system, the area of the human brain tucked in underneath our more evolved portions. Sometimes referred to as the 'lizard brain' because it controls our fight-or-flight mechanism."

"There's a lot more to how the limbic system operates. Your assessment is a gross oversimplification."

"We're not here to debate the finer points of neuroscience, Doctor. We're here because you've been withholding vital information."

Rosen was silent.

Cavanaugh stopped, leaned in and parked his face directly in front of Rosen's.

"We're talking about permanent damage here. Yes, I'm just an ignorant cop, but I have top scientific minds at my disposal, and this is what they're telling me." Cavanaugh stood and continued to pace. "If any of these infected men conceive a child in their future, those children will have smaller lizard brains. A diminished capacity for fear and anger and other basic human emotions. I'm not sure what you're telling yourself — maybe that this is justified because anger is an outdated biological survival instinct — but I assume you'd agree that whoever designed this idiotic plan had a limited grasp of how the human brain operates. This could spell disaster for millions of newborn babies. This bothers me, Dr. Rosen. You don't fuck with babies. That's some sick-ass Nazi shit."

Rosen looked at his lap.

Cavanaugh continued. "The only reason I can discern as to why you'd try and hide this information from me is because you knew about the mole at the CDC."

Rosen closed his eyes and spoke mostly in a whisper. "They said they would kill me. Kill my family."

"Who?"

"I can't. My family." His speech fragmented. "You don't — I can't."

"Dr. Rosen. I don't think you understand." Cavanaugh slid a manila folder across the table. "These documents here," Cavanaugh said, "are all files from your work computer — which we didn't need a warrant to search since it's property of the U.S. Government — and courtesy of Dr. Bendel. Conclusive evidence you knew about the specific genetic modifications."

Rosen mutely glanced through the papers, then set the folder back on the table.

"In fact," pressed Cavanaugh, "I think you knew the specifics before anyone else did. Anyone except Dinesh Mehta, that is."

Rosen grew pale.

"Dinesh found the information in the bunker and knew what it meant, but he wouldn't talk to anyone until you confirmed his suspicions. So he brought it to you. And then both he and the information disappeared."

Dr. Rosen put his head in his hands. "I didn't have a choice. They told me to destroy the notebook, to stall. They threatened my children. I thought the encrypted scans would be safe to keep. Insurance. But now that you've found the pages I scanned in—" he paused, terrified—"what if they find out?"

"Where's Dinesh?"

Rosen was quiet. "I don't know. We were going to meet again yesterday morning, but he never showed up. Then—they told me to say I hadn't seen him."

"And you listened to them." Cavanaugh pinched the bridge of his nose, weighing his options. Telling Rosen about Dinesh might do more harm than good. They needed to focus on stopping these people right now. He went to the door and called in Jake and Paige, who had been waiting outside the conference room, and as they entered turned back to Rosen. "You're in a lot some serious shit here. We also found the UAV remote piloting records on your computer. Turns out you did more than withhold critical information from the FBI."

"It wasn't me. He used my computer."

"He?"

"The man they have watching me."

"Tell me his name. What he looks like. Anything."

"You have no concept how powerful these people are," Rosen said, speeding through his words, desperate, pleading. "I have kids in college. They threatened to hurt them. I didn't know what to do."

"Tell me who 'they' are," Cavanaugh said, leaning in.

With chin trembling, Rosen said, "All I know is her first name. Tracy. Some hidden secret underground society." He wiped his forehead. "They're going to kill me and my family if I tell you anymore. No. I can't—"

"We'll protect you. You should have come to us with this long ago, Dr. Rosen, but keep talking."

Rosen stiffened his neck, looked at the table and continued. "Fine. She had her people deposit money into an offshore account for me and promised not to harm my family. All I needed to do was help delay the investigation to give the virus time for maximum impact. She's the one who set up the UAVs. Those four attack drones." He shot a glance at Jake. "She said there'd be no way to track the pilot because of the remote connection." Rosen covered his face, hunched over and cried.

Cavanaugh looked at Jake.

"Tell us what you know about Willis," Cavanaugh said.

Rosen wiped his cheeks and whispered. "I can't."

Cavanaugh held his phone to his cheek. "Bring him in," Cavanaugh said to the agent waiting outside. A moment later, the door opened again. One of Cavanaugh's agents escorted Willis into the room but remained inside with the door open.

Willis darted glances to each of the men. When Willis saw Rosen, he reached for something underneath his pants near his ankle.

The agent yelled "Knife!" and stepped away from Willis, drawing his weapon.

Cavanaugh pulled his 9mm Glock from his leather holster, dropped to one knee, and ordered Willis to drop the weapon. But when Willis lunged for Rosen, fired two shots to his center mass.

Paige screamed.

CHAPTER 60

August 20th
12:16 p.m.

Viktor confirmed, first with Selim and then his Sacramento associate, that everything was on schedule.

After ending the second call, he tossed the burner phone onto the passenger seat of his airplane — now fully fueled, signed-off by the mechanic, and ready to fly — and thought back to the CDM attack two years ago. All his failures with Jakey Boy. A gross underestimation of the man's intellect, gut instincts, and survival skills.

But his assumptions — and cockiness — ultimately caused the plan to fail.

Viktor knew this now. Lesson learned. Praise Allah. But Viktor had no intention of making the same mistakes with Jake. This time Viktor needed to keep his plan to kill Jake simple, effective, and with a high probability of success.

He turned the ignition key, fired up both 210 horsepower Continental engines, and pushed both black throttle knobs forward.

Sacramento, here I come.

One last time.

CHAPTER 61

August 20th
12:25 p.m.

Jake held Paige in a firm embrace outside the war room, glancing through the doorway at Willis' corpse. Between giving statements, waiting for their equipment to be released, and waiting for Cavanaugh, they'd had to stick around for over an hour after the shooting. She buried her face in his chest and he tried to avert his gaze, but curiosity got the best of him. A pool of blood the size of a small couch reflected the fluorescent lights from the ceiling. Willis' dead eyes stared straight up as he lay on his back.

Cavanaugh caught up with the two engineers as they made their way to his office.

"How you guys holding up?" Cavanaugh asked.

"Fine, I guess," Jake said.

"Our plan worked. Willis was the mole. We're rolling now, getting some breaks. Rosen's spilling his guts and we finally got a ping on the phone Viktor used to call you," Cavanaugh said. He glanced at his phone, reading a message from one of the techs. "Looks like he's heading north toward Sacramento, going about a couple hundred miles an hour."

Jake nodded, releasing Paige from their hug. "He's on a plane."

"I had the same hunch," Cavanaugh said. "There's a flight plan filed for a Piper Seneca V. No pilot info, but it's headed to SAC, which I think is the Sacramento International Airport, a few miles north of Sacramento. Should be landing in just over an hour and a half, barely enough time for us to drive there—with the reds and blues on—surprise him, and take him down once and for all."

Cavanaugh handed Jake another 9mm Glock and three extra magazines, all tucked in a smooth, brown leather pouch. "We found your Tesla filled with bullet holes in another bunker two miles away from Viktor's hideout, burned to a crisp. The other weapon I gave you was inside, so I'm issuing you a new weapon. Same as the last one and for the same reasons. Just in case," Cavanaugh said. "Forty-five rounds total. Only if your life is threatened." He patted Jake on the side of his shoulder.

He handed Paige a black object the size of a deck of playing cards.

"This is a newly developed, covert, portable GPS triangulation device used to track cell phones in the field." He paused. "Well, it's supposed to be. Haven't field tested it yet. Guess you get the privilege." He gave her access rights to the shiny black electronic gizmo before they tore out from the Federal Building. She asked him how to use the device.

"It pairs with your iPad. You're a smart engineer," Cavanaugh said. "Figure it out."

CHAPTER 62

August 20th
1:45 p.m.

A three-car squad packed full of FBI agents blazed eastward along I-80 toward Sacramento. They used an emergency preemption device that allowed them unimpeded access along the rightmost side freeway lane formerly known as the "slow lane." Jake and the other developers of the Sûr System had included a mechanism in the algorithm to allow for emergency vehicles to drive in their own dedicated lane as fast as necessary. Safety had always been a top priority in everything Jake worked on.

An agent drove a loaner Prius from Cavanaugh, as Jake sat in the passenger seat reviewing aeronautical maps of the Sacramento area, while Paige sat in the back, fiddling with the tracker. She'd plugged the black metallic rectangular box into the data port on her iPad and told him she'd figured out how to use the device without a hitch.

"Either this sucker has a bug or, like, we're tracking two phones," she said, leaning forward to show Jake the screen as they zoomed on the freeway at over ninety miles an hour, following three FBI SUVs.

Jake took a quick glance at her iPad that showed a satellite map of California, with two red dotted lines shown as a layer.

The lines started near L.A. and went north to the southern tip of Sacramento.

"Gotta be a glitch," he said, white-knuckling his phone while clenching his jaw. "Cavanaugh said they just got that thing last week and hadn't tested it yet."

"I'll take a screenshot and text it to Cavanaugh," she said, but then she noticed something else. "This is odd. Looks like one of the phones stopped moving. Or this thing is broken." She reverse-pinched the screen to zoom in. "S-A-C."

"I don't understand," Jake said. "Sacramento airport?"

She continued to poke and pinch at the iPad screen. "Yes and no. Sacramento has two airports."

"Can't be. Cavanaugh said we're all headed to the airport."

Paige read details from her map. "The big one, SMF, is the international airport about seven miles north of downtown. But there's a second airport. S-A-C is an executive airport about five miles south of downtown."

Jake checked the map on his phone and confirmed, before looking up to see them riding the tail of the black SUV in front of them.

"Sounded like he thought there's only one. Hope someone checked before we went on this little jaunt across the state."

Jake called Cavanaugh, who confirmed he'd received the text from Paige with the map.

On speakerphone, Cavanaugh said, "Yes, of course I'm aware of two airports. Probably a glitch with the two phones, but listen, we found Dinesh and it didn't end well for him."

Jake hated getting news about the recently deceased. "No, not another one."

"Found his body floating in the California Aqueduct in Palmdale, near the Pearblossom Highway. Willis looks good for the kill, so dead end there." He took a beat. "Dinesh had a message carved into his chest, just like Dave, but Jake, are you sitting down?"

"I'm the SUV right behind you," Jake said, shaking his head slowly at Paige.

"The carving said: BENDEL IS NEXT."

Chills ran up Jake's spine and a heightened sense of urgency to find Viktor grew in Jake's belly. "That's disgusting."

"Agreed, but that's not all," Cavanaugh said.

Jake swallowed, wondering if he could stomach more bad news. He shot a glance to Paige, who gave him a firm nod of confidence, and his mind turned to the pistol in the back seat. A brief fantasy appeared, similar to his many dreams over the years, where he had the chance to shoot Viktor between his cold, heartless eyes, and watch as the man's twisted, rotten brains blew clean out the back of his skull. Only then would he be free of Viktor's torment. Or would he regret the act of murder?

A sense of numbness washed over him. "You might as well tell me," Jake said.

"Linda Bennett was found by her maid, drowned in a bathtub. Initial evidence seems to point to a murder suicide by her husband, Frank, but you and I both know who's behind this."

Absolutely.

Cavanaugh continued, "Either way, I'm ordering you to peel off at the next exit and head south on I-5 toward that little executive airport. I'll send backup your way ASAP, just in case. If you see Viktor, which I suspect is not at all likely, do not engage, just observe. Copy?"

The agent responded, "Copy that, sir."

Jake took a beat, taking in the new data about Linda, and calculating what Viktor's next move might be. "I want to follow you to SMF."

"Negative. This'll be safer for you guys. Trust me. The tracking device shows Viktor's flying over downtown right now; he's coming here, and we'll get him. We gave instructions to ATC to hold him on the tarmac until we get there and we have a team waiting on the ground right now with a weaponized FBI helicopter and all. We called in the big guns, literally. This is it, Jake. We got the bastard."

Jake formed several arguments in his head, but before he could blurt out the first, Paige spoke.

"Something tells me we need to be at this other airport," she said, patting him on his shoulder.

Jake agreed, but turned back toward Paige. "I thought you believed in logic, not intuition."

"This is something else. Can't describe it," she said.

Jake sighed dejectedly.

"Okay, Cavanaugh. Try not to get shot. And get that son-of-a-bitch once and for all."

Jake ended the call.

The agent exited I-80 and sped up onto the southbound I-5, leaving the FBI caravan.

Ten minutes later they exited I-5 and drove through several residential areas toward the executive airport.

"Stop!" Paige said. The agent slammed on the brakes and pulled to the side of a suburban street. Two kids played jump rope on a driveway between two overgrown brown lawns. "The signal stopped moving again. Says Viktor's phone's not at the airport. It's two blocks from here. East."

They accelerated north, then turned right onto another street lined on both sides with 1950s era middle-class single-family residences.

With no idea what to expect, Jake's mind played out potential scenarios happening at that very moment at the international airport. Maybe Cavanaugh was chasing Viktor. Maybe Viktor was already dead. Maybe Cavanaugh had the guy in cuffs and would call Jake any second.

Maybe.

CHAPTER 63

August 20th
1:55 p.m.

Cavanaugh was in the front passenger seat of the lead vehicle of the FBI caravan, speeding north on I-5, passing thousands of cars and trucks going sixty-five miles an hour, all packed inside the Sûr System.

With the freeway exit to the airport looming a quarter-mile ahead, a barrage of bullets peppered the FBI vehicles.

Loud pinging noises echoed throughout Cavanaugh's SUV, causing immediate ringing in his ears.

On instinct, he yanked his service weapon from the holster and whipped around to see his attackers.

Two dark green Humvees followed, swerving side to side. A man wearing dark sunglasses hung out the passenger side window of the front vehicle, to the side of Cavanaugh's SUV, and fired an automatic weapon, probably an M4. Bullets ricocheted off the tempered, bullet-proof glass. The second vehicle pulled up around the right side onto the freeway shoulder, creating a mushroom cloud of dust and debris behind both vehicles. Cavanaugh's driver, Agent Bulinski, swerved right to prevent them from overtaking the FBI caravan.

"Get as far away from these civilians as possible," Cavanaugh ordered, scanning the area through the windshield.

"Gotta take this fight somewhere else to minimize casualties." He jerked his arm and pointed front right. "There. That alfalfa field. Drive through that cattle fencing."

The driver followed the order. All three FBI vehicles careened off the freeway in succession into a massive open area studded solid with rows of short green plants. The lead SUV plowed into a dirt berm, jamming Cavanaugh's head against the ceiling. He craned his neck, turning back around to get another view of the assailants. The two assault vehicles followed and the man in the window sprayed more bullets at them, but the bullet-proof glass held.

For now.

A black mass rose from the center of the second assault vehicle. Cavanaugh wiped his eyes and took a second look, then with his fist, tapped the knee of Agent Horsfall sitting behind him and pointed to the rear of his vehicle.

"Tell me that's not some fucked-up hidden gun turret," Cavanaugh said, drawing his eyebrows together and staring for a better look.

Before the agent could turn around, the rear window of Cavanaugh's SUV exploded and the back quarter of Agent Horsfall's head disappeared, spraying blood across Cavanaugh's face and chest. Horsfall slumped down to his side, limp.

Realizing they had no cover where they were, Cavanaugh turned to his driver. "You either get us the fuck out of here or we stop and make a stand. Right here."

"We can't make a run for it, sir," the driver said. "Too many goddamned rows of dirt slowing us down."

"Then stop," Cavanaugh said. He pressed his finger onto his earpiece to talk to the rest of the team. "We're stopping. Focus all firepower on that gun turret. We take that thing out we might have a chance."

Cavanaugh grabbed his radio tuned to the private FBI frequency. "Helo-1, this is Ant Trail," Cavanaugh said into the mic. "We're taking heavy fire from a fifty-cal southwest of your position. Request assistance."

Static.

Static. Beep.

Static.

"Roger that, Ant Trail," Helo-1 said. "Inbound hot. Two minutes."

"Get out," Cavanaugh said to the two remaining agents. "Cover us." The second agent in the rear seat pushed Horsfall's torso out to the left side of their vehicle, leaned out his window and emptied his fifteen-round magazine at the Humvee, while Cavanaugh and the driver exited and ran in prone to the opposite side of their SUV for cover. The other two FBI SUVs skidded to a stop, in a U-shape, one on either side of Cavanaugh. Those agents followed suit through a hefty beige dust cloud, then took position behind their respective SUVs, firing at the turreted Humvee.

"Got one," Cavanaugh heard in his earpiece. "Me too," said another agent.

The turret rained nonstop fifty-caliber rounds at the SUVs.

Thirty seconds.

Cavanaugh looked north toward the airport. A small black dot hovered above the horizon and grew larger with each passing second.

He stood, aimed at the turret operator, fired five rounds, then ducked back behind his SUV. He popped out his mag and counted the remaining rounds. Five. He shoved the mag back into the handle and chambered a round.

Ten seconds.

The sound of chopping copter blades filled the air.

The converted UH-60 Blackhawk chopper flew overhead and opened up its own arsenal of automatic fire, all aimed squarely at the Humvee and fifty-cal turret. The M134 minigun hanging beneath the body of the copter spewed out hundreds of rounds in a matter of seconds, kicking up dirt and turning the Humvee into nothing more than a chain-link fence, but somehow missed the shooter who'd ducked behind the steel shield at just the right angle.

The turret operator rotated his gun and aimed up at the copter.

Distracted. And exposed.

Cavanaugh stood on the running board of his SUV, set his elbows on the roof, closed one eye, took careful aim at the shooter and fired his last five rounds. A shower of blood erupted from the man's back and he folded forward onto the massive gun barrel.

With the fifty-cal out of commission and all but two of the attackers out of the fight, Cavanaugh allowed himself to feel a sense of hope. He wiped the dripping sweat from his forehead, backed away and listened. No more shots. His posture perked up and his situational awareness increased.

With extreme caution, he stepped out from behind the SUV and looked up at the copter which finished a large radius turn and headed back toward them.

A searing shot of pain bolted through Cavanaugh's right shoulder. He found himself on the ground, head buried between two leafy green plants. Smelled like a healthy salad. His breath hitched, but he craned his neck down at his shoulder, where crimson liquid bubbled toward the front, above his vest, out of a round hole in his pressed white dress shirt. He rolled onto his back and looked up at the blue sky, where the black chopper hovered directly above. The gushing wind felt cool on his face.

CHAPTER 64

August 20th
2:00 p.m.

"Right here," Paige said, looking up from the iPad and triangulation box. She pointed to the corner house on their left. The agent guided the Prius to the curb as they all rolled down their windows and the driver pushed the off button.

The sounds of multiple bird chirps floated through the air as the sun drifted across the peak of its daily arc. Short shadows lay flat beneath various trees and shrubs planted in the residential front yards.

Jake studied the house from his position across the street. Nothing out of the ordinary. A faded gray asphalt shingle roof mounted atop the cream-colored exterior of a single-story home with dark brown trim and a large, covered, open front porch. The overgrown bushes could use a decent clipping and the grass a good mow. And a few hundred gallons of water. A wind chime hung from the awning above, off to the side of the front door, as a light breeze wafted through the neighborhood, forcing the wind chime to sing its tune.

"Nothing here," Jake said. "Show me the map. Must be an error."

Paige leaned forward and placed the iPad into Jake's hands. He pinched in on the screen to zoom.

"According to this," Paige said, pointing at the map, "the cell phone, or whatever this thing is tracking, is around the back of that house, off to the side."

Jake tugged at his earlobe and furrowed his brow.

"Something's not right," he said.

"Patience. I'll bet if we—"

The front door to the house opened and a decrepit, bald man stepped on to the front porch.

The man they'd been searching for.

The one who'd killed Cynthia and threatened Jake and Paige in the Tesla outside the Modesto Bunker.

The mastermind behind two separate plots against Americans.

Viktor Johnston.

Without the beard. But definitely him.

"Holy. Fucking. Shit," Paige said.

"That's him." The agent sounded surprised. Jake blinked rapidly, his heart pounding hard, bouncing around inside his chest as he did a double take.

Viktor smiled, slowly waved to Jake from the shade of the porch, then retreated inside of the house.

"Call Cavanaugh," Paige said to the agent. "We need the cavalry down here. Now."

The agent tried the radio while Jake fumbled his cell from inside his pocket and dropped the phone onto the front floor. He reached near the accelerator pedal and grabbed the device. He called Cavanaugh. Four rings. Voicemail.

Dammit!

"Cavanaugh, it's Jake. Viktor's here. Here in Sacramento. Near the small airport. To the south." He gave the address. "You're at the wrong airport. Bring the troops."

"Shit. What do we do now?" Paige asked, ducking from the back seat.

The agent rubbed his chin, studying the house.

Jake thought back to his wife. Murdered by Viktor. He thought of the missed opportunities to catch Viktor. To kill the man who'd caused so much pain to him and his family. The man who'd now murdered his good friend, Dave, although Viktor denied doing so. The psychopath responsible for Professor Everton's death. All the pain the man had caused to the millions of suffering men because of the viral attack in the drinking water. All the hate. So much hate.

Paige leaned forward between the front seats. "You have that look in your eyes again," she said. "Calm down. We're gonna sit here and wait for Cavanaugh and the cavalry. We got Viktor's cell signal. He's not going anywhere." She checked the iPad. "Wait. Crap. The signal's gone."

In a shaky, halting voice, Jake said, "You're right, but . . . I have to confront him. I'm going to lose my mind sitting here waiting. It's been two years. I'm tired of the sleepless nights. The depression. The anxiety of not knowing where, when, if he's coming after me. Or what he'll do to me. Or Carlie. Or my grandson. No matter what, one way or another, this stops today." He felt the pressure of tears of pain, anger, and frustration welling up in his eyes. Deep, vengeful fire raced through his blood.

He reached around to the back seat of the Prius, past Paige, grabbed the gun pouch and pulled out the 9mm Glock. He jammed a fifteen-round magazine up into the grip, chambered a round, and stuffed the two extra magazines into his rear pocket.

"Dr. Bendel, you need to stay here. Cavanaugh's orders." The agent finally seemed to remember why he was there.

Jake ignored him.

"I'm coming with you," Paige said. "Last time you went all macho, you left me in the car and I got attacked. And drugged. Forget that, dude, ain't no damned way that's happening again."

Jake only heard the faint whisper of her words as he opened his door and exited the Prius.

"We need to get ahold of Cavanaugh first," the agent said.

While the agent stayed in the car, conflicted, trying to call Cavanaugh again, Jake jogged, bent double, to the side of the house, behind a four-foot-tall juniper bush. Paige crouched beside him.

"How the hell did Viktor know we would come here and not the big airport?" Paige asked in a whisper. Seconds passed while Jake contemplated an attack strategy. She shook Jake's shoulder. "Give me that Sûr System pen."

Now crouched and with his eyes focused on the front door, Jake slid the pen out from inside his jeans pocket and handed it to Paige. She set the pen on the ground and slammed a rock onto the center, cracking the pen in half, then picked up one end and showed the parts to Jake.

"Bet you a hundred bucks these wires and tiny circuit board here are part of tracking device," she said, jiggling the pen before other electronic parts slid out into her palm. "Pens aren't, like, supposed to have chips inside." She eyed a tiny black object the size of a fire ant. "Micro-antenna. And this is a micro-transmitter. Wow. Viktor knew where you were the entire time, dude."

This revelation enraged Jake further. His left eye twitched uncontrollably and his mouth went dry. Total cotton.

Jake's phone vibrated.

UNKNOWN CALLER.

Jake pushed the green button but remained silent.

"C'mon inside, Jakey Boy. I have something you need to see," Viktor said. "Bring your gun. Bring Paige. I'm not going to hurt you. I promise."

A loud crack thundered from the porch window. Crimson exploded inside the Prius, covering the windshield, and the agent slumped over to his left, head dangling out the window, blood streaming into a puddle on the pavement.

"Jesus Christ!"

Jake and Paige ducked further, slamming their faces onto the dirt, and Jake flipped the safety on his 9mm to red.

Paige sent a text to Cavanaugh: Under fire, agent down, where's backup??

"Carlie looks so sweet," Viktor said. "All tied up here in the basement. Mascara running down her pretty little cheeks. She keeps asking for you. Saying you're going save her. I thought I'd help you out. You can be her little hero."

"Bullshit," Jake said, renewing his grip on the Glock. "You didn't have to kill that agent. And Carlie's in New York." He set his teeth. "With your IQ, I thought you'd have a little more creativity. Pathetic."

Jake took a knee, phone pressed against his ear.

"Your choice, Jakey Boy. You willing to take that chance? When was the last time you talked to Carlie? About nine hours ago, yes? Hmm. She told you her babysitter had been slaughtered? Yes, I believe so. Heard the entire conversation."

"That pen had a mic, too," Paige said, still in a whisper. "He's been one step ahead of us this whole time."

Good luck charm, my ass.

Wheels turned in Jake's head, contemplating the possibility of Carlie somehow making the six-hour flight out here today after he specifically told her to follow their plan with the burner phone, secret place, et cetera. Why would Daniel let her do that? Perhaps she was physically abducted from New York? Someone would have to then get her on a private plane and fly all the way out here and for what? *To force my hand? To make me do something I don't want to do?*

"I'm going in," Jake said.

Paige grabbed his forearm and restrained him.

"What the hell is going on?" Paige asked. "This psycho just murdered an FBI agent in cold blood. He's the least trustworthy person on the planet. This is a damned set up. Has the word 'trap' written all over it. We need to sit tight and wait for backup. Carlie's not in the basement of this old house." Jake took another step toward the front door. "Don't tell me you're just gonna, like, walk on up to the porch and — "

Before Jake could change his mind and do what any reasonable person would do, two large German shepherd dogs ran toward Jake from across the street, barking, baring their teeth.

Jake wiggled his arm free and pulled Paige behind him, toward the front door.

"No time to argue. Get inside. Now!"

They hopped up onto the concrete deck of the porch and ran through the front doorway to the inside of the house, angry dogs in pursuit close behind. All the window coverings were drawn down, giving the room a yellowish-orange tint from light filtering through the paper. No lights were on and the smell of musty air filled his nose.

Jake tried to close the front door, but something caught the bottom and he sneezed.

"It's stuck," he said to Paige. The dogs jumped onto the porch, claws scraping the cement, barks echoing inside the house.

Without a word, Paige ran toward the center of the house and Jake left the front door open, following close behind her.

She darted into an open doorway halfway through the main hall.

"In here," she said, waving and crouching.

Jake slid through the jam as the dogs weaseled their way through the front door and ran toward Jake. Paige pulled the handle and slammed the inner door closed.

Darkness. Stale air filled Jake's lungs.

Claws scratched at the door from the outside, dogs snarling and barking.

The humans paused a few seconds to catch their breath as Jake fumbled in the inky darkness for a light switch.

"Something's not right with this ground," Paige said through the darkness as a crunching sound, like popcorn or potato chips, emanated from their feet again and again as they stepped.

"I feel it too." His pant leg vibrated the way it would if tiny creatures crawled around on your clothes.

"Got it," Paige said as Jake heard a click. Dim light illuminated their immediate area. Paige's hand was grasping the bottom of a chain that went up to a single yellow bulb. Jake looked at the floor and Paige screamed.

The dogs continued to bark and growl from outside the door.

Jake and Paige stood, hopping up and down, at the top of a narrow wooden staircase that led into to a shoddy basement. The landing they stood on had several dozen beetles crawling around at their feet. Carrion, clown, bone, and rove beetles.

"It's just a few bugs. Not even spiders," Jake said, brushing off their pant legs.

"Bugs freak me out, dammit. Let me outta here, I'd rather take my chances with those dogs," Paige said.

A blue glow emanated from below. The air felt hot entering his lungs. Stifling.

Jake blocked the doorway and gave a patronizing look to Paige, knowing full well the dogs would chew her tiny frame to pieces. No, the bugs were a minor threat, so nowhere to go but down, unless he wanted to shoot the dogs. Not an option.

Jake grabbed hold of Paige's wrist and led them down the steps toward the basement where, at the bottom of the staircase, he pulled on another tiny light chain, illuminating the rest of the basement with two more dim yellow bulbs.

Paige screamed again. This time, a different pitch altogether. Primal.

The basement room, the size of a small school classroom, had six-foot tall poured concrete walls on the perimeter, exposed wood floor joists for a ceiling, and a single six-by-six-inch vertical wood column in the center. The ground looked like a moving swamp of black flesh as thousands of beetles covered the entire concrete surface.

Paige made several noises, gasping for air.

To Jake's left, an open laptop sat on a stack of boxes, at chest level. A familiar Zoom window took up the entire screen, with a video call already started.

A video image of Viktor's head filled most of the screen. He smiled.

On the opposite side of the basement, a four-foot diameter circle of fire pulsated from the floor, surrounding a human figure—slumped over—sitting on a chair. A brown burlap sack covered her head, hands tied behind her waist to the chair.

The dogs continued barking and clawing at the door at the top of the staircase.

Paige sounded like she'd hyperventilate and pass out any second.

"Welcome to the last few minutes of your life, Jakey Boy," Viktor said from the computer screen.

CHAPTER 65

August 20th
2:07 p.m.

Jake took a step toward the computer, crunching more bugs as he peered into the pinhole camera and renewing his grip around the Glock handle.

His phone vibrated. Governor Fairchild.

Eyes wide with disbelief, he put the phone to his ear.

"Jake, thank God you're alright. Listen, there's been a shootout and I need an update and—"

The line went dead.

Through the computer speaker, Viktor said, "Jakey Boy. We can't have you chatting with your friends during our little game. Wasn't sure if I'd need to activate the cell jamming device, but hey, you can never be too careful."

Jake scanned the rest of the basement, looking for clues or ideas. He cocked his head and stared at the woman in the chair. He took a step toward her to get a better look.

"Not so fast, Jakey," Viktor said. "Stay right where you are until you know the rules of our game."

Jake stopped dead and swallowed hard.

Paige shivered.

The hand holding the Glock dripped with slippery sweat.

"Carlie," Jake yelled to the person in the chair. No response. Not even a twitch.

Viktor chuckled.

"Here's what we're gonna do, Jakey," Viktor said. "I'm gonna give you one chance to save your life. Just one."

Jake licked his dry lips, studying the seated person while his heart raced inside his chest, causing the room to spin with dizziness.

"You're going to shoot Carlie three times in the chest from exactly where you stand," Viktor said.

"Tell me why the hell I'd do that," Jake said.

"If you do, I promise I'll let you and your little friend go. Two lives for the bargain price of one. Today's special. Only good for two more minutes. Better act quick."

"These bugs don't bother me," Jake said, referring to the various species of beetles crawling on and around his shoes. "Cavanaugh knows where we are. I'll just wait for him."

"Oops. I forgot to mention the bomb," Viktor said.

"How cliché. Surprised you couldn't come up with something better."

"You know me, Jakey. Always gotta have a few pounds of plastic explosives in my games. Specifically, the twenty pounds of Semtex underneath the chair your daughter's sitting in."

Jake studied the chair in the dim light. Sure enough, there was a pile of something set beneath it. As he tried to see exactly what was there, he noticed the wood column in the center of the room, between him and Carlie—or the person Viktor claimed was Carlie. It was just dark enough not to be sure. He recognized the standard six by twelve-inch girder resting on top of the column and followed the beam to the perimeter wall. Structural calcs automatically ran in his head: dead load, flexural stress, moments, shear, and column stability factor.

But he had to keep Viktor talking.

"That's not Carlie," Jake said.

Viktor laughed again.

"You may be right. You may be wrong. You willing to gamble with your daughter's life? And Paige's?"

"Sounds like she dies no matter what. Either I shoot her, or you blow us all to kingdom come."

"Oh, how I've missed our little chats," Viktor said with a large yellow smile. "You never cease to amaze me, Jakey. Here, let me help you with your decision."

A countdown timer appeared on the laptop, with red digital numbers.

"You have thirty seconds. Less if you move toward your daughter. Got my finger on the trigger right here."

Jake leaned toward the seated person and stared, evaluating every detail. The height seemed accurate. Matched Carlie. Shoulder width, too. Ankles. Carlie had a tiny tattoo on her left lower shin right above the ankle bone with a triangle as the primary shape, something symbolizing peace or love.

Jake leaned forward even more to get a better look.

"Twenty seconds, Jake!" Paige said.

The dim light bulbs cast a shadow onto the area where the tattoo would be, but his eyes hadn't adjusted to the darkness yet.

Jake slammed his eyes shut and counted.

Five.

Four.

Three.

Two.

One.

With fourteen seconds left on the timer, Jake opened his eyelids and peered close at the person's ankle. He slid the Glock into the front of his pants, retrieved his cell phone, turned on the flash, snapped a pic of the ankle, and zoomed in.

No tattoo. Definitely not Carlie.

"Ten seconds, Jakey Boy."

Jake pocketed the phone, slid the Glock out from his waist, and took dead aim at the center of the column. He hoped Viktor would assume the shots were meant for the person in the chair.

Instead, Jake unloaded all fifteen rounds at the wood, chipping away at the column, while yelling "I'm sorry," over and over. Then he swapped out the empty mag for a fresh one and fired another fifteen shots at the same place on the column. One mag remained. Two-thirds of the wood had been obliterated.

Six seconds remained on the timer.

He swapped out the second mag for his last one and planned to fire fifteen more rounds at the nearly obliterated wood.

On the fourteenth round and with two seconds remaining, the column collapsed, unhinging the main supporting girder above, along with the entire floor of the house.

Jake turned around, grabbed Paige by her waist, and hoisted her up to a pocket above the perimeter wall, but below the floor joists. He jumped up and covered her body like a cocoon.

The beam supported by the broken column cracked in half. A thundering boom crashed onto Jake's eardrums as the first floor of the house collapsed onto the basement below, crushing whoever the hell was in that chair. Bright white sunlight bathed the scene.

"Quick!" Jake said to Paige. "Get up before the bomb goes off."

Dozens of beetles crawled across her chest and thighs as he helped her stand.

They climbed through an opening to the front yard and took several steps toward the neighbor's home, shaking off bugs as they ran.

Viktor's bomb detonated.

The force of the concussion wave blasted them both to the ground, sliding them along the dead grass into a fire hydrant. Jake tried to cover Paige again, shielding her body as shrapnel, mostly shards of wood and metal and chunks of concrete, rained down and the neighboring home caught fire.

The air smelled of charred kerosene.

A stabbing pain emanated from Jake's right knee and he looked at it, wrenched outward, sideways at an unnatural angle.

The pain intensified by a factor of ten once he saw his lower leg in a position it was not supposed to be in.

He rolled off Paige and looked at her.

She stood and helped him to stand on his left leg. He thought the pain might lessen if he set his knee back in place.

Do it now while the adrenaline is still flowing.

He reached to his calf, clenched his jaw and with both hands, snapped his lower leg straight. The pain caused his vision to narrow and for a second he thought he might pass out.

Even with a strong ringing in his ears, Jake heard a loud, guttural word fill the air.

"NO!" Viktor screamed from the other side of the collapsed, smoking house, as he threw an object, likely the detonator, toward the smoldering blaze and hobbled toward Jake. He held a twelve-inch scabbard knife in his left hand.

Jake searched the ground for his gun and spotted the weapon ten feet away, toward Viktor. He hopped on his left leg and fell to the ground, landing on his side and grabbing the pistol.

Viktor approached, trying to come down with the tip of his knife into Jake's belly. But Jake held the pistol tight in both hands, aiming up at Viktor a split second before the knife would have plunged into vital organs. Viktor froze in an attack position, then moved his arm slowly back to his side as he smiled, laughing.

"You're out of ammo," Viktor said.

"Might be. Might not. You want to gamble with your life?"

Viktor laughed again. "Touché. But you're not gonna shoot me," Viktor said, taking a step back, away from Jake and toward the smoldering hot mess behind them. "You didn't shoot me on the plane two years ago. You don't have it in you."

"A lot's happened since then," Jake said while struggling to get up and stand on his good knee while keeping dead aim at Viktor's chest. "I've had a lot to think about." Jake wiped a nagging piece of charcoal from his brow. "This exact scenario has unfolded in my head thousands of times and always, without hesitating, I shoot your sorry excuse for a human. I send you back to hell."

"Shoot him now," Paige said, loud, over the sound of the flames licking charred wood from nearby. "Shoot that sick bastard once and for all."

Sirens blared in the distance. Cops.

"Smart thinking," Viktor said. "For a woman."

She sneered at Viktor.

"If you shoot me now, you won't get answers to those burning questions in your mind. Why I did this. Who else is involved? Who's really in charge?" He looked at his wristwatch and raised his eyebrows. "Clock's ticking, Jakey."

CHAPTER 66

August 20th
2:18 p.m.

"Another innocent person," Viktor said, regripping the long-bladed knife in his hand. "That poor woman in the chair. You just let her die."

Paige helped Jake continue to stand on his left leg by supporting his right side to keep the weight off the wrenched knee.

"Bullshit. You detonated a bomb. You killed her like you killed my wife. And Paige's dad. And Dave. And that FBI agent. And Dinesh. And Linda. You sick son-of-a-bitch." Jake cocked the hammer on the Glock, keeping solid aim at Viktor's chest.

Jake tried to put up a good defensive front even though guilt, which helped mask the extraordinary pulsing pain from his knee, raged inside him for failing to save the seated woman in the basement.

The volume of the sirens increased. Several squad cars skidded to a halt in the street.

Viktor ignored the cars, instead staring at Jake and moving the knife from his left hand to his right. He panted, out of breath, but continued to speak.

"Tracy wanted to do what she thought was best for mankind," Viktor said. "She wanted to eliminate wars, genocide, anything so-called 'bad' caused by our collective egos." Viktor inhaled, baring his teeth. "I didn't give a damn about all her bullshit. Just wanted to do my part for Allah. See the Jihad through to the end. Eliminate your pathetic infidel way of life. Make the world great again. The way it was when the prophet Mohammed walked this earth."

Viktor sat on a thick, tilted wood beam resting on broken chunks of concrete as fire blazed behind him. Jake hobbled forward a few feet closer, Paige at his side.

"Tell me why you killed my wife," Jake said, hearing a tremble in his voice, but still pointing the gun at Viktor.

Viktor stared at the ground, back up to Jake.

"Was my brother, Syed's idea. He met with Tracy. Months before the Long Beach fire. They decided taking out your wife would give us a reason for the public to believe the story of you turning to the dark side. Wasn't my idea at all."

The lack of pride in Viktor's speech piqued Jake's attention. After all this time, Viktor was finally telling the truth. Possible?

Paige squeezed Jake's shoulder. "We don't believe you, dude. You're nothing more than a pathetic, loser terrorist. You've hurt more people than I can count. You deserve death."

Viktor nodded. "Paige Turner, judge, and jury. You could be right. If that is Allah's will." His eyes moved toward the knife, and he bit his lower lip.

A loudspeaker crackled through the hazy air, interrupting the conversation. "This is the Sacramento Police Department. Put down your weapons, get on the ground, and put your hands behind your head. Now."

Viktor made no sign of hearing the command, as though his brain had a mute button. He moved the knife again back to his left hand and gripped hard, with white knuckles.

Paige retrieved her phone from her rear pocket and tapped the screen. She aimed the phone's camera lens at Viktor.

Jake kept his eyes on Viktor, turned his head toward the police, and yelled, "This is Viktor Johnston. Check with Agent

Cavanaugh at the FBI. San Francisco. This man is a wanted terrorist."

The police ignored Jake's information and repeated the commands for the trio to drop their weapons.

"I've done my part, Jakey Boy," Viktor said. "I will not rot in jail for the next twenty years. I want to go home. Be with my mother and sit on the right knee of Allah."

"No," Jake said. "You're not getting off that easy. You still have some explaining to do. You owe me."

Paige continued to film with her phone. Jake shot a quick glance. Facebook Live.

Smart. Stream evidence of the entire scene live to the cloud.

The police repeated their commands a third time, but halfway through, Viktor raised the buck knife to his throat, sharp edge against the front side of his neck.

"I'm in control, Jakey Boy. Me. This ends my way so I can haunt you from the great beyond," Viktor said before he tilted his head back, lifted his chin, looked up to the sky, said something in Arabic, and grinned and grunted as he swiped the blade across his neck, slicing open his jugular vein. Paige gasped and turned the phone away an instant too late. At first, deep crimson liquid spurted out in an arc several feet in front of Viktor, toward Jake, then several pints of liquid oozed from his neck, onto his front upper torso.

Jake contemplated whether to fire his last round into Viktor's head, to live out his own sick fantasy, and watch the psychopathic brains scatter across the dead lawn.

No. He was better than that.

Viktor slumped forward. His body landed with a small thud five feet in front of Jake and Paige.

Still, a sense of relief came over Jake. The evil from this man's soul, all the pain he'd inflicted onto the masses — gone.

Jake tossed the Glock onto the grass and put his hands in the air.

CHAPTER 67

August 21st
Noon

"I can't believe these mouth breathers won't even talk with us," Jake said, sitting on the floor of a holding cell in the Sacramento Police station, with his leg in a knee-brace, elevated onto a chair.

In an adjacent cell, separated only by thick, cream-colored, vertical steel bars, Paige sat cross-legged with her head resting on her palm, elbow on her knee.

"Cavanaugh should have vouched for us by now," she said. "This is, like, frickin' ridiculous. I watch *Law and Order*, man. We're supposed to have an attorney for them to hold us this long."

An echo of boots shuffling along concrete bounced off the concrete walls, keys clanked, and Jake turned around.

A short, stocky man wearing a stereotypical FBI get-up that included a black suit, white dress shirt, and a black and gray striped tie stood, holding a pair of crutches, at the cell opening next to a Sacramento police officer.

"I'm Agent Bulinski." The officer unlocked both cell doors and the agent handed the crutches to Jake. "Please come with me, Dr. Bendel." The agent looked at Paige and she stood. "You too, Ms. Terner. And both of you, not a word."

Several quiet minutes later the three stood outside the police station ten yards down a wide, sloping concrete ramp, underneath an expansive beige canopy. Jake leaned on his crutches and wondered where Cavanaugh had disappeared to. Why hadn't he shown up?

Jake stared out across the parking lot, weight mostly on his left leg, with an unfocused gaze toward a California black walnut tree. The fresh air felt good inside his lungs, but a pressure had built inside him, a missing piece to their entire ordeal. This entire time, Jake had assumed Viktor was the top shot-caller. Jake had spent the last two years of his life under the constant stress of not knowing whether Viktor was alive or dead, or whether another attack would occur, or what Jake would do if given the chance to confront Viktor one last time.

But now Viktor was dead, and Jake had a hard time wrapping his head around it. Viktor had alluded to puppets and strings, but Jake wanted to believe otherwise. Viktor had to be in charge. Right? Was Tracy the same Tracy Ciacchella that Everton had written on the fax? Was she really the one responsible—ultimately—for killing Jake's wife? And the CDM two years ago? And now the viral attack on millions of innocent California men?

Are there truly people with that much power?

These questions swirled around inside his tired brain like a looming tornado, making it hard to focus on any particular question. He needed more information. More data. He needed someone to trust.

But after Jake and Paige had spent the night in jail—a total slap in the face to the two engineers after what they'd endured—the thought of trusting another government official sent a wave of nausea through Jake's abdomen.

"I can tell by the look on your faces you're pissed," Agent Bulinski said. "I don't blame you. Either of you."

Jake clenched his jaw and Paige crossed her arms as they both glared at the agent.

"Thank you for neutralizing Viktor. That bastard had it coming for years. Wish I'd been the one to—"

"I'm gonna stop you right there," Jake said, putting his hand up. "First, we didn't kill Viktor. He killed himself. With a buck knife. Probably one of the worst ways to die. And second, where the hell is Cavanaugh? Why isn't he here picking us up? Vouching for us?"

The agent rubbed absently at his arms.

"We're getting conflicting information," the agent said.

Paige whipped out her phone and tapped the screen a few times. She shoved the phone in the agent's face.

"This is a video of Viktor's suicide," Paige said. "Went viral. Over a hundred million views. Surprised you people haven't watched yet."

The agent said, "Yeah, we've seen it," before taking a hard swallow. "Agent Cavanaugh was just released from the hospital. We were attacked near the airport and he sustained a bullet wound to his right shoulder, blew the whole thing apart."

Paige covered her mouth. Jake shifted his stance from one side of the crutches to the other, tilting his head in confusion.

The agent continued. "He was in surgery for the better part of the night. The doc wanted to keep him there for another day, but you can't keep Agent Cavanaugh down. He needed to get back to work. Thought you might need some help."

Jake and Paige exchanged worried glances.

The agent explained and shared details of the shootout near the other airport. "He's lucky to be alive, but he's actually the one who cleared up the confusion with our friends here at the Sacramento P.D. Apparently they had no idea who you were."

"Jesus, we tried to tell them," Paige said. "But they wouldn't even let us talk."

The agent waved his hand and took a step toward the parking lot. "C'mon. Let's discuss the constitutional violations on our way back to the Federal Building in San Francisco. We have bigger fish to fry. Cavanaugh's there and we need you guys to debrief. Something big is going down and I'm afraid we're a bit in the dark. Since you actually spoke with Viktor, you might have information that could prove helpful."

Paige leaned into Jake, limping toward the agent's car as they followed Bulinski. With her mouth hidden behind the back of her hand, she whispered, "Typical."

Two hours later, Jake and Paige hurried with Bulinski up to the seventeenth floor of the Federal Building.

"Can't use the same conference room as yesterday—the crime scene techs are still down there wrapping up their investigation of that shooting," the agent said, opening the door to a different conference room, where Cavanaugh sat at the end of the table. Must have been his favorite seat. "They removed the bloodstain on the carpet, and they got this god-awful wild rose air freshener to mask the scent of shit and death. Anyway, have a seat."

Cavanaugh's right arm hung in a navy blue sling. The dark circles under his eyes told Jake the man was sleep deprived or on heavy-duty pain meds. He waved to Paige and Jake to enter.

Paige walked and Jake hobbled into the room and sat. "Thanks, Agent Bulinski, I'll take it from here," Cavanaugh said before Bulinski closed the door.

Cavanaugh stared at Jake and blinked several times.

"The hell happened to your knee?" Cavanaugh asked.

Jake glanced at Paige, back to Cavanaugh. "The hell happened to your shoulder?"

"They got me on some mild pain meds. I want to figure out the big picture." He looked at Paige. "I'm sorry about your dad. We checked his apartment, no copy of the fax, so a dead end."

Jake slid the crutches to the side, leaned forward and steepled his fingers. "Viktor wasn't working alone."

"We know. That Gunther asshole back at the bunker and—"

"No," Jake said. "I mean someone hired him. And Gunther. And God knows whoever else. Same person Willis worked for. The Wizard of Oz woman behind the curtain of death. Some hidden cabal, run by Tracy."

"I've never bought into all that conspiracy crap. There are no secret societies with that kind of power. Trust me," Cavanaugh said, easing back in his chair and exhaling. "The human part of the viral attack is fully contained and, with the information and stockpile of vaccines from the bunker, we have a plan. Linda, to her credit, had already converted one of her manufacturing plants—one that made polio vaccines—to mass produce vaccines. We'll be ready in case this virus pops up anywhere else. And, although Viktor probably killed billions of dollars in crops, we've neutralized the weaponized water and we're flushing out the entire water system again just to be sure. This little terrorist attempt of theirs is a done deal."

"Any of the men who attacked you near the airport still alive?" Jake asked.

"We had one. He'd been shot in the hip, just a graze. We bandaged him up and hauled him into an interrogation room down on the first floor, but—" Cavanaugh said, staring at his finger swirling on the desk " —we found him dead an hour ago. Poisoned himself, supposedly. Still trying to figure out how. And some kid named Selim was flying the plane that led us to the Sacramento International Airport. He's clammed up tight, though, I'm not expecting to get any info from him."

"While you were playing *Cowboys and Indians* with the terrorists," Jake said, "we had a pleasant chat with Viktor."

"Before he committed suicide," Cavanaugh said, nodding. "I watched the video. Horrific shit. We'll get you both some heavy-duty counseling after this is all over." Cavanaugh rubbed his eyes. "By the way, for what it's worth, two different eyewitnesses and forensics confirmed the woman in the basement was already dead by the time you got there."

Jake darted a glance at Paige, back to Cavanaugh. Jake's eyes went up, looking heavenward. "Thank God."

"Strangled to death behind a strip club yesterday afternoon. We found the Nylon rope in a nearby dumpster and matched the DNA. Same diameter rope we found in a car parked around the corner from the house Viktor incinerated. We're testing the car for Viktor's DNA but I'm sure it's his. We're also testing the rope now for DNA. I have a feeling the evidence will prove Viktor killed her."

Paige blinked several times. "Who was she?"

"Prostitute. She'd been picked up multiple times for solicitation in some of the seedier areas of Sacramento. Twice for possession, too. Meth."

Jake remembered the burlap sack over her head, covering her neck. He told Cavanaugh details of the bomb, the laptop, and how he skirted Viktor's death trap and save Paige by doing structural engineering calcs in his head, then blowing that wooden column to hell.

"Glad you made it out. Both of you. Now let's focus on Viktor's last words. Tell me exactly what he said."

Jake pulled up the scene in his mind and recited Viktor's words verbatim to Cavanaugh.

"Sounds like this Tracy person tried to be some holier-than-thou savior. The part I have a hard time believing is how someone could have been behind all this—the CDM attack, this viral attack—and completely stay off our radar. Except for that incinerated fax from Everton, our investigations led us to Viktor. Only Viktor. Nobody else. He was supposed to give us all the answers, but now he's dead. Thank God. But we have no file on Tracy. Any other details?"

Jake shook his head.

"You're sure Tracy's a woman?" Cavanaugh asked.

"That's what Viktor said."

Cavanaugh rubbed his chin and pursed his lips.

"And these long-term effects from the virus," Cavanaugh said. "The so-called permanent genetic modifications."

"We need to do a scientific study," Jake said. "Someone we can trust at the CDC." Jake stood and looked up at the ceiling tiles. "But since we don't know what we're looking for, that could take years." He let out a heavy sigh. "We need answers and I was hoping Viktor could give us some clues, but since he's dead, I guess this Tracy person is the only one who can shed some light on all this."

Cavanaugh turned to Paige. "I haven't forgotten about my promise to take care of your dad."

But before she could acknowledge the thought, the door bolted open. A computer tech ran in and skidded to a stop in front of Cavanaugh.

"Sir. We got something."

CHAPTER 68

August 21st
Afternoon

Jake found himself in the rear passenger seat of another FBI helicopter, his leg and swollen knee in a brace jammed tightly into the rear next to Paige's lap, hovering above a caravan of seven black FBI SUVs a thousand feet below, all heading toward the San Francisco International Airport. Cavanaugh sat in the front left seat, in front of Jake, next to the helicopter pilot, while Paige sat next to Jake in the rear, staring at her iPad. All four passengers wore green headsets and the copter floated up and down with the wind currents. Choppy. But no air sickness.

"She's still at the airport," Paige said into the mic with the tin-can pitch and speckles of static typical in aerial radio communications.

Jake leaned over and looked at her screen showing an aerial satellite view with a red circle pulsating around a slowly moving red dot on top of the San Francisco airport.

Jake turned to look out the front bubble glass windshield of the chopper where the airport loomed halfway out on the horizon below, in the middle of an earthen tapestry of buildings, roads, trees, and other structures.

"Two miles out," Cavanaugh said into his mic.

"Guess the drone attack two days ago was good for something, other than turning my Tesla into a holey mess," Jake said.

Paige looked up from her iPad to Jake. "I thought dud jokes were my thing." A tiny smile made its way onto her lips.

The chop-chop of the rotating blades vibrated the cramped interior, but while Jake performed a self-evaluation, he still noticed zero nausea, no motion sickness.

"We got the best techs working for us," Cavanaugh said. "Our guy found a proverbial needle in the haystack when he reverse-tracked the drone attack software from Rosen's computer and found the link to the true source of the data feed. Rosen said Tracy sent the order to attack your car with those four drones. If that's true, Tracy's at the airport."

On the ground, directly below the copter, the caravan blew past the security gate at the airport and headed onto the tarmac toward the Fixed Base Operator parking area where several private jets sat idle, awaiting orders from their owners, but none showed any life.

Except one.

"There," Paige said, pointing below to her right at a Gulfstream G650, a hundred million-dollar plane with a range that could easily span the Pacific Ocean. Each side of the white fuselage had eight windows and a dark blue underbelly, which made the craft stand out from the other, older planes. The red and green navigation lights blinked on the outer tips of the wings, and a guy hung out the cabin door, pulling up the boarding stairs as the plane lunged forward.

"If that's Tracy's plane, the caravan's not gonna make it," Paige said, referring to the accelerating snake of FBI vehicles below, a good mile and a half away from the jet. The caravan was approaching the end of the runway from the side.

"They have to," Cavanaugh said to them, but to the caravan on the ground, he said, "Ant trail five, Stinger one. The target is on the move."

"Roger that," someone said.

"The source of the tracking signal is definitely coming from that plane," Paige said, exchanging glances between her iPad screen and the tarmac below.

"Put us down in front of the plane," Cavanaugh said to the pilot.

The plane sped along the tarmac, crossing taxiway 'K' and turning left onto runway Ten, an easterly vector. The helicopter descended toward the accelerating craft.

"They're not following any of the normal ground maneuvers," Jake said.

"Exactly," Cavanaugh said. "The pilot's violating a ton of aviation laws every second."

Tracy was on that plane.

The chopper descended and hovered twenty feet above the surface, moving at the same speed to the left of and on a parallel path to the plane. As Jake looked out Paige's window, their craft tilted forward and accelerated, faster than the plane. For now.

"I'm gonna try to get in front before it's too late," the copter pilot said.

A mile away, the seven-car caravan turned onto the runway and headed west, straight toward the Gulfstream. Like a high-stakes game of chicken, Cavanaugh's apparent strategy was to pinch the jet between their FBI copter and the black SUVs on the ground, forcing the plane to stop and keep Tracy from taking off.

The copter flew at fifty knots toward the FBI caravan, but then a loud thunder emanated from the jet and the plane's engines blew out tight orange flames, accelerating it eastward toward the approaching black SUVs. The chopper lost ground to the plane.

"Faster, goddamnit," Cavanaugh said into his mic. The chopper tilted forward, speeding up, but could not keep up with the plane.

The FBI cars on the ground would be the only obstacle keeping the jet from possibly taking off. If they could get there in time. The SUVs split and formed two lines of three, with one

SUV in the front middle like a spear of vehicles, heading straight west at the approaching jet.

Jake ran calculations in his head. Basic physics. Acceleration, distance, velocity. He knew the plane needed at least a mile of runway to lift off but Tracy, assuming she was aboard the plane, had about that same distance before the caravan closed the gap.

Gonna be close.

"Stay back," Cavanaugh said to the pilot. "We can't stop them. Let's hope the agents on the ground can, then we'll come in from behind to surround the bastards."

The copter pilot ascended to a couple hundred feet above the runway to get a better angle of the impending collision.

The Gulfstream plowed down the runway just shy of the speed needed for lift off and Jake calculated failure. A massive collision would occur if the SUV drivers kamikazed into the jet.

The nose of the jet rose, tilting skyward. Jake recognized the short-field take-off tactic — all pilots practiced this technique as part of their training. *Popping a Wheelie*, Jake's instructor used to say.

With the SUV caravan less than 300 yards away, speeding toward the jet at over seventy miles an hour, seconds remained until the crash.

But the jet lifted off from the ground a nanosecond before colliding with the front car, the rear wheel of the landing gear crushing the windshield of the leading SUV and forcing the vehicle to swerve left. The driver overcorrected and rolled multiple times.

"Shit," Cavanaugh said.

The jet ascended, heading east at bearing 1-0-0.

Jake dropped his head, eyes closed, before hammering his fist into the rear of Cavanaugh's seat in front of him.

"There goes our only lead," Jake said into the mic. "The only person on the planet who could give us answers."

Someone, another agent, spoke into the FBI channel. "Sir, their flight plan shows they're headed to China."

"Wonderful," Cavanaugh said, combing his fingers through his hair. He barked orders to get rescue personnel to the overturned SUV.

The helicopter circled the area, descended, then at fifty feet above the ground, a female voice came over the com channel.

The pilot stopped, hovering.

"Agent Cavanaugh," the voice said. "I do hope your people are all right. I did not intend to ruffle your feathers."

"Who the hell is this?" Cavanaugh asked.

"My good man, I believe you know beyond a doubt."

CHAPTER 69

August 21st
Afternoon

The FBI helicopter touched down near the collision site.

"I do apologize for miscalculating how long you'd take to get to the airport," the voice, with a hint of an arrogant British accent, said through the com. "Thought I had a few more minutes, so kudos to you, Agent Cavanaugh. Very impressive work."

Jake looked upward out the left-side window of the chopper to the jet ascending into the sky as it banked hard to the left for a half-turn.

"Tracy Ciacchella," Cavanaugh said. "The so-called mastermind."

The voice chuckled. "My good man, I am not behind anything. I merely coordinate, facilitate, and motivate people to do certain tasks they were already planning. And I help raise money to pay for said tasks. That is all."

"You've infected the sperm cells of millions of Californians. Changed the DNA for their offspring."

Cavanaugh thought about telling her his team found BioStall's repurposed polio vaccine plant in Cupertino and unlocked the security system with the entry code: *90-93-96,* but decided against it.

"Indeed. Rumor has it the research done at BioStall concluded that the only way to save mankind from obliterating—no, annihilating—itself is to eliminate the source of hatred. In the brain itself. No more egos. No more anger. With these outdated primitive survival instincts and emotions all rendered moot, humans can finally ascend into something far greater than our current state. Evolve into our destined being. Homo-spiritus. Imagine a world with no possessions. No religion. No wars. Just compliant souls doing what we want."

"You sound like a John Lennon song," Cavanaugh said.

"Indeed, sir. That great man was on to something, I must admit," the voice said. "But I do encourage you to consider one important fact."

"You're playing God with innocent lives the same way Hitler and Himmler did. I'm not sure where you got your research from, but your plan won't work. Instead of saving mankind, you just might have planted the seeds to destroy us all. And who the hell—"

"May I finish, Agent Cavanaugh?"

Pause. "I'm listening."

"Assume California finishes these five plant-combos and they all go online in a few months as our dear Dr. Bendel has promised the good Governor. In theory, clean fresh water is provided to a substantial portion of the population. In time, the energy created by the Molten Salt Reactors will provide ample proof of a safe, efficient, inexpensive power plant. An alternative to solar, wind, hydroelectric, and the existing nuclear power plants that create more nuclear waste than we know what to do with, the ones Nixon should never have allowed to be constructed. But I digress. What's keeping other states, or the federal government and the energy commission for that matter, from building more of these?"

"Nothing. That's the point. The energy is cheap and safe and—"

"Stop thinking like an insect, Agent Cavanaugh. Which companies would be harmed financially with these MSR's?

Which companies would do anything to prevent MSR's from becoming mainstream? Companies that generate trillions of dollars per annum selling so-called energy all across the globe. Companies with more influential grit than you can imagine."

Jake knew the answer before Cavanaugh could respond.

Big Oil.

Cavanaugh shifted the conversation. "Bottom line here, lady, is you've violated basic human rights. Who the hell are you to determine the fate of mankind?"

A booming laugh came through the com. "You shall see, Agent Cavanaugh," the voice said. "This is only the beginning. Units of people all over the world are working hard right now on an even more grand plan. The CDM attack two years ago was intended to be a wake-up call. A few million deaths in exchange for a better society. A safe, wholesome America. But Dr. Bendel thwarted that effort. Because of his actions, my people will now be forced to plan an attack on such an immense scale it will put the CDM and this virus mess to shame. An attack to end all other attacks. It's going to be . . . let me find the right word . . . ah yes. Powerful." She chuckled. "Ooh, I'm getting shivers just thinking about it."

"The next time you visit us, lady, we'll be all over you like fur on an ape," Cavanaugh said. "You'll wish you'd never messed with the Federal Bureau of Investigation."

A short, light laugh came through the com. "Do say 'Hi' to my brother for me," she said, her words lingering in the air, as Cavanaugh looked at Jake, both confused as hell.

Is Selim her brother?

Seconds later the plane disappeared behind several clouds, heading west toward China.

EPILOGUE

Three months later, Jake leaned back in a comfy leather La-Z-Boy chair, sipping a hot cup of tea in Carlie's new apartment in downtown Manhattan. Baby Andy crawled in circles on the thick carpet, sucking on a blue pacifier before stopping, sitting, then looking up at Grandpa Jake with a huge, two-toothed grin.

From her kitchen, Carlie walked in bringing along the fresh aroma of roast turkey, homemade biscuits, and apple pie.

"I'm super glad that total mess is behind us now," she said, pulling up a chair from her dining room set and sitting. "Daniel should be home from the station any minute."

Jake's stomach rumbled in anticipation of the impending feast he planned to enjoy. He took another sip of tea. Too hot.

"Cavanaugh said they're already up to full production on the Cupertino vaccine plant and they have more than enough vaccines for everyone."

"Awesome."

"And he's still working to take care of that mess with the IRS," Jake said, licking his throbbing lips. "Within the next few months, I hope all my bank account balances are cleaned up. Back to normal."

"And your plant combos seem to be humming along with outstanding success. In fact, they had a nice article in the New York Times about how the new tech could revolutionize water treatment and energy generation." She leaned over, picked up Andy, and sat the little man on her knee. "And your reputation—sounds like Viktor failed to drag your name through the mud. Again."

"Did you read the L.A. Times exoneration article I sent? The one that detailed how I was drugged when they filmed the video?"

"Twice. I liked the quotes from your doctors about the Trihypnol and how dangerous it is."

"The FBI confirmed with Linda Bennett before her husband supposedly murdered her that she was in on the drugging with the Trihypnol. She named and pinpointed the exact date, which matches up perfectly with the digital date stamp on the video of me attaching the virus canisters to the chlorine tanks at the San Francisco plant. FBI techs also found Viktor's backup plan in case I failed to cooperate."

Carlie bounced Andy on her knee and his little pacifier fell out. She bent over and picked it up.

"Man, that guy was always crazy prepared," she said.

"Apparently they were going to sabotage the trunk line that connects that plant to the aqueduct."

"No idea what a trunk line is, Dad."

He tried to take another sip of tea. Still too hot, so he blew on the surface. "We have three eight-foot diameter pipes running underwater for about fifty miles that carry the fresh water from the plant up to the aqueduct and we didn't think about putting any protective security devices on the pipe, but next time I'll be sure to think like a criminal first and make sure anything I design and build is terrorist-proof."

Carlie tossed the dirty pacifier aside and grabbed a clean one from the counter.

"They find anything else?"

Jake blew on the surface of his tea and nodded. "They were also thinking of destroying the power supply to the San Luis Obispo plant once it went online."

Carlie shrugged. "I don't understand."

"In a traditional nuclear power plant design, there's a colossal risk of meltdown if the power supply dies because the water-cooling pumps fail. But in a Molten Salt Reactor, if power is cut, the liquid salt cools and solidifies and actually prevents a meltdown. Totally safe. That's how dumb they were, they thought they could cause a meltdown.

"And everything else is back on track. Worked the political bugs out with the governor. She's super happy with the progress. All five plant combos are officially online as of earlier this week. The California drought is over. I've been approached by people from several other countries looking to build similar facilities on their coastlines, too. There are over a dozen major countries around the world running out of fresh drinking water, it's crazy."

A timer beeped from the kitchen and Carlie stood and stepped toward her dad. "Here. Hold Andy for a bit while I go check on the apple pie." Jake set his tea on the end table and accepted his grandson onto his lap. Jake looked into Andy's eyes and saw Cynthia. He felt privileged to still be alive, to enjoy this moment with the baby boy.

Jake's phone vibrated. He stood and, holding Andy in one arm, answered the call with the other.

"Dr. Bendel, I'm not sure if you remember me or not, we've never met, but this is Barbara Bazmi. I saw you at the ribbon-cutting ceremony for the plant combo in Point Pinole."

Jake bounced Andy in his arm several times as he thought back. "Yes, of course. Happy Thanksgiving to you."

"Sorry to bother you on a holiday so I'll be brief. I want you to know our primary competitor, the man you met that same day, Tex Murphy, is, well, let's just say he's smack dab in the middle of the Big Oil family of companies."

"I don't follow," Jake said, bouncing Andy in his arm.

"My family is investing heavily in alternative energy. We've done quite well for ourselves with solar and wind investments and right now it looks like we'll be all in on the MSR tech. We see this as the way of the future, something to revolutionize the energy production industry."

"Couldn't agree more. But what do I have to do with this?"

She paused.

"I understand you're getting calls from other countries requesting your expertise to construct MSR/DP's, and I'm calling to offer, financially, in any way I can. We'll end up putting guys like Tex out of business. They have too much power. Too much influence. In my world, there's a rumor going around that someone named Tracy is the leader of a handful of powerful people, a secret society if you will, and is working with Big Oil to fund Big Pharma to do experiments on humans in countries with dictatorial regimes."

Jake walked toward the kitchen. The fresh scent of apple pie hit his nose and he salivated like a Pavlovian experiment.

"Thank you, but I'm not a conspiracy theorist and I don't really want to get involved at that level. I'm just an engineer trying to do my small part to help humanity."

"I appreciate your modesty, and I do have to run, but before I go, I want to reiterate my offer. You need anything, financial or otherwise, you call me. Understand?"

Carlie slid the pie out from the oven. The crisscrossed crust covering had turned a golden brown and Jake's stomach growled again.

"I'll keep that in mind. Always good to have a friend in the energy industry."

They ended the call, but before Jake could start another conversation with Carlie, the front door burst open.

"I'm home. God, it smells amazing in here," Daniel Cavanaugh said.

They exchanged pleasantries and over the next hour, Jake and Daniel helped Carlie finish cooking their feast. Then she put

Andy down for his afternoon nap and the trio started in on their Thanksgiving meal.

"I overheard you talking on the phone about conspiracy theories," Carlie said.

Jake finished chewing a tender morsel of dark turkey meat and swallowed, nodding. "Don't want to bore you with the details, but suffice to say, we have a wealthy friend in the energy industry. Might be something there for me. The next phase of my career. Who knows?" He scooped up a forkful of mashed potatoes and stuffed them into his mouth.

"Speaking of conspiracy theories," Daniel said. "There are some heavy-duty rumors going around the fire department, and City Hall, for that matter, about how all the facts on the 9-11 attack aren't adding up."

"Why now? It's been decades."

"Apparently, the California weaponized water attack has revived some of the 'Big Brother' conspiracies."

Jake took a swig of Budweiser and set the glass on the tablecloth. "There's no conspiracy. Al-Qaeda planned the attack. Those brain-washed extremists hijacked the planes and crashed them into the Twin Towers. Thousands of innocent people were murdered on American soil and millions more were affected. We all know this."

"That's what they want you to think," Daniel said mischievously.

"Your brother works for the FBI. There is no 'they.' Trust me," Jake said.

Jake severed a thick piece of turkey with the side of his fork and slid the bite into his mouth. So tender. Carlie took after her mom in the cooking arena. Wow.

"You're an engineer," Daniel said. "Tell me how the rate of collapse of the upper stories was equal to freefall speed. The kinetic energy should have been converted to building damage, which would have slowed the speed of the collapse. Since that didn't happen—there was no resistance as the building crumbled—how can you explain that?"

Jake's mind turned to basic physics, specifically to the conservation of momentum principle and Newton's Third Law of Motion. If an object, like a ball, were dropped from the top of one of the Twin Towers, the time to travel straight to the ground would be eleven seconds. He recalled watching a documentary on the Twin Towers and they said each tower fell during an eleven-second time interval.

Jake stopped chewing, then furrowed his brow, impressed with Daniel's grasp of physics.

Daniel smiled and pointed his fork at Jake.

"You're right. Something seems off there," Jake said.

"How about the fact that some of the tenants in the Twin Towers included the Secret Service, the CIA, the Department of Defense, and the Office of Emergency Management? Or that fire has never, in the history of all humankind, ever brought down a steel building?"

Jake glanced at Carlie. She shrugged. "Don't look at me. I'm a drama teacher. Engineering's your thing."

Jake continued to do calcs in his head. He replayed the 9/11 attack in his mind.

Daniel continued. "Anyway, there are a ton more facts like that. Building Seven didn't even get hit by a plane and somehow it was destroyed by a mysterious fire? Doesn't add up. The only reasonable explanation is that those two buildings were brought down by controlled demolition. But who would do that? And why?"

"Let's talk about something else, please," Jake said. "That's a very sore subject for millions of Americans. Not sure if we're ready to have this discussion just yet."

Jake finished his beer.

"My brother says because of the water attack there's a bunch of men in California who might not be able to have kids," Daniel said.

"We're still sifting through the data and doing a ton of research, but right now it looks like they're not sterile and can still have kids. But if they do, there's a high probability the children will have mutated brains, different than what we have. The CDC is working on an antidote that should reverse the effects, but as of today, we're recommending anyone contaminated by the virus to try not to conceive, which feels like something from Nazi Germany—absolutely horrible. But hopefully, in a few more months the antidote will be available. The advice should hold for most people, but accidents happen. I guarantee you in six more months some babies will be born. And they'll be different. We'll have to see. Not looking forward to that. And anyone want to guess the final tally on the damage inflicted on the California agriculture industry?"

"Five billion," Carlie said.

"More," Jake said.

"Ten billion?" Daniel asked.

"Twenty-five billion. About half the size of the industry. Thousands of people out of work. The homeless population is gonna go through the roof. And the results of the AI report showed over a hundred different investment companies had shorted the Ag stocks in California, so Cavanaugh couldn't point the finger at any single one. It's like they all knew about the plan which is impossible."

"Viktor didn't lose after all," Carlie said.

Jake turned his thoughts to baby Andy.

They finished their meal, talked more about politics, family histories, and the latest technologies for fighting fires.

Four hours after finishing dinner, Jake fell asleep in Carlie's guest room. For the first time since the CDM attack, he slept all night without waking up.

Not once.

Teaser for book two:
BLACKOUT

CHAPTER 1

8:49 a.m.

The dark seeds of anarchy thrive in a country devoid of electric power.

Tracy tapped her watch, satisfied with the text from her team on the ground. A smile eked its way to one side of her face as she walked her tall, lean body down the center aisle of her Gulfstream G650, past several young men wearing black combat uniforms. Cruising at a safe altitude at Mach point seven, eastward over the coast of Venezuela, she leaned in toward Boris, her lead coordinator, as he typed inhumanly fast on a laptop.

Boris looked up at Tracy, now standing erect, arms crossed, giving him a nod. Both knew the gravity of their impending actions.

"My good man, in five minutes we are a go on my signal," Tracy said, tucking several strands of straight red hair behind her ear.

If this operation went according to the plans polished ad nauseum over the last two years, her name could go down in history with two of her most infamous predecessors: John Wilkes Booth and Lee Harvey Oswald.

And Tracy Daniela Ciacchella.

Maybe. But she needed to ensure someone smart enough connected the dots.

Indeed, the true motivation driving her dedicated, secretive efforts was to implement a larger strategy — her brainchild.

"Your yacht is in position at Old Tampa Bay," Boris said. "All four hundred drones are ready for deployment from the deck."

Airplanes attempting to land on runway 1R at the Tampa International Airport, about 1,600 miles northwest of Tracy's location, typically approached from the south, over ocean waters in the Gulf of Mexico. Sailing Tracy's eighty-foot Sunseeker yacht into the adjacent Bay had been remarkably uneventful. And the two-pound bricks of homemade Semtex explosive — one for each drone — proved relatively easy to make with coal, water, air, and her team's solid knowledge of chemistry.

Nobody — not the FBI, CIA, or Homeland — was prepared to defend against the impending assassination. Sure, there'd been talk at various committees and meetings held in D.C. of trying to protect America's airports with anti-drone tech. But as was typical with US leadership, nothing actually got done. No decisions were made. Only political wrangling, posturing, and dick measuring.

Men. One more reason to raise my curtain of death.

In four minutes.

CHAPTER 2

President Whitehead slammed the front section of the New York Times onto a small round table near the middle of Air Force One and stood, staring down at his press secretary and three assistants cowering in front of him. He ground his teeth and turned away before looking out the window, to the swampy coastline of eastern Florida rising beneath him as his 747 descended.

Squinting to bring the landscape into focus, he kept his attention out the window, his back turned to his staff. "Do your job. Make this go away."

"But Mr. President," the press secretary said. "The evidence is more than damning and our 'fake news' excuses only work for so long. They have video of you actually making the deal with the sex trafficker. Your money. His fourteen-year-old. Clear as day, it's—"

"I know what the hell it is," he said, slapping the side wall of the fuselage. "Make something up. I don't care. I've only been in office a year and already the damned Democrats dig this up? Change the media's focus to something else."

"To what, sir? This is solid criminal evidence, we can't just—"

"*We're on final approach to Tampa,*" the captain announced over the loudspeaker. "*Need everyone to please take their seats.*"

Whitehead leaned his handsome, Hollywood-ish, tanned face forward to the press secretary, practically touching his nose with hers, pulse pounding in the side of his neck and head flush with boiling blood. "Make. This. Disappear. After we land, you have two hours or you're history."

He waved the team of spin doctors away, threw on his black suit coat, and sat in his favorite leather seat. He straightened and massaged the knot of his favorite navy blue tie—for good luck—then downed the last ounce of Kentucky bourbon, baring his teeth as the soothing liquid drained down into his gut.

CHAPTER 3

8:54 a.m.
One short minute remained.

Tracy confirmed again with her ground team that they were ready to raise the *curtain of death*. She grabbed her iPad and opened the video chat app connected with her two generals: the captain on her yacht in Old Tampa Bay and her trusted, longtime friend Bob Huffington—nicknamed Huff—on the roof of a Macy's near I-275. Huff was perfectly positioned a mile south and directly under the flight path of the final approach for runway 1R at Tampa International.

Both video feeds were clean, sharp, and streaming smoothly, one from the boat and one of the airport.

Still flying above the Venezuelan coast, thoughts of the planning, coordination, bribing, frustration, negotiations, money—all swirled through Tracy's mind.

This is my opening act. My chance to finally bring down the mighty US of A.

Her skills had been tested during the presidential primaries, but she'd managed to get her man, Jonathan Goldberg, as the running mate with candidate Whitehead. Goldberg owed her big time and she'd made sure he knew full well that she had him by the balls. Talk about some strong strings on that brainwashed puppet; hers were like steel cables. No way he'd ever cross her. With Goldberg as president, she would have full control over the US military while her cabal rose to the peak of power on the global stage. Behind the scenes, of course, lurking in the shadows.

Confidence billowing inside, Tracy pulled her iPad close and said into the tiny speaker, "Green. Repeat, we are green for operation White Out." On her screen, both men nodded. She watched the feeds as workers on the boat peeled off a massive blue tarp to reveal the four hundred off-the-shelf drones made in China, all spaced two feet apart in four stacked layers—each in a ten drone by ten drone grid—and held together by a customized carbon fiber lattice. Each quadcopter had a two-pound payload of Semtex and a preprogrammed set of GPS-coordinated waypoints to travel to, so no input was needed by an operator.

Once the drones were given their orders, they'd follow them using precise signals from GPS satellites, which were all in perfect working order as of five minutes ago, according to her inside man at the Department of Defense.

Boris leaned back in his chair, away from his laptop, looked to Tracy, smiled and said, "I still think we could have come up with a better name for the op." She nodded. "How about operation kill the racist pedophile?"

"Oh come now, Boris. Way too on the nose."

But accurate.

A second later on her iPad, red and green blinking lights shone from every craft as propellers spun fast, creating a buzzing sound similar to a swarm of bees. The crowd of drones lifted off skyward. Crews on the yacht removed lattice layers as each wave of one hundred drones lifted off from the boat deck, east toward the Florida coast a half-mile away. The camera feed panned away, south, and zoomed in on the target: a baby blue and white 747 descending for its final approach.

She tapped Huff's video feed and enlarged it to see him viewing the swarm from his unimpeded Macy's rooftop viewpoint as the dense black cluster of drones sped toward the department store. Now the grid of drones, which did, in fact, look like a curtain of sorts—two-hundred feet square—flew closer to the grassy fields in front of runway 1R, the center drone dead nuts at two-hundred feet above the ground and in the path of the approaching aircraft.

"Detonate on my signal," Tracy said into the iPad. She watched as Air Force One flew closer and closer to the curtain, over Macy's, toward the runway, toward the curtain, toward its certain doom.

When the president's 747 was fifty yards away from the wall of drones, like a bird flying into a window, Tracy gave the order.

ACKNOWLEDGEMENTS

First and foremost, I need to thank my best friend, business partner, and wife of three decades, Tammy, for her continued encouragement to finish this book, for being my alpha reader, and making sure the overall story made sense. To my three editors over the four years it took to polish the book, Christine Fairchild, Marsha Zinberg, and Trinity Huhn Freeman, your wisdom, guidance, and patience are deeply appreciated. Special thanks to my daughter, Carley Logue, who somehow convinced me to take improv acting classes at the Groundlings School in Hollywood in order to tighten/enhance the dialogue. Thank you to my parents, Richard and Linda, who always lovingly pushed me to do my absolute best in all of the crazy endeavors I've embarked on. Of course, a dear thank you to my publisher, Reagan Rothe at Black Rose Writing, for taking a chance on a new author and gently guiding me along the traditional publishing route. Finally, thanks to you, the readers, for taking the time to finish this book; I sincerely hope you enjoyed the story and it opened your mind to opportunities for improving our society.

ABOUT THE AUTHOR

A veteran civil engineer, Bennecke has spent his career helping people by improving Southern California roadways. In his role as philanthropist, he awards scholarships annually to high school seniors at his alma mater. He lives in Southern California with three spunky cats and his wife of 30 years, whom he enjoys traveling with. In his leisure time, he spends his hours flying, learning about innovative technology, playing golf, and catching up with his grown daughters.

NOTE FROM THE AUTHOR

Word-of-mouth is crucial for any author to succeed. If you enjoyed *Waterborne*, please leave a review online — anywhere you are able. Even if it's just a sentence or two. It would make all the difference and would be very much appreciated.

Thanks!
J. Luke Bennecke

Website: www.jlukebennecke.com
Facebook: www.facebook.com/jlukebennecke
Instagram:@jlukebennecke

Thank you so much for reading one of our
Terrorism-Thriller novels.
If you enjoyed our book, please check out our recommendation
for your next great read!

Jihadi Bride by Alistair Luft

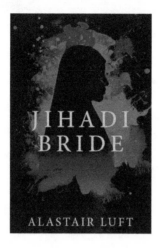

"A timely edge-of-your-seat terrorism thriller that plays on every
parent's worst fears. This cinematic thriller is destined for TV."
–*Best Thrillers*

View other Black Rose Writing titles at
www.blackrosewriting.com/books and use promo code
PRINT to receive a **20% discount** when purchasing.